The Subterranean Stratagem

ALSO BY MICHAEL PRYOR

10 Futures

The EXTRAORDINAIRES series
Book One: The Extinction Gambit

The LAWS OF MAGIC series
Book One: Blaze of Glory
Book Two: Heart of Gold
Book Three: Word of Honour
Book Four: Time of Trial
Book Five: Moment of Truth
Book Six: Hour of Need

For younger readers

The CHRONICLES OF KRANGOR series
Book One: The Lost Castle
Book Two: The Missing Kin
Book Three: The King in Reserve

For more information about Michael and his books,
please visit www.michaelpryor.com.au

The
Subterranean Stratagem

two

THE EXTRAORDINAIRES

MICHAEL PRYOR

RANDOM HOUSE AUSTRALIA

A Random House book
Published by Random House Australia Pty Ltd
Level 3, 100 Pacific Highway, North Sydney NSW 2060
www.randomhouse.com.au

First published by Random House Australia in 2013

Addresses for companies within the Random House Group can be found at
www.randomhouse.com.au/offices.

National Library of Australia
Cataloguing-in-Publication Entry

Author: Pryor, Michael
Title: The subterranean stratagem/Michael Pryor
ISBN: 978 1 74275 819 0 (pbk.)
Series: Pryor, Michael. Extraordinaires; 2
Target audience: For secondary school age
Dewey number: A823.3

Front cover photograph © Simpli/Flickr/Getty Images
Back cover photograph © iStockphoto.com/chalabala
Cover design by Astred Hicks, www.designcherry.com
Internal design by Midland Typesetters, Australia
Typeset in Bembo by Midland Typesetters, Australia
Printed in Australia by Griffin Press, an accredited ISO AS/NZS 14001:2004
Environmental Management System printer

Random House Australia uses papers that are natural, renewable and recyclable
products and made from wood grown in sustainable forests. The logging
and manufacturing processes are expected to conform to the environmental
regulations of the country of origin.

For Meredith Gill

The waters lapped, the night-wind blew,
Full-armed the Fear was born and grew,
And we were flying ere we knew
From panic in the night.
—Rudyard Kipling, 'The Rout of the White Hussars'

ONE

The giant steel jaws on either side of Kingsley Ward were quivering. Being suspended upside down as he was, it was difficult to judge the trap's eagerness to close on him, so he ignored the metal monstrosity and focused his attention on wrenching himself free from the straitjacket. At the back of his mind, he was ticking off the seconds, keeping track of the three minutes he had before the Jaws of Death snapped shut.

Through strenuous flexing of his shoulders, he'd managed to heave his right arm – the one in the continuous restraining sleeve – up and over his left. If he could stretch the leather and canvas enough to push his head through the gap he'd made, he was halfway there. The problem was, however, that his writhings had sent him swinging, pendulum-like, bringing him uncomfortably close to the metal teeth on either side.

1

The mantrap was finely machined, a giant saw-toothed clamshell driven by a spring coiled tightly enough to work ten clocks the size of Big Ben. He'd seen it demonstrated and the crash of the jaws when they shut had made his ears ache.

Kingsley was sweating, and glad of it. The slickness helped him drag his arm up and over his forehead. Immediately both arms were looser. He attacked the buckles on the sleeve with his teeth, tearing at them in a way his wild self approved of. His shoulders ached and his lips hurt, but he soon had the sleeves undone. This let him claw for the fastenings at his back. His fingers slipped, and he cursed, but he soon had the buckles open. After a combination of further teeth work, twisting and wriggling, he was free of the jacket and reaching for the belt that was cinched tightly around his feet.

When he yanked the belt free, he dropped, flipping so he landed on all fours. Immediately, he sprang from the platform just ahead of a monstrous crash behind him. The sound echoed around the exposed rafters of the workshop, sending the chains and ropes swaying.

Success! Kingsley stood, panting, muscles aquiver with exertion and more than a little relief. He glanced over his shoulder at the Jaws of Death, which he imagined looked disappointed, frustrated at not fulfilling their existential purpose, viz. slicing him in two.

Once he'd gathered his breath he struck a pose that he hoped was both debonair and devil-may-care. 'How was that?'

Evadne Stephens was ensconced amid a mountain of papers at a long table near the window. A large diary detailing their performances sat on top of a metal box. She held a document in one hand while the other juggled three or four small brass cubes without her apparent attention. If not for that subtle movement, she might have been a statue – especially given her marble-white skin.

She lifted her head from her reading and pushed back her glasses on her admirable nose. 'Sorry,' she said, and she caught the brass cubes in her palm, 'I wasn't paying attention.'

Kingsley threw his arms wide in indignation that began as mock but soon decided that it deserved to be genuine. 'But I escaped from the Suspended Straitjacket! I defied the Jaws of Death!'

'You did?' She went back to her document. 'That's splendid, Kingsley. Well done.'

'Of course, it was made more difficult by having to fight off the tiger while I was upside down.'

'Mmm. I imagine it would.'

'And the spitting cobra didn't make things any easier, either.'

'I loathe spitters.' Evadne put her document on the pile in front of her. 'You're testing to see if I'm paying attention, correct?'

'I'd never dream of testing you. I was giving you an opportunity to show how well you were listening, that's all.'

She sighed. 'While I would infinitely prefer supervising your practice and making sure the machinery works perfectly, I admit I was giving time to a problem and a mystery.'

'You do look distracted.'

She held up a letter. 'It's from the current Mrs Oldham. She's resigning.' She refolded the letter with one hand. 'That's the third Mrs Oldham since we rebuilt the school.'

3

Kingsley understood Evadne's pique. As part of her desire to help lost children, she had used her considerable fortune to set up Mrs Oldham's School for Girls, a boarding school for orphans and other unfortunates. When it was burned down by agents of the ancient, evil trio known as the Immortals, and all the children were abducted, it had roused a superhuman fury in Evadne. Singlehandedly, she rescued the girls and destroyed the lair of the Immortals. Some months after that, with liberal application of money and the goodwill she'd accumulated in the Demimonde, she was able to reopen the school with a new Mrs Oldham in charge – the headmistress needing to take on the name in order to maintain the brass plaque at the front of the school, according to Evadne. However, being in charge of forty or so children from circumstances that could charitably be described as "difficult' was not the easiest of positions.

'You need another Mrs Oldham; I assume that's the problem.'

'Correct.'

'And the mystery?'

Evadne gestured at the metal box on the table. It was the size of a large family Bible. 'I've had many deliveries lately but this one, it appears, was never meant to be here.' She waved this away. 'Never mind.' She gave him the sort of appraisal he had seen her direct at temperamental machinery. 'The Jaws of Death operated smoothly?'

'As in nearly bisecting Kingsley Ward? I suppose you could say that.'

'I'm glad my design meets your approval.'

'And I'm glad I didn't take any more than the three minutes you set on the timer. Beastly, those jaws.'

4

'Timer?' Evadne stood and sauntered towards him with her accustomed grace. She'd unaccountably thrown herself into what she called a military phase, and was wearing a blue linen sailor suit that reached to her ankles and a jaunty nautical cap. Her hair was braided so it hung down the middle of her back. Kingsley found the combination of the winsome and the martial both charming and deeply unsettling. 'I discarded the timer notion,' she continued. 'When I gave the plans to my Demimonde foundrymen, I made a few revisions to your notes. The jaws won't close until you step off the platform.'

'Really? I thought I'd gauged it perfectly. I'm crushed.'

'No, you're not, and that's the whole point of my emendations.'

Kingsley tried to step off the tiny stage. 'My tails are caught.'

Evadne balanced herself with a hand on his shoulder and peered behind him. 'So it would seem.' She tugged. 'There.'

Kingsley dusted off his lapels while Evadne crouched and adjusted a lever on the side of the machine. It had been delivered in the middle of the night by a gang of navvies who wore their furtiveness as others would wear cloth caps. The metal jaws gleamed, looking deadly enough for the most bloodthirsty audience – at the Alhambra, say. The entire mechanism was encased in an elaborate grid of ebony and silver for the appropriate blending of drama and menace. It overtopped his tallness by a good two feet. Kingsley thought it was magnificent. 'I think we now have a fine centrepiece for the Extraordinaires,' he said.

Evadne straightened and wiped her hands together. 'If we could only get a booking, we'd find out.'

TWO

'Don't worry, you two, this new act will be a stunning success, I'm sure of it.'

A small bespectacled man stood in the doorway. He brandished a paper bag and, even at that distance, Kingsley could smell that it was packed with fresh currant buns.

'I'm glad you're back, Mr Kipling,' Evadne said. 'But these Hindi texts we've been puzzling over can wait until after Kingsley and I have sorted out a few things.'

'I see,' the famous author said. He touched his moustache with a finger and looked from Evadne to Kingsley. 'It appears that I've walked in on a contretemps.'

'Only a mild disagreement,' Evadne said. 'Kingsley here is still a babe in the theatre world and doesn't understand that we're officially what's known as "between engagements".'

Rudyard Kipling, the writer whom Kingsley had come

to count as a friend and a confidant, looked at them both and Kingsley had the distinct impression that he'd summed up the awkwardness of the situation in an instant. Kipling placed the paper bag on the table. 'I think I'll make the tea it would seem we all need. Later, we can get back to sorting through your correspondence, Evadne.'

'There goes a discreet man,' Kingsley said as the author disappeared into the small kitchen. He used both hands to push back his hair, snagged on a curl and disentangled his fingers. *A haircut, soon,* he told himself. 'Back to my point: it seems that we're doing a lot of betweening and not much engaging, lately.'

'And pish to you,' Evadne murmured, but her head was down again, the brass cubes were looping and she was giving a fine impression of having dismissed him.

Bridling, Kingsley turned away – even though he knew that the patchiness of their bookings over the last six months had been his fault and she was restraining herself from pointing this out.

The Extraordinaires – their magic and juggling duo – initially had some success. Perhaps it had been due to the exhilaration that came from saving the world, and possibly saving it twice, but their skills had blended beautifully in those early performances. Despite constant uneasiness about possible vengeance from the sorcerers they'd defeated – the Immortals – a well-received week at the Theatre Royal in Bath had resulted in their climbing above the bottom of the bill for a fortnight at the Everyman Theatre in Cheltenham and as 1909 began, their star was on the rise.

Kingsley first began to struggle during their time at the Peterborough Hippodrome a week later. Not with the mechanics of his escapes – he continued to sweat over them, practising maniacally between performances – but with the re-emergence of his wild side.

After his adventure the previous May, in which he'd smuggled himself into the headquarters of the Immortals, he'd thought he'd reconciled his inner wildness with the rational, civilised Kingsley. He'd acknowledged this wild side as part of himself, and had accepted that it provided him with a useful way to see the world. He'd thought that his inner struggle was over.

At Peterborough, he'd discovered otherwise. If it hadn't been for Evadne's magnificent juggling, the performance would have been an utter disaster. As he struggled within a metal chest that was swinging across the stage, Kingsley's wild side panicked. He had barely mastered it.

After that, he had to admit that he was growing more wild, not less. Sometimes he found himself at his window at night, listening for the call of the pack and trembling at the sounds that came to him through the darkness. His sense of smell was even better than ever, too, and he experienced an awareness of his surroundings that made him feel as if he'd spent much of his life half-blind. He could smell *fear* in people. But these benefits came at a cost as his wild side continued to strive for dominance.

More subtle than the nagging desire to howl was the longing that came to him at unexpected times, a craving for a world less civilised, a world of tractless wilderness far from the touch of humanity. It would take him unawares – while rehearsing, while trying to sleep – and would overwhelm him with an unbearable sense of loss for something he'd never had. Each time, he had to catch himself lest he fling everything aside, abandon civilisation and set off to roam the untouched lands for good.

He grew even more worried when he found himself studying steamship schedules in the newspaper and considering how long it would take to get to the north of Canada, or to India, or even far-away Australia.

Kingsley had soon learned how difficult it was to arrest downhill motion. The Regent Theatre, Salford. The Nottingham Empire. The Buxton Opera House. Her Majesty's, in Aberdeen. By this time, it was only Evadne's supreme skill and otherworldly appearance that kept audiences at all satisfied. Gradually, though, their stage partnership began to show the strain.

After an embarrassing performance at the Grand Theatre in Wolverhampton (the irony of which didn't escape him) Kingsley had called a halt. Time was needed, he declared, to refine their act, to develop new material. The dressing-room was where he made this announcement – with the angry stage manager outside and Evadne arranging a blanket around his trembling shoulders, then agreeing without an argument.

Kingsley was convinced the Jaws of Death was the beginning of their return to the stage. Escaping from such an elaborate and dangerous device was sure to win an audience – and it would be a step towards saving himself.

In those painful moments when he was candid with himself, Kingsley admitted that he was at various times on the verge of slipping away, being torn apart or breaking down, and sometimes all three at once. All these hurt, but more painful was the knowledge that he may not be as robust in temperament as he had thought – or as he wished he were.

What he wanted, above all else, was to unify himself, to bring his wildness and his civilised self together. He wanted to be sound. Once he achieved this, he was sure his showmanship would return but, in all honesty, he knew that this wasn't his major consideration.

He didn't like disappointing those whose esteem he valued and he was determined not to let it happen any longer.

He cleared his throat, turned and presented himself to Evadne. 'I confess that I've been a little distracted lately.'

Evadne looked up, but kept a finger on the document she was reading. 'In your line of work, that's unfortunate. Possibly lethally unfortunate.'

'I apologise. It's my wildness again.'

She put the document on the table and laced her hands. 'I know.'

'I thought you hadn't noticed.'

'Please. The snarling, the growling, the way you look at cats? It was hard *not* to notice.' She was trying to look stern, Kingsley could tell. 'Do you have any explanations?'

Kingsley shook his head. 'I fear that any explanations are hidden in my past.'

Evadne quickly stood. 'And that's what I've been waiting for. Mr Kipling! I think he's ready!'

Kipling re-entered the workshop carrying a tray complete with cups, saucers and teapot in a jaunty tea-cosy that Evadne admitted she'd knitted years ago in a fit of unaccountable domesticity. He was smiling broadly. 'My boy. I'm glad to hear it.'

'Hear what? And I'm ready for what? For tea?'

'That you're ready to confront your past,' Evadne said. Kipling put the tray on the table next to the bag of buns. 'In preparation for this moment,' Evadne continued, 'I've been investigating your history with a view to restoring it to you and making you a whole, integrated and content young man. With help from Mr Kipling, of course.'

'Since you were raised by a wolf pack in India,' Kipling said as he poured the tea, 'and I, as it happens, have some knowledge of such things.'

Kipling had heard rumours of Kingsley's origins. Fascinated by the parallels with Mowgli, the hero of *The Jungle Book*, he had sought out Kingsley and introduced himself, thereby beginning a friendship that began awkwardly but had become staunch.

Evadne plucked a document from a pile. '*Exempli gratia*: we've just had a shipment from Madras, with some more information about the military career of your father, Major Greville Sanderson. Letters, some personal recollections, and this.'

She held out a photograph. Kingsley took it and sat, all the strength leaving his legs. While he battled tears, he gazed at a tall man in military uniform, a man whose eyes were distant, but whose mouth – under a rakish moustache – was on the verge of smiling. Kingsley turned it over: *Major Greville Sanderson, attached to Madras Light Cavalry.* 'You've been investigating my past?'

'Kingsley,' Evadne said with some heat, 'you've been in a funk for some months now. Since you've had trouble dragging yourself out of it, I took matters into my own hands.'

'For purely professional reasons, of course.'

She glanced at him sharply. 'If my partner can't hold his end up, then the Extraordinaires is in trouble.' She

11

pointed at the deliveries. 'This is part of my funk-ending enterprise.'

'I'd prefer to call it a brown study rather than a funk.' Kingsley took the cup of tea and the currant bun that Kipling offered. 'It sounds rather more stylish.'

'Brown is rarely stylish,' Evadne said. 'Practical, perhaps, but rarely stylish.'

'I think this could be for the best,' Kipling said, slipping himself into the exchange much as a referee would step between two boxers. 'Your current state suggests a life with much unresolved. You admit you know little of your parents or your upbringing, even your very survival in the wild. With knowledge of these things should come understanding. With understanding comes peace.'

Kingsley stared at the table with its stacks of letters, its assorted books and ledgers and the mysterious box that had irritated Evadne so. 'All this is part of your investigation?'

'I've been working for months,' she said, 'on several fronts, including various regiments and civil service departments, and getting nowhere until I asked Mr Kipling for help.'

'The Indian Civil Service ...' Mr Kipling spread his hands. 'It's a vast and mysterious thing.'

Evadne went on. 'Mr Kipling introduced me to the head of the Indian Forestry Service. Eventually I was able to correspond with the two officers who found you as an infant.'

'These were the men who actually discovered you with the wolf pack. The ones who gave you to Dr Ward as a three-year-old who could run like the wind,' Kipling said.

'Windy Kingsley,' Kingsley said faintly. 'That's me.'

'They found a box a year after Dr Ward left India with you. In a cave, near the lair of the wolf pack,' Evadne said. 'Someone had been living there for some time, maybe half a dozen years ago.'

'And inside this box?'

'A journal.' She looked at Kingsley seriously. 'Belonging to your father.'

She held up a small, leather-bound volume, much worn and battered. Kingsley found it hard to breathe. All he could make out were the stamped letters that spelled 'Sanderson'.

While Kingsley gaped, Kipling shot to his feet. 'Good heavens! You arranged for it to be sent to you? How splendid!'

'That's the puzzling thing,' Evadne said. 'I tried to obtain it but couldn't. The Forestry men said they'd already given the box to someone from the Army.' She rapped the mysterious box with a knuckle. 'And now here it is, an unaccounted-for delivery containing the very item I've been seeking.'

'I don't understand,' Kingsley said.

'And nor do I,' said Evadne. 'And that vexes me. And when I'm vexed I want to do something about it, and quickly.'

'Oh, I agree.' Kingsley realised he was grinding his jaw, as if attempting to reduce all this to manageable pieces. As a whole, it was too much to cope with.

'A shipping mix-up, no doubt, but one that has worked to our advantage,' Kipling suggested. He peered at the shipping marks on the box. 'It's from India, but there's no indication of who sent it. Finding the shipping agent used to get it into the country could be useful. He'd know who sent it in the first place.'

'Shipping agent?' Kingsley asked.

'The firm that handles shipments in and out of the country, liaising with the steamer companies, warehouse owners and Customs.'

'I've used Morton's in the past,' Evadne said. 'And from this manifest it appears the box was handled by the same firm.'

'Indian specialists, no doubt.' Kipling took out his pocket watch. 'Ah, my two hours are at an end. I'm afraid I must leave you.'

'Must you, Mr Kipling?' Evadne said. 'You've been so helpful.'

The author stood and brushed bun crumbs from his jacket. 'I'm afraid so. When you invited me to help you today, I told you I could only spare a few hours and I've already stayed longer than I should have. I have an appointment that I'd like to pretend is both clandestine and dangerous, but is actually with my bank manager – and it doesn't do to cross your bank manager. You must promise, however, that after you've read Major Sanderson's journal you'll tell me everything, or I will expire with curiosity.'

Once Mr Kipling had left, Evadne took the journal. Kingsley was eager to read it, but he was moved by what Evadne had done for him and so allowed her first perusal. The decision was made easier by a perverse reluctance that had come upon him. He had wanted such a document so badly that now it was in his grasp he was hesitant to confront it squarely, half-afraid at what it might hold.

Waiting was difficult. In part, he blamed his inner restlessness on his lack of knowledge about his past. It was as if he had a great hole inside him – and the journal Evadne had found for him could fill in that hole.

When he considered this, he was nearly overcome with gratitude. Evadne had gone to remarkable lengths. He tried to frame an appropriate statement of thanks, something that she would understand was heartfelt and not flippant, but he was distracted by a sound from the basement.

He peered towards the stairs. 'Did you hear something from downstairs?'

'No, and you've interrupted just as I was beginning to make sense of your father's complex lines of reporting – but that's no matter, as we appear to have visitors.' He turned back to find Evadne crouching and listening to one of her rat-like Myrmidons.

Kingsley grimaced. He'd never warmed to Evadne's creatures. No matter how helpful they were as sentries and messengers, they were far too ratty for his liking.

A familiar scent told Kingsley who the visitors were before he saw his foster father's limping gait and leonine countenance. The other, though, was a stranger. His wild side, almost automatically, was wary, but his father beamed and waved his walking stick. 'Kingsley! Evadne! I'm glad you're here!'

'Father!' The title was odd on Kingsley's lips after the recent topic of conversation. He had great affection for Dr Ward, but the recent revelations about his true father left him confused. He owed the old man so much – his upbringing, his education, and a great deal of tolerance, for instance. The ordeal of Dr Ward's kidnapping had angered Kingsley, but had also renewed his respect for the strength of the man who had raised him as a civilised, rational being.

Dr Ward looked well recovered from the injuries inflicted upon him by the Neanderthals, but Kingsley had never seen the slim, dark woman on his arm. He took her to be half Dr Ward's age, but he revised that figure upwards to middle thirties, then down again by several years before giving up in confusion.

She had eyes like polished coal and Kingsley barely kept himself from staring at the green jewel in the side of her nose – an emerald like a drop of dragon's blood. She was wearing a dark grey-blue silk dress and she had a black taffeta bag at her side. She sought Kingsley's gaze and held it with an intensity that nearly made him gasp.

Dr Ward beamed. 'Kingsley, I'm proud whenever I hear you call me Father.' He gestured grandly at the woman on his arm. 'And now I'd like you to extend it a little.'

'I beg your pardon?'

'Kingsley, I'd like you to meet your new mother.'

THREE

I'm suddenly suffering a surfeit of family, Kingsley thought, as he weighed up whether he felt as if he'd been hit behind the ear with a sock full of sand or run over by an elephant. He hardly heard Dr Ward's addendum: 'Or mother-to-be, more correctly. Getting ahead of myself, there.'

Kingsley had never known his mother, Alice Sanderson. He'd never known a foster mother, either, as Dr Ward had never married. So he was quite unaccustomed to the entire concept of a female parent. Of course he'd seen the mothers of other boys when they visited the school at end of term, so he was aware they existed and that they came in a variety of shapes and sizes. He understood from these experiences that mothers were treated in many ways, from aloof disdain to unashamed affection, and that their duties with their sons mostly entailed dabbing at faces with moistened handkerchiefs.

17

Confronted by this exotic woman, however, he had no idea how to behave, so he assumed all the characteristics of a statue while deep inside his wild self bristled with wariness.

Dr Ward coughed. 'Now, I might be getting ahead of myself, Kingsley, but introducing Mrs Winter as your mother-to-be didn't quite have the theatrical impact I thought you'd enjoy.'

Mrs Winter held out a lace-gloved hand. 'Kingsley,' she said in a voice that was lower than he expected. 'At last.'

Kingsley regained control of his body enough to decalcify his movements. He took her hand and bowed over it while silent explosions of confusion bounced around inside his skull. Who *was* this woman? Why had his foster father never even *mentioned* her before?

He straightened to find Evadne leaning forward as if she were on the edge of a diving board, every atom of her being demanding an introduction. Dr Ward cheerily performed this duty. 'Evadne, I'd like you to meet Mrs Selene Winter, my fiancée. My dear, this is Evadne Stephens, my son's partner.'

'Mrs Winter,' Evadne said, emphasising the title just enough for Kingsley to add 'possibly widowed' to the jigsaw image he'd assembled, right next to his vague stab at her age. He was rather more certain of 'Anglo-Indian', thanks to the nose jewel that was prompting unsettlingly vague memories, but he was sure that he was missing many, many pieces. He was impressed, nonetheless, at how she accepted Evadne's curious appearance with equanimity.

He wanted to do the right thing – for his foster father's sake – so he gathered himself and smiled. 'Congratulations, both of you. And when's the wedding to be?'

Dr Ward relaxed minutely, and Kingsley knew then that despite his bonhomie his foster father had been anxious about Kingsley's reaction. He also took in a tiny nod of approval from Evadne. His cheeks went warm.

'Soon, but we haven't set a date yet,' Dr Ward said.

'I'd like our wedding to be in one of your lovely English gardens,' Mrs Winter said. 'And I'm not fussy about a date.'

Dr Ward beamed, then took Kingsley by the arm. 'Do you mind if I have a word with my son, my dear?' he said to Mrs Winter. 'A little business to attend to.'

Mrs Winter smiled and nodded, then Evadne whisked her away. Kingsley saw that they were immediately deep in conversation and he had the disconcerting feeling they were talking about him.

'Now, Kingsley,' Dr Ward said, and Kingsley had to turn away from the two vastly different females. 'I want to reassure you about Mrs Winter.'

'There's no need, Father. While this is all a little surprising, I wish you every happiness.'

'I'm glad about that, but it's the stories I'm worried about.'

'Stories?'

'You know how rumours fly in the Demimonde. You must promise me not to believe everything you hear about Mrs Winter.'

Kingsley was about to point out that his foster father was being needlessly cryptic when a hollow boom resounded from the basement.

Kingsley looked at Evadne to find her looking at him. He shrugged at the same time as she did, much to the amusement of both Dr Ward and Mrs Winter, but

Kingsley had only taken a few paces towards the stairs when the source of the noise became all too apparent.

'Spawn!' Evadne cried as a long-limbed, roughly human creature mounted the stairs three at a time. Its head was hairless and its skin was dull and greyish. It wore a dark blue suit that Kingsley decided had definitely seen better days and better occupants.

Kingsley had never overcome the revulsion that the servants of the Immortals invoked. The creatures were made by infernal magic, created from severed parts of the Immortals' own bodies. Their origins stayed with them, even though they were strong, enduring and totally obedient to the will of their masters. Kingsley thought that they always carried a taint of corruption.

'Kingsley, look out!' Dr Ward cried, but Kingsley had already seen that more of the horrid creatures were bounding up the stairs behind the first. Kingsley leaped for a length of chain dangling from one of the rafters. He'd been using it in his escaping practice and he knew it was strong and trustworthy. He swung it in a vicious arc. The first Spawn stopped its headlong rush and reeled back, hissing, and fell on its comrades. They tumbled backwards in a tangle but in an instant they were on their feet again and boiling out of the stairwell.

'They'll not take you, Selene, not again!' Dr Ward cried out and stood in front of his wife-to-be. Kingsley caught a glimpse of her face and while she was horrified, there was no surprise there at all. He had no time to consider this, for the Spawn were still coming. Kingsley advanced, swinging the chain around his head as if he were a hammer thrower. Without hesitating, the first Spawn leaped. The chain struck and wrapped around its torso. The creature howled, its features contorted with pain, but its companions grabbed the chain and clung to it with ferocious strength; Kingsley was engaged in a furious tug of war. He was unwilling to drop his end of the chain and surrender his weapon, but four or five more of the creatures were already swarming over the tangle at the top of the stairs.

Kingsley snarled. He yanked at the chain with such force that it was torn from the grasp of his foes, then he cracked it like a whip, sending the foremost of the creatures backwards. Its comrades hesitated. Kingsley was congratulating himself for presenting a fearsome picture, Horatio at the bridge, but then he became aware of a presence at his side. A sabre was extended, point and edge held unwavering by a slim, snowy-white wrist.

'Where did you find a blade so quickly?' he said without taking his eyes from the Spawn, who were again massing at the head of the stairs.

Evadne wove the point of the sabre in an elegant figure of eight. 'Really, Kingsley. Keeping weapons nearby is just common sense when in the Demimonde.'

The Spawn chattered, and a dozen more pushed up from below, groaning in their eagerness to join battle. Kingsley risked a glance behind him and saw that his foster father had taken Mrs Winter to the far end of the room and was brandishing a broom. Kingsley was startled to see, however, that she was struggling and arguing vehemently with him. He had no further time to wonder at this, for the vanguard of the Spawn, reassured by the reinforcements, charged out of the stairwell.

The workshop became a melee. As the creatures closed, Kingsley's chain became useless and he had to resort to his fists. He drove a jab at the face of the quickest of the Spawn and as its head snapped back he advanced and crashed a round-arm blow into its ear. The Spawn slammed against its comrade, as Kingsley had hoped. It kept them both from attacking Evadne from the side while she herded two more back with her flashing blade, her booted foot stamping a rhythm that signalled peril for those in front of her.

Kingsley heard Dr Ward shouting, and he hoped his foster father was either fleeing with his intended or calling for help, although the good citizens in the district were more likely to take the chance to nip in and make off with anything not nailed down than they were to lend aid. No likelihood of police, either, as police only entered the Demimonde on important missions, and then only reluctantly.

More Spawn pushed up the stairs and they yammered wordless cries as they came. Kingsley waded into the press, trying to stop them spreading and surrounding Evadne and him. He used shoulders and elbows as much as his fists, and he was also happy to employ knees and boots. Gradually, though, both Evadne and he were forced back until Kingsley felt the table behind him. He grabbed a clawing arm and dragged its owner sideways. This tripped the Spawn and gave Kingsley a little room to work in. He turned and grabbed a chair, which he immediately used to batter his assailants while giving thanks for the solid woodwork and good craftsmanship – thanks that were just a little too early, as the chair splintered on the head of a particularly red-eyed Spawn who was making a dive under Evadne's blade.

'Remind me to buy better furniture next time!' he shouted.

'I'll get you to read "A Guide to Furniture as Weaponry" before you do!' Evadne cried. She lunged, and disengaged. A Spawn spun away, screeching.

Three Spawn tackled Kingsley at once and rammed him back against the table. It toppled, and Kingsley threw himself into a back somersault but slipped and sprawled upon landing. They leaped on him. He grappled on hands and knees, doing his best to keep fingers from his eyes and teeth from his throat as the hideous creatures pounced. His fists were raw and bloody and he was pretending that the rib low down on his left side wasn't cracked at all. Evadne was nearby, still taunting the creatures, which he took as a good sign – not for them, but as an indication of her relative safety.

A stone-like fist took him on the temple. While a vast, cosmic ringing seized him, all the strength left his muscles and black curtains began to draw across his vision. He heard his name, dimly, as if the speaker were miles away on a foggy day in a world made of smoke.

Kingsley struggled to hold onto the last vestiges of consciousness and his wild side panicked, whimpering to find a safe place, a cave, a lair to hide in. He tried to keep his fists up, but they felt as if they weighed a hundredweight apiece, and he understood, then, that he was actually on his back, on the floor, and he had three or four Spawn on top of him who were doing their best to tear him apart.

At that moment, he had a curious sensation. Stirrings. Pluckings. Shiftings around and about, as if thousands of tiny fingers were pinching him. It began in the parts of his body touching the floor, but soon the rustling swarmed all over him. While not gentle, the sensation wasn't painful.

23

The Spawn, however, reacted differently. They began to shriek – not with triumph, but with dismay. Those on top of Kingsley ceased their clawing and scrambled away, careless of where they put their hands and feet.

Bruised, gasping and relieved at the retreat of the hideous creatures, Kingsley dragged himself to his knees.

Evadne was panting hard a few yards away, her back to a pillar. She wiped her cheek with the back of her hand and waved wearily at him. Once he'd established that she was safe, he was able to gawp at the sight before him.

The Spawn had all been knocked off their feet. They were in a great untidy heap on the floor, squealing and gibbering, but they were doing their best to crawl back towards the stairs. Kingsley shook his head, cleared it a little, and looked again. *They're not doing it themselves. It's being done to them.*

The Spawn were clawing at the floor, at the balustrades, at each other, at anything to *stop* their progress, but their efforts were futile. Slowly but inexorably, despite all their struggles, the Spawn were being dragged by invisible hands as carelessly as if they were old rugs on the way to the rubbish heap. They tumbled down the stairs, shrieking all the way. When an echoing *boom* came from below, Kingsley realised he was quite dizzy, so he let out the breath he'd been holding and sagged to the floor on all fours.

'Thank you.'

The voice was low and intense. Kingsley straightened and looked up, ready to modestly decline Mrs Winter's gratitude, but he deflated when he saw that she wasn't addressing him. She was addressing the blank, white-washed wall of the workshop.

Now, that's odd. What was even more odd, however, was that he was finding it difficult to focus on her. He put a hand to his brow. *Concussion. That must be it.*

It was the only explanation for his seeing double in such a peculiar way. Mrs Winter was blurred, as if two images of her were overlapping. He went to draw attention to this curious phenomenon when he noticed that his foster father, standing a few paces away from Mrs Winter, was startlingly unblurred.

Still dazed, he went to point it out to Evadne, but she was already looking in the same direction – and with more than a touch of concern. Then he saw that Dr Ward was also a picture of apprehension.

Mrs Winter continued to address the blank wall.

Nothing, Kingsley thought, bemused. *She's staring at nothing.*

Then he squinted, shaded his eyes and nearly choked. Was the air *twisting* in front of Mrs Winter? She faced what looked like a small whirlwind, but a bizarrely slow whirlwind; one that was spinning with the regularity of a metronome, a column of glassiness, hard to see and harder to hold in one's vision, nearly reaching the ceiling and an arm span wide.

'We thank you.'

Kingsley shivered. Mrs Winter's voice was deeper, more resonant, and altogether more *present* that it had been previously.

'Thank you,' Dr Ward and Evadne echoed in a manner Kingsley found unsettlingly ritualistic.

He straightened his jacket and winced at his bleeding knuckles. He was more than happy to acknowledge aid. 'And who is it we're thanking?' he said as he went to Evadne's side. He was relieved to see that she was unharmed.

'The lar of this place,' Mrs Winter said without turning her head, 'the guardian god, long gone, from when this was a Roman outpost. I opened the way and it performed its duty. It protected us from the intruders.'

'A god? Here? In our workshop?' Kingsley said. Evadne's elbow caught him in the side, where a massive bruise was taking up residence. He managed to turn his yelp into a cough, then he saw his father's frown. 'And I'd just like to add my thanks for a duty well done.'

Mrs Winter held her hands up in front of her, palms out. Kingsley once again had the disturbing impression of her duality. He caught Evadne's eye and she discreetly held up two fingers and raised an eyebrow.

Mrs Winter bowed to the shifting air. She began to speak softly; Kingsley couldn't make out the words. Then she brought her hands together. The whirling column of air – the lar? – vanished.

Dr Ward hurried to her side and took her arm. He turned her around slowly. She staggered a little, and clutched at him before glaring at Kingsley and Evadne. 'If it weren't for Malcolm, I would have let the filthy brutes take you.'

Kingsley held up both hands, apologising – but then he realised he didn't know what he was apologising for.

'I'm sorry,' Evadne said, 'but what have we done?'

'Malcolm said your dealings with the Immortals were over. From the appearance of the Spawn creatures, that is evidently not the case.'

In the awkward silence this brought about, as Kingsley grappled with astonishment, bewilderment and hurt and Evadne cleaned her sabre, Dr Ward looked from his intended, to his foster son and the juggler and back again before pursing his lips. 'I don't know about the rest of you,' he declared, 'but I *definitely* need a good cup of tea.'

'No.' Mrs Winter disengaged herself from him. She brushed herself off and straightened her hat. 'We must go. Now.'

'Now?' Dr Ward. 'Where?'

'The Hebrides. You said you wanted to go there for your linguistic research.'

'I did, but we just arrived here. And – just in case you'd forgotten – we have a wedding to arrange.'

'That can wait.'

Kingsley felt as if he were stumbling about in a cellar, blindfolded, trying to catch a horde of black cats. 'You can't leave so promptly. You've only just arrived.'

Mrs Winter glanced at him with a look so ferocious that his wild self immediately wanted to turn tail and flee. She took Dr Ward by the arm. 'Malcolm. Now.'

'Now, eh?' Dr Ward shrugged to Kingsley and Evadne. 'Mrs Winter had some ugly encounters with the Immortals while in India. I understand why she needs to stay well away from them, if they're about. We'll write and let you know when we'll be back.' He coughed. 'We'll sort this out, don't you worry.'

Kingsley was having trouble putting words together. He'd just found evidence of his true father, been presented with a potential foster mother he'd never heard of, one who had run up against the Immortals in the past, then he had been attacked by Spawn and rescued by a god. The world was suddenly a much stranger and much more disconcerting place than it had been an hour ago.

27

Evadne touched Kingsley's arm as he grappled with his astonishment. 'Don't worry, Dr Ward,' she said. 'Just let us know if there is anything we can do about the wedding.'

'Wait,' Kingsley said. 'What?'

They were gone and Kingsley was left with his unresolved bewilderment.

Evadne lifted his hand and studied his knuckles. 'Don't worry. They'll be fine.'

'Didn't that seem strange to you?' He ran his free hand through his hair. 'She just called up a god and overwhelmed a horde of Spawn, then she says we're awful and announces that it's time to visit some Scottish islanders.'

'It's hard to say if it's strange. I don't know her very well. Perhaps she does that sort of thing all the time.' Evadne shrugged. 'She could just be a nervous bride.'

'She didn't strike me as a nervous bride. And, besides, how is running off to the Hebrides a good way to deal with pre-wedding nerves?'

'Everyone is different, Kingsley,' Evadne said solemnly. 'I thought you, of all people, would appreciate that. Now, let's get you cleaned up.'

Kingsley looked at the upturned table and the general destruction wrought by the Spawn. 'You understand, of course, that this suggests that the Immortals are back.'

'Back and looking for revenge after our efforts last year. Call me foolish, but after all that waiting, I'm actually relieved they've shown themselves again.'

Kingsley heaved the table to its feet, then he stooped and searched in the mess. He held up the metal box. 'The journal's missing.'

'It must have been knocked aside in the fight.'

Ten minutes of sorting through papers, books, wires and tools was enough to convince Kingsley. 'It's definitely gone,' he said, and he had that peculiar feeling one has upon finding something one didn't know was lost – and then losing it again.

Evadne slotted a screwdriver into the rack that Kingsley had lifted back into place against the wall. 'What would the Spawn want with your father's journal?'

'The implications of that horrify me, but it's the other possibility that worries me more.'

Evadne frowned. 'You don't think Mrs Winter took it, do you?'

'All I know is that she didn't look surprised when the Spawn appeared. Angry, perhaps, but not surprised.'

'And that's enough for you to suspect her? Kingsley, you worry me enough as it is. I don't need the extra burden of worrying if you're seeing enemies everywhere.'

'I could be being unfair, but we can't discount the possibility.'

'It's far more likely that the Immortals have gathered their resources and are up and about again. Remember: they want you for your brain.'

Kingsley hesitated. Evadne didn't always see clearly where the Immortals were concerned. 'And when they couldn't get me they took my real father's journal?'

'They must have found out it was here. It was a second-best prize. Finding out about your past mightn't only answer your questions, you know, it might answer theirs about how you gained your wildness, and how you manage it.'

Kingsley wasn't entirely convinced. He remembered how Mrs Winter had behaved after she'd seen the godling off. The fury in her eyes when she accused them of bringing the Immortals down on her was formidable – and confusing.

'We'll get it back,' Evadne said, mistakenly believing his silence came from concern for Major Sanderson's journal. 'We'll need a plan. But not here, not now that the Immortals know of the place.'

He saw a shiny corner projecting from under a ledger that had been thrown aside in the fracas. He bent and plucked the photograph of his father from the mess. He straightened it and, then, with a forefinger, touched the man who had been his father. He managed a smile. 'D'you know anywhere safe?'

'It so happens that I have an underground refuge that is highly secret, filled with alarmingly destructive weapons, and possessing a very fine bath.'

'Perfect.'

FOUR

Leetha clung to the memory of the smells of her home. The spiciness that hung in the moist, warm air there was different from the metallic coldness that surrounded her in the lair of the sorcerers. The others of her people, the ones who had been taken when she had, looked to her for leadership. Their expectations were heavy on her shoulders. The chill, the dark, the confining walls, nothing was like their home. She wept over it. Leader's tears, she explained. The others understood.

Leetha had not known that she and her people were small until she was ten years old. That was when her parents let her see her first stranger, one of the big people from the other side of their island. Her mother and father held her hand as they travelled for two days. They ghosted through the thick, lush greenery until they came to the river where the women washed at the stones.

Leetha heard the singing first. It made her heart light. She wondered who it was and why they were singing nonsense, words she could not understand. When she saw the singers, she was not afraid; not at first, not hidden as she was in dense undergrowth. Then she felt the hand of her mother tighten on her shoulder. She looked up to see her alert and ready to flee.

The women pounded bright fabric on the rocks, flailing rainbows and laughing when a dog wandered past and was splashed. Then Leetha could see that even the shortest of the washerwomen was twice her own height.

'Big people,' her father whispered. 'Never let yourself be seen by them.'

Using their skill for hiding, they eased back through the bushes. They ignored the path. They hid themselves again in the byways of the jungle until they reached the caves that were their home.

That night, young Leetha, the Leetha who was happy and free, scratched pictures on the stone wall next to where she slept. Charcoal black lines, flickering in the light of the fire she loved so much. One was Leetha, smiling. One was a big person, towering over her. The big person was smiling, too.

She grew and her friends grew around her, but she knew she would never be as tall as the big people. Her people kept to themselves in the rocky, unloved heart of the island. They were few, ten or twenty families, but life was good. The land gave them what they needed, if they listened closely enough. In return, they tended it with their hearts, never taking too much. They were part of the world and they measured their lives in ways foreign to the clocks and calendars she was forced to worship in the lair of the sorcerers.

Her people had three gifts that had allowed them to survive. They could hide, avoiding notice if they chose. They were eternally curious, which meant they learned much of the world around them. And they loved fire and were good at making it wherever they were, from whatever was available. These skills gave her people a place. They were happy in their world, living apart from the big people who spread over most of their island. Safe, secure and hidden.

Then she, and thirty of her kin, were taken away from their home.

Leetha lay in her bed, clutching the sheet beneath her chin and holding onto her memories. She waited for the bell. As every morning, she had woken before it shouted at her but still she was shocked when it yammered. Its metal voice demanded that she rise and report to the factory floor. She sat on the edge of her bunk and watched the others of her kin rise, grumbling and complaining.

She ate while assembling the machine parts. The food had no taste, no texture, no smell apart from the sour odour of paste. While she screwed and tightened, she let her mind wander. She needed to know more about her captors. They made Leetha and her kin work hard with their machines and their electricity. Leetha had learned much about this world, but she knew there was much she still did not know. This hurt. It was a hole inside her that ached, and only by finding out would it be filled. Of course, the more she found out, the more likely she would be able to help her people escape – but finding out was more than that. It was something she needed to do, or else she would be itchy, jumpy, incomplete and on edge.

She sighed and chose another nut to match the bolt she was tightening. She needed to risk much – again – and go exploring.

A guard came and pointed at her with his sparky stick. 'Report to the testing area,' he said.

She had never been able to learn the guard's name, but she called him Glass Face – to herself – for he wore the spectacles to help him see. She had learned that he liked the black sweet called liquorice and often kept some in his pockets. She had overheard that he had a brother, too, and it made her wonder about the rest of his family.

She did not linger at her bench, not even to tidy. She let the bolt fall from her hands. It bounced on the floor then skittered away like a beetle finding a home under a leaf.

With Glass Face and his sparky stick behind her, she trotted on bare feet across the concrete floor. She grimaced. So cold. So smooth.

The big steel doors at the end of the corridor awaited her. She never thought of running away, no matter how her insides folded up on themselves at the thought of more tests. She would last through them as she had the other trials. Some had been hurtful, others harmless. She had once been left in a room, alone, on a chair, with a jug of water and a cup. The door was locked but no-one came, not even when she gathered the courage to call out. When she finished the water, many hours later, the door was opened and she was led back to her quarters. No-one told her what the test meant. Leetha took it as she took a monsoon: something to be endured for the future that lay on the other side of it.

Part of her cried out to know what the tests were for,

but the guards never explained. She wanted to know. She wanted to know so hard it hurt.

This time, Glass Face did not leave. After he led Leetha to a bare table, he stood inside the door. The room was small and white, with hardness everywhere in the walls and the floor and the ceiling. Sounds were strange in these places, not like in Leetha's home where they disappeared into distances, or were swallowed by greenery. Here, they bounced and came back sharply, with edges that hurt.

She wondered what the walls were made of, and how they were made, and who made them. Was she happy at what she had done? Had she done it with love? With care?

Two of the big people entered the room through another door. One was female, one had the hairy growths on his face that Leetha had come to understand were normal, not an illness. Gompers was his name and he was a blank. She had been unable to learn anything about him, try as she might.

Gompers studied Leetha for a time. Then he grunted like a bush pig and sat opposite her. He was wearing the heavy garments that so many of the big people did, and like them he was afraid of colour. His clothes were all black, and grey, and white. Perhaps he did not want to draw attention. Or did he not want a mate?

That was a question that needed an answer, but she had learned better than to ask Gompers anything.

Gompers held a packet made of the paper they were so fond of. He tapped it on the table while Leetha sat still, waiting for the test.

Gompers looked over his shoulder at the female who had entered the room with him. She was small for one of the big people, but would still tower over Leetha. She, too, had no colour. She had the lenses on her eyes, like Glass Face.

'Are you ready to record?' Gompers asked the lens woman.

She held up a pencil and a slab of paper.

'We shall proceed.' Gompers opened his packet. 'Number One.'

He held up an image, one of the magical photographs of these people. It was a picture with all the colour washed out. Two grey dogs were sitting on grey grass. Their tongues were grey and hung out of the side of their grey mouths.

'Pay attention,' Gompers ordered. 'Look at each photograph as I present it.'

Leetha did, for she wanted to have a reputation for obedience. She wanted all of the big people to look at her and think that she would do what she was told, that she was trustworthy and would not make trouble. The more they trusted her, the better chance she had of finding a way to escape.

Leetha stared at the dogs. She glanced at Gompers, who was watching her as a hunter watches prey. Leetha quickly looked back at the dogs. She bit her lip and nodded.

'Did you get that?' Gompers said to the female.

'Yes, sir. Lip biting and nodding.'

'Good.' Gompers put the dogs away. 'Number Two.' Gompers held up another photograph, a ship like the one that took Leetha and her people away from their home. She shuddered.

'Noted, sir,' the female said. 'Trembling.'

'Number Three.'

A big person beating another big person with a stick. Leetha gasped. She trembled at the grey pain in the face of the beaten one and the grey rage in the face of his attacker. Her people were peaceful, hiding rather than fighting, running away rather than attacking. Small children sometimes hit and hurt, but they knew no better. The big people were violent. She had learned that, but she had never grown used to it.

The face in the photograph was an adult with the rage of a child. She sat back and hugged herself, arms crossed over her body.

'Noted, sir.'

'Number Four.'

Gompers presented photograph after photograph to Leetha. She was good and willing. She looked at the images, never turned away.

The test stopped when Leetha was shown a photograph of her home.

Gompers was growing weary, drooping. Leetha was feeling sorry for him. She could never tell how old the big people were, but Gompers had years on him, had seen many winters. He should be home with his family who would take care of him.

He croaked, 'One hundred and fifty-five.'

She looked at the photograph. Suddenly her voice was not a part of her. It cried out, all on its own, a wordless sound like that of a bird, wounded and lost.

The grey image was that of the rocks near the river, near her home. The large rock, shaped like a nose, next to the two small ones and the four trees that leaned just so. There could be nothing else like it in the world.

She reached out slowly. She took the image from the hands of Gompers. She brought it close, but only realised she was weeping when the tears fell onto the shiny, grey image. It was her home, washed free of colour and scent and life, but it was her home. Unable to stop herself, she whispered: 'Where did you get this?'

Gompers did not answer. He peered at her with hard, flat eyes.

She wept. Far, far away, she heard the voice of the female. 'Noted, sir.'

'And pay attention,' Gompers said. 'Wild though these people may be, they have traces of civilised responses. I want each response recorded, tabulated and cross-matched by the time I get back from the north. I *will* find if they are human or not.'

FIVE

Evadne's underground refuge was beneath the immense Olympic Stadium at the White City. Construction was a boon to the Demimonde as, with a measure of cunning, it could mask subterranean building of many sorts. While Evadne's retreat was an impressive defensive redoubt, constructed with battleship-like walls and an impenetrable triple door system, Kingsley was glad she hadn't stinted on the creature comforts.

'That's better.' He propped his walking stick against an armchair, dropped into it and stretched, pushing his hands up over his head. He was tired, and hurting from the wrenching straitjacket escape on top of the assault from the Spawn. He knew he'd soon be sporting a splendid set of bruises.

Evadne finished bolting the last of the three successive heavy steel doors. 'Don't relax too much,' she said. 'We have a journal to find.'

Kingsley took one look at her face. *And that's your excuse for going up against the Immortals again.*

As well as being a virtuoso juggler and an astonishing weaponsmith, Evadne Stephens was an implacable foe of those like the Immortals; those who hurt children. Kingsley had seen her lose her customary poise and fly into a fury when given the opportunity to attack the Immortals, the age-old sorcerers whose continued existence depended on a supply of children.

As a matter of simple humanity, Kingsley was on her side, but he also knew he'd never match her level of fervour in her crusade. In a moment of anguish, she had divulged that she thought herself responsible for the loss of her younger sister, Flora, who had been taken by child stealers while in Evadne's care. She'd never been seen again.

Kingsley remembered how greatly satisfied Evadne had been after she believed she'd destroyed the monsters. Her habitual restlessness had been subdued, and for weeks afterwards she was relaxed. She'd instigated long picnics where they did nothing at all but look at clouds. When she learned that he enjoyed music she insisted on taking him to concerts where he learned to love Elgar and to laugh at Gilbert and Sullivan.

'The Immortals,' he said, as Evadne took up the green velvet armchair on the other side of the parlour, the one directly underneath what Kingsley had decided was a particularly fine Millais.

'The Immortals have your journal,' Evadne responded. She'd tucked her feet up under her and was resting her chin on her fist. 'You know that every day since I managed to demolish their lair under Greenwich, I've been expecting to hear of them.'

'I thought I was the only one who expected them to turn up at any minute.'

'Now, *that* can't have helped your equanimity.'

'Now that you mention it – no, it hasn't helped.'

'None of my usual informants have heard a whisper. They would have let me know.'

'I see. So where do we start?'

'I'll send out my myrmidons to see if they can find anything.' She brushed at the armrest of the chair, eyes on an invisible spot. 'But you're not convinced, are you?'

'I beg your pardon?'

'You're thinking that I'm being over-zealous in my hatred of the Immortals. You're still wondering if Mrs Winter might have stolen the journal.'

Kingsley blinked. *She's done it again. Just as I think I have Evadne Stephens all sorted out, she whirls around and confronts me unexpectedly.* 'I'm worried about my foster father. I don't want anything to happen to him. She's had some sort of run-in with the Immortals in the past. Who's to say they didn't turn her into an agent of some sort?'

'Kingsley, would you say that Dr Ward generally knows what he's doing?'

'I suppose so. Generally.'

'Then can you accept that he wouldn't be with Mrs Winter if she were an agent of the Immortals?'

What if she is and he simply doesn't realise it? 'I suppose so.'

'And since we have no idea where they are, let's assume – with our fingers crossed – that they're safe and well.'

'All that magic she did has me worried. Conjuring up a guardian spirit like that?' He shivered.

'Not a guardian spirit, a lar,' Evadne said. She'd plucked

41

four thumbnail-sized white balls from her belt and began cascading them from hand to hand.

'I've never heard of lars.'

'Lares is the plural. Latin.'

'Lares then. Jupiter, Juno, Venus, I'm familiar with. Vulcan, Apollo, Neptune. Lar? A stuck-up fellow, was he, the god of de dahs?'

'Lares were the guardians and protectors of locations. Worksites, meeting places, things like that. They were little gods, but within their circumscribed realm, they were powerful enough.'

'As we saw. And it was Mrs Winter who controlled it.'

'I'm not sure if control is the right word. I'd prefer summoned, or something like that.'

'A nice distinction.'

'It could be important. Control suggests a level of authority. She was too respectful for that, too cautious.' Evadne tucked the juggling balls back behind her belt. 'I know that the Demimonde is the realm of the outlandish, but having a god appear in one's workshop is dumbfounding.'

'Oh, good, I'm glad you say that. I thought I was the only one who was utterly nonplussed. A god? A real god walloping a horde of Spawn and banishing them? All organised by a woman who's going to be my mother, sooner or later? It sounds like a fairy tale.'

'Believe me, Kingsley, I share your astonishment. And I take it that you were almost equally stunned by your foster father's announcement?'

'About getting married to a woman I'd never heard of before? Imagine you were told that the King was really a giant lizard in disguise and he was about to marry a crocodile. That's about how surprised I was.'

'I thought so, which explains your being at sixes and sevens.'

'I decline to think I was thirteen,' Kingsley said.

'And that, Kingsley, I'll allow to pass.' She pointed. 'You brought your walking stick.'

'I've been practising.' Kingsley took it crosswise, in both hands. 'This may look like a simple walking stick, but in the hands of a master it can be deadly.'

Evadne looked at him slantendicular. 'It's not a sword stick,' she said, 'so you must be going to learn single stick or *canne de combat*.'

He shook his head. 'I'm favouring a more recent variation, following the work of the Swiss professor of arms Monsieur Vigny. It's called "bartitsu". The magazine claimed it's possible to sever a man's jugular vein through the collar of his overcoat with an ordinary Malacca cane.'

'I see. And how do we get him into his overcoat if he's not wearing one?'

'That, my dear Evadne, is one of the mysteries of the art that I suspect will be revealed if I ever find the next edition of the magazine.'

She pursed her lips. 'I'm glad that my weaponry for our visit to Morton's is a little more substantial.'

'The shipping agent?' He tapped himself on the forehead with the head of the cane. 'Of course. If we don't know where the journal has gone, we should find out where it came from.'

'Exactly. While we're waiting for my myrmidons to

learn what they can, let's investigate the origins of this mysterious delivery.'

'Especially since this is a mystery that the Immortals might well be interested in too.'

She smiled slowly. 'That, my dear Kingsley, is a consummation devoutly to be wished.'

SIX

Leetha remembered being brought to this place in the city, the lair of the sorcerers and the home of their machines.

All her life, Leetha had spied on the big people who lived on her island. Their ways fascinated her; how they differed from her people's and how they were alike. The big people who took them from their home, however, were nothing like those who shared the island with her kin.

They came to the caves at dawn, when Leetha was still asleep. They were bigger than the islanders. They wore strange heavy clothes all over their bodies. Some had hair on their faces, so that Leetha wondered if they were demons, especially when one of them used a metal rod to make a noise like thunder.

Some of her people ran and escaped. Most were too afraid. Some were too curious and peered from bushes, wondering what these intruders wanted and where they were from. They were captured in nets.

Leetha and thirty of her kin were put in chains. They were marched through the jungle, which was silent except for the wailing of those left behind in the caves.

They were taken to the sea and then the nightmare truly began. They were herded onto a boat, then rowed to the biggest thing Leetha had ever seen, all made of iron, spewing smoke as it floated outside the reef.

Leetha and her kin were locked in the belly of this ship for a month, trapped in the stink and the heat and the misery. When the boat finished its journey, they were locked in boxes. When the boxes were opened, they were in a large place made of metal and the hard stone called concrete. The only light came from a globe far above, just like the one in the hold of the ship, faint and sickly. The man she came to know as Gompers was there, hands behind his back, face like a slab of stone. 'That's all of them?' he asked the guards.

'Thirty-one,' the chief guard said. He had a tattoo of a fish on his left arm and had done the most of all the sailors to teach Leetha and her kin the language. He liked the sea because it gave him time away from home, but Leetha never found out why that was good.

'And their leader?'

The chief guard pointed at Leetha.

Gompers grunted. 'Bring her with me.'

The chief guard unlocked Leetha from the others, then made sure her shackles were secure. He took the length of chain attached to the metal collar around her neck and, not unkindly, led her after Gompers.

The room was big, with many windows full of the glass the big people loved so much. High overhead, the ceiling was painted with pictures. Even seized by terror as she was, her curiosity was not still. Leetha wanted to know who the people were in the pictures and why they were dressed like that.

Ahead of her, Gompers turned and beckoned impatiently. The guard brought her close. When Gompers pushed her forward to confront the three figures on the platform at the front of the room, Leetha's insides became a cold hollow full of fear.

They sat on a three-seated gold throne, propped up by cushions. At first – but for only a moment – she thought they were children. Then she saw their eyes and she understood that these were only the bodies of children. They held the souls of creatures much older and much less innocent. They were monsters, sitting on gold thrones and looking at her as if she were a worm.

She clutched her hands and began to wail. Gompers took a step and cuffed her behind the ear.

'This is what you wanted?' one of the horrors asked Gompers. It was a female, dressed in bright silk robes. She looked about six years old and everything about her was wrong.

'It is. From the island of Flores in the Dutch East Indies. I can learn much from these creatures.'

Another of the horrors spoke. This one was dressed in

furs. His hands were bandaged. Red seeped through, but he ignored it. 'We've had other sub-humans for study in the past. Neanderthals.'

'Are they sub-human?' Gompers asked. 'That is the question. What makes them so? What makes them different from us?'

'We tried to find out the same from the Neanderthals,' the female said. 'A waste.'

'What *you* can learn from these creatures isn't important,' Gompers said. 'You have found them for me and for my investigations as part of our bargain.'

The third of the horrors was eating berries from a bowl. He looked up at Gompers's words. 'Be careful, Gompers. We are not accustomed to such insolence.'

Gompers snorted. 'You need me for your plan. I need you for what you can provide me with — creatures like these and the resources to experiment on them.'

'We have many plans,' the female snapped. 'We could abandon yours in an instant.'

'You wish to rule the world,' Gompers said. 'Your other plans might achieve this, but only mine promises to achieve it soon. No-one else can blend wireless telegraphy with your magic and your supply of phlogiston to create a mindless army to do your bidding. No-one.'

The fur-wearer laughed. Leetha wanted to clap her hands over her ears, so awful was the laughter, but the manacles would not let her. 'Three months it has been, Gompers, since you first came to us. Only three months! We are moving faster than we have for years. I like it! You shall give us an army and soon this country shall be ours!'

'Which will be just a beginning,' Gompers said.

'Continue to support my endeavours and the world shall be in your hands.'

'Hah!' The female thumped the arm of the throne with a tiny fist. 'It is worth enduring your impertinence for this!'

The white-robed one, in a gesture that shocked Leetha in its childishness, put both hands on his cheeks and rested his head in them. 'When the world was younger, we were rulers. When we demanded sacrifices so we could continue to rule, our subjects rebelled. We fled, but we never forgot. The world today is full of the descendants of those who wronged us. They shall pay the price.'

Gompers tapped Leetha on the shoulder. 'Pay attention. These are the Immortals. Jia, Forkbeard and Augustus.' The female, the fur-wearer and the berry-eater. 'If you fail to cooperate you will not only lose your life, but your soul will be forfeit to them in ways that will have it screaming for eternity.'

At that, Jia, Forkbeard and Augustus smiled awful smiles. 'Our souls are everlasting,' Augustus said. 'When we wear out one body, we move to another. Thus, we have learned much about souls and how to manipulate them. We would put yours in a jar and keep it in an oven, just as a beginning.'

Leetha whimpered, but still her curiosity scurried about wondering who these Immortals were and where they came from. They were magical, of that she had no doubt, but what was the range of their powers? They were mad, too, she was sure of that. Ruling the world? Whatever for?

'They must be close to the wild,' Augustus said. 'Look at her. So primitive.'

'Human and wild. We can learn from them,' Forkbeard said. 'For another plan, Gompers, nothing to concern you.'

Jia pointed at Leetha. Leetha quailed. 'I hope we can learn more than we could learn from the wild boy and the ghost-skinned girl. Ward and Stephens. They nearly destroyed us, Gompers, can you believe that?'

Leetha was keen to hear more of this. These horrors had enemies?

Gompers, however, shrugged. 'As you wanted, the Spawn are looking for those two. We shall have them soon.'

'Good,' Jia said. 'The wild boy still might be useful to our plans. In him, civilisation and the wild are united. I am sure it is something in his brain. Augustus here says it is due to his upbringing.'

'Raised by wolves,' Augustus said. 'How would that change a person? Not for the better, I should think.'

Jia scowled. She pointed at Leetha. 'Take it away,' she said to Gompers. 'Make it learn English.'

'She has been, on the voyage.'

'And find work for them,' Jia said. 'We won't have them sitting idle.'

'Do we need their brains?' Augustus asked.

'Perhaps,' Gompers said. 'Let us wait until after the tests.'

'They are biddable?' Jia squeaked.

'Oh yes. Very biddable.'

In her cell, waiting for the new day's work and trials, Leetha remembered that day she first came into the presence of the Immortals. She was afraid of them, and they made her sick to behold, but she recalled the anger with which the sorcerers spoke of the wild boy and his friend. It was the sort of anger that had more than a touch of fear, the anger of the bully who suspects he will not always have his way.

Wild boy and ghost girl, the enemies of the Immortals. Even then, standing at the awful feet of the awful sorcerers, Leetha had wanted to know more about them. And now? After nearly half a year of looking for a way to escape, of gathering what knowledge she could, now was a good time to look for these enemies of her enemies.

SEVEN

In the armoury, Evadne flung open a large metal cabinet and reached inside. 'Here's the Angry Hammer. I think it will suit you as a hand weapon.'

The Angry Hammer was far more discreet than its florid name. Kingsley found that he could hide it in his closed hand. It was shaped like a regular pistol, but showed no sign of a magazine. Made of black metal, the grip was inlaid with cross-grooved wood. 'It's compact,' Kingsley observed.

'It'll stop an elephant if you need it to. Each round is packed with explosive phlogiston, so be careful with it.'

'I shall.' Kingsley gingerly put it in his pocket. After the affairs in the Neanderthal den, when he had used some of Evadne's phlogiston-based explosive to destroy their time machine, he had a healthy regard for the power of the substance. 'With it and my trusty walking stick, I'm ready to take on anything. You, I take it, are ensabred?'

She touched the scabbard she'd belted to her side, which neatly matched the light grey coat she'd put on. 'And I'll have the Swingeing Blow in my pocket.'

'"Swingeing" as in forceful?'

'That's the one.'

'So let us sally forth and broach the mystery that is Morton,' Kingsley said.

Evadne looked pained. 'As cod Shakespeare goes, that was about the fishiest exit line I've ever heard.'

He bowed. 'At your service, fine lady. Forsooth. Verily. Hey nonny.'

She pushed him towards the door. 'Keep that up and I'm calling the Theatre Police.'

Morton's offices were in Rotherhithe, a short distance away from their workshop. Evadne insisted that they snatch a quick meal first, and over bacon sandwiches Kingsley listened to her tell of how – while Kingsley had been testing his Angry Hammer – her myrmidons had been overjoyed to see her, as they were every time she presented herself at her underground lair. The thought of her being swarmed over by excited ratty creatures made him extremely uneasy.

The afternoon was drawing in by the time they made their way down Jamaica Road. Morton's offices were in a depressing slab of buildings facing the rear of the seventeenth-century St Mary's Church. A figure was clearly outlined against the first floor window. Evadne hissed with satisfaction and led the way.

The man who opened the door would have only been in his twenties, but he affected the dress of someone four times that age. His knee-length frock-coat and high collared shirt could have come from the middle of good Queen Victoria's reign, while his spectacles looked like antiques. He opened the door, however, with a broad smile and Kingsley noted that his teeth were so even they could be used as some sort of measuring instrument.

The man's expression quickly changed from delight to puzzlement. 'You're not them.'

The door was open, so Evadne marched straight in. Kingsley said, 'Evidently not,' and followed.

The office had three arched windows overlooking the church gardens, but their griminess made it clear that those in the office rarely looked outside. The walls were lined with shelves jammed with volumes bearing labels such as 'Invoices Sept–Nov 1899' and 'Deliveries Pending'. Four desks looked as if they were especially reinforced to support the massive stacks of ledger books that towered on them. The most modern aspect of the office was the telephones, one on each desk.

Evadne took this in with one sweep. She turned on a heel in the middle of the room, aided by carpet so threadbare that it was more of an idea than an actual floor covering. 'You are Mr Morton?' she asked the frowning man who still held the door.

He closed the door. 'I am.'

'And who is them?' Kingsley asked.

This inspired an additional frown, and Kingsley began to worry about the well-being of the man's brow. *Any more fissuring like that and his skull could cave in.*

'Them?'

'The them that we aren't,' Kingsley explained.

'None of your business.' Morton gathered himself. 'Now, look here – who are you people?'

Evadne held up a finger in mild admonishment. 'Oh dear, is that any way to treat customers?'

Morton immediately became unctuous. 'Customers? I'm sorry. I didn't realise. How may I be of service? Please take a chair, all of you. Remove the cat, first, though.'

Kingsley started. What he'd taken for a furry bag was an immense grey Persian cat. He shook the back of the chair, but the cat merely fluffed up and hissed at him. Something deep inside Kingsley wanted to take its throat in his teeth and shake it, but he had an inkling this could create a bad impression.

'I'll stand.' He took the opportunity to move around the room and look menacing. Morton tried to keep an eye on him, but he was torn by the natural attraction Evadne exerted on most males. As a result, his head kept moving from side to side, twisting around, like a cobra following a snake charmer's flute.

'Now,' Evadne said. She was sitting demurely, her hands in her lap. 'We don't have to involve the Port Authority Police, do we?'

Morton started, jerking his elbows and knees and neighing in a remarkable display. 'The police? What? You said you were customers.'

Evadne shook her head. 'I simply asked if that was any way to treat customers. I didn't say we *were* customers.'

'You tricked me.'

'I was prepared to bribe you, but since the tricks seem to be working I'll stick with them.' She waved a hand at Kingsley. 'You won't need your pistol just yet, Mr W. Rest easy.'

Kingsley heard the cue and patted his pocket in as ominous a fashion as he could muster.

'Pistol?' Morton's voice was strangled. 'Who *are* you people?'

Kingsley sensed that Morton was nicely off balance and it would be handy to keep him that way. 'You have special arrangements with the East India dock, do you, Mr Morton?'

Morton swivelled right around in his chair, hanging an arm over the back. 'I'm a shipping agent. Of course I do business with the East India dock.'

'That's not what I asked.' Kingsley nodded, and Evadne caught it.

'Your reputation is important to you, isn't it, Mr Morton?' she said. 'Without it, you wouldn't get the extra business that you seem to enjoy.'

'Now, listen here,' Morton said in a voice that missed being a bluster by a good splutter or two. Instead, he sounded both desperate and pathetic, as if he'd been caught cheating on a test. 'I demand to know who you are and what you want. Otherwise I'll ask you to leave.'

Evadne thrust the shipping manifest under his nose. 'This is yours, is it not? Imagine what damage your reputation would suffer if it became known that you deliver goods to the wrong people.' She whisked the document back before he could focus on it. 'And I'm sure that damage would be particularly serious in the Demimonde.'

'Demimonde? Who said I had anything to do with the Demimonde?'

'Just about everyone in the Demimonde, which must be good for you, as long as your reputation stays intact.'

Morton chewed a lip and glanced first at Evadne, then Kingsley and finally Evadne again. Finding nothing helpful, he sagged where he sat, his shoulders doing their best to migrate towards his waist. 'We have so many deliveries coming in and going out. Things go astray sometimes.'

Evadne reflourished the shipping manifest. 'What do you remember of this shipment?'

'I monitor all shipments personally.' He nudged his spectacles with a knuckle. 'I remember this like it was yesterday, Miss . . . Stephens.' He looked up. 'You're one of our most regular recipients of items from India.'

'And I haven't had cause to complain until now,' Evadne said.

Kingsley was lost in admiration. In the face of her certainty and indignation, Morton hadn't realised that Evadne was the beneficiary of the delivery gone astray rather than the injured party.

Morton ran his finger down the columns of the manifest. 'All seems to be in order. Letters. Documents. Indian newspapers.'

'And a box.'

'A box? It says nothing about a box here.'

'And yet one was delivered to me along with all these other items.'

'What?' Then Morton's eyebrows shot up. 'Wait. I do remember this box.' He rubbed his jaw. 'It was meant for you.'

'It couldn't be. Everything that has come to me from India was from a known correspondent. This was a mystery, unattributed and not appearing on this manifest.'

Morton crossed his arms on his chest. 'Nevertheless, it was yours.'

'Your memory is that good?' Kingsley growled.

Morton was regaining some of his composure. 'I pride myself on it.'

'Then you'll remember who sent it,' Evadne said.

In a series of movements so transparent that Kingsley thought they'd give glass a run for its money, Morton looked at the manifest, then at Evadne, then at the nearest ledger. 'We respect the privacy of all our customers, Miss Stephens. You can't expect me to divulge such information when the customer paid for anonymity.'

'Don't be tedious, Mr Morton. Eventually, you're going to tell us because you won't want us to let everyone in the Demimonde know how indiscreet you are.'

'Indiscreet? But telling you the identity of the party you're after would be indiscreet.'

'Precisely. You could argue about it, complain and protest about it, but eventually you'll tell us because you have no real choice. I'd simply prefer that you do it now rather than subject us all to such dreariness. Mr W over there is easily bored, and when he's bored he tends to become violent.'

Morton swallowed. 'I'll need to consult our records.'

While the slumped-shouldered Morton opened the ledger, Kingsley's sides were trembling with the effort of not laughing, and his bruised rib was aching. Evadne kept a hand over her mouth, but her eyes were bright with suppressed humour.

'Here we have it,' Morton said. He looked over his shoulder, but kept a finger on the page of the ledger. 'One of our most regular customers. Does the name "Jabez Soames" mean anything to you?'

58

The snarl that leaped into Kingsley's throat was not entirely a product of his animal self. Jabez Soames had been the Immortals' foremost underling, a vile go-between who was prepared to deal with the amoral sorcerers for the gold they paid him. Kingsley despised the man, and not just because he'd had plans to sell Evadne into slavery, but because of his utter lack of scruples. Kingsley had shed no tears when Evadne told of his death when she had flooded the lair of the Immortals last year. Part of Soames's work for the Immortals had been shipping items from India, magical and otherwise.

Evadne's voice was steady. 'I have heard of Soames. He has been arranging shipment of items of an unusual nature from India for some time. He would have emphasised the items' value – and the extreme displeasure that the owners of said items would feel if said items were damaged or went astray.'

Morton sat up, ashen-faced. 'But we haven't! I haven't! It wasn't us!'

'That's not what we've heard. Isn't that correct, Mr W?'

Kingsley nodded and crossed his arms on his chest.

By now, Morton was actually wringing his hands, an action Kingsley had never been able to understand. Were they wet and in need of drying? Was it an attempt to mould them into innocence? 'I haven't done anything,' Morton croaked.

'I'm sure you have,' Evadne said.

'It's not my fault.' Morton put both hands to his head and squeezed. 'This box was sent to you on behalf of Mr Soames.'

Kingsley started. 'On behalf of?'

In his outpouring of denial, Morton didn't appear to

hear. He went on. 'I want it recognised that, as stipulated, I held every other shipment until Mr Soames came for them. It's not my fault that he hasn't collected them yet.'

Evadne was half out of her chair. 'Think carefully, Mr Morton. Are you saying that you have more items for Mr Soames waiting in your warehouse?'

'Safe, I say. Absolutely safe. If you don't believe me, I'll show you.'

EIGHT

The next day, after the test with Gompers, Leetha was exhausted. Even though some of her reactions were feigned, she had been surprised by the force with which others took her, a storm that left her shaking.

The morning gathering was in a room bare of comfort, a room typical of the dwellings of the big people. The walls were hard, red brick. The floor was cold. The air was stale and without life. On the bench, her feet dangled well above the floor, something she had grown accustomed to. Slowly, her tiredness faded. Inside, she was empty, as if she had not eaten for days. She stared at the brick wall, tired of not knowing what was on the other side. Her curiosity nibbled at her like an ant. It demanded she find out more about their surroundings.

The door opened and her cousin Mannor trotted in – bright, smart Mannor. When he saw her, he gave a quick shake of his head and glanced back to let her know that a guard was behind him. He joined her on the bench and the door closed.

'You were tested yesterday?' Leetha asked. Mannor was a fine rope maker, and his nimble fingers had much work in the factory of the big people. He was quick to learn, too, and already understood much about the machines and the science of the big people.

He sighed and put his hands on his knobbly knees. 'Sounds. From a box. Animals. They watched me listen to them.'

Leetha hissed between her teeth in sympathy. She patted him on the back and felt his shoulder blades sharp as ever. Mannor never ate enough at home. How was he managing here? 'They caused you no pain?'

'Not this time.'

More of her people joined them and their stories were similar. More tests, mysterious in their intent. Calli was the only one who suffered, having been made to run around the outside of a room until she collapsed, after which her breath was captured in a jar.

Leetha saw how tired Calli looked, and her mind was made up. Now was the time to do what she had been planning for days.

A few minutes later, Ubbo was pushed through the door. His tale of being asked about his family was interrupted by a guard barging into the room. 'Right,' the guard said, slapping a sparky stick in one hand. 'It's the factory for you lot today.'

Leetha was on her feet. Her hands were already sweaty because of what she had decided to do. She lingered at the back of the group, her heart pounding. As they left the room, she called on her hiding skill. She kept her head down and thought of walls and floors, of greyness and hardness, brick and stone. Through lowered lids, she watched the guard gesture in the direction he wanted them to go, but she eased her way to one side, close to the wall. Her people nearly blocked the corridor as they moved closer together, enjoying the nearness, something they were often deprived of in this world of big people. Leetha, however, sought the shadows that lingered even in this brightly lit place, the places where the electric lights did not reach. She slowed in her walking, thinking about the clay that made the bricks, the heat that baked them. She thought unimportant thoughts for she was not worth noticing. She belonged there. She was not a threat. She could be forgotten.

She was drawing on an age-old talent of her people. When they chose, they remained beneath the notice of those around them and could hide even in plain view. It had helped them to survive, allowed them to slip away whenever big people blundered near in the jungle.

As long as no-one could hear the drumming of her heart, Leetha thought that she was safe. The guard glanced at her once, but his gaze found nothing to see. His attention slipped across her like water on a smooth stone.

When her people reached a corner, Leetha hung back. When they rounded it, she hurried away in the opposite direction. She needed to find a way out of the place. She needed to find the outside. She needed to find help.

She felt in her pocket. The gold she had clipped from the small sheets used in the electrical machines – a bit here, a bit there, over many weeks – was still there. She knew the big people were greedy for it. She hoped to use that greed.

Panting, with fear gripping her throat, Leetha crept from the place where they slept and were tested, casting around as if she were in an unfamiliar part of the jungle. If she could find a way to the outside, she would be a step closer to her dream.

She strained her senses, afraid she would be discovered. She would be beaten, at the least. Worse, she could be taken in front of the Immortals.

Down stairs and past open doors, she came to a stone way roofed with glass. It led to the hard metal and the machines of the factory. Leetha slipped past the wires and tables. She came to the rear, the place she had glimpsed through open doors, the place where big people came with their carts and their boxes to bring material for the factory. It was the place where the world of their captors touched the wide world.

When she stepped outside, she almost cried. She stood in the grey light and shivered. She looked up to see a sky that disapproved, clouds unlike those of her home, clouds that were not moving at all. The narrow alley was bridged by walkways, high overhead. Ropes and chains hung from them like vines.

A young voice spoke from behind the crates stacked against the brick wall opposite. 'Blimey, you're small.'

'I am small,' she replied in the language she had learned. 'But I have gold if you want to earn it.'

'Gold?' A boy, still young but already approaching her height, straightened from the rubbish he had been picking through. He pushed back a cap, soiled and ragged, and stood with his hands on his hips. 'I'll bet you don't have gold.' He screwed up his face. 'You're funny looking as well as small.'

Leetha took the gold strip from her pocket and held it in front of his face. His eyes narrowed. He swallowed. 'If you take this and run,' she said, 'you will have something, but you will miss out on much, much more.'

'More?' He did not take his gaze from the gold. His whole body quivered with greed. 'What do I have to do for it?'

'I want you to find two people and bring them to me. Here.'

He chewed on this, frowning. 'You got anyone in mind?'

Leetha smiled. 'A wild boy and his ghostly friend.'

NINE

Fog lingered about the river like layabouts looking for a job – not with any real intent, mostly through having nothing better to do. Kingsley could make out the lights of Limehouse without any trouble, and several large steamers were waiting to berth. His gaze lingered on them, and he realised he was trying to read the port of origin on the bow, hoping to find them from exotic realms, far, far away.

He wrenched his gaze away. *I am* not *stowing away*, he told himself. He thrust a hand into a pocket and came out with a pair of coins. He concentrated on palming them, moving them from the tips of his fingers to the back of his hand until the desire to run away to the wilderness faded away.

During the short walk to the warehouse, Kingsley was afraid Morton would cut and run at any moment. The shipping agent jumped at any noise, be it a bell from the river, a snatch of song from a house nearby, or any one of a hundred sounds of the streets at night.

This was not a man with an easy conscience, Kingsley decided, and he was also unlikely to be a man without enemies. He acted as if he expected to be set upon at any time, but whether it was from divulging too much information or simply his normal state, Kingsley had no way of telling. All he could do was walk close alongside him, with Evadne just behind prodding him with her sheathed sabre whenever he looked like stopping.

Morton produced a key and the doors of the warehouse opened noisily. This excited no interest from anyone inside or nearby, so Kingsley assumed such sounds were commonplace. While the warehouse looked shabby, Morton was able to turn on electric lights to illuminate the place, so some effort had been put into making the place modern and efficient. The efforts simply didn't extend to paint.

Without hesitation, Morton led them through the towering rows of crates and boxes to the rear of the warehouse. He stopped at a concrete wall running right across the breadth of the building. This wall was newer than the rest of the warehouse, and a heavy steel door was set into it. Three keys were needed to unlock it. 'This is for my most valuable shipments,' Morton explained over his shoulder. 'One hundred per cent secure.'

The electric lights here illuminated more concrete walls. With the concrete floor and ceiling, this was a box within the warehouse. 'You see?' Morton said. He rapped on a wall with his fist. 'Nothing can get in here.'

'Not unless you let them,' Kingsley said darkly. 'Soames's goods?'

'There's just the one shipment waiting.'

'Mr Soames won't be collecting it,' Evadne said.

'He is indisposed?'

'Very.'

The crate was a waist-high cube. Morton handed Kingsley a pry bar. 'I suppose you want to see what's inside.'

'Of course.'

Kingsley removed his jacket. He looked for a place to hang it; Evadne stepped up and draped it over her arm. He rolled up his sleeves and went to work. Five minutes later, Evadne and he were peering at a dodecahedron.

Kingsley recognised it immediately. After their experience with the Immortals and their obsession with Platonic solids, he had made a point to research these regular polyhedrons. The five Platonic solids had been known since ancient times, and were the subject of study, inspection and even worship. Each of the five Platonic solids – the tetrahedron, the cube, the octahedron, the dodecahedron and the icosahedron – were convex shapes with faces entirely made up of regular triangles, squares or pentagons. Plato's followers considered the solids to be mystical objects, full of power and majesty – and magic.

The dodecahedron was similar to the other Platonic solids that Kingsley had seen in the Hall of the Immortals under Greenwich. It was a yard or so across and looked as if it were made of dull metal. If it were the same as its relations, however, Kingsley knew it was capable of hovering in the air unsupported, and that was only the beginning of its powers.

Evadne straightened after leaning over and peering inside the crate. 'I think the Immortals would pay a pretty penny for this.'

A yelp from behind made them whirl. Morton was staring at them, eyes wide. 'The Immortals? What is this about the Immortals?'

Kingsley tapped the pry bar in his other hand. 'I would have thought that you, as a middleman, would have thought about the possibility that your client, Mr Soames, was a middleman himself.'

'Yes, but the Immortals?' Morton looked at the door, as if he were wondering exactly how far he could run in a short space of time. 'I don't want anything to do with them.'

'I see,' Evadne said. 'You only want to do business with the nicer sort of Demimonder, is it?'

'I . . .'

'You understand that will limit your clientele quite substantially?'

'Ah.'

'And so far, I've been unable to detect any such scruples in you at all.'

'Um.'

'And if you can utter anything more than monosyllables, we can discuss what we're going to do next.'

'Next?'

'Yes. You're going to help us.'

Morton considered this while a dozen different expressions flitted across his face. 'And why would I do this rather than simply go about my business? Unclaimed goods, you understand, are forfeit to the carrier.'

'You could do that. Of course, it would bring the wrath of the Immortals down upon you. In fact, simply having this object in your possession for so long without passing it on is likely to bring down the wrath of the Immortals very, very soon.'

'They're very wrathy,' Kingsley said. 'Wrathful,' he corrected when he saw Evadne's pained expression.

'Or,' Evadne continued, 'we could take this object off your hands. If you help us in this matter, I'm sure you won't go unrewarded.'

'Unrewarded? By you, young lady?'

'That's right.'

She said it with such aplomb that a retort visibly died on Morton's lips.

'She's very, very wealthy,' Kingsley put in.

Morton looked as if he'd bitten into a lemon but had found a lump of sugar inside. 'Exactly *how* well rewarded?'

This was where Kingsley saw the value of the bribe over the threat, at least where Morton was concerned. Evadne mentioned a sum that made Kingsley gape and Morton grow enthusiastic to help. Despite the late hour, he rustled up the manpower to shift the re-crated dodecahedron, and found an empty warehouse nearby in which to store it. Kingsley was impressed by the way the surliness of the dockers disappeared thanks to Morton's liberal distribution of sovereigns.

Evadne noticed Kingsley's staring. 'It's ever the way,' she said softly. 'Those who are bribed feel that bribing is a way of life.'

'It's pernicious.'

'Of course, and a harmless honorarium sometimes opens the door to malfeasance. But who, among the poor, can resist a bribe? Money is money.'

'I would never take a bribe.'

'You speak as someone who has never been poor,' Evadne said gently.

The shifting concluded; the men were paid and vanished. Morton stood in front of the second warehouse and eyed it suspiciously. 'And now?'

Evadne handed him a large sheaf of banknotes. He counted them, and tipped his hat.

'A pleasure doing business with you,' he said, 'but forgive me if I hope never to see you again.'

Morton hurried off into the night.

Kingsley rubbed his hands together. 'Please excuse my obtuseness, but what exactly is the plan?'

Evadne walked to the door of the warehouse. She prised up the switches for the electric lights, but the darkness was immediately alleviated by the electric light she always carried, an elegant silvered device the shape of a pen. 'We have something that the Immortals want. They have something that we want.'

'You're going to bargain with them?'

'I wouldn't trust them for an instant. I was thinking, rather, that we now had a perfect lure.'

'I have it. When the Spawn come for it, we can then track them back to their lair.' Kingsley straightened. Amid the rope and tar, the lingering scent of Morton's pipe tobacco and the hint of orange blossom that Evadne was wearing was something else, something new. 'Unless they find us first,' he said. Evadne was about to query this, but he held up a hand. 'Hush. I hear something.'

Evadne snapped off her electric light. Kingsley took her by the hand and together they slipped into the shadows of the warehouse. They found a position behind crates that, according to the stamped marks, had come from Burma and Ceylon.

Kingsley took out the Angry Hammer. Evadne already had her Swingeing Blow.

A figure appeared in the large, open doorway. Against the light cast by a gas streetlamp, it was a silhouette, devoid of features, and Kingsley's heart thumped in his chest.

Two more figures joined the first, and another two slipped into the warehouse proper. The last of these turned and caught the light so that Kingsley's wolfish sight, in that tiny split second, saw a normal human dressed in shabby black clothes, scarf and a woollen cap pulled low on the brow. He relaxed somewhat, but it was almost disappointing to think that he'd wasted such alertness on an ordinary gang of thieves.

He caught Evadne's attention, but before he could whisper to her a voice cried out from nearby: 'They're here!'

Kingsley whirled and bounded towards the shadows whence the voice had come. A wiry stranger saw him coming and ducked just enough to avoid the worst of Kingsley's charge. They grappled, Kingsley striving to clamp a hand over his mouth, but the stranger was fast, wrenching his head to one side and crying out again: 'Over here!'

They rolled against a crate and Kingsley managed a short jab to the jaw of his assailant, then he flipped him over on his stomach, pinning him to the wooden floor.

Evadne came out of the darkness and flicked on her electric light. 'She's not Spawn.'

'I know she's not,' Kingsley said, then he eased up on the knee he was pressing on the stranger's back. *'She?'*

His prisoner twisted like a snake. She was out of his grasp and on her feet in an instant. She snapped a kick at him. He was quick enough to escape the worst of the blow but it still glanced off his cheekbone and made his head ring. He reached for her. 'Now, look here.'

She spun away but Evadne interposed a hip, following it with an elbow swing and an artfully angled leg. The stranger tripped and Evadne had her lantern and sabre on her as she landed on her back.

Four electric beams darted out. Evadne, Kingsley and their prisoner were caught in a web of illumination. Immediately, Evadne tumbled backwards beyond the reach of the lights, and before they could capture her again the air was ripped apart in a whirlwind of electric discharge. The entire front half of the warehouse was swallowed in a bubble of garish purple-white light. Four tall figures in coats and cloth caps – two on either side of the entrance – were caught as it crackled around them, their lanterns feeble amid the electrical harshness. Two held pistols, one a rifle, and all of them had expressions of wide-eyed shock.

Then the roof fell in.

Kingsley sat with his back to the lamp post. With eyes reddened from the dust thrown up by the collapse, he eyed the half-ruined warehouse. 'That was the Swingeing Blow?' he asked Evadne, who was sitting on the cobblestones nearby. 'Does it come with a warning: Do Not Use in Confined Spaces?'

Evadne pursed her lips. 'It might need some adjustment,' she conceded.

All five of the strangers had escaped the collapse, thanks to the roof undertaking a slow and groaning descent rather than a precipitous one. The worst injury looked to be some damaged egos among the men, as the young woman Kingsley had thrown was admonishing them with gusto. For some lapse of thievery tactics, he assumed.

'We should be leaving,' he suggested to Evadne.

'Not until we make sure the dodecahedron is safe.'

Kingsley nodded, then was startled to see the young woman approaching them. She stood, hands on hips, then coughed before jabbing a finger at them. 'You two are in strife,' she croaked. 'Assaulting an officer of the Crown like that.'

'Oh my.' Evadne put a hand to her mouth. 'Have we just assaulted a police officer?'

'Police? Hardly. I work for the Agency for Demimonde Affairs.'

'The Agency?' Evadne repeated. 'What's the Agency doing here?'

Kingsley remembered his foster father speaking about the Agency. It was one of a thousand things about the Demimonde he'd wanted to pursue with Evadne, but he'd simply not had the time.

'I'm the one asking questions,' the officer said sharply. She was younger than Kingsley had thought at first, probably not much older than he was. She wore a long black coat over men's trousers and Kingsley decided that these plain clothes officers wore very plain clothes indeed. Coppery-red curls hung from under the brim of a battered bowler. She had freckles and an impishness that Kingsley would have found decidedly attractive if she weren't so angry. She looked around at her four

74

colleagues, who had sidled up and were still looking sheepish. They were well-groomed and fit-looking, young and with the sort of confidence that went with expensive schools and family backgrounds that could be measured in centuries. 'Now, you're interfering with an investigation and should be well and truly locked up but we don't have time for that, so hop it.'

'Wait,' Evadne said. Her pistol had vanished. 'How do we know you're truly from the Agency?'

The officer had turned her attention away from them and was peering towards the entrance to the warehouse. 'Eh? Oh.' She reached inside her coat without looking and thrust a card at Kingsley – again, without looking.

'Christabel Hughes,' he read in the light of Evadne's electric illuminator. The photograph looked like the officer in front of them, he decided. More or less. 'You're sixteen years old,' he blurted.

'Seventeen next week,' she said, and snatched the card from him. 'And before you ask: yes, it's a little young for this kind of business but I'm perfectly capable of carrying out my Agency duties.'

'Kingsley didn't have any trouble dealing with you,' Evadne pointed out.

Kingsley couldn't help noticing how the young officer shot him a glance when Evadne said his name. Then she looked again at Evadne, appraisingly.

'But who's in charge now?' she said. 'It's not who strikes the first blow who is always the winner. Plan for eventualities and the details take care of themselves.'

'Really?' Evadne said. 'That's what I always say.'

'I see.' The young officer frowned. 'I know you. And you.'

Kingsley couldn't help himself: he bowed. 'The Extraordinaires, at your service.'

'Extraordinaires? What on earth are you talking about?'

'We are the Extraordinaires; juggling and magic together on the stage.'

'No, that's not it.' The young officer's eyes widened. She pointed at Evadne. 'You were the one that smashed the Immortals under Greenwich last year.'

Evadne tilted her head a little. 'Perhaps.'

The young officer eyed Kingsley. 'And you must be the one that the Immortals are mad keen to find.'

Kingsley didn't forget his manners. 'Kingsley Ward. How do you do?'

One of the young officer's colleagues trotted over and murmured in her ear. She grimaced. 'Well, that's that, then.'

'What's what?' Kingsley asked, intrigued by the way the older men deferred to this young woman.

'You've messed things up good and proper tonight. The whole docks area is alert thanks to your indiscreet display with that weapon.' She pursed her lips. 'What was it, by the way?'

'Something I've been working on,' Evadne said.

'And something she'll continue working on,' Kingsley added.

The young officer looked torn between curiosity and duty, with duty eventually winning out. She grimaced again. 'I'm going to have to ask you to hand it over, and any other weapons you have on your person.'

'I beg your pardon?' Kingsley said.

'Interfering with an Agency operation is a serious offence. You're under arrest.'

TEN

Leetha's curiosity was buzzing, set alight by the prospect of rescue. Every aspect of their surroundings had become even more interesting. She pondered the large pipes that brought water into the factory and imagined making a flood that would work to their advantage. She paid new attention to the pipes that brought the foul air the guards called gas. The big people were afraid of this and were always careful to keep flames away. Leetha thought such a thing could be useful.

Her curiosity also led her to discover the moving cage.

While she was obtaining more copper wire to coil around the tiny cylindrical magnets, Leetha saw several guards gathered around the hole in the wall that divided the factory from the building that housed the hall of the Immortals. When they slid the panel up, inside was a cage with a rope on one side. When the rope was pulled, the cage slid upwards and soon returned with pots of their tea.

The cage was small, but so was Leetha. She could haul herself up to the place where the Immortals were.

She took a step towards the panel and the cage, then she stopped. Why would she do something like that? Why did she want to see the Immortals again?

The more she knew about them, the better the chance of escaping their clutches, ghost girl and wild boy or not.

She hissed, examined herself and shook her head. She was wise enough to know that while this was true, it wasn't the real reason: curiosity needs answers like an itch needs a scratch.

The bell rang for mealtime. Leetha straightened and every bone in her back cried out. The supervisors began walking along the aisles between the benches. Their sparky sticks swung, ready to hasten Leetha's people to the meal room. The big people worshipped their schedule. If the meal was to be taken now, now it would be – which was why the big people were so startled when the bell rang again. This time, it was a different signal, the signal for a delivery – but mealtime was not the time for a delivery. Some stood still, some shouted. Leetha watched with the closest she had had to amusement for a long time. Usually her people would be herded well away from the doors before the delivery bell rang. Clearly, the delivery was unexpected. More big people with sparky sticks appeared at the far end of the workshop. Again, they were unexpected, if the shouting from the others was any guide.

Ubbo was working at the bench on her right. As usual, he was singing very softly under his breath. She caught his eye as he finished one of what the big people called 'capacitors' and placed it carefully in the box that cradled the completed items. He nodded, then pointed his nose at the nearest guard. Leetha was sure this one was a newcomer, with curly hair the same orange shade as the apes in the jungle at home. Was he unfamiliar with Leetha and with her people? It was a chance, especially with the uproar around them – a chance for her to get to the moving cage.

Leetha slid off her stool. She sidled along the bench, hardly even thinking of what she was doing. After all, she belonged there, was no danger, was not worth worrying about. The orange-haired guard looked at her, but his gaze slid away in search of more important things. He barked orders and brandished his sparky stick. When Leetha dropped to all fours and crawled away underneath the benches, he did not notice. Leetha was a shadow's breath, that was all.

Leetha's journey through the workshop was a fearful test of her heart. The big people were alarmed and upset and that meant they were alert. The ability of Leetha's people to slip about unnoticed worked best when the others were at ease. Leetha had to concentrate on her smallness, on her lack of interest, on the fact that so many more impor-tant things were going on. Every time one of the guards paused, her breath caught in her throat, but Ubbo must have spread the word, for at those moments one of her people always managed to trip, or to upset a collection of parts. They drew attention away from Leetha.

Leetha crept to the north side of the workshop. She kept away from the doors that led to the residence and the doors that led outside. Too many big people there, too alert.

Finally, she reached the panel that hid the moving cage. No-one was watching. She pushed the panel up, climbed in and then dragged the panel down again. In the dark, she found the rope and pulled the cage upwards.

The shaft was dark and dusty, but Leetha was not afraid. As she hauled herself up she could hear sounds all around her – the clattering of machines, but also people talking, moving about, ordinary sounds of people living. Smells other than dust came to her, too, and the smell of cooking made her mouth water.

The darkness receded as she rose. Thin beams of light came from above, enough for her to see the panel when she reached it. She heard voices just outside.

She did not hesitate. She sprang and grasped the rope overhead and hauled herself up just before the panel slid open. Voices talking about the weather came first, and then white-hatted big people pushed covered dishes into the cage.

Leetha bit her lip and scrambled higher, but the rope began to go down, taking her with it. She peered about and saw another rope not far away. She grabbed it, but it took her up! She would soon crash into a grooved metal block that the rope looped through. She wanted to chide her curiosity for putting her in such a position, but it ignored her and instead asked: *What is that slot in the wall we are just passing?*

Leetha saw it then, a narrow gap. Without thinking, she swung across and tumbled into it, rolling face-down in dust and muck between two walls.

Leetha picked herself up. The gap was narrow, but not close for someone of her stature, as long as she shuffled sideways. The walls on either side were unfinished. She could see the narrow timbers and the plaster that had oozed between the cracks.

An old house. Who knew what was in it? Secret ways, perhaps?

She looked back at the shaft. The rope had stopped moving. She could probably climb down now, but her curiosity would never forgive her.

With a sigh, she edged into the darkness, stepping from beam to beam as she went.

Leetha had not gone far before the gap widened. Underfoot, boards had been laid. Light came from slits up high, enough for her to see that the walls here were finished, well plastered and whitewashed. A little further, and she found two chairs, both ancient and thick with dust.

She frowned. A room? Here? Of what use would that be?

She looked about. In the stillness, she saw her footprints. No-one had been here for many, many years.

Then she saw them. Tiny doors the size of her hand were set in the wall, well above her head. She dragged one of the chairs closer and found that the doors slid aside. She put her face to the slot this revealed. She almost choked on the dust when she gasped at what she saw. She was looking down at the hall of the Immortals, where she had been presented to them. The hall was empty, but she felt her humiliation and shame all over again; the way they mocked her, how helpless she had been. She cried a little, then slid the door closed.

She had found a spying room, just like the tree platforms her kin used to spy on animals for hunting. She went to leave but after only two steps her curiosity asked: *What about the other wall? The one opposite the peepholes?*

Now she knew what she was looking for, she found the doors easily. This time, though, she was looking down

on a room unlike the throne room. No gold, no paintings, no carpets – and no windows. Only a screen at one
end of the room.

The Immortals were there. As before, they were sitting
together, but not on a golden throne. They were on a
single stone bench and they looked sick.

Augustus and Jia had reddened bandages on their
feet. Forkbeard had them on both hands and feet. They
all looked as if they had been working in the hottest
noonday sun with no water. They were pale and shaking.
Their skin was waxy. Augustus was trembling and when
he put his hand to his head, hair came away in clumps.

He was speaking, but Leetha had to bring her ear close
to the slot to make out his words. 'It's true, I tell you,' he
squeaked. 'The bodies are wearing out even faster than
before!'

'We knew that,' Forkbeard grumbled. 'As we accumu-
late our experiences, they grow too much for the bodies
to endure.' He grimaced and then, to Leetha's disgust, he
spat out a tooth. 'We must change. Now. While we can.'

Jia winced. 'I do not like being in bodies this young.
So many limitations.'

'Younger is stronger,' Augustus muttered. He mopped
his brow with a sleeve, but Leetha could see he was not
sweating at all.

'Hah!' Jia snapped. 'Even the six-year-old bodies are
wearing out quickly now.'

'So we continue to look for a solution,' Forkbeard said.
'The Neanderthals . . .'

'Were a stupid idea! You two are obsessed with the
wild and civilisation. Pah!'

Forkbeard struggled to sit up. 'The wild is strong. The

82

wild has vigour. If we can tap that essence, we can strengthen the bodies we inhabit and inure them against decay.'

'The Neanderthals were primitives,' Augustus said. He was struggling for breath. 'Primitives do not have the civilised self that controls the wild self. They were as close to the wild as humans could be. They had no civilising influence.'

'Didn't they?' Jia said. 'They proved you wrong. They weren't primitive, just different.'

'Perhaps. Probably. But the Ward boy – ah, he is different.'

'So you say. Brought up in the wild and he has a gland in his head that means he can reconcile his wild self and his civilised self? Convince me that this isn't just wishful thinking.'

'We get him,' Forkbeard said. 'We'll find out. Who knows? His wildness may mean his body is strong enough to withstand transfer. Be patient and we can find out.'

'Patient!' Jia was red in the face. 'I have been patient! I want to get out of this Demimonde and reign again where I can feel the sun on my face! I want to find a way to stop our host bodies decaying around us before we reach a point where none will sustain us! I want everything! I want it now!'

'You are not the only one who wants this,' Forkbeard said, 'but you are the only one who is dangerously impetuous.'

'At least I do not go around clutching at foolishness!'

'Stop this!' Augustus squeaked. He waved his chubby hands. 'Stop this! We have been united for a thousand years. We must not war with ourselves now.'

'And you!' Jia screeched. 'You're obsessed with this woman, the god-opener! Years wasted on such a danger!'

'Wasted?' Augustus said. 'She may be just what we need.' He took a deep breath. 'Regardless, we must work together, not apart. And be calm – or else you jeopardise the process.'

An uneasy silence fell. None of the three looked at the others. Their baby scowls were hideous.

'What is keeping them?' Jia asked. 'They must be ready by now.'

Augustus clapped. 'Bring them in.'

This time, Leetha had to clamp a hand over her mouth lest she scream. Three creatures staggered out from behind the screen at the end of the room and Leetha's stomach churned at their unnaturalness. Their arms were too long, their shoulders moved in ways shoulders should not, their skin had the appearance of something buried for far too long.

But this was not what made Leetha fear that her heart would burst. No, it was the tiny burden that the horrors held in their arms. Each one held a child, lolling bonelessly like a doll.

'Bring the soulless vessels here!' squeaked Jia. 'It is time for us to migrate our essences!'

Leetha ran, heedless, and for the first time in her life she cursed her curiosity. Helpful though it had been, her curiosity could never help her unsee what she had just seen.

ELEVEN

The Agency offices were in a jumble of government buildings near Victoria Station. While not technically situated in the Demimonde, they were as hidden and unobtrusive as if they were.

After being deposited in a dingy lane, Kingsley and Evadne were hustled through a portico and then swept through a foyer replete with columns and decorative friezes. Hughes led, and the dishevelled officers brought up the rear. They mounted a grand set of stairs to emerge into a world of corridors. Kingsley could imagine future civil servants shuffling cut-up squares of paper in their nurseries and dreaming of working in such a place. These halls, and countless others like them, were the heart of the empire. Far more than the obvious statements of the Houses of Parliament or Buckingham Palace, these offices drove the great engine that kept far-flung lands united under the British flag. Bureaucracy was at work, making sure the sun never set.

That may be. Kingsley's nose twitched at the staleness of the air. His wild self was uneasy and keen to know where all the exits were. He found the place stifling, as if the walls were edging in on him, subtly, the longer he stayed.

He pushed the feeling aside. He couldn't afford to be below his best, not after the warning Dr Ward had given him about dealing with the Agency.

While the relentlessly unspeaking young men watched Kingsley and Evadne, Hughes went through a pair of inlaid doors. She was soon out again, accompanied by a lean man with a beard so pointy Kingsley decided that he probably risked serious harm every time he dropped his chin to his chest. He wore a very fine black topcoat over black trousers, and his tie was a subdued grey marble. He studied them for a moment, not at all startled by Evadne's appearance. 'I'm Buchanan,' he said abruptly, 'and you're Dr Ward's fosterling, aren't you?' His Scottish heritage was clear in his voice.

Before Kingsley could answer, or register his surprise at the question, Evadne cut in. 'And what's all this about? Why have we been arrested? Do I need to contact my very expensive and notoriously aggressive firm of solicitors, the ones who have excellent relations with the press and who delight in exposing government foolishness?'

'Arrested? I'm sorry, Miss Stephens, did our officers lead you to believe you were under arrest?'

'She did,' Evadne said, pointing at Hughes, 'by using the words "You're under arrest" and confiscating our weapons.'

Buchanan shot Hughes a glance. She shrugged. 'It seemed like the best way to bring them in, sir, once I realised who they were. The bulletin and all that.'

Ah, so she did recognise us! Kingsley thought, and then wondered about this bulletin Hughes mentioned. Had their descriptions been distributed willy-nilly? And, if so, why?

Buchanan barely looked at her. 'Quite right, Hughes.' He stroked his beard. 'And your mission? What of that?'

Hughes squirmed, and Kingsley was reminded of her youth. 'It was a bit of a mess in the end, sir. A waste of time.'

If Buchanan had pursed his lips any tighter, Kingsley decided, his mouth would have disappeared.

'That's a shame, Hughes. We *must* find these sorcerers,' Buchanan said. 'Best if you hurry your unit down to General Staff and debrief.'

When Hughes and the rest of her unit had filed off, Buchanan spread his hands. 'You'll have to forgive us. While Hughes might know her way around the Demi-monde, she's not quite our sort of people, really. Useful, but limited.'

'Which is a way of saying we're not actually under arrest,' Evadne said.

'Of course not,' Buchanan said. 'A wretched misunderstanding.'

'So we can go?' Kingsley said.

'I'd be honoured if you wouldn't. Not right away. We've been looking for you for a long time.'

Kingsley was feeling the effects of a tumultuous twenty-four hours – he was barely holding back a barrage of yawns that threatened to engulf him.

Evadne and he were taken to a room rather better decorated than a typical government office. It was long, with dado rails along the walls and stiff leather chairs guarding the immense table in the middle of the room. The walls above the panelling sported a collection of large paintings, mostly of curly-wigged noblemen posing with swords and horses and some extremely fine sneers. They gazed directly out from the frame, promising a damn good smothering if their wigs ever broke loose and went on a rampage.

Buchanan saw them seated and left.

'The Agency was looking for us?' Kingsley kept his voice low. The place encouraged such artifices. 'Why didn't they just drop into our workshop? Or send a letter?'

Evadne yawned, covering her mouth with an elegant hand. 'I'd heard hints about the Agency's lack of effectiveness, but I thought that was just talk.'

Evadne's yawn set off Kingsley, and he had trouble mastering his jaw enough to ask: 'Are you saying the Agency is incompetent?'

'Sh. Someone's coming.'

The someone was a tea lady, a motherly looking woman resplendent in apron, mob cap and cheeks red enough to make a heart surgeon think he had an immediate case on his hands. She was smiling when she wheeled in a trolley, giving no indication that it was nearly five o'clock in the morning. Without a word, she served tea that was hot, strong and undistinguished. She gave each of them a digestive biscuit.

Kingsley lifted the biscuit until it was in front of his face. He stared at it. Then it was gone. *Sometimes hunger is just as good as sleight of hand.*

The double doors banged open. A man strode in. He was well-built, with a mane of silver hair artfully swept back in great wings that made him look as if he were travelling a hundred miles an hour. He propped and put a hand to his forehead in a manner so theatrical that Kingsley thought it would have drawn applause from the most hardened of stagehands in the most raffish of music halls. 'Tell me it's not true! Malcolm Ward! Married? I don't believe it!'

While Kingsley stared, Buchanan hurried in behind this apparition. 'Miss Stephens, Mr Ward, this is Colonel Congreve-Knollys, the head of the Agency for Demi-monde Affairs.'

'Delighted,' Congreve-Knollys declared as he shook Kingsley's hand manfully, then grasped Evadne's and bowed over it at an angle that was somewhere between knowingness and mockery. He straightened. 'Is that tea I see before me?'

'I'll fetch a cup,' Buchanan said and went out of the room.

'A fine man,' Congreve-Knollys said, chuckling, 'but a bit of a worrier. Still, that's a fine thing in a second-in-command, eh?'

Buchanan shepherded the tea lady and her trolley back into the room. She smiled benignly as she took up the dirty plates and dished out new cups.

Congreve-Knollys sat at the head of the table. He laced his hands on his chest and leaned back in the chair. 'Now, I need to let you know that as well as being in charge of this important government instrumentality I am an old friend of the esteemed Dr Malcolm Ward, your foster father, my lad, and I've been hearing rumours of nuptials.'

An old friend my father never mentioned? Just like the wife-to-be he never mentioned? Kingsley declined a second cup of tea and the tea lady moved onto Buchanan. 'My father has many friends,' he said carefully.

'Oh, he does indeed. A remarkable man. And might I say it's a pleasure to meet you again, Kingsley, a true pleasure, even if the circumstances are a little unusual.'

'Again? I'm sorry, sir, I don't remember ...'

'Of course not. You were far too young at the time. India, eh? How I miss her.' He shook his head. 'Well, that's in the past. The present, though ... Malcolm Ward, married, a victim of *le coup de foudre*. Well, I never.'

'They're not married yet, sir,' Kingsley said and he felt Evadne's elbow in his side.

'No?' Congreve-Knollys raised an eyebrow. 'I'd been led to believe that they were.'

Buchanan, on Congreve-Knollys's right, cleared his throat and slid a folder to him. While the Director undid the string, Kingsley took in the man.

Congreve-Knollys's frockcoat was carefully cut to display an outstanding waistcoat, which was paisley, black on black. His ascot was a rich purple and cleverly tied to look almost, but not quite, hastily done. A small black pearl pin kept it in place.

Before Congreve-Knollys started reading the papers in the folder, he took a gold-rimmed pince-nez from the lapel pocket of his coat. Kingsley noted his exceedingly well manicured nails and concluded that this wasn't a man who took shortcuts with his appearance. Only a sense that he was treating it all as a joke stopped him looking like a dandy.

Evadne tapped the table. Congreve-Knollys looked up from his reading. 'Colonel,' she said, 'I think it time you tell us what we're doing here. I need to get some sleep.'

Congreve-Knollys blinked at her, then he looked down at his documents. 'I'm sorry, Miss ...' He ran his finger down one. 'Stephens. Has this not been explained to you? Buchanan?'

Buchanan tsked. 'We were working up to it, sir.'

Congreve-Knollys brightened. 'Ah, of course! Now, Mr Ward and Miss Stephens, we understand you've had a bit of an encounter with some notorious Demimonde identities: the Immortals.'

Evadne glanced at Kingsley, and he could see she was about to wither the man where he sat, so he jumped in. 'That was six months ago, sir.'

'Eh?' Congreve-Knollys pawed at the papers. 'Ah, quite so, quite so. Indeed. Of course.' He frowned. 'We're keen to find them, because we've heard that these Immortals are about to deploy a project which will provide them with a vast, mind-controlled army that they will use to conquer the country.'

Buchanan leaned forward and broke the silence this created. 'We have hints that they're on the verge of using modern science in combination with their sorcery. After conquering Britain, they aim to bring all humanity under their control.'

'How?' Evadne snapped. Kingsley could see she was only remaining seated through a titanic effort of will. 'How are they planning to do this?'

'We don't know,' Congreve-Knollys said. 'We've sent

almost all our operatives out into the Demimonde to try to find them, but it's been futile. Hughes's unit was the closest, but after tonight we may have to start all over again.'

Say what you like about them, Kingsley thought, agog at these revelations, *these Immortals don't think small.*

Kingsley had no desire to be a lapdog to the Immortals. With such power, the Immortals would only corrupt humanity and reduce every man, woman and child to baseness and depravity.

Evadne was still, her hands clasped in front of her. She studied Congreve-Knollys and Buchanan as if every word was suspect. 'So you don't have any details about the Immortals and their plans,' she said with a steely calm. 'You've only heard rumours.'

'I'll admit we've had trouble finding out what they're up to,' Congreve-Knollys said. 'But we've had this titbit confirmed independently from a number of sources.'

'Unlike some of the other rumours,' Buchanan said. He found a list. 'According to what we've heard, they're living in the drains under Buckingham Palace, they have a floating island off Land's End, they rule over the Forest of Dean, they're responsible for the dreadful weather, a series of attacks on barbers and wigmakers, and a reported outbreak of dancing sickness in Leicester. They're also planning to attack London via airships, the sewers and by way of a flotilla of gravel barges, apparently.'

Congreve-Knollys smiled. 'The arrival on our shores of someone in whom we've long had an interest has brought things to a head, so to speak.'

Kingsley's eyes widened as he leaped ahead of the conversation. 'Mrs Winter.'

Evadne immediately saw what he meant. 'Oh.' She turned back to Congreve-Knollys. '*That's* why you're so interested in her. You think that Mrs Winter is one of their minions.'

Congreve-Knollys wasn't at all embarrassed. 'Of course I'm interested in what old Malcolm is up to, but I'm *very* keen to put the kibosh on these Immortals. We think that if we find her, she can lead us directly to them.'

Buchanan tapped a folder in front of him. 'We have very good evidence that your Mrs Winter, while in India, was an accomplice of the Immortals.'

Mrs Winter involved with the Immortals? Kingsley remembered her disgust when she thought that Kingsley and Evadne had some association with the sorcerers. And yet, couldn't all that be a ruse designed to make them think she *wasn't* an underling of the sorcerers?

Despite the misgivings Kingsley had had about her, he was distressed to learn it was true. Or, at least, that the Agency believed it was true.

'They've gone,' Kingsley said, torn between wanting to help his foster father and to protect him. 'They've left London.'

'Your foster father and Mrs Winter?' Buchanan had his pen ready. 'Where?'

Evadne glanced at Kingsley. 'We don't know. They had some dialect studies they wanted to pursue.'

'That makes things difficult.' Congreve-Knollys shuffled his papers together and shut the folder. 'You'll let us know immediately when you hear from them?'

'Then what will you do?' Kingsley asked.

'I think we'd best take her into custody.'

After a short sidelong glance, Kingsley had the measure of Evadne's concern and it was substantial. He longed to take a good long walk with her, somewhere they could talk. What should they do? He didn't want his foster father, the man who had been so good to him, marrying an acolyte of the Immortals! And, if she wasn't, he didn't want his soon-to-be foster mother suspected of being in league with the worst of the Demimonde.

So many questions, but one presented itself above all the rest. Kingsley tapped the table in front of him with such authority that everyone looked at him. 'Why is Mrs Winter marrying my father?'

'Because she *loves* him,' Evadne said without hesitation.

Congreve-Knollys gave a little chuckle at that. To Kingsley's mind, he might as well have said: 'Miss Stephens, would you please throttle me?'

'We're thinking that he must have something they need,' Buchanan said. 'So they've sent her to work her way into his trust.'

Kingsley winced.

Congreve-Knollys drummed his fingers on the table. 'You wouldn't have another way of finding the Immortals, would you?'

Now, that's starting to sound like desperation. 'We found them last time, and Evadne nearly destroyed them.'

'But I didn't,' she said. 'Something I regret.'

'From all reports,' Congreve-Knollys said, 'you are an extremely capable young woman. I'm sure you'll be able to remedy this situation.'

'It sounds to me as if you're encouraging her to do your work for you,' Kingsley said.

'I wouldn't put it as bluntly as that,' Congreve-Knollys said. 'Let us just say our interests and yours coincide where the Immortals are concerned.'

94

But not necessarily where Mrs Winter is concerned.

'Our resources are limited,' Buchanan said. 'And stretched.'

'We are sometimes forced to use unconventional avenues to achieve our ends of protecting the realm from threats from the Demimonde,' Congreve-Knollys said. 'And you two definitely fall under that heading.'

'We're not working for you,' Evadne said flatly. 'We have another calling.'

'The stage? Of course, and good luck to you.' Congreve-Knollys nodded. 'We'd simply appreciate any information you could provide on your progress towards finding these Immortals.'

'And in return?' Evadne said.

'In return? Dear girl, I'm appealing to your patriotism!'

'What about somewhere to sleep?' Kingsley said, and they all looked at him. 'It's the early hours. I'm exhausted and I'm sure Evadne is too. I can tell you that we're not going out into the Demimonde to tackle anyone without at least a few hours' sleep.'

TWELVE

Later that morning, Kingsley found Evadne with Christabel Hughes. They were in what could have been a High Street tearoom, if it weren't for the outlandish characters at the tables around them. Three dusty folk swathed Bedouin style were talking with an earnest, pale-faced young man who couldn't have been much older than Kingsley. Two heavily moustachioed gentlemen were speaking in low voices with a young woman Kingsley was sure he had seen singing at the London Coliseum. A large brown bear was eating a currant bun and chatting with a monkey. The monkey seemed to be making a point, jabbing a finger and gesticulating with the other hand, but the bear kept speaking with her mouth full, which made the monkey angry.

This is definitely *the Agency for Demimonde Affairs,* Kingsley decided as he slid in alongside Evadne. She was bright-eyed and rested, and smelled delightfully of violets.

'Good morning, Kingsley,' she said. She adjusted her dark blue spectacles and patted him on the arm. 'I think I've cleared the air. Christabel and I are on the way to a usefully mutual relationship that could help restore the good name of the Agency.'

Kingsley blinked. 'Good morning, Miss Hughes.'

'You're right, Evadne,' the young Agency officer said. 'He is well-mannered.'

'Mostly,' Evadne said. 'I find good manners a pleasing quality in males. It's difficult for some of them, of course, but there you have it.'

Kingsley immediately vowed to polish his manners until they shone. 'And what's this about restoring the good name of the Agency?'

Evadne sobered. 'Christabel has told me that the Agency chaos isn't solely because of incompetence,' she said, 'even though there's been a lot of that.'

Christabel shrugged. 'We don't have as many good, experienced officers as we should. Most of the new blood hasn't even visited the Demimonde, let alone had experience in it.'

'Congreve-Knollys believes that one's school is the most important criterion for a job at the Agency,' Evadne said. 'As a result, they don't approve of Christabel.'

'I'm not really their sort of person,' Christabel said.

'That's true,' Evadne said. 'You're extremely capable, for a start.'

Evadne and Christabel both burst out laughing at this. Kingsley felt excluded, not through any malicious intent but through the gulf that sometimes divides the sexes.

He took this philosophically; he was a devotee of these differences, and so an occasional bewilderment was a small price to pay for the glorious benefits.

'They've let some important departments run down,' Christabel went on. 'The Ancient Languages section, for instance, and the Science section. It's appalling.'

'Agreed.' Kingsley looked about. 'I'd enjoy a cup of tea.'

'You should have risen earlier, then, slugabed,' Evadne said. 'We're leaving.'

'We are? And you, Miss Hughes?'

'If we're going to work together, you must call me Christabel. None of this "Miss Hughes" nonsense.' She rose. She was wearing a peaked cap on her mass of red curls, with the sort of skirt Kingsley imagined useful for playing tennis.

'We're working together?'

Evadne stood. 'Christabel and I agree that our sharing information and helping each other is the sensible thing to do, especially after I told her about how new you are to the Demimonde, and your reactions to it, and the mistakes you've made. She realised then that your blunder last night was understandable.'

'My blunder?' Kingsley gave Evadne a look that he hoped conveyed his desire to have words with her later about this. 'She lies,' he said to Christabel. 'She can't help it, poor thing. It's a condition, and we're seeking help.'

Christabel looked from Kingsley to Evadne. 'Do you two need a moment alone to sort things out?'

'No,' Kingsley and Evadne said at the same time. Then they repeated it, again at the same time.

Christabel laughed. 'You do work well together, at least. Now, the Demimonde awaits.'

Kingsley caught Evadne's eye. 'Err . . . I'm afraid we have some other business. An item in a warehouse, remember?'

'That?' Evadne said. 'Oh, pish. After I explained, Christabel was willing to overlook the whole incident.'

Christabel grinned. 'There are some things it's best not for the big nobs to know, or so I've found.'

'Quite so,' Evadne said. 'I've arranged for some people I know to guard the place for the time being, before some other useful people move a certain valuable object to my underground refuge.'

'All overseen by your myrmidons?' Kingsley asked.

'Of course. Now, go and fetch your hat and cane, then we can be off,' Evadne said. 'Here.'

Kingsley caught the small black object Evadne tossed to him. It was his Angry Hammer. 'I don't know why you give me your weapons. I never get to use them.'

'Never mind.' Evadne's eyes were merry. 'I feel better knowing that you have something useful in your pocket.'

'We need to go to St Giles Under,' Evadne said, as they pushed through a basement door onto a set of stairs that soon led them into a large, red-brick-lined tunnel. Two gas lamps were embedded in the wall directly opposite, enough to show that the tunnel floor was dry. 'In my experience it's the best place to chase down news of Demimonde goings-on.'

'St Giles Under? Near Great Russell Street?' Christabel asked.

'That's right. The great rookeries – the slums – were there until they were cleared in the 1840s,' Evadne said.

'But the authorities didn't appreciate that the place was like an iceberg.'

'Only a tiny part of it showed above the surface.' Kingsley remembered: St Giles Rookery had been a notorious haunt of thieves and ne'er-do-wells, the sort of place that the police only went in numbers, and only when they couldn't avoid it. If one needed a cut-throat, St Giles Under was the place to go for an embarrassment of choices. 'No chance of getting breakfast there, I take it?'

'A beggar's breakfast,' Evadne said. 'If you're lucky, the water will be clean.'

Christabel led off, holding a kerosene lantern to light their way.

Kingsley swung his stick as he walked behind Evadne. He tapped it against the walls of the tunnel, enjoying the 'tock-tock-tock' and its echoes. The noise helped him gauge the spaces ahead and behind them. His wild side needed such reassurance, as it shrank from the confines of the tunnel, whimpering, and the smell of heavy, dead air ahead did little to cheer him either. This was the sort of situation where he was glad of his civilised self. Even though the tunnel had every potential for being unnerving, he was able to tell himself that all was safe, that the tunnel was well made and unlikely to collapse, and that nothing frightful was going to appear from out of the darkness and swallow them up.

Repeat that enough to yourself and you'll start to believe it, Kingsley thought. He tugged on his collar, which had grown unaccountably tight. The air here was uncomfortable, too, really far too hot and stuffy.

Five minutes later, to Kingsley's relief, the tunnel opened out into a large area the size of a village green. Overhead

100

was swallowed in shadows, but Kingsley could just make out a riot of beams, rafters and makeshift buttresses at all angles, cascading downwards to an erratic collection of pillars and columns that made the expanse look like a forest with a particularly insane canopy overhead. Many of the supports were timber, some lashed together from many parts. Others were piles of masonry drunkenly stacked up to take the weight of the street above.

The area was dimly lit by a multitude of crooked shafts of light. It was as if they'd entered the ground floor of a large abandoned building, one where the upper storeys had partially collapsed. Kingsley could see flickering lights about them, both at the level of the ground, and on the walls stretching up to the heights. *Some must be oil lamps*, he thought, *which means the walls are populated by nerveless and tenacious observers*. Others had prime position on what remained of the upper floors, their small claim of horizontality almost serving as balconies. Rope hung from beams above, and water dripped unstaunched from a thousand places.

Kingsley could see the tunnel again on the other side, its mouth a black O. Between the supports, the ground ahead was a mish-mash of broken bricks, masonry and timber, none of it useful enough to be scavenged.

As soon as Christabel stepped out of the tunnel, she was besieged by small figures, some with lanterns, all piping for her attention. 'Miss! Miss! Miss!'

Evadne turned to Kingsley. 'Do you have anything in your pockets? Anything important?'

'I have my pistol. And a handkerchief.'

'Keep anything you want in your hand. Otherwise it'll be lost.'

'I beg your pardon?'

'This is the home of the best urchins in London. They'll steal your belongings and then try to sell them back to you.'

'I appreciate the warning,' Kingsley said, but despite this he was unprepared for the insistence and number of children who came at him, and of the smell that accompanied them.

'Sir, oh sir! I have handkerchiefs, fine handkerchiefs for you!'

'Sir, what about this ring? Suits you, it does!'

'You all right, sir? You look peaky. Want to try a tonic?'

And, more than once: 'Can you spare a copper?'

Few of them were more than waist-high and they had perfected the art of jostling, buffeting him on all sides in a manner that wasn't painful, or distressing, but was disconcerting. Hands waved up at him, but he also felt fingers plucking at his clothing, searching for valuables.

Kingsley wondered about the urchins. Was this the sum of their lives? He was sure they had to spend time on the surface, but if this was their home, what were their prospects?

He studied Evadne. She talked to a few of the urchins, and smiled at them all – but it was a troubled smile. *You want to help every one of them*, he thought. *I can see it in your face.*

He took her arm. 'You don't have much money left in your purse, do you?'

'It's empty. How did you know?'

'A guess.'

'Those rascals. You have to admit, they're very skilful.'

'So skilful they'd take your purse, empty it of money and replace it?'

'Whimsical creatures.'

'You gave all your money to them.'

She hesitated, then shrugged. Kingsley saw the sadness there. 'All the money I had with me.'

'Why? They'll only spend it.'

'That is the purpose of money, or so I'm led to believe.' She pursed her lips. 'Unless you have some radical new economic theory I haven't heard of.'

She looked into his face. A number of light-hearted retorts came to him, but he abandoned them. 'You know,' he said with a sense of recklessness, 'I don't think I've admired anyone more than I admire you.'

'In a purely professional sense, of course,' she said softly.

Kingsley saw the way the wind was blowing. 'In a purely professional sense,' he echoed.

That was not *disappointment I saw*, he thought as they resumed their journey. *I'm merely hopeless at interpreting facial expressions.*

An urchin, taller than most, pushed his way through the mob around them. He used his elbows with alacrity until he finally was able to pluck at Kingsley's sleeve. 'Mr Ward,' he said. 'Mr Ward – that girl, over there, she's asking for you.' Startled, Kingsley was about to ask how the boy knew his name, but the urchin ducked, squirmed, and then vanished into the mob.

'He may have seen the Extraordinaires,' Evadne said as Kingsley craned his neck and looked for the lad. Many bobbing, pleading faces, none that resembled his.

'I hope so,' Kingsley said. 'I'd hate to think I'm gaining a Demimonde reputation.'

Christabel was thoughtful. 'Too late. I'd heard of you, even before the bulletin went around the Agency.'

'And?'

Christabel shrugged. 'I heard you had a wolf.'

'Isn't it remarkable how facts and rumours work in the Demimonde,' Evadne said, giving Kingsley time to recover from Christabel's words. 'Now, let's see who's wanting to chat to Kingsley so much.'

The urchin was far removed from the cocky creatures on the floor of the open space. She was tiny, with dark huge eyes. Her hair was sparse, with large patches of scalp showing through, and her clothes were the oldest of rags.

Kingsley couldn't help himself. Both his wild self and his civilised self went out to her. His wild self saw a cub, helpless and needing the protection of the pack. His civilised self saw a human being who was less fortunate than himself.

He knew then that he was feeling just a portion of that Evadne felt. 'What is it, child? What do you want?'

She pointed at him. 'You're the wild boy.' She looked at Evadne. 'And you're his white friend.' Kingsley could see tracks of dried tears in the grime of her face. 'Please,' the tiny girl said, 'a friend of mine needs help to destroy the horrible sorcerers.'

~ THIRTEEN ~

Leetha was walking on her toes, jumping at sudden noises, living alert for far longer than one should while she waited for the boy to find her champions. The delicate wiring that the big people had found her people so good at eluded her. She ruined the final stages of an important piece of equipment – a 'microphone', they called it – when she fumbled putting the black carbon in between the two metal plates. She was berated and threatened with the sparky stick. She cried and cried some more when she decided that the boy had betrayed her, had taken the gold and fled never to return.

That afternoon, she was taken to another of the tests for the Gompers man. A woman was with him, a different one this time, notebook on her lap. She sat on a chair next to a table. On the table was one of the machines of the big people, one that Leetha was unfamiliar with.

A squat box, with a great horn emerging from it. A row of cylinders stood next to it.

'Music,' Gompers said through his whiskers as soon as Leetha was brought in, 'is the highest expression of civilisation.' Leetha was unsure if he was talking to her, to the notebook woman, or to an unseen audience somewhere in the shadows of the poorly lit room.

She nodded, just to be sure. Then she looked at the box and horn again.

'Pay attention,' Gompers snapped. He glared at her. 'Your people make music?'

Leetha nodded again. 'We sing. We have drums and pipes.'

The woman made a note. Gompers grunted. 'Crude, no doubt, and lacking sophistication.'

Leetha shrugged. 'We like it.'

'I care not for what you like and what you don't.' Gompers pointed at the notebook woman. 'Play selection one.'

The woman put her notebook on the table, next to the machine. Then she took one of the cylinders and arranged it in the box. Immediately, the room was full of singing.

Leetha's mouth fell open. 'You have captured a voice?'

'Pay attention,' Gompers repeated. 'Listen.' He pointed at the notebook woman, who had resumed her seat. 'Ready? The subject is straining to hear, clearly responding to the music. Her hands are beginning to move. Her nostrils are dilated.'

Leetha knew what to do. She listened hard to the music, while wondering how it was made. The music changed each time the woman changed the cylinder, from the voice to shrill and brassy instruments, then to a combination of voices with the musical instruments still playing along. She made sure that Gompers had something to describe.

She watched him, too, sidelong, and was amazed. In all his dealings with her and her people, Gompers had been a stone. He showed no concern for their weariness or distress. He had the cold, hard patience of an eagle. Yet now, his attention narrowed with the music. With a lively tune, she was sure his foot was tapping – not with joy, but with furious focus as if it were a puzzle he was trying to solve.

After the final cylinder had been removed – a loud piece that made Leetha want to get up and march across the room – Gompers glared at the woman. 'I hope, for your sake, you took note of all that.'

The woman wet her lips with the tip of her tongue.

Gompers sat back in his chair. He pinched his nose. 'Now note this: opera, music hall, military band. They all move the subject, which shows she is not insensible to the finer emotions.' He scowled. 'But how does it work? What does it do inside her people? I shall have the answer, if it takes me forever.'

The next day, Calli took her aside. 'You are driving yourself too hard,' her cousin said. 'You must let us take some of the risks.'

Leetha should have known it would be Calli who would approach her. Calli was the one who noticed hardship in others. Tall and slim Calli was never afraid to speak up. 'I suppose you will not let me say no?'

'Of course not. Tell me who I should look for outside.'

'A boy. With a cap. And a hunger for gold.'

Mid-morning, in the next lull in their telegraphic construction work, Calli took her chance. Calli crept under the benches towards the doors, and Leetha was proud of how her cousin pushed her fear aside and refused to let it master her.

While the rest of her people swept and cleaned the workshop, they chattered and moved about, making it difficult for their guard to count numbers, even if he had been interested. The way he sat on a stool by the door, smoked his cigarette and read the large sheets of his newspaper, however, suggested he had few concerns about the little people – the good, dutiful little people.

Leetha took her sweeping seriously. She searched for metal shavings with all the intent she used when looking for sweet gum in the jungle. Even though the broom was heavy and sized for big people, she applied it with vigour. She swept past the lathes, past the coils of wire, around the hammering of the metal punch. Each time she turned with the broom, she cast a glance at the doors at the far end. It was when she was sweeping the ghastly hair from around her workplace that she saw Calli lingering just inside, grinning. A few moments later, Calli was with her, a dustpan in hand. While she helped, she reported, bright-eyed and breathless. 'The boy wants you.'

Leetha's heart beat like a moth's wings. For a moment she was dizzy. She gripped the handle of the broom and her fingers ached. 'Here.' She handed the broom to Calli and found a rag. She polished the mirror above her workplace, then the electric light on its metal stand, and gradually worked her way along the row of benches. She kept her head down. She belonged there, after all. She was doing the work expected of her. She was not worth noticing, or worrying about, as she drifted away. She was forgettable.

Outside, she found the boy leaning against the wall, under the poster that showed elephants much larger than the ones Leetha knew. 'You have someone for me to meet?'

This boy with his ragged cap and bare feet had the look of stubbornness Leetha had seen many times before. This one would not give up. 'P'raps,' he said. 'If you've got more gold.'

Leetha sighed and gave him a strip. She thought about how much she had and when she could find some more without being detected.

The boy set off down the lane, then stopped and crooked a finger at her. She came to his side. He looked around, as if surrounded by watchers. Then he reached into a pocket and pulled out a short iron bar, flattened at one end. With this tool, he knelt and lifted the round metal plate at his feet. A shaft opened and Leetha could see rungs.

The boy advised her to hurry.

Leetha swallowed. She put both hands over her chest, to stop her heart bursting free. She looked back down the lane at the door to the factory. She had closed it. What if the guard decided to shift himself and lock it?

The boy urged her on. He was angry.

Leetha looked up at the sky. Grey and flat though it was, the light reminded her of freedom.

~ FOURTEEN ~

Evadne put herself in front of the urchin. 'Where do you want us to go?'

The small girl was almost entirely a pair of large eyes. She pointed ahead. 'It's up there.'

'Is it far?'

'No. Yes.' She bit her lip. 'It's underneath a lane behind Lambeth Road,' she said in a sing-song voice that signalled a lesson well-learned.

Christabel looked horrified. 'You're actually going with her?'

'How could we resist?' Evadne asked. 'A chance to meet someone who wants to destroy the Immortals? Just what we need.'

'And you agree with this?' Christabel asked Kingsley.

'Of course.' Waifs and strays were Evadne's weakness. He was honour bound to support his partner.

Christabel threw up her hands. 'But she's an urchin! She'll most likely pick your pocket as soon as your back's turned. Or she might just lead you into a right den of thieves.'

Evadne touched the small girl on the shoulder. 'You wouldn't do that, would you, dear?'

The small girl shook her head hard.

'There,' Evadne said. 'What better guarantee could one have?'

'If you're committed to this, someone needs to know where you're going. I need to notify the Agency.'

'Very well,' Evadne said. 'If you think it best.'

'I think it essential.' Christabel gave a salute that was only half in mockery, then she was off.

Kingsley was ambivalent about her departure. He'd come to enjoy the company of the young Agency officer but he did see the sense in having their whereabouts known. It was like the safety net he'd seen aerial acrobats using – not elegant, but occasionally life-saving.

Kingsley lifted his lantern and peered down the tunnel. 'So, a couple of miles as the crow flies? Or the worm creeps?'

'A stroll, in Demimonde terms,' Evadne said.

'Perhaps.' He addressed the small girl. 'Are you sure you know the way?'

She put a hand to her mouth. Her gaze darted from one side to the other. She trembled, and Kingsley suddenly saw her as a small animal looking to flee.

Evadne glared at him and dropped to her knees, heedless of the muck underfoot. She took the girl by the shoulders. 'It's all right. We trust you. Show us.'

The girl looked at her feet and slowly she stopped shivering.

Evadne pushed the girl's hair back from her face. 'What's your name, dear?'

The girl shrugged, a tiny jerk of a gesture. 'They call me Mouse.'

'But what's your real name?'

'Don't know.'

'Mouse it is, then.' Evadne took one of the girl's hands and stood. 'Lead on, Mouse. We're with you.'

Since his introduction to the Demimonde, Kingsley had become accustomed to subterranea. Tunnels, pipes, shafts and access points were familiar places to him. Even though the confines were uncomfortable to his wild self, they provided further exercise for his growing olfactory senses. Smell was useful in such places, even if the odours were hardly refined.

Mouse, true to her name, scurried through these underground byways in an unhesitating but tangled route. She wasn't afraid of emerging into the open air, either, and she took them through mazy lanes and even through a course of abandoned buildings linked by makeshift bridges that were mostly open air and wire.

They reached Lambeth Bridge and, again, Mouse didn't hesitate. She scuttled down the stairs at the bridge abutment and shepherded them to an ancient waiting wherry. The boatman grunted, threw a stub of a cigar into the water, and pushed off as soon as Kingsley had stepped from the embankment.

On the south side of the river, they were soon underground again and, eventually, Mouse brought Kingsley and Evadne to an opening in the wall. It was a workers' room off a large sewer, with curved walls and bricked benches set into the side, and a place for lamps to sit, sconce-like, just overhead. A metal ladder opposite led to what Kingsley assumed was the upper world with its streets, carriages and sunlight. At the foot of the ladder, reeking water rushed along the middle of the drain, filling the space with a sound that reminded Kingsley of wind in trees.

'We wait here,' Mouse said. The young girl took up a position on the bench opposite. She looked at her feet instead of at them, and she fumbled at a frayed sleeve. Kingsley sat next to Evadne.

'How long have you been down here?' Evadne asked Mouse.

'Don't know. Always?'

Kingsley's heart went out to her. The child was lost and didn't even know it.

'How would you like to be somewhere different?' Evadne asked. 'A school where you'd have a bed of your own and hot food three times a day?'

'No.'

'No? Why not?'

Mouse squirmed on her seat. Her chanting tone of earlier returned: 'If anyone says they'll take you some-where nice, run away as fast as you can.'

Kingsley thought Evadne was going to cry. 'You're not running away, Mouse,' she pointed out.

Mouse slid off the bench and stood, eyeing the sewer. 'I should. Scratcher said we should.'

'Then why don't you?'

Mouse bit her lip. 'Scratcher said it was monsters what want to take us away. You're not a monster. You're nice.' She glanced at Kingsley. 'He's not bad, neither.'

'And who's Scratcher?'

'That's me. Mouse is one of us.' A boy was descending the ladder opposite, testing each rung as he came. A grating noise signalled the cutting off of the light from above, and the descent of another figure.

The two stood on the other side of the drain, and Kingsley recognised the lad as the one from St Giles Under, the one who'd pointed out Mouse. He was about ten years old, bare-footed and wearing short pants, braces, a shirt that had once, in another life, been white, and a waistcoat that was far too large but once had pretensions of gaudiness. His cap was ragged.

He must have signalled to Mouse and then gone to fetch ... who?

The lad's companion was small, less than four feet in height, but not a child. Her skin was a milk coffee colour. Her black hair was pulled back and tied behind her head. She had almost no chin, and her nose was extremely broad. As she stood peering across the drain, her shoulders were raised, as if she were constantly shrugging. She wore grey calf-length trousers and a simple high-collared blouse hung loose at her waist. Her gaze was calm, steady and intelligent.

Kingsley at first assumed she was a foreigner, maybe even from India, afflicted with dwarfism, but the more he stared the more he realised that he'd never seen anyone like her before, and it took Evadne's elbow in the ribs to make him realise he was being unseemly. 'A Demi-monder?' he asked her softly.

'Perhaps, but not one that I'm familiar with.'

Scratcher waved. 'Now, Mouse, time to go.'

Mouse was on her feet straight away, but then she hesitated. She held her hands out, palms up, and spoke without looking at Evadne. 'Scratcher takes care of us.'

114

Evadne looked across the drain. 'Do you?'

Scratcher grinned, but it evaporated when he saw Evadne's expression. He shrugged. 'Best as we can.'

'Make sure you do.'

Evadne patted Mouse on the back. It was all the urging the small girl needed. She leaped over the drain and landed on both feet, like a rabbit. She went to Scratcher. He pointed. She trotted off into the darkness with no lantern and no hesitation.

Scratcher held a hand out to the small stranger. She counted five small rectangles into his hand, each the size of a playing card. They glinted yellow in the light from the lantern Mouse had left in the workers' niche.

'Done,' Scratcher said. He hurried off in the direction Mouse had gone, keeping to the narrow walkway alongside the drain.

Evadne was following Scratcher's indistinct shape as the shadows closed in around him. For a moment Kingsley was worried that she was about to succumb to her need to protect lost children and dash off after them, but when she looked away he knew the moment had passed.

She caught him looking at her. She shook her head, her lips pressed tightly together.

'Children hurt your heart, no?' The small figure opposite had her hands by her side but her eyes were inquisitive. Her voice was high and reedy. 'You want to help them.'

Evadne held her hands out, palms up, and Kingsley wondered if she knew she were mirroring Mouse's gesture. 'They need our protection. They *deserve* our protection.'

'Ah, they do. If we do not care for our young ones, what does that say about us?' The small stranger moved both hands horizontally, as if pushing something aside, a clear indication she was changing the subject. 'Please,' she said. Kingsley knew straight away – from the stumbling elision of the p and the l – that English was not her first language. 'The male. Walk a little, for Leetha to see.' She pointed up the drain. 'That way.'

Kingsley spoke to Evadne from the corner of his mouth. 'You have your Swingeing Blow?'

'All ready.'

Kingsley then did as he was bid. He strode away along the walkway. Halfway, he was suddenly conscious of being watched and when he wheeled about the small stranger's eyes were bright.

'Good,' she announced once Kingsley had returned to his starting point.

'Well walked,' Evadne murmured. 'Anyone would think you've been doing it all your life.'

'The female, now, please.'

Evadne pursed her lips and took her hand from her pocket. As she walked off, Kingsley called after her. 'Just one foot in front of the other. Don't try anything fancy.'

Her sniff of disdain echoed from the bricks.

Kingsley watched the small stranger (Leetha?) as she studied Evadne. She bobbed her head in time with Evadne's steps, her mouth open a little as if she were tasting the motion. She moved from foot to foot, almost miming, and Kingsley noticed that her feet were long for someone of her diminutive stature.

Evadne reached Kingsley's side. Hardly thinking, he sought for her hand only to find hers looking for his. A brief, clumsy moment of embarrassment and they intertwined.

'You are both dangerous,' Leetha declared.

Kingsley blinked. 'Well, we're armed, if that's what you mean.'

'No.' Leetha flapped a hand, making a motion like a butterfly. 'You hunt, when you need to. You are powerful. You are strong. You can make others afraid. You are what we need.'

'And you can tell all of that from a little bit of walking?'

A sharp hiss came from Leetha, and was repeated several times. Laughter. 'In the jungle, you must judge quickly, or you become someone's meal.'

'A good point,' Evadne said, and Kingsley filed away the jungle reference for later cogitation. 'And now to business?'

Leetha held up a hand. 'The male. He is a beast.'

'Well,' Evadne said, 'he can be abrupt at times . . .'

Kingsley squeezed Evadne's hand. 'What do you mean?' he asked the small stranger.

'The animal inside you. The animal outside you. You are both. The female,' Leetha said abruptly. 'You are a storm.'

Evadne considered this. 'Well, when all's said and done, that's not half bad.' She eyed Kingsley. 'I think I have the better option.'

Kingsley ignored her and spoke to Leetha. 'If you mean she's unpredictable and uncontrollable, then I want to talk to you about doing a spot of fortune telling at the next spring fair.'

More laughter, then the small stranger was abruptly solemn. 'My people want to go home. I want you to help us.'

~ FIFTEEN ~

'Home?' Evadne said, 'Mouse said you wanted help to destroy the Immortals.'

'Yes. They have us captive,' Leetha said. 'Destroy them, and we shall be free.'

Kingsley considered pointing out that such things were more easily said than done, but instead asked: 'How many of you are there?'

'We are thirty. We are lost.'

'Do you know where your home is?' Evadne asked.

The small stranger was silent for a moment, her head cocked as if she were listening to a distant sound. Her movements were sharp and precise and Kingsley had the unsettling feeling that she was fully aware of her surroundings – and that if he took his eyes from her, she'd disappear. He could smell her – a faint cinnamon odour, not unpleasant. 'I know where my home is, but I do not know how to get there. Those who work on us, for the Immortals, say it is in the East Indies. They call our island Flores.'

'You are a long way from home, then,' Kingsley said. 'But *you* seem to have escaped. Why don't the rest of your people just nip out the same way you did?'

A small smile. 'One at a time and our keepers will not notice if we return before long. But even they will see something if we all leave at once.'

Evadne leaped on this. 'That would suggest that the Immortals are based somewhere near here, if you can't be away long.'

'They are. Once I have your word that you will help me, I shall show you.'

'You don't have to convince us to help you,' Evadne said, 'we are sworn enemies of the Immortals.'

Kingsley raised an eyebrow. '"Sworn enemies?"'

'What would you prefer: "on the outer with"? "loggerheaded"?'

'Sworn enemies it is. I like the grandeur of it.' He held out an open palm to Leetha. 'What is the project the Immortals are working on?'

'Project?'

'They want to enslave humanity. How are they going about it?'

Leetha frowned. 'They make us work with metal, with your electricity.' She shrugged. 'We do it or we are beaten.'

Evadne made a small sound, half-sigh, half-cry. 'We shall help you.'

Kingsley put a hand on her shoulder in mute agreement.

'I have gold,' the small stranger said. 'I shall give it to you.'

'No need,' Evadne said. 'Wiping out the Immortals shall be a reward all of its own. How many children do they have imprisoned? We'll have to free them, too.'

'Ah. I have heard them, seen them, but do not know how many they have. Poor, poor things.' Leetha looked up towards the manhole cover, stricken. 'The Immortals are cruel.'

'We want to end that cruelty,' Evadne said. 'Find the children. Help us free them. That is the price for our help.'

Kingsley covered his mouth. 'Journal,' he murmured.

Evadne caught this smoothly. 'Do you know the Spawn?' she said to Leetha. 'They are magical slaves who do the bidding of the Immortals.'

'The not-alive creatures? I have seen them.'

'They have stolen something of ours. A book. We need it back.'

'How will I know it?'

'Can you read?'

'I have learned. A little.'

Kingsley wasn't convinced. He took out his notebook and wrote down the title of his father's journal. He tore out the page. 'Here. This is on the cover of the book. Just look for this word: Sanderson.'

Leetha took the slip of paper and studied it. 'Children and a book.' The small stranger unclasped her other hand and pointed at the gold in it. 'You do not want this? Your people love it.'

'Keep it,' Evadne said. 'You may need it when you're free. For travel.'

The gold disappeared. 'We are agreed?'

'We are,' Kingsley said. 'Now, if you'll show us the way.'

'No.' Leetha shook her head. 'Only the head of the

tribe can make an agreement that binds.' She pointed to Evadne. 'The head of the tribe is a female. Always.'

Evadne managed not to look smug, but Kingsley could tell it was taking a monumental effort. She took a small step forward, so she was right on the edge of the drain that separated them from the small stranger. 'I am the head of the Extraordinaires tribe. I agree to your terms.'

'You promise this?'

'I promise. For both of us.'

'Come with me.' Leetha climbed the ladder. At the top, she panted with effort for some time, long enough for Kingsley to consider climbing the ladder to help her, but finally she was able to shift the cover. She disappeared.

'What do you think?' Kingsley asked Evadne when they stood at the foot of the ladder.

'Peculiar,' Evadne said, 'but no more peculiar than a thousand things in the Demimonde, and half as peculiar as another thousand.'

Kingsley shaded his eyes at the disc of light above. 'I suggest that we investigate first. We get some idea of location, the lie of the land, the disposition of the Immortals, then we report back to Christabel and the Agency. We can come back with numbers.'

'An eminently sensible idea.' Evadne's gaze, too, was on the entrance to the shaft.

A nice sentiment, Kingsley thought, worried that Evadne may not be able to restrain herself if she came face to face with the Immortals, *but it's nothing like agreeing with my strategy*. 'We should inspect the place for entrances and exits as soon as we can, and find any access points to the Demimonde while we're at it.'

'Splendid,' Evadne murmured. Her hand was in her pocket.

Kingsley took her shoulder and made sure she was looking at him. 'Evadne. Listen. I don't want you going off half-cocked.'

'I know I have a tendency to go off half-cocked. But I decided, a long time ago, that whenever I went off half-cocked I'd go off fully half-cocked, so to speak.'

This did not reassure Kingsley at all. 'You know what I mean.'

'I do, but do you realise what you're doing?'

'Standing here wondering what you're getting at?'

'Besides that.' Evadne glanced at the ladder. 'I'm wondering if it's your Inner Animal speaking.'

'Now I'm completely lost. My Inner Animal?'

'You call it your wild side, or your wildness, or half a dozen other names. Trying to avoid the issue, most likely. I call it your Inner Animal and right now I think it's being protective of your other pack member.'

'My other pack member?'

Evadne blushed her unique blush – a pinkening of her white skin like the inner petals of a rose. She cleared her throat a little and looked away. 'That would be me, it seems.'

Kingsley actually swayed back on his heels, narrowly avoiding banging the back of his head on the brick wall of the tunnel. 'I see. You and I are Extraordinaires. We belong to the same pack. I'm protecting you.'

She looked back at him with a steady, even gaze. 'As a good wolf should protect other pack members.'

'My Inner Animal at work.'

'Since we're so professional about our partnership, what other explanation could there be?'

Kingsley was spared any prevaricating by Leetha's face appearing at the top of the ladder. 'We are safe. It is time to come up now, please.'

Kingsley went first, gripping his cane in his teeth and tilting his head sideways, a thousand thoughts sky-rocketing around as he tried to look beyond Evadne's words, beyond the nuance, to understand exactly what she meant.

This isn't what I need right now, he thought as he pulled himself up and into the world. He stayed low and scanned the surroundings. *I need to concentrate on the task at hand.*

The lane was dingy in the feeble midday sun. Ware-houses crowded in on either side, two and three storeys of shabby red brick. A cold wind whipped through it, and the grit it carried made Kingsley squint. He could smell hot oil and coal smoke.

'Kingsley?'

Evadne looked up at him, her hand outstretched. He grasped it and with hardly any effort, lifted her straight out of the shaft, catching her around the waist to steady her. 'Thank you,' she said. She wouldn't meet his eyes and he cursed himself. He'd obviously missed the moment, or said something he shouldn't, or not said something he should have.

Leetha interrupted his clatterfall of thoughts. 'This way.'

She led them to a wooden door in the side of a red-brick edifice, a two-storey warehouse or factory. From the inside came an industrial clangour mixed with shouts and the whirring of engines – and the harsh ozone smell of electricity. A row of dirty windows looked down on them. A handful of uninterested pigeons did the same from the peak of the gable before taking flight in search of something more edible. The flurry of movement caught the attention of his wild side – or Inner Animal – and he barely stopped himself from leaping at them. Evadne noticed and put her hand on his arm.

Leetha paused. 'We must be careful. Guards and keepers will be about, watching over my people as they work.'

The door was little-used, to judge from the formidable sound it made when Leetha edged it open. Kingsley's heart almost took flight at the groaning, but he reasoned that this meant they'd be unlikely to encounter anyone just inside, and the noise of the nearby workshop was enough to obscure a thousand creaky doors.

And so it proved. Leetha brought them into a narrow, filthy corridor stacked on both sides with barrels, boxes and lengths of tarry rope. A slit window, equally filthy, admitted light begrudgingly. The walls quivered with the hammering that came from the workshop.

'Stores,' Leetha said as she led them through the narrow aisle the corridor had become. 'Things we use to make what the Immortals need.'

'Are there any more places like this?' Evadne asked. She shifted the lid on a barrel and plucked out a handful of long brass screws. Automatically, she looped them from hand to hand before dumping them back.

'Many, many,' Leetha said. 'I have explored them all.'

'Can you show us? I might be able to deduce something about the whole from the parts.'

Over the next hour, Kingsley was glad they had the diminutive Leetha with them. As it was, his wild side was driven almost to howling by the number of times guards passed an instant after Leetha had found a hiding spot for them. At times, he became convinced that the small woman had abandoned them but she always reappeared just as he was about to cry foul.

In contrast, Evadne had entered a state of intense musing as they moved from store room to store room. Her brow was perpetually furrowed as she examined heavy machinery and tiny crystals alike. She muttered words like 'transducer' and 'microphone diaphragm' and she even produced a small brass gauge to measure wires and couplings.

Kingsley was very much aware that he was watching over her and, more than allowing him to do such, she was relying on him to. In the middle of the danger of discovery, in the noise and the acrid stink of burning rubber, he enjoyed the responsibility. Knowing that Evadne was concentrating, he refrained from interrupting her thinking. After Leetha had asked question after question, he advised the small woman to do the same, a request she acceded to with good grace.

When they found a room full of small glass vials betraying the presence of phlogiston – that half-mystical component of air capable of providing unparalleled power – Evadne merely nodded, as if she'd been expecting to find such a thing.

Eventually, they found a room full of large metal cylinders. 'Ah.' Evadne clapped her hands together. 'This settles it. Compressed nitrogen, for the spark gap generators.'

'Obviously,' he said, understanding a response was needed. 'Do go on.'

'Wireless telegraphy,' she said. 'The Immortals are turning Hertzian waves to their own ends, using phlogiston for power and efficacy.' She shook her head. 'They'd still need receivers, though. What am I missing?'

'Hertzian waves – radio?' Kingsley pointed his cane at the nitrogen cylinders. 'The Immortals want to talk to the world? I know that Congreve-Knollys was convinced about this, but I'm not so sure.'

'There must be more to it than that. Leetha, what about magic? Do you know of any magic the Immortals are using?'

The small woman shuddered. 'They make the not-alive creatures, the Spawn, but they also do other things.'

Leetha took them through a wretched ceiling crawl-space until they reached the end of the building. After a moment, she led them across a cobbled laneway, over a wooden fence she scaled with no hesitation and into the rear of a large warehouse. Pigeons roosted in the rafters and narrow spears of light slashed down from holes in the roof. Stacked around the steel pillars were square bales almost as tall as Kingsley. 'Wool? Cotton?' he wondered aloud.

Evadne had her hands clasped in front of her. 'Can we find out?'

Kingsley patted his pockets. 'I thought everyone in my position carried a penknife,' he muttered.

Leetha grinned and stepped up to the nearest bale. She shook her sleeve and a sliver of bright metal fell into her hand. 'A blade? I have one.'

She slashed at the hessian cover, then jumped back with a small cry of alarm. Kingsley crouched and used his cane to prod at what had spilled from the bale. 'It's hair.' Steeling himself, he scooped up a handful and sniffed. 'Ordinary, brown human hair.'

He dropped the hair and wiped his hand on his trousers. 'I'm at a loss.'

Evadne bit her lip, still thinking.

Leetha trotted some distance away and slashed at another bale. More hair tumbled out, glossy black this time. After four more samples, Kingsley was ready to admit that the Immortals had a warehouse full of human hair.

He remembered. 'Buchanan said that barbers and wigmakers had been attacked. Perhaps this is the result.'

'Hush,' Evadne said. 'Please.'

She turned in a full circle, taking in the bales that were stacked almost to the rafters in some places. Kingsley was nonplussed by what it represented. Thousands of shorn heads? Tens of thousands? Hundreds of thousands? And was this all of it or was there more?

'I have it,' Evadne announced. 'I think that this time the Immortals are uniting the most modern of technologies – radio broadcasting – with sympathetic magic, one of the most primitive forms of sorcery.'

Kingsley felt as if he were standing in a sub-Arctic draught. 'Sympathetic magic? That's using effigies and the like, isn't it? Poking in needles?'

'That's part of it. Another aspect of sympathetic magic is using things that have once been part of someone to influence their action at a distance.'

The full import struck Kingsley. 'Hair. The hair of thousands of people.'

'If the Immortals can use all this in conjunction with phlogiston-powered radio, then they could control every person the hair came from. This way, their phlogiston-powered technology wouldn't need radio receivers. Their commands could work directly on the person.'

'They'd have the mind-enslaved army Congreve-Knollys was afraid of.'

'It could be worse than that. What if some of the hair came from Whitehall barbers? The Immortals could control members of Parliament, even the Prime Minister himself.'

Leetha looked at them anxiously. 'It is good that the sorcerers are bad. You will be more ready to stop them, yes?'

'Oh yes,' Evadne said with an ominous calm. 'We'll certainly stop them.'

SIXTEEN

The heavy tramp of booted feet sent them fleeing down a corridor. Leetha pointed at a door, urging them towards it, and then she waited behind. Hurrying, with Evadne right behind, Kingsley wrenched at the door-handle and barged inside just as he caught the flat smell of corruption that signalled the presence of Spawn.

The room was dark – even darker when Evadne closed the door and stood with her back to it. She went to speak, but Kingsley hushed her. He held his hand in front of him as he peered into the blackness, skin prickling, his Inner Animal struggling to assert itself. This was its realm, after all, darkness and the unknown, with a scent in the air that spelled danger.

An electric light snapped on and Kingsley's lips drew back in a snarl. A dozen Spawn stood unmoving, clad in bedraggled overalls – and one stood at the rear, in a

129

shabby suit, with a fist around a long cord attached to the electric light.

Spawn in storage! Kingsley couldn't help seeing the advantages of such a system, while his wild side sought frantically for the best way out.

As one, the dozen overalled Spawn blinked in the light. Then they advanced.

Kingsley took the first of the Spawn on the side of the neck with his cane, then jabbed it in the throat with the next thrust. It fell, but was instantly replaced by another of the dead-faced creatures. Evadne cried out as the door behind them was battered open. She fell into him and her Swingeing Blow flew from her hand.

The Spawn howled and the din hammered at Kingsley's head, nearly splitting it. Shouts came from behind him as Evadne struggled to hold the door close.

We're trapped!

The realisation sent his Inner Animal rebelling. It screamed, hot and full-throated, and instantly he forgot all the trappings of civilisation such as weapons and scientific combat. He flung his cane at the nearest Spawn and followed by launching himself at its throat. Together, they went backwards. He wrenched at the creature and then he rolled to all fours to find himself surrounded by more. For an instant, his more civilised self was frozen by the hopelessness of the situation he'd put himself in, then his Inner Animal responded. He attacked.

Bruised and aching, Kingsley was mired in the shame that came from his inability to control his wildness. He tried

130

to distract himself by contemplating the fact that, while the new Hall of the Immortals lacked the grandeur and mystery of their previous premises deep under Greenwich, it had a baroque opulence that was daunting in a traditionally British way. False columns lined the walls and the ceiling was covered with paintings of alarmingly jolly hunters who were spearing deer and boar. The frames were gilt, as were those of half a dozen tall mirrors on the walls. The floor was the very best parquetry, while a long blue carpet marked the way from the door to the foot of the thrones.

Armed guards stood with their backs to the walls. They were garbed in a uniform that Kingsley had never seen before. They had dark blue shakoes, each sporting an intricate brass badge, while their tunics were heavily draped with braid. Rows of brightly polished brass buttons studded their fronts. Their breeches were black, as were their knee-length boots. Kingsley thought it all looked foolish, a caricature of a uniform, but the guards' steady, distant gaze dissuaded him from laughing. The way they held their rifles was not that of make-believe soldiers. They were ready to use them, too: the bayonets were locked in place.

He put a hand to his forehead. His wild side was afraid and angry, a bad combination. It was as if it were scratching inside his skull, whining to be let out.

To do what?

Evadne's face was set as they were marched towards the canopied dais at the other end of the room, and Kingsley was sure it wasn't just because they'd been divested of all their weapons before being brought here. A golden throne stood on the dais; the feet of the occupants didn't

131

reach the ground. Two guards stood on either side of the triumvirate of evil.

The Immortals were pleased. Two were giggling, while the fur-clad one was actually clapping his pudgy hands, ignoring the red-splashed bandages that covered what had been his fingers.

As they neared the sorcerers, Kingsley was saddest about Evadne. As well as the world being poorer without her, any idea he'd had of a future with her was now pointless. Could you miss something you never had? Was that a form of pre-emptive regret?

Pointless though it may be, he scanned the room for possibilities – a friendly face, a convenient trap door, an overlooked cannon. Then he straightened, ignoring the complaints of his abused body. With an effort that came from reason and will, he threw off his resignation as if shrugging off a shawl. Their fate might be inevitable, but he was dashed if he was going to go to it shuffling and spiritless.

I refuse to be cowed.

The five guards marched them until they reached a line on the carpet a few yards away from the steps that led up to the dais. Kingsley glanced over his shoulder – and noticed that Evadne did the same – to find that the guards were extremely professional. They were standing a good distance behind them, far enough to forestall a backward stumble and grapple. Thoughtfully, still sizing up possible escapes, he returned his gaze to the Immortals. Two of them were whispering to each other. The fur-clad one was mumbling to himself, his head bowed.

Kingsley steeled himself to maintain his reserve. Their grotesqueness was one thing, but his insides contracted at the unnaturalness in front of him. The vile way they had taken the innocence of children and used it to sustain their own, foul lives was deeply repugnant. Small and fat, and younger than when Kingsley had seen them last, they lolled on the long bench that was their throne. They were supported by many rich cushions, without which Kingsley suspected they may have had trouble sitting upright. They looked to be about six years old this time, with chubby cheeks and limbs, but their eyes were still ancient. Kingsley could feel the malevolence rolling off them like mist from a glacier.

While his civilised, rational self could cope with the horrors, his wildness whimpered at the sight. They were wrong – stomach-turningly wrong. They smelled wrong, they looked wrong, they didn't belong in the world and yet here they were.

In the months after the Greenwich destruction, Evadne and he had talked about the Immortals, wondering if they would reappear. Evadne scraped together enough details from her friends in the Demimonde to suggest they would, and that they would certainly seek revenge.

The female, who Evadne had learned was called Jia, was in an embroidered robe. Her hair was black and hung in a short pigtail over one shoulder. She pointed. 'You! Ghost girl! You thought you had seen the end of us!'

Evadne didn't flinch. 'It's to my great disappointment that I find this not true.'

'You are not the first to be in this position,' said Forkbeard, the one wrapped in furs. He was scratching underneath them with a distant, fixed look on his face. 'You will not be the last.' He turned to Jia. 'I don't see why we're wasting time on these fools. We have more important things to deal with.' He held up a hand. 'I don't think I can feel my fingers.'

Jia ignored him. 'We have had many enemies,' the other male said – Augustus? He had a bowl of grapes in his lap. He examined each fruit before eating it, holding it up to the light. 'None of them is alive now.'

'How unexpected to hear such boasting,' Kingsley said. 'I thought you'd be more modest.'

Jia rounded on him. Her eyes were not the eyes of a child. Kingsley could see years of depravity in them, and not a single tinge of mercy. 'Brave words, wild boy, for one who has been stupid like you. Caught when you were blundering about in the home of your enemies? To think, we do not have to hunt – you come to us to find a book to read.'

Two of them found this hilarious. They giggled, while the fur-clad one scowled. The giggling was chilling.

They lured us here. Kingsley wanted to kick himself. *They used my father's journal as bait.*

'The Sanderson man,' Jia said when she had recovered from her laughter. 'He interfered with us, in India, setting back our plans. We saw to him, you know.'

Kingsley's lips pulled back from his teeth with anger. His father had crossed swords with the Immortals? Now, as well as wanting to know more about the man, Kingsley wanted to shake his hand. Anyone who went up against the Immortals was brave enough to do the right thing even when it was dangerous. In short, a man that Kingsley would like.

'I know,' he lied. 'And I'm glad he set back your plans. Remind me – how long have you been trying to achieve your ends? A thousand years? More?'

'We are patient,' Augustus said, 'and our prize shall be the sweeter because of our waiting.'

'You know,' Evadne said, 'that sounds frightfully as if you're trying to convince yourself of something.'

'Your taunts are as nothing to us,' Augustus said, but Kingsley heard more than a hint of irritation in his voice, squeaky though it was. 'We're so glad you brought your head with you. We want to look inside it. To settle a wager, if for no other reason.'

This set them off again. Jia and Augustus laughed until their plump faces were red. Jia gripped the arm of her throne until she regained her breath. 'It's his brain we want, not him. His brain!'

Forkbeard muttered and studied his hands.

'It's a pity,' Evadne said to Kingsley. She went to reach out to him, but one of the guards behind them growled. 'You've had so little use of it.'

'It should be in good shape then,' Kingsley added. 'Nice and fresh.'

'Do not play lightly with us!' snapped Forkbeard, looking up. 'Guards, take them away.'

Kingsley saw his tactic as clearly as if he'd written it down. He'd wait for a guard to come close. He'd wait to be nudged, then he'd twist to the left and while the guard was off-balance he'd bring him down with an elbow behind the ear . . .

Then one of the guards reached out and grabbed Evadne by the hair, laughing.

Kingsley's wild self exploded again.

135

The cell was makeshift. The smell of furniture polish, soap and methylated spirits told Kingsley that it had once been a cleaner's cupboard, hastily but securely converted.

He gathered this slowly. It took him some further time to realise that the reason his wrists were aching so much was that he was manacled to the wall and dangling from them. One knee was throbbing, too, and he found it difficult to open his right eye. His back felt as if he'd been dropped onto a bag of cricket balls and his ribs were hurting all over again. The inside of his mouth was raw and – as he discovered when he probed with his tongue – still bleeding in places.

Evadne was sitting on the floor opposite, her back to the wall. Her head was bowed. She was sobbing.

'Evadne?'

She lifted her head. Her hand went to her mouth. 'Kingsley? Oh!'

In an instant, she'd thrown her arms around his neck. Her tears were wet on his skin.

He gasped and when he spoke it was through gritted teeth: 'As much as I've dreamed of such a display, would you mind stepping back for a moment? It feels as if these shackles are sawing through my wrists.'

Evadne tottered backwards, dashing tears from her eyes with the back of her hand. 'Oh, Kingsley, I'm so sorry.'

'Why? Was it you who beat me?'

'No ... I ... What?'

'Never mind.' Kingsley had never seen Evadne befuddled before. 'Before we explore things any further, could you get me a pick or two from inside my collar?'

Evadne straightened and, with a visible effort, composed herself. 'That's what I was trying to do when you interrupted me.'

'It felt like an embrace to me.'

One of her nails was suddenly intensely interesting. 'I'm not responsible for what you feel.'

And that's a statement so jam-packed that it could take me a year to sort through. 'My lock picks, please?'

The last thing Kingsley wanted to do was to embarrass Evadne, but he was beginning to suspect that she was also feeling the confusion he was. Her customary assurance had vanished. He wasn't about to draw attention to it, nor describe her as being flustered, but that was the distinct impression he had as she stood on tiptoes and fumbled behind his neck.

He lowered his face to her cheek. She still smelled of violets.

She skipped backwards, brandishing two lengths of wire. 'Here we are,' she said brightly. 'Can I do anything to help?'

'If you could put them both in the fingers of my right hand, that would be most useful.'

It took Kingsley nearly a minute to free himself, but he blamed that on the battering he'd apparently taken at the hands of the guards. He rubbed his wrists and eyed the manacles balefully. 'This has all gone outstandingly wrong, hasn't it? I'm sorry for messing up like that.'

'Ah. Your outburst was unfortunate.'

'Unfortunate? It was shameful.'

'Don't berate yourself. You couldn't help it.'

'Couldn't I? Then that's a sad story. It's happening too often. I'm worried where it will lead.'

'And don't wallow in self-pity, either.'

Evadne was right, and Kingsley knew it. He'd always held that self-pity – while seductive – was singularly pointless.

'I'm not wanting to be horribly trite, but do you know where we are?'

Evadne gestured at the small window, which was grimy and barred. 'I can see the dome of Bethlem Hospital. We must still be near Lambeth Road.'

Gingerly, Kingsley went to the door. It was reinforced with steel bands. The lock was a heavy-duty four-tumbler model with a hand-driven bolt for extra effect. 'We'll be out of here before you know it, and probably before Christabel gets back to the Agency.'

Kingsley heard an ominous thud some distance away. He blinked, then wrapped an arm around Evadne's waist, pressed her against the door, seized the top of the door-frame with one hand, pressed his back against one side and grabbed the other side with his free hand.

Muffled by his body, Evadne said, 'What on earth are you ...'

The whole world roared and the floor bucked, shattered, then fell away.

~⟡ SEVENTEEN ⟡~

Leetha crouched in her cell, smelling smoke. She cried out, seized by the shivering that came through fear. She was afraid that the Immortals would know that she was the one who had caused the disaster. Then she was afraid that her people would be left behind to die in the fire she had caused by setting the gas free and setting rags to smoulder.

Just when she had given up hope, one of the guards flung open her cell door. She was herded, along with the rest of her people, to a room where the smoke was not as dense as in the corridor. She was relieved to see them all. Mannor, Calli, Ubbo and the others were all there, red-eyed and coughing, but together. It was a moment of happiness just to be close with them, but it wasn't long before they were shouted at and driven into darkness, finding stairs to take them down and down and down.

Ahead, Leetha was sure she could hear the crying of children, but the noise was faint and distant. Her heart ached for them.

The guards had lanterns that shone like stars, and they used their sparky sticks to move her people along a narrow metal walkway. The tunnel echoed with their passage. A ladder took them down to where a dozen more guards were waiting. They were nervous, strutting about and shouting when there was no need. Leetha watched as, one by one, her people were pushed into what looked like small metal canoes. Each of her kin was forced to lie down in their shiny little pod, then a door slid over the hole in the rock. The pod disappeared with a whoosh and a blast of air. This was just the sort of mystery to set all her kin chattering, making guesses as to the construction and purpose.

Leetha's turn came soon enough. She lingered, but when a guard brandished his sparky stick she saw he was afraid. She sniffed, smelled smoke, and understood why.

Leetha felt the draught. A breeze was sucking smoke from above. She sought for the source of the draught and found it when the guard raised the alcove door again. Then Leetha had it. The pods were being sucked along the tube that enclosed them, like water through a reed.

The guard helped her into the pod. As soon as she lay down, sweating and trembling at the strangeness, a cover slid over her face. When the pod started to move, the jerk made her stomach turn over. The motion was frightening in the darkness, but she tried to imagine being swept along a river in a strong current, a ride full of laughter.

A clang and a jerk signalled the end of her ride, which could only have been a few minutes' duration. The cover

140

was removed and she was lifted out, a guard taking her under the armpits. She looked about to find a chamber with floor, walls and ceilings covered with the flat white stones that the big people called tiles. They were slick and hard underfoot. Leetha sniffed, but the only smoke she could smell came from her tunic and trousers.

The single guard shut the cover on the pod. He glanced over his shoulder. 'Through the door. Hurry!'

Stairs took Leetha up a level. Another guard was standing in front of an iron door, waiting with a notebook and pencil. 'You're Leetha?'

Leetha was surprised. She had not realised that any of the guards knew her name. She nodded, and the guard made a mark on her paper. Then she stood aside and opened the door.

Four guards were standing in front of a large lorry, just like the one that had taken Leetha and her people from the docks to the lair of the Immortals. She shrank away, but the guard behind prodded her forward.

Then she saw Ubbo and Calli and three of her cousins inside the lorry. She climbed in and they huddled, embracing, in the far corner, surrounded by metal and hardness.

One by one, her people joined them. They smelled of smoke and fear, but it did not matter. Leetha counted. When all thirty of them were inside, the doors were locked and the lorry lurched off.

She hoped that it had all been worthwhile. She had risked much to set the gas free so their young champions – the ghost girl and the wild boy – could have a chance to escape.

Even though her journey was in the dark, in the metal shell of the lorry, her sense of direction did not fail her. They were travelling north, far north.

While they travelled, they sang songs of their home and songs of their family. Ubbo told stories. Mannor made them laugh. All of them were curious about their destination and played guessing games; most guessed they were being taken home, but that was through hope, not through knowing.

Leetha was calm. She had hope because she believed in her young champions. They would find Leetha's people and set them free.

Leetha had kept the knowledge of her young champions to herself, uncertain whether telling of it would be a good thing or not. As she listened to the songs and saw the resolve in the faces around her, she decided she would tell her people about the wild boy and the ghost girl. When they arrived at their destination, she would share the news, and the hope.

It was the right thing to do. It made her feel content, but she knew, too, that an agreement like the one she had made with her champions worked both ways. Leetha had to do her part.

She hoped that the sorcerers had remembered to take the book with them, the book that belonged to the wild boy. Leetha needed to find it.

She'd promised.

⤞ EIGHTEEN ⤝

Kingsley had the door open in seconds. The corridor outside was rapidly filling with smoke, while the remains of windows and mirrors sparkled on the carpet. Raised voices were coming from nearby. Kingsley looked both ways and thought the corridor to the right was marginally less smoky. He took Evadne by the hand and they ran.

They stumbled upon a set of stairs and hurtled down them while the building collapsed in a chaos of smoke and flame. Coughing, they pushed on until they blundered into another locked door. He motioned for Evadne to crouch to find sweeter air, while he applied himself to the lock. For a moment, his Inner Animal threatened to take over, panicked by the smoke and heat. He had to beat it down, to impose himself on it, which interfered with his work on the lock. Evadne was beginning to cast worried looks his way when he finally had it, taking two or three times longer than was his wont and, in the end, using brutal rather than deft movements of his lock pick.

Kingsley hit the door with a shoulder. He nearly yelped with pain, but he pushed Evadne through into blessed fresh air. With his arm around her shoulders, they stumbled into a crowd that had gathered.

'This way, this way,' a motherly grey-haired woman clucked. 'Give 'em some air, now, air!'

Kingsley sagged with relief. The crowd was a motley mixture, but they were not uniformed guards of the Immortals, nor were they Spawn. Neighbours and the few passers-by had been attracted by the explosion and by the flames that were consuming the house and the factory at the rear. He couldn't imagine that the Immortals would be caught in such an ordinary manner, but he was dismayed to think of Leetha's people and what could be happening to them – and to any children the Immortals had imprisoned.

He coughed, and each spasm was sublimely painful. Through the hurt, he wondered at the source of the explosion. He'd seen no evidence of magic, but this raised more questions than it answered. He refused to believe it was a simple accident.

A motor fire engine roared up. Several of the more eager firemen brandished axes and bounded into the smoke, their brass helmets gleaming until they plunged into the gloom. The more taciturn went to work uncoiling their hoses and priming the water pump.

Evadne thanked their grey-haired saviour and assured her that they were well. They stood and watched the fire brigade at work.

Kingsley approached a fire officer. 'Any people inside?'

The fire officer harrumphed through his moustache and unhooked his sleeve from Kingsley's grasp. 'Not as far as we can make out, young sir. The buildings at the rear are clear, too.' He squinted at Kingsley's somewhat sooty and dishevelled appearance. 'You know the residents, do you? The workers?'

'The basement. Did you check the basement?'

'No-one anywhere, but what's your reason for asking?'

'Civic duty.' Kingsley tried to look appropriately noble. The fire officer snorted and went to join his fellows.

'They've fled, haven't they?' Evadne said. She produced a scarf. She wrapped it around her head and knotted it under her chin, to protect herself from stares. With her dark blue spectacles, Kingsley thought it made her look exotic, a visitor from the East.

'It looks so. The Immortals are good at that, it would seem.'

'I suppose that changing from body to body for centuries makes shifting location seem a simple task.'

'We've lost them,' Kingsley said.

'For now, but not to worry. We have a lure that I'm sure the Immortals won't be able to resist.'

'Not my brain, I hope.'

She took his arm. 'Not yet. I was thinking of a certain dodecahedron.'

Together, they slipped away while all attention was on the fire, finally stumbling – exhausted, dazed and not a little sooty – into Evadne's underground refuge.

Kingsley was wakened from a doze by the bathroom door being flung back. An immense cloud of rose-fragranced steam billowed out and Evadne emerged. She was clad in a startling blue satin robe and she was drying her hair vigorously on a towel. Her forearms, where her sleeves had fallen back, were pinkish from the heat, as were her cheeks. 'I cannot exist without a bath,' she announced in a voice that was muffled by the towel. 'Starve me and I laugh, take away my liberty and I care not, but keep me from a bath and I'm liable to do anything.' She dropped the towel. 'Don't you agree?'

Right now, I'd agree with anything you said. Kingsley had trouble formulating an answer, so overwhelming was her appearance. Unearthly, but altogether human, he decided, after rejecting a number of comparisons, mostly to do with goddesses and the like.

He noticed that her gaze was roaming across the chamber uncertainly, seeking him out but moving on when it crossed him.

'You don't have your spectacles,' he said.

'La.' She kicked the towel into a corner. A large rat (*myrmidon!*) scuttled out from behind the bench, seized the towel and disappeared into the bathroom. 'I have spares everywhere here.' She held up her arm. 'Would you assist me to my bedroom?'

Kingsley leaped to her side. 'This way,' he said and hoped she didn't notice how hoarse his voice was. He dropped his gaze and was actually dizzy when he saw her bare feet peeking out from under the hem of the robe.

'Was that another myrmidon I saw?' he asked with what he hoped would pass for nonchalance.

'Of course.' They reached the bedroom door. She

146

stretched out and touched the doorframe. 'I keep a few about to make sure the place stays tidy, while the others are out there sniffing for information about the Immortals. And your father and Mrs Winter.'

'Ah. When good help is hard to find, I suppose a rat will do.'

A laugh. 'The bathroom is free. Towels are on the rack.'

'I beg your pardon?'

'You need a bath. Doesn't your highly attuned wild nose tell you so?'

Kingsley sniffed.

'Trust me,' she said. 'You do. Go and attend to it and I'll see you in the morning.'

'The morning? Shouldn't we be doing something about the Immortals, now, before they get too far away?'

She grasped his arm, hard. 'Kingsley, we've just been outrageously lucky, escaping the Immortals like that. Now, I'm exhausted. You're exhausted and aching. Any decisions we make now are bound to be bad ones. When we're rested we'll be in a far, far better state to do something.'

She closed her bedroom door behind her. Kingsley was left uncertain of everything except a desire to replicate the experience of the ten-step walk with a satin-clad, barefoot Evadne Stephens.

Both startled and warmed by this notion, he took the thought, folded it, folded it again, made a crane shape out of it and put it on a shelf to look at some time in the future.

Then he went to have a bath.

The next morning, Kingsley was touched to find that Evadne had stocked a wardrobe with clothing for him. Such thoughtfulness helped lighten the despondency that had accompanied him all through a fitful night's sleep. As he donned a superbly fitting pair of black trousers, he fleetingly wondered how she'd managed to obtain his measurements. He also wondered about the tailor. No label proclaiming Jermyn Street premises, simply a discreet 'Mus, Gloucester' was enough for the remarkable craftsman (or craftswoman?) who made the garments. The shirt and the ascot bore the same label and were equally well made. After some thought, he eschewed a hat and completed his dressing with a handy walking stick from a selection by the door.

While he adjusted his cuffs and squared his jacket, Kingsley resisted the weight of dejection on his shoulders. On many fronts, he had cause to be grateful about what had happened at the factory of the Immortals – they had escaped, after all, and they had learned something of the Immortals' plans – but he sank into gloom when he thought of the missed opportunities. Their botched incursion had allowed the Immortals to up stumps and take their machinations somewhere else, somewhere even more difficult to find.

And even though the search for this father's journal had been demoted in importance, he'd always harboured some hope that, if they could find the Immortals' whereabouts, he'd have a chance to find it.

Even worse was the possibility that the journal had been consumed in the fire. Only two days before, he'd had a tantalising glimpse of his past in diary form, a battered book that could hold the secret of a life that had always been in shadows for him. Now, at best, it was still in the hands of his enemies. At worst, it was gone forever – and with it the chance to restore part of himself. Kingsley remembered his prep school days as a solitary time. He was never lonely, as such, and his athletic prowess made him popular enough, but he had no true friends. For a time, when he first discovered his love of sleight of hand, he gathered a group around him. They were impressed by his feats of legerdemain and chaffed him appropriately when he fumbled or forgot a routine, but they remained only an audience; none of them ever approached and wanted to learn with him.

He was envious of the other boys when they were fetched by their families for holidays. Dr Ward was generous enough, but coming home to the large Bayswater house, mostly empty apart from books and servants, wasn't the same as the homecoming he imagined the other boys enjoying. Sometimes, despite his foster father's best intentions, he felt afloat, by himself, in unfamiliar waters.

Now, perhaps, he had lost his chance to fill in that hole in his soul.

He realised then that his past had become murkier, rather than clearer when the Immortals claimed to have killed his father. He was unable to summon the rage that such a claim should inspire because he was simply too uncertain of its veracity. He was ready to admit that he'd even entertained the notion himself. His father's work in India had apparently taken him into some dark places – the sort of places that the Immortals revelled in. Their crossing paths was only too likely.

On the other hand, lying just to inflict pain is precisely the sort of thing they'd enjoy, he thought glumly, still mired in confusion. And then, with a pang, he realised he hadn't given his foster father much thought at all. Immediately, he felt ashamed and wondered what Dr Ward and the bewildering and possibly dangerous Mrs Winter were up to.

He's been in far stickier situations, Kingsley thought, *if his stories are to be believed*. He decided that Dr Ward could take care of himself. Most probably.

Evadne was waiting for him in the small parlour. She had a cup of tea in one hand and a small, black-bound book in the other. She cocked her head and inspected him over her spectacles. 'You can be presentable, can't you?'

'I do my best.' He bowed and took in her trim white skirt and blouse, both of which could have been silk. If they weren't silk, he decided, they were definitely silkish. Over this she wore a scarlet coat, and her white hair was tied into a loose knot and hanging past her ear. Any hint of the demure was undercut by her boots, which were black patent leather and on the table in front of her as she lounged in the stuffed velvet chair.

Lily of the valley, Kingsley thought. 'And I thank you. It's why I take a charwoman with me everywhere I go. I hand her a stiff brush and she transforms me in no time. I always say that there's no scrubber like a professional scrubber. It's all in the elbow, apparently.'

'You're a fast learner.' Evadne snapped her book shut, took a sip of tea, placed the cup back on the saucer on the table, and rose to her feet. 'Not long ago, you would have been tongue-tied if I'd commented on your appearance.'

'I've had a fine teacher.'

'Tut. Now you're on the verge of overdoing it, but I appreciate the sentiment, nonetheless.' She frowned.

'You're trying hard, but I can see that you're wearing your disappointment like a very heavy hat.'

'It's that apparent?'

'Not to most people, no.' She tapped her chin with a finger. 'I can understand your frustration, and I share it. We had a chance to deal with the Immortals and we failed.'

'That's part of it, true.'

She touched his arm. 'I know, I know. Your father's journal. We simply have to hope that the Immortals took it with them when they decamped.'

'You're sure they escaped?'

'No doubt about it. I've had my myrmidons nosing about in the ruins, avoiding sundry investigators from the Agency. Everything they found indicates that the Immortals were ready to move, and they moved quickly. With Leetha's people and a handful of children.'

'Clever rats.'

'They're not rats,' Evadne said patiently. 'I've told you: they're mechano-rodental constructions of my own devising and very handy for scouting like this.'

'Very handy for looking like rats,' Kingsley said darkly.

'They're indispensable for taking messages to some useful people I know, and some useful non-people.'

'Non-people?'

'Some not exactly human members of the Demimonde.'

'Such as Lady Aglaia?'

'I wouldn't call Lady Aglaia non-human.' Evadne touched her lips with a finger, thoughtfully. 'I'm not sure I'd call her human, either.'

'You know,' Kingsley said, 'I'm looking forward to meeting this Lady Aglaia. She sounds remarkable.'

'You have no idea how remarkable.'

'Any chance of a cup of tea with her any time soon?'

'Don't you think it should wait until after we save the world?'

'Probably. I don't want her to feel as if I'm slighting her, though.'

'I think she'll understand if we save the world before dropping in on her. She reassures me that she doesn't believe half of the things she hears about you, Kingsley.'

'Me? What half? And who's talking about me?'

'That's much better,' Evadne said. 'Less unhappiness and more Kingsley.'

He couldn't help it. He smiled. 'You're a tonic, but I can think of something that would complete my uplifting.'

'And that would be?'

'A solid and workable plan to find the Immortals.'

'Then you've come to the right place.'

~ NINETEEN ~

Walking across London gave Evadne plenty of time to present her plan to Kingsley, while she gamely carried an enormous carpet bag the contents of which she was unwilling to divulge. He immediately saw the genius of her plan, but he also saw where he could add his own particular expertise and the right touch of showmanship he felt would guarantee success.

South of Victoria Station, near Tatchbrook Street, Evadne plunged down an unmarked lane – more of a gap between two leaning whitewashed houses than a thoroughfare. Not far down this lane, a grim-faced man was sitting on a doorstep. He wore a battered tweed suit and he had a wandering eye. As he watched them approach, Kingsley had the uncomfortable impression that someone was behind them, or beside them or, sometimes, floating overhead.

'Hello Xerxes,' Evadne said. 'Is he in?'

Xerxes looked at them, grimaced, then put a hand over his wandering eye. 'Last time I looked, he was,' he said in a voice like a handful of gravel. 'You've business with him?'

'A proposition. One I think he'll like.'

'I've given up trying to guess what he likes,' Xerxes said gloomily. He jerked a thumb over his shoulder. 'Careful on the stairs.'

As they descended into the Demimonde, Kingsley was grateful for the warning. The stairwell was unlit and so narrow that his shoulders brushed the walls on both sides, and Evadne had trouble with her awkward carpet bag. The stairs began as uneven wood, but soon became stone that was damp and slippery. Just as he was about to ask how far they had to go, he had to grab Evadne's collar as her feet went out from under her.

'Remind me to thank my dressmaker,' Evadne said after she found the stairs again. 'Good stitching on that collar.'

Kingsley let out a long breath. He hadn't meant to test his ribs that way, but they were healing well. 'Perhaps I'd better go first.'

'We should have thought about that before we started down. It's too squeezy to change positions now.'

For a moment, Kingsley enjoyed an image of the proximity required for this manoeuvre. 'I'm willing to try. It's a good cause, after all.'

'In another time and place, perhaps,' Evadne said. 'Here, it's important that he sees me first, not you.'

'A pity,' he said as Evadne plucked her pen light from a pocket. They started down again. 'And who is he, by the way?'

'He is the person we're going to see.'

'I gathered that. He has a name?'

'He has many names.'

'Like most of the Demimonde, in my tiny experience. What should I call him?'

'Not Rupert the Bloody,' Evadne said, 'that's likely to offend him.'

'I can understand that. Awful name.'

'An awful name and it's not his, which is why he'd be offended.'

Kingsley saluted her – an awkward gesture in such a confined space and one that Evadne couldn't see anyway but one he couldn't help offering. 'I stepped right into that one, didn't I? Are we thinking of changing our act? "Laugh Your Heart Out with the Extraordinaires", that sort of thing?'

'Not really.'

'It might be worth it. I'll be the straight one, you can be the funny one.'

'That would be the most logical arrangement. Ah, here we are.'

The wooden door was as ordinary a door as Kingsley had seen for some time – dark wood with no distinguishing features, not even a knocker – so he was surprised when it dissolved at Evadne's touch and allowed them to step into a room that wouldn't have been out of place in a bank, apart from the faintest trace of a smell of peppermint.

A small angular man was sitting behind a desk. He looked up and Kingsley saw the very model of a clerk. He had a green visor, a white shirt with sleeve garters, ink-stained fingers and wildly bushy eyebrows. He wore a black waistcoat over his shirt.

He didn't look like the sort of person who could help them lure the Immortals. He looked more like a bookkeeper.

'Ah!' he said, standing. 'Miss Evadne!' He clapped his hands together and rubbed them. 'You like to buy a bridge?'

Evadne smiled. 'Which one?'

'Which would you like? London? Blackfriars? Tower Bridge is shiny new, you know. You can have it for a song.'

Evadne shook her head. 'I've no need for a bridge at the moment, but if that situation changes, you'll be the first person I'll talk to.'

'Excellent. And who's your friend?'

'This is Kingsley Ward, escapologist. Kingsley, I'd like you to meet ...'

The gap Evadne left so intentionally was filled in by the small man. 'I'm Cleghorn – Oliver Cleghorn.' He plucked a card from his waistcoat and handed it to Kingsley.

'So, you're a scrap metal merchant, are you, Mr Cleghorn?'

'Scrap metal?' The small man took the card back. He blinked when he read it and with two decisive movements tore it to pieces. 'I'm sorry, lad,' he said, handing Kingsley another card. 'I've no idea where that came from.'

The new card had the same discreet black lettering as the first, with a significant change. 'So you're a poet, Mr Cleghorn. Much less noisy than scrap metal.'

'That's what I thought. I have no love at all for brass and copper, not currently. Wandering lonely as a clown, that's more to my taste.'

'That's enough, Finny,' Evadne said. 'I've come to you for advice.'

'On matters poetical? I could knock out a sonnet or two, if you like, but it'll cost you.'

'Of course it shall, Finny, but I'm after something more in your line of work.'

'Finny?' Kingsley echoed.

'That's his real name,' Evadne said. 'Or the name I first knew him by. And he's not a poet.'

Finny rubbed his chin for a moment, then crossed to the door. He bent and tapped on the frame about a foot from the bottom. 'There,' he said. 'We won't be disturbed now.'

He went around to the wooden chair behind the desk. He gestured at the two chairs in front of it. 'Why don't you sit and tell me what you're on about, Miss Evadne?'

They sat. Evadne placed her carpet bag on the floor, but then spoke to Kingsley instead of Finny. 'Kingsley, Finny here is the Demimonde's foremost dodger.'

'Dodger?'

Finny grinned. 'I am what our American cousins might call a confidence man. I separate fools from their money. By the way, lad – do you have the time?'

Kingsley reached for his watch only to find it not in its pocket, nor on its chain. He looked up to find Finny dangling it in front of him. He applauded as Finny handed it back to him. 'Well done. I assume you took it when you crossed to the door?'

Finny shrugged. 'One of my lesser skills, and handy when I need to switch an envelope or somesuch.'

'Finny is the master of Demimonde deception,' Evadne said. 'He knows all sorts of people who can help lure our targets out of their hiding places.'

Finny sat forward. 'You want to set up a bait and switch, do you, Miss Evadne?'

'We had some excellent bait, but we're willing to be advised by you,' Evadne said to him. 'Kingsley, Finny is renowned for his dodges, both long and complicated and short and sharp. Isn't that right, Finny?'

'It is, but I'm not altogether happy about that "renowned" bit. It's made my job all the harder.'

'I take it,' Kingsley said to Evadne, 'that you want Finny to help us lure the Immortals.'

'Having the bait is just the start. Finny can help us with the rest. Isn't that right, Finny?'

Finny wasn't there.

Evadne rubbed her forehead. 'You shouldn't have said it.'

Kingsley hadn't seen Finny move and yet the man was gone. 'What? What did I say?'

'You mentioned the Immortals.'

⸎ TWENTY ⸎

They arrived at journey's end after travelling all night. Leetha and her kin blinked in the light, while the big people who herded them out of the lorry grumbled about the move. Their voices were low when they complained, with many a glance about to see who was listening. They paid no heed to Leetha and the others, seeing them as no threat, so Leetha knew it was the sorcerers who the guards were afraid of. This was not foolish, Leetha decided. The sorcerers were clearly mad and dangerous.

She hoped the ghost girl and the wild boy had not been hurt in the fire. It might slow them down. For an instant she wondered if they might not have simply given up, but she shook that notion away. They would not. Not the girl, and not the boy either. They were true. Fierce and true. They were coming to help.

Still, she wondered if she might need another plan to escape. Perhaps it was time to talk to Mannor, and Calli, and Ubbo. More heads together might be a better way.

She and her kin chattered, for the air was cleaner than that they had become accustomed to and their hearts were uplifted. Smoke, and the smell of cooking, came from the buildings. She sniffed again. She could smell little of the stink of the city. The richness of growth was close by, and animals. The sky over their heads was big, not crowded out by the great buildings of the big people. Green surrounded them, with wide expanses of grass. Many trees grew not far away. This was good country, good for living.

While they waited under the reach of a broad, leafy tree, Leetha crouched and plucked a blade of grass. It was soft and juicy, different from the tough grass of her home, and it was a welcome thing after the city of stone and glass. She cast her gaze around. The green was different, too, from that of home. Not as bright. Softer. Or was that the light from a more mellow sun? It did not matter. It was a joy to be in a place like this.

A bird in the tree chirped. Another answered. Life was all around and Leetha was, for a small moment, almost content.

Her kin were feeling happy, too. Laughter that had been a stranger for so long – fleeting, never lasting on lips – had returned. Calli sang a song that made them all sing along, even though the guard scowled like an angry boar. Ubbo found a small white flower with a yellow eye. He pushed it into his hair.

The wagons went on to what the guards called the farmhouse and Leetha watched with interest. The two men guiding the animals jumped down and shifted large wooden boxes. They were heavy and the men swore and grunted. The men took the boxes into the farmhouse one by one. When the boxes were all taken away, the men climbed back onto their wagons and drove past on their way to the gate in the distance.

A guard came out of the farmhouse and waved. Their guards growled and pointed and then Leetha and her people were off, marching along the track, arms swinging, wrapped in the outside world they'd almost forgotten.

She recognised the guard who waved to them as Glass Face, from the factory in the city. His sleeves were rolled up and he looked almost happy when the other guards handed him a sheaf of papers. Perhaps the air here was good for him, too?

Then Gompers came out of one of the other buildings, one of the newer ones. His black hat and long coat were gone, but otherwise he was the same. It would take more than country air and sunshine to change him. 'They're here,' he said. 'Good.'

Glass Face had not realised that Gompers had stepped into the yard behind him. From the way he stiffened, Leetha saw that the guard was afraid of Gompers. 'Yes, sir,' Glass Face said, turning smartly. 'And the boxes from the city base, too.'

'All of them?'

'This should be the first shipment. There's more to come.'

'Now, this is important: nothing was lost in that infernal explosion?'

Glass Face flipped through the papers. 'The documents and the artefacts that the Immortals collected in

India had already been packed ready for the transfer. They were unharmed.' He swallowed. 'The stockpile of hair, though, all went up in the fire.'

'Gah! That will affect our schedule badly.' Gompers stamped off a few steps and then came back. 'We're expecting more deliveries next week, which should help, and we have stockpiles in the underground storage areas here, enough to start compressing and embedding it in the transmitter core.' He rubbed his chin. 'The base of the transmission tower is ready. We can begin assembling the pre-fabricated sections almost immediately. That should make the Immortals happy, especially after the debacle with the dodecahedron.'

'Yes, sir,' Glass Face said. He was sweating, even though the day was barely warm.

'Continue,' Gompers said. 'Do not be distracted.' He glanced at Leetha and her people but he showed no recognition, then he stalked back into the farmhouse.

The guards took Leetha and her kin around the back to a yard with smooth stones underfoot. A long bucket was full of water, and the guard said they could drink. Chickens wandered about. These could have been from home, so alike were they to the birds that pecked and clucked around their caves. These chickens behaved the same way – a glance, and then Leetha was unimportant. Or, at least, the possibility of a tasty worm or forgotten grain or insect was far more interesting.

Leetha shrugged. To a chicken, a person was less important than a beetle. It did one good to remember such things.

Buildings surrounded the flat, open area. Most were old and dusty – homes for animals, Leetha guessed from the smell. Guards were still shifting boxes into the largest of them. Three other buildings were new and reeked of fresh paint, the same sort of smell that had given her a headache in the city. These buildings were large and many-windowed – but all the windows had bars on them.

Calli nudged Leetha in the side and pointed, carefully, barely a twitch of her finger. Leetha followed her gesture. A group of small children, some barely older than infants, was being taken into one of the buildings. The wail of one of them tugged at Leetha's heart. She took a step towards them, only for Calli to seize her arm and shake her head. She turned away from the children even though it hurt every part of her.

Mannor pointed at what Leetha had thought were thin vines running between the buildings.

'Electricity runs in those wires,' Mannor said. He scratched his head. 'I cannot hear a generator, though. They must have another source of power.' He grinned. 'No smoke, no noise. It is good.'

Leetha was relieved. If clever Mannor believed they were safe, she was happy.

Light began to shine through the windows of the front building. 'See?' Mannor said. 'It is all electric!'

They were taken to one of the new buildings. Her heart sank when she saw it had a long central corridor with doors on both sides. They were herded into a large room, all together, then the door closed behind them. Leetha heard the sound of a heavy lock and she dropped her head. They were further from home than they had ever been.

~ TWENTY-ONE ~

When they caught up with Finny, he was scurrying along a tunnel that had been hidden by an illusory wall behind his desk. Kingsley admired the cleverness of the magic that had concealed the escape route, even while they were pushing through cobwebs in pursuit of the dodger.

Finny yelped when Evadne caught his collar.

'What's the matter, Finny?' she asked as she slowly turned him around. She trained her pen light on his face. 'Has the Demimonde's greatest dodger lost his nerve?'

He shook his head so violently he had to grab at his green visor to stop it flying off. 'I'm not having anything to do with those Immortals! And you're bleeding doolally if you do! Both of you!'

Evadne was a model of disappointed patience. 'Finny, you wouldn't like certain aspects of your life to become public knowledge, would you? How would it sound if it were known that you were a major contributor to Miss Oldham's School for Girls? Finny, the hard man of the Demimonde, the man without a conscience, helping little orphans? You'd be laughed into the mundane world.'

As far as dark secrets are concerned, that's not so bad. Kingsley supposed that among blackguards, helping little old ladies instead of robbing them would be seen as a weakness.

Finny was appropriately crushed at the prospect. 'That'd be the end of my business. The end of everything I've worked for.'

'Most probably,' Evadne said. 'But cheer up. With your background in deception and double-dealing, you could always go into politics.'

Back in Finny's office, Evadne was brisk. 'Yes, Finny, we're pitting ourselves against the Immortals. But never mind – you won't have to do a thing. We're just looking for some advice, some help setting up, then we'll handle everything else.'

Finny shook his head gloomily. 'I don't know. The Immortals and all.'

'It'll be all right. It's not as if we haven't gone up against them before.'

'What?'

'Kingsley and I had a run-in with the Immortals last year.'

'Wait – you had a run-in with the Immortals and you're still here?'

'And thriving. Did you hear reports about a little incident under Greenwich?'

Finny gaped. 'That was you?'

'That was us,' Kingsley said, hoping to remind Finny that he was there. 'Greenwich was mostly Evadne, while I handled the Neanderthals.'

Finny's eyes actually bulged. 'You were the one who took it up to the Neanderthals? Not the League of Righteousness?'

Evadne crossed her arms. 'Are they claiming that they were responsible? The League of Righteousness?'

'That's what I heard,' Finny said.

'Wait until I catch up with Sir Donald,' Evadne muttered. 'That's just too much.'

'So you've managed to tangle with the Immortals and come out all right,' Finny said. 'That sheds a different light on it, so to speak.' He leaned back in his chair and gazed at the ceiling. Kingsley was astonished to see his face undergoing a series of startling contortions. His lips wobbled about and his cheeks sucked in and out alarmingly.

'Don't worry,' Evadne whispered. 'He's just thinking.'

'Thinking? His face is exploding.'

'He's just moving his false teeth about. It helps him concentrate.'

It may help him concentrate, Kingsley thought, *but it makes me feel ill.*

A few minutes of this remarkable display were enough. Finny tilted forward again, his false teeth clicked into place and he clasped his hands in front of him. 'You'll need money if you want to attract these Immortals.'

'I have money,' Evadne said.

'And you'll need daring.'

Evadne nudged Kingsley. 'We have daring in abundance,' he said smoothly.

'And you'll need premises deep in the Demimonde where no-one will ever find you.'

'What?' Kingsley frowned. 'Don't we want to be found? By the Immortals, for a start?'

Finny shook his head pityingly. 'You have so much to learn, my lad. In my line of work, the best way to draw attention to oneself is by not drawing attention to oneself.'

It took a moment, but then it came to Kingsley. 'It's like stage magic. A little misdirection, a few key gestures, and suddenly the audience is looking exactly where you want them to look.'

'That's it exactly,' Finny said.

Evadne rapped the desk with a knuckle. 'So we have money and daring and I'm sure you can find us premises. What we don't have is time.'

'Go on,' Finny said, frowning.

'I want this bait and switch up and running by tomorrow morning.'

Finny snorted. 'Can't be done.'

Kingsley let out a deep breath. 'That's that, then.'

'That isn't that, Kingsley. Finny's response was automatic. Now I get to tell him exactly how much money I'm prepared to put into this enterprise and after a while he finds a way to do what we want.'

Finny laced his hands on his stomach. 'That's usually the way it goes, lad. Lucky for you that I was setting up a nice little bait and switch of my own. If it's worth my while, I could turn it your way.'

'And I assume you have a sculptor on your books? Someone who can work fast?' Evadne plucked a piece of paper from the carpet bag at her feet and passed it across the desk.

Finny squinted at it. 'Sculptor? I've plenty of 'em.' He picked up the paper and turned it around. 'Is this accurate?'

Kingsley nodded. It was an entirely accurate representation of a dodecahedron.

After a day spent delivering hundreds of cryptic letters to dozens of Finny's colleagues, both seedy and upstanding, and negotiating purchases that ranged from the bizarre to the humdrum, Kingsley slept poorly. He lay awake for hours worrying about Dr Ward. His foster father was an immensely capable man, but Kingsley couldn't help remembering Mrs Winter's bearing during the attack of the Spawn. The way she summoned that little god spoke of great magical power, something Kingsley was still wary of. However, after hearing Christabel's scepticism about her superiors, he wasn't willing to accept the Agency's suspicions, either. Mrs Winter could be fleeing the Immortals, or she could still be in league with them.

His doubts chased his hopes around and around until he finally fell asleep.

The next day, Kingsley and Evadne entered the Demimonde via a service door in Charing Cross Underground. Once they were alone in the darkness, Finny trotted through a workshop, then led them to another door. More lock-picking, then stairs led downwards before opening onto a tunnel. Soon, they were deep under the city streets. The trips through the tunnels under Greenwich were mere superficial meanderings compared to this, but Finny – dressed in nondescript jacket, trousers, boots and a brown bowler hat – was convinced that this was just what they needed.

More stairs, down two separate shafts with rusty iron rungs inset, a winding sinuous ramp and several scrambles over falls of broken masonry later, they finally reached the level Finny was looking for. They passed several Demimonders as they went, but Kingsley soon guessed this wasn't the high-life area of the underground realm. Anyone they saw quickly hurried on, shrouding their faces in any way they could. The tunnels and stairs were quiet, with only the distant rumbling of the Underground to disturb the silence.

Finally, they passed through what looked like an abandoned cellar, half-full of broken wagon wheels, and into a flat area with a single door set into a rock wall. Finny handed Evadne a key. 'Cost a pretty penny this did. Extra for the basement, of course.'

Evadne frowned. 'Everything has a basement in the Demimonde.'

Finny shrugged. 'Everything costs extra in the Demimonde.'

Inside was a large room with an elegant plaster ceiling twenty feet overhead. Towards the rear stood a dark wooden counter and behind it was a curtain that Kingsley guessed led to another room. In front of the counter were three long tables. Green-shaded, double-headed lamps were arranged along the length of the tables, providing places for reading and study. The walls of the room were wall to floor bookshelves entirely empty of books. Two ladders on wheels were positioned on either side of the room to allow access to the uppermost volumes.

The establishment was the epitome of studiousness. Underneath the smell of gaslight lay the odour of beeswax and dust.

'The books'll be here within the hour,' Finny said. 'And then it's done.'

'It's impressive,' Evadne said after she'd surveyed the establishment and found a place behind the counter for her carpet bag.

'What's out the back?' Kingsley asked.

'Bit of a workroom,' Finny said, 'with newspaper racks, a sofa, map drawers, a tiny kitchen, stairs to the basement and a rear exit.' He looked smug. 'One last thing.' He went behind the counter and fumbled around for a moment before straightening. 'Here we go.'

He held up a small brass plaque, barely larger than Kingsley's hand. Kingsley went to the counter and took it from him. 'The Ficino Institute of neo-Platonic Studies,' he read and handed it back to Finny. 'Perfect.'

'It goes by the door, out the front. Nice and proper, you are, and respectable.'

Evadne went to one of the ladders and gave it a push. It rolled easily and without a sound. 'The Immortals won't be able to resist this place. Remember their lair under Greenwich?'

Kingsley would never forget it. The immensity of the main hall demonstrated that the sorcerers thought on a scale beyond that of ordinary people, but it also demonstrated that they had singularly poor taste. The hall had been a huge dodecahedron, a giant echo of the one Evadne and he had taken from Morton's shipping warehouse.

The previous day, Kingsley and Evadne had discussed every aspect of this plan with Finny, who had argued and probed until he was satisfied. Evadne told him about the niches around the colossal chamber under Greenwich. Two of them were the home of magical objects, others of the so-called Platonic solids. Kingsley told of the details divulged by Soames, the oily middleman the Immortals used: how the Immortals had been having trouble controlling the magic of the Platonic objects.

'They don't seem to be putting all their eggs in one basket,' Evadne had said, 'but I'm sure they'll be interested in any opportunity to increase their knowledge and understanding of neo-Platonic magic. Especially from people who have their own dodecahedron.'

'And once we've lured the Immortals here,' Kingsley said, 'we'll switch the real dodecahedron for a fake one.'

'With one of my myrmidons inside. When it reaches the Immortals' new lair it will free itself from its confines and then situate itself so it can communicate its location with me through the link it has with my electrical windows.'

Kingsley had been impressed by the windows in Evadne's refuge, which were almost magical examples of her engineering genius. Some of her myrmidons had a sort of camera that was able to convey what it saw back to its mistress, all without wires of any kind.

'I'm puzzled, though, about our location,' Kingsley said. 'How will the Immortals hear of our establishment?'

Finny cleared his throat. 'The brass plaque will help, but I've got Xerxes and some of my other cronies spreading the word out there. Won't take long for talk to get around, the Demimonde being what it is.'

171

'Finny,' Evadne said. 'I thought I'd let you know that I've asked the Free Trojans for help. They should be here shortly.'

Finny rubbed his chin. 'The Free Trojans, eh? You know 'em well?'

'Well enough,' Evadne said. 'We've worked together in the past.'

'I'm sorry,' Kingsley said. 'I'm not sure I know who you're talking about.' He held up a hand. 'I lie. I have no idea who you're talking about.'

'The Free Trojans are Demimonders,' Evadne said.

'That doesn't surprise me.'

'They're the last survivors of those who fled the sack of Troy a few thousand years ago.'

'That *does* surprise me. They'd be old, then?'

'These are the *descendants* of the survivors Aeneas led away as the Greeks plundered. The survivors spent ages trying to find a place to settle. Some settled in Rome. Brutus led a breakaway group all the way to Britain, but some of them weren't happy here and are still travelling, looking for the site to found New Troy.'

'After thousands of years?'

'They're picky.' Evadne ran a finger along a shelf, examining it for dust. 'But they're also extremely resourceful. They've done some good work for me in the past and they're looking forward to this little enterprise.'

'Free Trojans,' Kingsley mused. 'I suppose they won't come with armour and spears and the like?'

'They're so ordinary looking that you'll have to look twice. They'll pretend to be scholars, to make this place look worth visiting, and they'll be ready if any muscle is needed.'

'I see. We'll operate as a genuine Institute of neo-Platonic Studies.'

'That's the key, my lad,' Finny said. 'If you live the business, then the dupe won't suspect anything. The moment of truth will come out of the blue.' Finny rubbed his hands together. 'Oh, it's beautiful.'

'I still think we'll need to attract attention,' Evadne said. 'Of the right sort, of course.'

'I'm sure we could paste up some posters around the place,' Kingsley suggested. '"Pots of Plato at the Ficino Institute!" and the like.'

'That might need a little work,' Evadne said, 'but the idea is a first-class one.'

'I'm tickled by your praise.'

'No, you're tickled by the tag sticking out of your collar. Be a good fellow and tuck it in. You don't want to look untidy.'

Evadne's observational skills were eclectic: she noticed some things acutely, while others passed her by entirely. Kingsley did as he was told, intrigued by the knowledge that minor details of his dress lay within Evadne's scrutiny.

He was sure it meant something. He had an inkling what it was, but he didn't want to examine the possibility too closely just in case it was like a photographic negative. Cast too much light on it, and it would spoil.

~ TWENTY-TWO ~

The books arrived, along with a team of Finny's best hirelings, and were arranged by a system enforced by Mrs Kropotkin, one of Finny's recruits. She kept the large catalogue ledger at the front desk and was a genuine neo-Platonist scholar.

Evadne stood in the middle of the aisle between the tables and slowly rotated, looking at their work. Then she put her hands on her hips. 'Disguises.'

'You think we need disguises for this undertaking.'

She rolled her eyes. 'Believe it or not, I do have some notoriety in the Demimonde, and after the to-do with the Neanderthals and the Immortals, it appears as if you do too.'

Kingsley was amused. Only Evadne could have described the near deadly encounters of last year as 'a to-do'. 'I see your point. If we're recognised, then the whole enterprise could be ruined.'

'And our lives put in danger,' Evadne said darkly.

'Do you have any ideas?'

'I'm delighted you ask. Wait here.'

Half an hour later, Kingsley was interrupted in his efforts to make head or tail out of a translation of the works of Pseudo-Dionysius the Areopagite when a striking figure emerged from the curtains.

If I hadn't known we were alone, he thought, the book forgotten, *I'd think I was greeting a stranger.* 'Evadne, you are magnificent,' he said. 'Your mysterious carpet bag? You kept stage makeup in it?'

She curtseyed. 'Among other things,' she said in a voice that was deeper and huskier than her norm. 'I thought of trying subtlety, but I became carried away.'

Evadne had used a considerable amount of stage makeup to change the colour of the skin on her face, neck and hands to a deep olive. She was wearing half-glasses – lunettes – that made her eyes brown and mysterious. She had caught her hair up under a scarlet scarf that she'd wound with gold chain. She wore a long dark skirt that demanded to be swished dramatically, and a short dark jacket. She looked startling, exotic and more than a little unearthly; somewhat African, somewhat Asian, with a hint of mysterious lost lands of legend.

The effect was breathtaking. Kingsley actually rocked back on his heels and pressed against the bookshelf behind him. He replaced the works of Pseudo-Dionysius the Areopagite, vaguely wondering what the philosopher would say if he'd been confronted by such a transformed Evadne, then he decided that such a modern young woman needed a modern approach. 'We should go dancing later, when this is all done. You'd be the toast of the town.' He shrugged. 'As long as you wouldn't consider it unprofessional.'

'Dancing? There's nothing wrong with dancing.'

'With me, I mean. Your professional partner.'

Evadne put a finger so unlike her usual white one on her dark chin and tapped it thoughtfully. 'I'd forgotten that.' She looked at him. 'I can see I might need to consider revising my project.'

'Your project? Me?'

'That's right. I might need to move you onto the next stage. You seem to have become accustomed to the theatre and the Demimonde, after all.'

'And what would this next stage entail?'

'Oh, many things, but I think you can assume that dancing is part of it, if you're willing.'

'Of course. I'm light on my feet and I have a good sense of rhythm.'

'I meant: "If you're willing to advance as the next stage of my project".'

'And how many young men of your acquaintance have gone onto this next stage?'

'If this weren't a professional discussion, that could be construed as an impertinent question.'

Her smile took away the sting of the remark, but Kingsley sensed he was on sensitive ground. 'I assume Clarence reached Stage Two.'

'Clarence? Oh, he was certainly Stage Two.'

'And beyond?'

'Since he was an imaginary beau, I could imagine he was well beyond.'

'Lucky Clarence.' Kingsley was suddenly, unaccountably,

embarrassed. He turned away. 'I suppose I should consider a disguise, too.'

He turned back to find that Evadne had a hand over her face. 'Evadne? Are you unwell?'

She waved her other hand. 'Out the back. You'll find your disguise there. Give me a minute, would you, Kingsley dear?'

It was only some minutes later, while he was gazing at the assortment of clothes, false hair and makeup, that Kingsley realised the last word Evadne had said to him.

He stood still for a moment, in wonder. *I think we might be redefining what 'professional' means.*

The next day, two customers were waiting when Kingsley opened the doors. He welcomed them and led the way to the front desk.

He still had to tell himself that the beauty behind the desk *was* Evadne. Even though he knew she was in disguise, the change in her appearance was so remarkable that it made him question himself every time he looked at her.

He wondered if she had the same problem with him.

Kingsley's disguise made him look considerably older, thanks to a bushy beard and dark spectacles. It was enough, he thought. Even though Evadne encouraged him to alter his gait or his posture, he could never achieve this consistently and rather than draw attention to himself by suddenly becoming spry or taller, he opted to remain a bushy-bearded, bespectacled Kingsley.

Mrs Kropotkin was at the desk, too, next to Evadne. She wore a pince-nez and her greying hair was never out of a bun. Her dresses were severe – high-necked, dark grey and so devoid of shape or style that Kingsley suspected they'd been made by prisoners. He had trouble believing Finny's stories of the off-duty Mrs Kropotkin, who, he assured them, was an outrageous carouser and one of the best lady boxers in the Demimonde.

The two customers were Kingsley's idea of genuine down-at-heel scholars. They had worn but clean clothes. His sleeves were frayed, her dress was patched discreetly. They approached the desk earnestly and asked to use texts by Plotinus and Numenius. Mrs Kropotkin opened her catalogue ledger and directed them to the appropriate section of the shelves.

We have an institute, Kingsley thought. He beamed at Evadne, then realised she may not see through the bushiness of his false beard. As a signal, he gave his ear a tug, then hobbled to the front door again to see if anyone else was wanting to enter. The two scholars were already poring over their books, taking copious notes and contributing to an air of scholarship that that Kingsley hoped would help establish the credentials of their bogus academy.

The leaders of Evadne's mysterious Free Trojans arrived before noon. Evadne brought them to the workroom. 'Kingsley, this is Lavinia, and this is Troilus.'

Lavinia and Troilus were both taller than Kingsley, something he was unaccustomed to. They had the most remarkable grey hair he'd ever seen, despite their being only a few years older than him. 'Don't worry about staring,' Lavinia said easily. 'We're proud of our hair. It runs in the family.'

'I see. Oh. That is.'

'That's right,' Troilus said. He was wiry rather than well-built, but his handshake was firm. 'Lavinia here is my sister.' He looked around. 'This is no minor undertaking, Evadne mine. Plato, eh? What's inside that clever and pretty head of yours?'

Kingsley's wild self rose at that. He'd encountered brashness before, but Troilus had that special sort of know-it-all way about him that could have been designed to irritate.

'Troilus, enough,' Lavinia said, frowning at her brother. 'I'm sure, from what I've heard, that's it's Kingsley here who has this play in hand.'

On the other hand, Lavinia seems entirely sensible and thoughtful.

It was Evadne, after all that, who explained what she needed: a rotating cast of characters who would give the Ficino Institute an air of serious and credible study. Lavinia asked questions that Kingsley thought were incisive and intelligent. Troilus made inane comments, and jotted in a notebook, although Kingsley thought he was probably drawing rude pictures.

'Well?' Evadne said when the Trojans made their farewells. 'What do you think?'

'Lavinia is delightful. I like her thoroughness.'

'Hmm.

'Troilus is flighty, though. I hope he's up to it.'

'I see.' Evadne flicked at some dust on her cuff. 'You understand they're leading a band of like-minded Trojans on a search for the perfect place to found New Troy?'

'I'm sure she's doing a fine job.'

'They both are. Lavinia is serious, Troilus is light-hearted. They work well together.'

'Better light-hearted than light-headed, I suppose.'

Evadne rolled her eyes and marched through the curtain.

Kingsley followed, wondering if Lavinia enjoyed the theatre.

Kingsley shuttled between being on duty at the front desk and continuing their work behind the scenes – and even taking in a little neo-Platonic philosophy. For a time, it made him consider the connection between the Demi-monde and the mundane world, but his head started to hurt when he tried to determine which was a copy of which, and which was the more imperfect.

The neo-Platonist tracts also made him wonder about Mrs Winter and the encounter with the small god of their workshop. Perhaps neo-Platonic theory was a way of describing this notion of living in a god stew, with local deities, sprits and divinities in every nook and cranny. It made him shiver. London was enough to deal with, let alone other layers of reality.

Evadne made them take periods of rest, and insisted on his making tea. She'd bought an excellent Ceylonese blend but was firm in her opinion that he made better tea than she did.

Kingsley was disappointed when no minion of the Immortals appeared, even though their bait and switch scheme wasn't quite ready. The Agency people had fears that the sorcerers' plans were close to completion. The fire may have bought some time, but Kingsley wanted to see an agent of the Immortals – at least – very, very soon.

Otherwise we may be too late.

If a minion did arrive on the doorstep, Kingsley was ready. With Finny's help, he had a number of ruses ready. The Ficino Institute would present itself as credible, serious and well worth a second visit.

Once the doors closed for the day, Evadne, Finny and Kingsley immediately swung into putting the last aspects of their scheme into place. Kingsley was relieved when, just before midnight, the false dodecahedron was delivered by Finny's sculptor. She was a bohemian woman, very thin and with elfin short dark hair. 'Two hundred pounds,' was all she said. When Evadne gave her the cash, she disappeared out the back door without another word and left Kingsley to manhandle the crate into the middle of the back room with the assistance of some of the Free Trojans. When this was done, they too slipped out the back door and into the Demimonde night.

Early the next day, Kingsley finished his carpentry and donned his beard and spectacles. He settled a top hat on his head for good measure. He put on a long black coat, too, feeling every inch the undertaker, and took his walking stick.

He peeped through the curtain before leaving the rear room. Evadne was at the front desk, and Mrs Kropotkin was pointing out something in the catalogue. Two intense young men, both with long grey hair and bony fingers, were arguing in the far corner of the room. More of the Free Trojans.

Kingsley slipped through the curtain and joined Evadne as she stood at the desk, sorting photographs of Greek monuments. For a moment he enjoyed the sensation of being near her and the sandalwood-based scent she was wearing. Her fingernails were painted a dark red, the colour of Lancaster roses, a rather bold display in the upper world of London, but entirely fitting for her current appearance.

An older man was standing just inside the front doors. He was watching Evadne and his hands were clasped on the handle of the Gladstone bag he held in front of him. He removed his top hat and gloves. He had a light cane walking stick under one arm. As Kingsley watched, the man dismissed Evadne from his notice, then surveyed the room with a gaze so intent that Kingsley thought it could nail things to the wall.

Evadne's reaction took Kingsley by surprise. She was staring at the newcomer with such hatred that Kingsley was astonished that the man hadn't dropped dead on the spot.

He only had moments before the stranger would notice. Staying in character, he shuffled to interpose himself between Evadne and the man, then he approached the front desk. 'Don't,' he said softly when he was near enough.

She shook herself, almost as if she were waking from a dream. 'Don't what?'

'I recognise that look. You've just seen someone who you think deserves to be expunged.'

'Oh yes,' she breathed. 'Gompers deserves expunging, at the very least.'

Kingsley reached across the desk and put his hands

on hers. She was trembling. 'Perhaps so. You can tell me later.' He looked over his shoulder. The man was frowning at the other patrons. 'What I don't want is for you to fly into a fury right now. It would ruin everything.'

Evadne closed her eyes, took a deep breath, then opened them again. 'I won't.'

'Are you sure?'

'Before you intervened, I may have, but I'm in possession of myself now.'

'Who is it?'

'A nasty man who hasn't been afraid to conduct experiments on children.'

'Steady, now.'

'The unfortunate ones lived.'

'That's terrible, but you need to restrain yourself or all is lost.'

'It looks as if he's allied himself with the Immortals and he's a towering figure in the world of wireless telegraphy, which tends to suggest that the Agency's information has some basis.'

'How can you tell he's allied with the Immortals?'

'The Spawn bodyguards are a telltale hint.'

Kingsley turned. His eyes widened. Even bowler hatted and well suited as they were, the two gangly creatures that had just entered were unmistakeably Spawn. They stood either side of the door, a pace or two behind the old man. Kingsley could make out the peculiar putty colour of their skin, while their eyes had the lack of animation typical of the creatures. Their hands hung at their sides, as if forgotten, and completed their unsettling presence. With his heightened sense of smell he could detect the corruption on them. They were not alive, not dead, but something in between, created by the malignant sorcery of the Immortals – a sorcery that required the sacrificing of their own body parts.

At that moment, Kingsley's Inner Animal recoiled from such unnaturalness and he understood part of Evadne's antipathy for Gompers. Anyone who voluntarily associated with such creatures was, at best, a dubious character.

He was conscious, too, of the urgency of finding the Immortals. Kingsley's Inner Animal imagined bounding across the room, seizing Gompers by the scruff of the neck and shaking the truth out of him – but Finny's advice came back to him. This initial contact with a mark was a delicate time. Hasten slowly, was the arch-dodger's motto. Hasten slowly.

The two Trojans at the table didn't stop their arguing, but one glanced at Evadne. She very deliberately touched her ear.

The old man sniffed, quite audibly, then approached the front desk, with his Spawn in close attendance. 'Pay attention,' he barked. 'I need to know if you're going to waste my time or not.'

He was nearly as tall as Kingsley. His head was a massive dome, completely bald apart from a patch in the centre, a stubborn outcrop that had remained while all the rest of the hair had fled. He had great, billowing mutton-chop whiskers. His eyebrows were white and narrow. He didn't wear spectacles and his eyes were an unsettling deep blue: sharp and demanding. His frockcoat and the top hat under his arm were of the finest quality, and now that he had come close, Kingsley could see that the head of his cane was a dark rock crystal. Its facets caught the light and seemed reluctant to let it go.

Evadne smiled, and in the tightening of her neck, Kingsley could see how much it cost her. 'Here at the Ficino Institute, we endeavour to give our clients satisfaction, at a very reasonable price.'

'Reasonable, eh? I'll be the judge of that.' Gompers sniffed again. 'I imagine you're talking about a subscription, but I'll be hanged if you'll see a penny without some proof that it will be worth my while.'

'Naturally.' Evadne smiled again. Gompers didn't respond, which Kingsley found astonishing, for that smile could unman the most manly. 'Feel free to browse. I'm sure you will find our offerings to your liking.'

'That, as I said before, is for me to judge.' He rapped his cane on the desk. 'So pay attention. I won't waste time browsing, as you call it. Tell me what you have and I'll decide if you have anything to look at.'

'What are you after?' Evadne asked. 'We have Plotinus, Ammonius Saccus . . .'

Gompers snorted. 'Tcha! Everyone has Plotinus and Ammonius Saccus. If that's the extent of your holdings, I'll leave now.'

Evadne gestured to Mrs Kropotkin, who had been hovering not far away. 'Mrs Kropotkin? It sounds as if this gentleman is after items from our special collections. Can you think of anything that might interest him?'

Mrs Kropotkin stepped forward with a rustle of highly starched petticoats. Kingsley caught the lemon verbena scent he had come to associate with her. 'Our special collection has many highly sought after volumes,' she began, and she wasn't deterred by the snort from the old man. 'We have an original text of Porphyry of Tyre –'

185

'His "Introduction to Philosophy", no doubt,' sneered Gompers.

'No, sir. While we do have that esteemed volume, the one I was referring to is a scroll, handwritten, with marginal annotations in the hand of Porphyry himself. It's his "Launching-Points to the Realm of Mind".'

'You have that? Impossible.'

'If sir would care to take a seat, I'll fetch it for him to peruse.'

For the next hour, Kingsley and Evadne nervously busied themselves with needless re-shelving and tidying, while Mrs Kropotkin brought out an increasing number of scrolls and books – so many that the two Trojans volunteered to move to another table.

Another customer entered. Kingsley glanced at Evadne but her slightest of shrugs told him that this wasn't one of her Free Trojans.

Kingsley picked up a book from the front desk. He circled the room, careful not to disturb Mrs Kropotkin and Gompers. He shuffled along, using his walking stick, and eyeing the stranger who was working his way along the bookshelf in the other direction.

The man looked harmless. He had a huge beard and moustache and still had his hat jammed on his head. Kingsley shuffled towards him. 'Hello, good sir,' he said when he was close enough. 'Can I help you at all?'

The stranger started, which surprised Kingsley, for his progress hadn't been clandestine at all. The man's hand flew to his face, and he stroked his beard as if surprised to find it there. 'No, sir,' he said in a heavy accent that could have been Russian, if Kingsley were forgiving. 'I am correct here. Very good.'

Then the stranger leaned forward. Kingsley gripped the handle of his walking stick, but all the stranger did was gape. 'Kingsley,' he breathed in a decidedly non-Slavic voice. 'Is that you?'

Kingsley stared. 'Mr Kipling?'

~ TWENTY-THREE ~

His flabbergastedness threatened to floor him, but – with a huge effort – Kingsley managed to stay in character. He took the writer's arm and steered him towards the front desk and an alarmed Evadne. 'Sir! Please, come this way. I have something you might be very interested in.'

Kipling was no fool, for which Kingsley was exceedingly grateful. After a moment's puzzlement he saw the way things were unfolding. He threw himself back into his appalling Russian accent: 'I warn you, my good man – I am hard to please in the matter of neo-Platonic studies. You must be most excellent, surely!'

Ever the gentleman, Kipling tipped his hat to a puzzled Evadne, but not a trace of recognition crossed his face. Amused, Kingsley steered him through the curtain and to the large crate that had become the centrepiece of their workroom. When Evadne followed them, the writer was on his feet immediately, smiling and tipping his hat again. 'Rudyard Kipling,' he said, holding out a hand. 'At your service.'

Evadne laughed. 'Mr Kipling. It's Evadne. In disguise.'

'Evadne? My stars, so it is! What a transformation, my dear! You stagger me! I thought I was embarking on a spot of adventuring when I made my way here, but it appears as if I've joined yours instead.' He whipped out a notebook and sat. 'Would you care to enlighten me?'

'Things are much more diabolical than when we left you,' Evadne said. She sat, smoothing her long skirt around her legs in a way that Kingsley thought should be used as a lesson in elegance. 'The Immortals are planning something grotesque.'

'The Immortals? That doesn't surprise me, my dear, not in the least.'

Kingsley could see that tea was going to be needed and was grateful for the excuse to take his time. The desire to rush out and confront Gompers still burned in him. Kipling's presence was a helpful distraction.

Kingsley went to the sink to fill the kettle. 'We located their base. Their new base, I mean, to replace the Greenwich lair. But we were nearly killed when it caught fire.'

'So the first base – Greenwich – was consumed by water,' Kipling said, his pencil flying, 'and the second by fire. Fascinating.'

'We need to find them again,' Evadne said.

'They're aiming to conquer the country as a stepping stone to conquering the world,' Kingsley said, 'combining ancient sorcery and modern technology to do it.'

'And we're aiming to stop them,' Evadne said.

'Good heavens,' Kipling said, then he frowned. 'This is rather more than I expected.'

'You had some notion of the Immortals' plans?' Kingsley had found the matches, but Kipling's revelation stopped him before he could light one.

Kipling shrugged. 'Do you recall those Hindi texts I was helping you with, Evadne? Some of the lines we were puzzling over stayed with me, and I sought help from some of my more exotic sources.'

'In the Demimonde, you mean,' Evadne said.

'Precisely. I learned that the lines were concerned with the Immortals, and hinted at some evil they were responsible for in India. The lines also suggested that the Immortals were quite capable of vanishing completely and reappearing unexpectedly – especially to wreak revenge on their enemies.'

'That sounds like them,' Kingsley said.

'I admit to curiosity, but I knew of your interest in them.' Kipling looked at Evadne. 'Yours in particular, my dear. So I thought I'd try to help.' He shook his head. 'Given what you've found, I think I may have been overly ambitious.'

'In what way?' Evadne asked.

'Well, this is rather more than a spot of adventuring, isn't it?'

'Considerably more.'

Kingsley lit the tiny spirit stove. Blue flames appeared with a satisfying *pop* and he settled the kettle on the ring. Kipling took out a small knife and sharpened his pencil into a tobacco tin that Finny had left on the crate. He laughed a little. 'You two are responsible, you understand. Ever since meeting you I've been *stirred*, so to speak.

Certain impulses have been aroused in me that I wasn't sure that I had.'

'What do you mean?' Evadne asked.

Kipling tapped his pencil on his notebook, three times, sharply. 'I'm a storyteller,' he said finally. 'First, foremost and always, I want to tell stories to people. I imagine, I dream and then I craft a narrative designed to beguile, entertain, amuse and enlighten.' He coughed. 'I leave the judgement of my success to others.'

'You are one of our greatest writers,' Evadne said. 'You don't need to doubt your success.'

'I appreciate that, but it's not the success that is concerning me.' Kipling snapped his notebook shut and tucked it away inside his jacket. 'Since I've met you both, and particularly you, Kingsley, I've been impressed all over again by the power of story. My boy, you are my imagination made real. You could have stepped straight from the pages of one of my tales.'

Kingsley weighed the tea caddy in one hand, to save himself from answering straight away. 'I'm not Mowgli,' he said finally.

'I know you're not,' Kipling said. 'Even though there can't be many people raised by wolves, I'm not making the mistake of confusing fiction with reality. No, what's happening here is more subtle than that, much more complex.'

Kingsley was relieved. He admired Kipling and if the man had been turning strange, it would have been distressing.

Kipling continued. 'It's the other way around. Instead of someone stepping out of one of my stories, I want to step into one myself.' He grinned, a shy half-smile. 'Me, a forty-four-year-old duffer, wanting to be in a story. It's risible, I know, but I yearned for it.'

'Adventures can be dangerous,' Kingsley said. He brought the teacups and rested them on top of the crate. Once Evadne and Kipling were serving themselves, he peeked through the curtain to see the mound of papers and books on the table was nearly obscuring Mrs Kropotkin and Gompers. The two Spawn were still there, unmoving.

Kingsley hoped their preparations weren't in vain. Gompers hadn't left, at least, and he didn't look as if he were the type to suffer fools at all, let alone gladly.

He sat opposite Kipling, next to Evadne. *Tea is good for nervousness*, he told himself, but he found his fingers jittering on the handle. Waiting was hard. Doing something was much easier.

'Adventures aren't all fun and games,' Evadne was saying to the writer.

Kipling declined the sugar Evadne offered him. 'I saw enough in India to let me know that if I were to be a character in a story, I wasn't suited to being a hero of the more dashing type. That, Kingsley, is you.' He nodded at Evadne. 'And you, too, Evadne. A thoroughly modern, independent heroine.'

Evadne sipped her tea. 'Thank you, Mr Kipling. I don't think I'm quite right for an unassuming character. I prefer to live in a full and complete world, for all its dangers.'

She's right, Kingsley thought. What was the point of being bound in a paper bag, wrists tied with string? Escaping from such would be humdrum, whereas freeing oneself from a steel trunk riveted shut, bound with chains and lowered into a pool full of sharks – now *there* was a challenge!

192

'So you went looking for a Demimonde adventure,' Kingsley said to Kipling.

'A modest, but useful, one. I thought that if I discovered something more about the Immortals' interests then it might shine a light on possible weaknesses. When my informants told me of this place, I was simply compelled to come and investigate. Imagine my astonishment when I recognised you, Kingsley.' He looked about him. 'And what exactly *is* this place?'

Kipling once again made notes as Kingsley and Evadne took turns to explain their plan and the contributions of the talented Finny.

Kipling was thoughtful. 'Mr Finny is a cheat, a sharp, a dodger? That's someone I would very much like to talk to.' Then he sagged. 'All this is a sham? My usefulness has quickly become uselessness. Perhaps I'm not fated for a story of my own.'

'It's not as bad as that, Mr Kipling,' Evadne said. 'I'm sure you had a time simply getting here.'

'Oh yes, indeed. Remarkable, it was, once I found the right access door at the end of the right platform.'

'There you are, then.' Evadne put her cup back on her saucer. 'You've been vouchsafed something, then. And I'm sure we can arrange a meeting with Finny, to chat over this and that, when we're done.'

'And you're just in time to see our plans bearing fruit,' Kingsley said. 'We believe a minion of the Immortals is with us right now.'

Kipling leaned forward eagerly. 'Really? How can you tell?'

Kingsley waved a nonchalant hand. 'The Spawn bodyguards are a telltale hint.'

He ignored Evadne's dagger of a look.

'You have these Spawn creatures here?' Kipling said. 'May I see?'

Kingsley then remembered that Mr Kipling had only heard about the Spawn and not encountered them himself. *Otherwise he wouldn't be so eager to meet them.*

'Carefully,' Evadne said. She took him to the curtains.

'So these are the creatures made by magic? Astounding.'

'And very dangerous.' Evadne steered him by the shoulders away from the curtains. 'They're accompanying someone we hope can lead us to the Immortals.'

Kipling's fingers twitched. Kingsley could see him aching for his pencil and notebook. 'Are you going to wring their location from him?'

'We have something more subtle than that in mind.' Kingsley glanced towards the stairs that led to the basement. 'If you retire below, you may see something special.'

'How could I resist such a tantalising invitation?' Kipling hurried for the stairs. 'Good luck to you both.'

~ TWENTY-FOUR ~

After Kipling left, Evadne parted the curtain. 'Our brothers have been replaced by three more of the Free Trojans. Lavinia and Troilus are managing the roster beautifully. Mrs Kropotkin is reeling in that awful man wonderfully.'

Kingsley joined Evadne at the parted curtain. Mrs Kropotkin was hard at work with her atrabilious client, who was demanding another text. Three young grey-haired men were on the far side of the room, hunched over books and papers, intent on their imaginary work. They all looked moth-eaten and distracted. One had gone so far as to have different coloured fingerless gloves, a touch that Kingsley applauded. Another had an Astrakhan hat pulled down almost to his eyebrows. He read with his nose nearly touching the page, a picture of absorption. The third was making an art of copying text from a book the size of a sailor's sea trunk.

Evadne consulted her watch, a neat Dent repeater. 'Mrs Kropotkin can't stay much longer. She said she had an appointment.'

'Nothing serious, I hope.'

'She has a big fight coming up soon with the Holborn Hussy. She needs to get to the gymnasium for some last minute sparring.'

Images of Mrs Kropotkin whaling away at a punching bag danced in front of Kingsley's eyes. 'We can't stand in the way of that, can we?'

Mrs Kropotkin looked towards the front desk. Kingsley was immediately alert. He patted his beard to make sure it was secure. 'I believe it's our turn,' he breathed to Evadne.

He shuffled through the curtain, Evadne close behind.

'Ah, sir,' Mrs Kropotkin said. 'I'm glad you're here. This gentleman, Mr Gompers, has a few queries for the management.'

Kingsley rounded the desk. He put his hands together and bowed to the truculent old man. 'I hope that Mrs Kropotkin has convinced you of the utility of our collection?'

Gompers grunted. 'You have several volumes that my employers may be interested in. Minor interest, but that's something.' He frowned. 'What else do you have? Your woman here said I'd need to take this up with you.'

Mrs Kropotkin moved away. 'I'll be off, then.'

'Thank you, Mrs Kropotkin,' Evadne said. 'And good luck.'

Gompers watched Mrs Kropotkin leave and then, with a sniff, dismissed her as if she were a slightly useful animal of no further interest. Kingsley was repelled by the man's attitude, but he guessed that someone who worked for the Immortals was unlikely to be a soft-hearted man of the people.

Gompers glanced at his Spawn, who were standing on the other side of the table with their backs against the bookshelves, but then he dismissed them, too, with a sniff. He jabbed a finger at Kingsley. 'Now, pay attention. Do you have anything other than books? Artefacts, perhaps?'

It was all Kingsley could do to stop smiling. *The hook is in, now to play him gently.* This was one of the crucial moments that Finny had warned him about. Too much eagerness would arouse suspicions. Too cool a response would fail to reel him in. Gently, gently. Work on self-interest and greed.

Kingsley touched his beard. 'We do have certain objects,' he allowed. 'Our founder collected many over the years and has bequeathed some to the Institute, some that he thought useful for study. Tablets, inscriptions, odds and pieces like that. We have robes that once belonged to Marcello Ficino himself.'

'Which is of no importance to my employers.' Gompers waved a hand testily. 'Do you have anything more recent? Anything powerful? Anything from India, say?'

Bingo.

'Ah, objects of power.' Kingsley turned to Evadne, who nodded significantly. 'We have occasionally heard of such, and, once or twice, we have acted to determine the genuineness of such artefacts, tracing their provenance for discriminating buyers.'

'We? Who is this we?'

Evadne tensed. *Gently*, Kingsley told himself, *gently*.

'My colleague –' he indicated Evadne – 'and I have been curators of our founder's collection for some years. We have also acted as brokers, bringing together those who would purchase such items with those who would sell them.'

'My employers are in the market for such objects.' Gompers glanced at them sharply. 'As long as I'm convinced of their worth.'

'You would wish to examine any items we have?'

'I would wish to conduct tests.'

'We have something here today,' Kingsley said, 'but we couldn't show someone who isn't a member of the institute.'

'Pah! I will join, then. One guinea, correct?'

Kingsley relaxed. 'That's it, sir. One guinea for a lifetime of unparalleled scholarship.'

'I'll be the judge of that.'

Kingsley was startled to find Gompers was paying with a single gold coin. Kingsley flipped it in his palm to find the year 1813 incised on its obverse.

'Don't goggle at it like that,' Gompers said. 'It's good.'

Kingsley took out a ledger from under the counter. *Make it look proper.* 'Your name, sir?'

Gompers produced a card. 'Musgrave Gompers' it read, with a perfectly ordinary post office box number.

Kingsley returned the card after he'd entered the name in the ledger. 'If you will wait here a moment, Mr Gompers, I'll ready the object for your inspection.'

Kingsley and Evadne swept through the curtains to the back room.

'Gompers,' Evadne hissed. She stalked about, circling the large wooden crate in the middle of the room, fists on hips. 'Gompers, here and I can't do anything about it!'

Kingsley was happy for Gompers to wait a little, all according to Finny's dictums. 'Tell me what you know about him,' he said, more in a desire to calm Evadne than to elicit any useful information.

'I met him at the Empire Theatre in Oxford, two years ago.'

'He was in the audience?' Kingsley did some quick arithmetic. Evadne had been sixteen and performing on the stage?

'In the front row. I thought he was dreadfully angry with my performance, but he applauded well enough when I finished.'

'I couldn't imagine anyone being less than ecstatic at your act,' Kingsley said stoutly.

Absently, she touched him on the arm. 'I thank you, but Musgrave Gompers is hard to understand. He was in the same seat for each night of our two-week run, but I don't think I saw him smile once.'

'An admirer, then.'

'In a way. Perhaps. He sent letters to the stage manager, demanding that I be moved up the bill. He pointed out what an influential man he was, how much of an expert he was in what he called "minor variety acts".'

'I'm sure that worked in his favour.'

'Hardly. Stage managers rarely like being told what to do by the public, so I was let go.'

'You were dismissed? You? I'm sure the stage manager regretted his decision.'

'We'll never know. He disappeared the day after his decision to do without me.'

'Gompers?'

'Almost certainly. I was distraught. Lady Aglaia took me in and told me I was well off out of it. Gompers had a reputation of the worst kind. Many young people disappeared into his laboratories and never came out.'

'He experimented on them?'

'He wants to know why humans are different from animals. For years, he has conducted clandestine dissections, striving to find a physical explanation. Now, he suspects it is something in our brains.'

'Which would explain why he is working for the Immortals.'

'They'd allow him to do things that would get him arrested anywhere in the world.' She looked up. 'He does things to make sure he's human.'

'I beg your pardon?'

'I think he worries that he's not. He listens to music and he goes to the theatre not because he enjoys it, but because he thinks that such things are the mark of a higher order of being. He apparently feels that he needs to go regularly for it to have an effect. Like some sort of medicine, I imagine.'

Kingsley, then, had a glimpse of the darkness that was Gompers. Not enjoying music or the glory of Evadne's juggling, but simply enduring them as one would submit to unpleasant treatment, because it was good for one? 'That's both sad and frightening.'

'And that's Musgrave Gompers.'

Kingsley pushed through the curtains. Gompers was waiting at the counter. He narrowed his eyes. 'I hope this is not an attempt to do me harm. I have powerful allies.'

'The Ficino Institute of neo-Platonic Studies would

never attempt to do anyone harm,' Kingsley said, in what he hoped was a tone of dignified offence. 'While I'm happy to do business with you, I'm sure I can find others who are interested, if you are not.'

Gompers regarded him for a moment, cold and hard. 'I shall inspect this object.'

'This way.'

The crate was sitting on a rug in the middle of the floor of the back room. The chairs and the table had been pushed to the wall, leaving plenty of space around it. Before proceeding, Gompers stood just inside the curtain and surveyed the room. Satisfied, he strode to the crate, Gladstone bag swinging. While the Spawn watched Kingsley with flat, incurious stares, Gompers put his bag on the floor and raised the lid of the crate.

His eyes widened.

'Do you like what you see?' Kingsley said, coming to his side.

'Where did you get this?' Gompers said. His voice was hoarse.

'Discretion, sir, discretion. Suffice it to say that the person who wishes to sell this item has waterside interests.'

'The docks,' Gompers muttered. He pointed and the two Spawn heaved the lid off the crate. It tumbled and knocked over a chair, but Gompers was oblivious. He stalked around the crate, peering inside and scowling. 'Pay attention!' he said finally. 'I must test it. We must know if it is genuine.'

'As long as your tests are not damaging in any way, you're welcome.' Kingsley tapped his forefinger in the palm of his other hand. 'One point: we cannot allow it to leave the premises.'

Gompers grunted, without taking his eyes off the dodecahedron. 'I can conduct tests here. Stand back. Do not interfere.'

Gompers bent and opened his Gladstone bag. He took out an object that gleamed softly when light struck it. It was the size of an egg, and when Gompers held it up between his thumb and forefinger, Kingsley saw that it was a gold dodecahedron, a smaller version of the magical object in the crate.

Gompers lifted the object to his face. He opened his mouth wide and breathed on it.

If Kingsley had truly been a wolf, his ears would have pricked. It was as if the air in the room tightened, was drawn in and stretched towards the gold object.

A harsh tang made him wrinkle his nose.

Gompers placed the gold dodecahedron on the uppermost surface of the dodecahedron in the crate.

The tension in the room disappeared with an almost audible snap. Kingsley actually rocked forward onto his toes, a sign that he'd been resisting the ethereal stretching.

The crated dodecahedron began to glow. Softly at first, the grey surface became less grey, then the individual triangular surfaces took on a colour – red, green and blue, clear and bright. A second later, they all changed, creating an entirely different pattern of red, green and blue across the faces of the magical solid.

Kingsley was astonished to see a smile creep onto Gompers's face, then he saw that the crated dodecahedron was rising.

Gompers hissed through clenched teeth as the topmost edge of the large dodecahedron, complete with its tiny gold passenger, lifted itself up above the level of the crate.

He grimaced, then twisted the gold dodecahedron a full ninety degrees. The large dodecahedron stopped its ascent, then slowly sank again into the crate.

When it settled, Gompers detached the gold dodecahedron. He weighed it in his hand and scrutinised the version in the crate, which had resumed its dull, inert state.

Magic of this sort – sorcery, enchantment, arcane power – was still new to Kingsley. Despite having seen things he once would have counted as illusions, he was taken aback every time he came across it. It was unsettling, the sort of thing the pack would skirt or run a mile from.

Of course, he told himself, *a civilised person would be more rational, and examine the phenomenon as a chance to learn.*

Sometimes, he was sure that his Inner Animal was far more sensible than his civilised self.

'You are satisfied?' Kingsley asked and was pleased to hear how steady his voice was.

'It is what it appears to be.' Gompers slipped the gold dodecahedron into his pocket. 'We shall pay for it.'

During the haggling, Kingsley once again played the part to the best of his ability. He resisted, conceded, threatened to end negotiations, was offended, was amiable. Finally they arrived at a price that indicated that if the dodecahedron were a solid diamond, it would be substantially cheaper.

Kingsley found a hammer and a jar of nails near the sink. 'And where should we deliver the object?' he said easily. He slipped the lid back on, took a handful of nails and positioned the first to secure the lid again.

'You will not,' Gompers said. 'I shall take it now.'

Kingsley gave a silent cheer. 'Now?'

'Pay attention.' Gompers took a small metal box from his bag and put it on the table. With a sour face, he rummaged around and found another, which he placed on top of the first. 'The price agreed is in there, in gold.' Gompers pointed. 'This door, to the rear. We shall take it out that way.'

Kingsley was pleased with his haggling skills. 'If you wish.' Then he drove the nail home with one strike. He drove home another half a foot away, taking two blows this time.

Raised voices came to them from through the curtain. Kingsley paused. 'What is that?' Gompers asked.

Kingsley left the hammer and nails on the crate and went to the curtain. When he parted it, he saw the three Trojans wrestling on the floor, while the other patrons backed away in various attitudes of alarm and concern. Evadne was shouting.

'We have a brawl,' Kingsley reported. He shrugged. 'Neo-Platonic scholars can be an irascible bunch sometimes.'

'It is of no concern to me.' Gompers eyed the crate. 'I shall go and organise my carriers.'

'Wait.' Kingsley motioned to him. 'Something's happening.'

The front doors slammed back. The three grey-haired wrestlers attempted to look scholarly, despite the tangle they were in. Christabel Hughes strode in, followed by half a dozen uniformed men, all armed. The men looked as if they hadn't used their truncheons for weeks and were dying for an excuse to test their soundness.

'Please stay where you are!' Christabel announced. 'I'm from the Agency for Demimonde Affairs! I have reason to believe that contraband magical artefacts are on the premises!'

'What?' Gompers joined Kingsley at the curtain. 'The Agency, here? What do they want?'

Kingsley looked meaningfully at the crate.

Gompers glared. 'I thought you would have been more discreet.'

'We're in the Demimonde, Mr Gompers. Secrets are hard to keep.' Kingsley shook his head. 'I take it you wish to withdraw from our arrangement?'

'What? No! My employers would not be happy if I returned without it.'

Kingsley tugged at his beard. He took a peek through the curtains to see Christabel cornering Evadne, who was a picture of outraged dignity. The other patrons had been lined up against the wall and were uttering protests that ranged from the peevish to the furtive.

'Quickly then,' Kingsley said. 'Go out the back way. Get your carriers. I'll hold the Agency off for as long as I can.'

Gompers gnashed his teeth, something Kingsley had read about but never actually seen. 'Be ready!' He stormed out and left the door open.

Kingsley sprang into action. He pushed the door shut, then grabbed his hammer. He dropped to his knees, tapped the floor four times quickly, then he bounded to his feet and squared up the top of the chest. As fast as he could, just as a similar hammering came from below, he slammed in the remaining nails to secure the lid. He was just finishing the last when Gompers threw the door open and a dozen Spawn marched in.

Kingsley gave a quite genuine cry of disgust. 'Take them away!'

'Quiet!' Gompers snarled. 'Those Agency busybodies will hear you!'

The Spawn arranged themselves around the crate and seized it with their unnaturally long arms and fingers. Kingsley held his breath as they heaved it up. Crab-like, they scuttled to the door. With some awkwardness and tilting, they rammed it through, heedless of paint and timber, and then they were gone.

Gompers darted after them without a look back. Kingsley closed the door behind him and let out such a huge breath that he was surprised the seams of the room didn't give way.

I really should take a bow right now.

He pushed his way through the curtain to see Christabel threatening Evadne with a truncheon. Evadne, clearly, was barely restraining herself. Most of the other patrons were situated as far away from this contretemps as possible while still keeping their distance from the Agency officers at the doorway – apart from one of the grey-haired scholars, who was actually at the door, peering through a crack and holding one arm stretched behind him, palm out.

His hand became a fist. It shook, he straightened and bounded into the middle of the room. He threw his arms wide and roared: 'They've gone!'

Everyone cheered. The uniformed officers threw their caps high. The patrons broke out in smiles and pounded each other on the back. Christabel tucked away her truncheon. She and Evadne hugged, whirling each other around in a giddy reel that took them right up the middle aisle between the tables and back again.

Kingsley grinned at Evadne. 'Oh, well done, each and every one of you! Well done, indeed! They took the fake without thinking twice!'

A cry went up from one of the Trojans. 'Where's Finny?' It was seized by the others and soon a chant of 'Finny! Finny!' was rocking the room.

Finny poked his bowler-hatted head through the curtain. He, too, was smiling. 'What's all this commotion? I could hear you all from the basement.'

Kingsley dragged the master dodger into the room. 'All safe and secure? Did the accordion lift work properly? You secured the bottom of the crate?'

'You think I'm an amateur? Yes, yes and yes, if you really want to know.' He gestured to another figure pushing through the curtains. 'Your Mr Kipling was a great help in a time of need.'

Kipling was smiling so broadly Kingsley thought his moustache would disappear. 'I'm useful with a hammer, fortunately.'

'Useful?' Finny clapped him on the back. 'Basher Kipling, they'll be calling you! We would have been in trouble without you!'

'So the switch went smoothly?' Kingsley asked.

'Like buttery silk, lad. Like buttery silk.'

Another cheer, but Finny held up both hands. 'That's all well and good, everyone, but that's not the end of it, not by a long shot. This place must disappear, right now, if not sooner.'

'It'll be as if we were never here,' Kingsley vowed, grinning.

'I hope so,' Finny said grimly. 'I don't want the Immortals trying to find me.'

Kingsley's grin faded. 'No. That's something I wouldn't wish on anyone.'

⟶ TWENTY-FIVE ⟵

Christabel and Evadne wove through the maelstrom Finny's words had set off, with books being flung down from shelves and packed into crates, shelves being disassembled and chairs being hurried out through the open double doors. The deconstruction of the Ficino Institute was undertaken with the gusto inspired by success.

'I'm glad we could play a part,' Christabel said. 'Even if I did have to look twice to recognise you both.' She ducked to avoid a carelessly swung length of what had been a bookshelf until a few moments ago.

'We were glad to have you on board,' Kingsley said. 'Finny said it was crucial to hurry the dupe away once the switch had been completed. He favoured an appearance by the authorities as a useful hurry up.'

Christabel waved a hand at the rapidly disappearing institute. 'But I still don't understand how you convinced

Gompers to take a fake. Surely he was more suspicious than that.'

'Of course he was,' Evadne said. 'That's where Kingsley's art was important. Misdirection, deception, substitution.'

'We all played our part,' Kingsley said. 'Mine was on show. Evadne's wasn't but it was just as important. Even Mr Kipling helped.'

Christabel glanced at the writer, who was helping Finny's hirelings stack books into boxes. She still wasn't convinced. 'But didn't Gompers test the thing?'

'Oh, he did that,' Kingsley said. 'I insisted. But the dodecahedron he tested wasn't the dodecahedron he took away, and that's a sentence one doesn't have a chance to say every day.'

Christabel threw her hands up in the air. 'I give up! How do you swap a thumping great object like that when it's inside a sealed crate in the middle of a room?'

'This way.' Kingsley took Evadne and Christabel down to the basement. Even though there was no time to waste, he paused a moment to admire the work that had gone into their switch. 'Behold!' he said, and gestured with all the theatricality he could muster. 'The work of the great Evadne Stephens!'

Evadne bobbed a small curtsey, then trailed a hand along the steel limbs of the accordion lift. A platform on top of a neatly folding arrangement of joints, bolts and swivels, it was still positioned directly under the trap door they'd sawn in the floor. For something as functional as a hoist made in such a short time, Kingsley still marvelled at how elegant it was. Each of the supporting arms was inlaid with a strip of brass, while all of the pins that held the joints together shone silver. The entire hoist looked like a highly polished insect ready to spring into action.

Christabel stared at it, then at the trap door, and then at the large crate next to the stairs. 'Oh,' she said, and Kingsley was impressed by how quickly she'd apprehended the workings of a switch that Evadne, Finny and he had laboured over. She kicked the crate, gently. 'Your real dodeca-thing is in here,' she said.

'Correct,' Kingsley said.

'I'd guess that it was your friend Finny down here, operating the hoist, while you were up there making sure Gompers was alarmed by our arrival.'

'Also correct. Finny had the help of a brace of muscular lads he'd rounded up. They had the tricky job of lowering the hoist and bottom of the crate that was resting on it – and the real dodecahedron that was resting on the bottom of the crate.'

'The one that Gompers had tested.'

'Tested and found to be good. Once Finny's crew had lowered it, they heaved it off the lift and into the crate by your side. Then they heaved a prepared section of floor topped with rug, then the *fake* dodecahedron sitting on a carefully crafted crate bottom onto the lift.'

'The fake dodecahedron with my myrmidon inside,' Evadne added.

'But when the crate was lifted, why didn't the bottom simply fall out? It wasn't nailed in.'

'Evadne?'

'This was difficult,' Evadne admitted. 'I tried many approaches, but the one that worked was to have three spring-loaded pegs set into each of the four edges of the crate bottom. A sharp smack with a hammer and the pegs shot home, securing the base.'

'Finny and his men – and Mr Kipling – had to hammer quickly, and in an awkward position above their heads. They were heroic,' Kingsley said.

The swap may have been simpler if they'd chosen to lower the whole crate and substitute it instead of the more delicate manoeuvring of just the crate bottom and its contents, but Kingsley had insisted on the more difficult option. He maintained it was safer – if Gompers happened to glance into the room mid-swap, he would have seen nothing. Plus, a trap would have to be slightly larger than the crate and so might be detected. And besides, his final solution was, in a performance sense, much more elegant.

Christabel looked at them both. 'It was your idea, Kingsley?'

Kingsley remembered the discussions, arguments, proposals and re-proposals. 'We worked on it together.'

'And Evadne,' Christabel said as she slapped the accordion lift, 'this contraption is yours?'

'I designed it.'

'And constructed it,' Kingsley said. He remembered the way she had handled the welding torch, the goggles on her face dark against her hair. The basement had been full of sparks and screeches, an industrial Hades, but Evadne was at home tinkering with brazing or advising her helpers. 'She is astonishing,' he added simply.

Evadne's protests were interrupted by Finny's muscular helpers clumping down the stairs. One knuckled his forehead in a way that made Kingsley feel both lordly and embarrassed. 'Take the crate out the back way,' he said. 'And wait for us there.'

'I'll take my people out the same way,' Christabel said. 'It's time we were never here.'

'We appreciate your help,' Evadne said. 'We couldn't have done it without you.'

'I have the feeling you would have found a way. Still, I was glad to be part of it.' She hesitated. 'I suppose I should tell you, though, that the boss is keen to hear from you. Very keen.'

'Congreve-Knollys or Buchanan?' Kingsley asked.

'Both. My guess is they're getting some heat from above about the Immortals and they're desperate for something. Results, preferably, but I'm sure they'd be satisfied with some news. If you could find your way clear to dropping into HQ and bringing them up to date, I'd be grateful.'

'What is it, Christabel?' Evadne said. 'You're looking decidedly ill at ease.'

Christabel rubbed her nose, then sighed. 'After that mess at the docks, I'm in their bad books. To help you out here with this little exercise, I had to skive off from some pointless surveillance.'

'You disobeyed orders?' Kingsley asked.

'They were daft orders,' Christabel said, shrugging. 'Your show was much more likely to get results.'

'Be that as it may,' Evadne said, 'I'm not sure your superiors will see it that way.'

'A pity, that,' Christabel said, 'but I'd do it all over again if I had to.' She saluted easily. 'I'm sure I'll be seeing you soon.'

The crate went up the stairs after her, Finny's helpers grunting and swearing as much through habit as through genuine exertion. Getting the crate back to Evadne's underground refuge would be an adventure in itself, but Kingsley felt Finny would be equal to the task.

Kipling approached. He was still smiling. 'I must thank you, both of you. I've finally felt what being in the middle of adventure is like.'

'And how would you describe it?' Evadne asked.

Kipling referred to his notebook. 'Heady, exhilarating, breathless and daunting.' He looked up. 'That's just a beginning, of course.'

'So can we look forward to seeing Mr Rudyard Kipling in the newspapers as "Adventurer and Explorer" instead of "Writer"?'

Kipling slipped his notebook into an inner pocket. 'I'd say not. I've learned many things today, and one of them is that while adventuring may have its attractions, it has its dangers, too.' He shuddered. 'Those Spawn.'

'And they're only underlings of their much more dangerous masters,' Evadne pointed out.

'Quite so. No, I'm happy writing about such things instead of experiencing them. And now, thanks to you, I shall write about adventuring with a touch more verisimilitude.'

Kingsley shook his hand. 'That's probably a wise decision, Mr Kipling.'

Kipling stopped at the door. 'And you'll be careful, both of you? And let me know how it all turns out?'

'We'll do our best,' Evadne said. 'But even the best planned adventures have a way of going in unexpected directions.'

Despite Kingsley's wild side knowing the value of patience, he tended to fret, pace about and make a nuisance of himself at times such as these. So, while they awaited news from Evadne's myrmidon emissary, Evadne suggested going directly to the Agency headquarters. 'We need to make sure that Christabel doesn't get into trouble for helping us today,' she said as they strode along a dark and almost deserted Buckingham Palace Road.

'Of course. She could be very useful to us, with her insights into the Agency.'

'Oh, Kingsley, it's more than that. She's a fine person and simply doesn't deserve shabby treatment.'

'And how, exactly, have you come to the conclusion that she's a fine person?'

'We had quite a conversation over breakfast in the Agency mess, while waiting for you. I've learned a great deal about our Christabel.'

'Such as?'

'Such as the fact that Christabel Hughes much prefers living in the Demimonde to the ordinary world. She says the ordinary world lacks "spice".'

'She lives in the Demimonde?'

'Partly, I suspect, because she was brought up there by her mother.'

'Her father wasn't a Demimonder?'

'He was a merchant who did business with the sect of reclusive linen makers her mother belonged to. Rather romantic, their meeting up like that, when you think about it.'

'I enjoy a good romance as much as the next fellow, but perhaps she shared something a little more relevant to our current situation — her views about the Agency, perchance?'

'She's ambivalent. She staunchly defended its role, but admitted that it was mostly a shambles. She's convinced that ever since the Agency had failed to identify who destroyed the Immortals' Greenwich lair, Congreve-Knollys has been hanging onto his position by a thread. She says that he's desperate to save his position but he probably doesn't have the foggiest notion of what to do.'

Kingsley and Evadne had only a short time to wait before the doors of the meeting room burst open to admit the duo of Agency nabobs. While they were waiting, he sought for a slip of paper to jot a message to Christabel, but had to settle on one of the playing cards he kept on his person for practice.

Christabel trailed in behind Congreve-Knollys and Buchanan, and looked both embarrassed and impatient. Buchanan was thunderous, but Congreve-Knollys beamed as if he'd stumbled across them at a picnic in the park.

'Ah, Miss Stephens and young Mr Ward! Hughes was sure you'd be here after this morning's brouhaha. I'd let you have a copy of our report into the Lambeth incident but our investigators haven't returned from the site yet.' He took a seat opposite Kingsley and Evadne. Buchanan sat next to him, and Kingsley was dismayed to see Christabel taking up a position near the door – too far away to slip a message to.

Kingsley put that difficulty aside and decided that the front foot was the place to be. 'If you're going to discipline Christabel for what went on, I think you should know that her cooperation was vital in leading to important information.'

'Oh, I hope so,' Congreve-Knollys said. 'And I hope you'll be sharing this information, regardless of what happens.'

'She'll be disciplined,' Buchanan growled. 'She acted beyond her remit.'

'I understood you allowed your officers considerable latitude,' Evadne said.

Christabel offered a nervous smile at this, but didn't say anything.

'There's a difference between latitude and insubordination,' Buchanan said. Kingsley thought he looked as if he were ready to wrestle someone. 'You two are a bad influence.'

Congreve-Knollys waved a hand. It was a careful gesture, and Kingsley could see the man practising it in front of a mirror to get that combination of negligence and spontaneity just right. 'But that's a matter for us, and for another time. What we're most interested in is a progress report.'

'We have had contact with one of the minions of the Immortals,' Evadne said. 'Musgrave Gompers.'

Buchanan stifled an oath. Congreve-Knollys looked pained. 'We haven't heard of him for years. We thought he was dead.'

'Alive and working hand in glove with the Immortals,' Kingsley said.

Congreve-Knollys rubbed the bridge of his nose. '*Der ewige Friede ist ein Traum*, as von Moltke said. Eternal peace is a dream.' He sighed and looked down, and Kingsley felt sorry for him.

'With Gompers's expertise, that means wireless telegraphy in the hands of those beggars,' Buchanan said. 'It fits with what we suspected, and doesn't augur well.'

'It augurs very poorly indeed,' Evadne said, and she went on to explain their findings and her conclusions.

When she finished, both Congreve-Knollys and Buchanan had gone white. 'Sympathetic magic?' Congreve-Knollys croaked. 'On that scale? Unthinkable.'

'Of course, we'll have to get some of our experts to confirm your conclusions,' Buchanan said.

Behind them, Kingsley saw Christabel roll her eyes.

'More than ever it would appear as if we need to find these horrors,' Congreve-Knollys said, still ashen-faced. 'I hope you've made progress.'

'Indeed,' Evadne said sweetly. 'In fact, if we hadn't felt the need to come here and stop you from disciplining Officer Hughes over what was, in reality, an outstanding display of initiative, we may have discovered the location already.'

'Buchanan.' Congreve-Knollys's voice was strained. 'Make sure a commendation is entered on Officer Hughes's record.'

'Commendation?' Buchanan stared at Christabel who was, Kingsley decided, doing a fine job of keeping a straight face. 'Commendation. Of course.'

Congreve-Knollys tapped the table with a finger. 'And now, with that news I'm sure I'm in a position to share some with you.' He coughed. 'I'm sorry to tell you, but your father and his companion have been taken by the Immortals.'

TWENTY-SIX

'They never reached the Hebrides,' Buchanan went on, 'their professed destination. They were abducted from a house in St John's Wood.'

Kingsley hardly heard him through his shock. He immediately wanted to leap to his feet and go to help his father, even though he knew he didn't know where to start. His legs actually trembled, not through fear but through the frustration of not being able to act.

Congreve-Knollys smiled a little. Kingsley wanted to hit him. 'It appears as if our romantic pair abandoned their trip to the Hebrides. They lingered around Luton for a few days, then came back to London and set up in St John's Wood.'

'You couldn't know any of this if you weren't monitoring them,' Evadne said. She shot Kingsley a sympathetic look.

'A lovely villa, it is,' Congreve-Knollys said. 'Charming, really; quite private, with a well-established garden. Discreet neighbourhood.'

'Far too insecure. A bad choice,' Buchanan said. 'The Immortals' creatures simply battered down the front door and carried off Mrs Winter bound and gagged.'

Kingsley took several deep breaths to control himself and was still unable to speak properly. He saw that Evadne understood. She pointed at Congreve-Knollys. 'Your people, the ones who were monitoring Dr Ward and Mrs Winter. Did they simply watch this happen? Or are you merely guessing about this abduction?'

A detail hit Kingsley over the head and the fact that it was threatening to rifle his pockets finally stung him into speech. 'Wait – you said that they carried off Mrs Winter. What about my father?'

Congreve-Knollys put his hands together. 'It was he who told our operatives what had happened. Apparently he was stunned, or injured, or something of that kind by these Spawn creatures. They then seized Mrs Winter and fled. He set off after them on foot, roaring like a gorgon. Our people stopped him, he gabbled an account of what had transpired, then he knocked one of our men to the ground and ran off. He hasn't been seen since.'

Kingsley couldn't help but feel a touch of pride. Dr Ward wouldn't have been content to stand around and explain the situation to an Agency officer. 'So the Immortals weren't after him. They were after her.' Kingsley rubbed his forehead. 'When did this all happen?'

'Last night,' Buchanan said. 'We have our best people on it.'

Since Christabel was sitting right there, Kingsley doubted that very much. He sat back, unutterably weary and needing sleep, but nevertheless thinking hard. Saving humanity and saving his foster father now amounted to the same thing: finding the Immortals.

'We're doing what we can,' Congreve-Knollys said. He stood. 'And we'll continue to do just that.'

Buchanan was on his feet as well. 'We'll keep you informed if we hear anything. You'll do the same?'

'Could we do any less?' Evadne said.

Congreve-Knollys led the way, with Buchanan directly behind him. Christabel followed. Before she went through the doorway, she turned and spread her arms in mute apology. With a snap of his wrist, Kingsley spun the playing card like a horizontal propeller. It whipped through the air and a startled Christabel caught it in one hand. She glanced at it, grinned, pocketed the card and gave the thumbs up before exiting.

'Nicely done, Kingsley.' Evadne stood and adjusted her sleeves.

'I'm glad my misspent youth wasn't so misspent after all.'

TWENTY-SEVEN

Two fretful hours later, with night staking its claim, Kingsley and Evadne were lingering in Wood Lane, in the shadows of the great Olympic stadium.

'Yes,' Evadne said in response to Kingsley's question, 'I'm sure she'll come. And that's possibly the hundredth time you've asked.'

He straightened. 'Here she is.'

Christabel Hughes hurried out of the Underground station and stood for a moment. She spied them as they began waving.

'Sorry!' she said brightly as she bounced up to them. 'I had the devil of a time separating myself from Congers and Buckers.'

Buckers and Congers? The unlikeliness of these nicknames made Kingsley grin. It made them sound like a music hall act of the more dubious sort. 'Welcome to our cabal. Evadne, do you have a blindfold?'

'Whatever for?' Evadne said.

'I thought it customary when ushering a stranger to a secret refuge.'

'A stranger, perhaps. But, as you just pointed out, Christabel is now part of our cabal, a secret society of three working to defeat the Immortals.' She took Christabel by the hand. 'This way.'

'They were all business were they, your superiors, after we left?' Kingsley asked Christabel as they negotiated the passage under the stadium. 'Back to the grindstone, handing out tasks?'

'Not likely,' Christabel said. She looked about with great interest as Evadne unlocked a door that was marked 'Dangerous Electrical Installation' but opened onto a set of stairs leading downwards. 'They were all self-congratulatory – I can't imagine what for – and wanted to go out for a late dinner. The three of us. Together.' She shuddered. 'Congers probably wanted to tell me about the knighthood he's been promised after he fixes the Agency.'

'Ah. I didn't think he was doing the job out of altruism,' Kingsley said.

'He desperately wants the royal tap on the shoulder.' Christabel snorted. 'He's always going on about how all his school chums have been knighted and how he's sick of being overlooked. I couldn't think of anything worse than listening to it again. I pleaded that I had some reports to write up.'

'They believed you?' Evadne unlocked the door at the bottom of the stairs. It opened onto a tunnel narrow enough to make Kingsley stoop. Evadne found an electrical lantern on the floor and switched it on.

'There are *always* reports to write up,' Christabel said, following her. 'Those who say we don't achieve anything at the Agency don't know what they're talking about. We achieve absolutely gigantic mountains of paperwork. None finer, I'd say.'

They reached the end of the tunnel. A heavy slab of steel stood in their way, filling the tunnel completely. 'Welcome to my home,' Evadne said to Christabel with a flourish and an elaborate bow.

Once inside, Kingsley and Evadne gave Christabel time to recover from her astonishment. She stood in the armoured entrance area until she finally stopped goggling and instead stared at Evadne. 'You built this? All of it?'

'Personally? Not all of it. I hired help, but the plans were mine.'

'You haven't shown her all of it,' Kingsley admonished. 'Take her to the armoury. And the workshop.'

'Here,' Evadne said. 'I'll give you the full tour.'

Kingsley busied himself making tea. 'She's a wonder,' Christabel said to Kingsley when they entered the small kitchen twenty minutes later. 'I've never seen anything like it.'

'I second that motion,' Kingsley said. 'Here. A good Keemun, I believe.'

'My favourite.' Evadne took the cup and saucer and led Christabel to the parlour, where Kingsley joined them. He slumped into an armchair, tired and grateful for its comfort.

'Christabel,' Evadne said. 'We need your help again.'

'If it's anything like today, count me in. It was a lark.'

'We're afraid that what we're asking might put you in the bad books with your superiors,' Kingsley said. 'The even badder books.'

She shrugged. 'What can they do? Sack me? No great loss there. I'll get another job nipping between the Demimonde and the overworld. Maybe for one of those universities. Or I might go overseas and see how things work over there.'

'Much the same as here,' Evadne said, 'except in a different language.'

'Sounds like fun. Now, you asked me here – what for?'

Kingsley and Evadne looked at each other until Kingsley took the lead. 'After our narrow escape in Lambeth, we suspect that some assistance could be required if we encounter the Immortals again.'

Christabel sipped her tea. 'Go on.'

'Can you and your unit be on alert, if we need you?'

'You want us to come if you call? Might be a bit difficult, that, since we occasionally have Agency duties to perform. That paperwork won't do itself, you know.'

Evadne put her cup on her saucer. 'We were hoping, after today's commendation, that your roving brief could be extended. For instance, acting on your initiative, you may have to plunge into the Demimonde to investigate something or other. That would keep you away from their orders, wouldn't it?'

'That could work, especially if I tell Congers and Buckers that I'm hot on the heels of the Immortals.' She frowned. 'How will you let me now if we're needed? If I were at the Agency you could use the telephone, but things are a bit harder out there in the Demimonde.'

Evadne picked up her teaspoon. She rapped it on the table in a short, staccato rhythm. Kingsley steeled himself so that only the mildest expression of distaste crossed his face when the furry shape burst through the doorway and ran circles at Evadne's feet.

'That's an unusual-looking rat,' Christabel said, and Kingsley had to admire her sang-froid.

'It's not a rat,' Evadne said patiently. 'It's one of my myrmidons. They were once rats, but with some work they've become much more than that. They are perfect messengers and will find you wherever you are in the Demimonde.'

Christabel reached down a hand. The myrmidon stopped, looked up at Evadne, then scurried over to enjoy an ear-scratch from someone who knew what she was doing.

Kingsley didn't shudder – not very much.

'You made this?' Christabel said to Evadne.

'This one, and its cousins.'

Christabel grinned at Kingsley. 'I hope you realise just how much of a wonder she is, and how lucky you are.'

'She's the best partner anyone could wish for,' Kingsley said, and when the two young women looked at him oddly he was forced to examine his own words – and immediately thought he had only a few chances left to prove that all young men weren't buffoons.

'I trust her,' Evadne said when Christabel had left.

Kingsley picked up the teacups and put them on a tray ready for washing. 'She doesn't have the taint of the Spawn about her, at least.'

'The taint of the Spawn,' Evadne repeated. 'What is that? An ingredient in a recipe? "A pinch of salt and just a taint of Spawn"?'

He picked up the tray. 'It's just something I've noticed more of late. I can smell the Spawn. It's distinctive.'

'And what's it smell like?' Evadne took her sabre from the umbrella stand near the steel door and moved into a hanging guard position before whipping into a parry and then, blindingly, a horizontal belly cut.

'Ghastly. Dead and rotten.'

Evadne stopped her lunge and thrust. 'Thank you. I'm enlightened, but I don't know if I'm better off for it.' She re-sheathed the sabre. 'I want to check the electrical windows to see if we have a report yet. I'll help dry the dishes later.'

Kingsley was putting away the last saucer when Evadne came back. 'You look troubled.' He hung the tea towel on the rack by the stove. 'I take it we don't have a report yet.'

'It's more than that. I should be able to see the inside of the dodecahedron at least, even if it's dark, but I can't.'

'Nothing? What's that mean?'

Evadne opened a drawer and took out three teaspoons. She began arcing them from hand to hand. Kingsley was about to point out that he'd just dried them and she'd leave smeary fingermarks, but he decided that the juggling was important – it seemed to soothe her when troubled.

'My communication apparatus has a limit,' she said. 'Twenty miles, more or less. It doesn't extend much beyond that.'

'That's a huge area.'

'Exactly. I assumed the Immortals would relocate somewhere in London. But what if they haven't?'

'Oh. I see.'

'That's not the worst of it. Kingsley, I have a confession.'

Kingsley's breath caught in his throat. 'You do?'

Evadne's noble face was miserable and Kingsley's heart went out to her as she said, 'I don't have an alternative plan.'

The rest of the night was spent watching and waiting in front of the bank of electrical windows. Eventually, Kingsley thought he could be doing something other than sitting so he found a walking stick, located the appropriate pages in the old edition of *Pearson's Magazine* he'd come across on his previous visit and ran through a series of defensive positions while keeping an eye on the blank window. He was practising at 'Another Way to Avoid being Hit by Retiring out of Range of your Adversary's Stick' when Evadne asked him to stop. Thereafter, he confined himself to running through his range of flourishes, cuts, forces and fans, hardly looking as his fingers turned through the familiar movements.

Evadne sat like a statue, knees drawn up almost to her chin, apart from one hand, which hung over the arm of the wooden chair and kept three brass cubes looping, looping, looping.

When the cubes clattered on the floor, Kingsley was there immediately to catch the sleeping Evadne before she fell. With hardly an effort, he took her into his arms and carried her to her bedroom. He removed her spectacles, took off her boots, covered her with a blanket, shut the door behind him, made a cup of tea and resumed his watch.

As the hours wore on, he was more and more like a wolf – not quite asleep, not quite awake, resting in that state of awareness where any flicker from the blank and ominous electrical window would rouse him. Drifting, he tried not to worry about his foster father, an army of magical slaves and the loss of his own past.

Kingsley gently shook Evadne's shoulder. She groaned, sat up and rubbed her eyes. 'Any news?'

He handed her spectacles to her. 'I think we have a messenger.'

Kingsley had seen the furry creature on one of the electrical windows that showed the approaches to Evadne's refuge. Slightly longer than the usual myrmidon, and rather bulkier, this one reminded Kingsley of a ferret who had given up and really gone downhill. As it neared, keeping to the shadows of a service shaft to the west of the refuge, it waddled instead of scurrying, often stopping as if to draw breath.

He took Evadne to the window room and pointed. 'There.'

'Thank goodness,' Evadne breathed.

Kingsley knew that Evadne loved her myrmidons. He appreciated their utility while never warming beyond a wary tolerance. He was certain that if one ever leaped into his lap while he was reading, a scene of considerable agitation would follow, replete with cries of 'Eeerugh!' and 'Getoffgetoffgetoff!'

Evadne rushed out of the window room and across to the workshop. He followed as she hurried to the rear wall. A heavy grate was set there, covering a six-inch pipe outlet. Evadne seized the massive lever next to the grate and, throwing all her weight onto it, heaved it down. She was rewarded by four consecutive, dull thuds, the last being nearest, and then the grate shot up.

A blunt, three-eyed head poked out of the pipe. It half-swarmed half-tumbled onto the floor.

Evadne scooped up the myrmidon. If she had cooed, Kingsley wouldn't have been able to contain himself. He would have been forced to say something, probably along the lines of 'Get it away from your face!' or 'Good Lord, those teeth!' Fortunately, she just looked it in the eyes. 'It's Beanie, all right.'

'Beanie? I didn't know you had names for them.'

'I don't, generally, but Beanie is special. He's the oldest myrmidon I have.'

'I thought he was looking a bit long in the ... A bit grey around the muzzle.' Kingsley scratched his head. 'Wasn't the job a bit dangerous for an old timer?'

'He might be old, but he's one of the cleverest. And he is the most experienced.' She frowned. 'He's dreadfully grubby.'

'I thought that was part of being a rat.' Kingsley looked at Beanie and for a moment felt envious of the thing. It wriggled in her arms in obvious adoration.

She wagged a finger at the creature. 'Beanie, you need a bath.'

At the kitchen sink, Evadne dabbed the myrmidon with a wet rag. Kingsley vowed to scour the entire area repeatedly with carbolic soap before it was *ever* used again.

'There,' Evadne said. 'That's *much* better.' She found a

dry cloth under the sink and gently dried the uncomplaining creature.

'It can lead us to the Immortals, can't it?'

The myrmidon shook itself and would have jumped off the bench if Evadne hadn't restrained it. 'Oh yes,' Evadne said. 'Beanie knows where they are, but he doesn't want us to go.'

'He doesn't?' Kingsley was aware that he'd begun talking of the creature as 'he' instead of 'it' and he wasn't entirely happy with the development.

'It's dangerous, apparently.' Evadne sighed. 'He doesn't want *me* to go, really. He's not too fussed about you.'

Kingsley eyed the creature. He could see that very soon Beanie and he would need to have a little talk.

TWENTY-EIGHT

That night, a woman was brought into the farm. Leetha saw it all, through the window, in the darkness. The woman was taken from a motor vehicle by two of the Spawn creatures she had seen in the Immortals' secret chamber. Horror struck her as soon as she recognised them and she gripped the bars on the window so hard her hands hurt.

Only a stone's throw away, across the yard, the woman was bound with ropes, wrapped tightly so she could not move. Cloth was tied across her face so she could neither see nor speak, but she was not fear-crushed like Leetha. She flung herself about and she kicked. It made no difference. The creatures handled her as if she were nothing more than a rolled-up mat. They carried her into the farmhouse and the motor vehicle drove off.

Leetha was sorry for the woman and wondered who she was and what she had done to bring her to the attention of the Immortals. Soon, though, her heart was hurting even more. The cries of children echoed from the farmhouse. The pain and loss in those voices made her wrap her arms around her head, but the cries still came to her, full of loneliness and fear.

Later, Leetha was woken by shouts from the farmhouse. At first, she was surprised at having managed to fall asleep, then light flared – light that was fierce and orange, an unnatural and hard shining. It was followed by a great crashing noise, as if a hundred cooking pots had been hurled from a cliff to fall on rocks. More shouts, more panic, more rushing about in the night.

Leetha was half-afraid and half-welcoming, and nearly overcome with curiosity. What was happening? Nothing the Immortals and their guards were happy with, that was certain.

She hoped the children were safe.

Big people rushed about. They were green and blue in the light coming from the windows of the farmhouse. Some of the frightful Spawn creatures shambled around as well.

Leetha still had no idea what was going on. She bit her lip. Could this be a chance to explore, while the place was in uproar? Not to escape – they had to wait for their young champions for that – but finding out what lay where was always a good idea.

She sat up and saw Calli looking at her. 'I can open the lock,' Calli whispered.

'Good. Then you stay here.'

'No. I shall go with you.'

Danger was out there, but Calli was brave. 'I hoped you would say that,' Leetha said.

Hand in hand, they crept along the side of their sleeping quarters. Big people were still blundering about. Some were wild-eyed and babbling about the unnatural lights. Others had weapons, but did not seem to know where to point them. Great groans came from under the earth, as if the world itself were in pain. The windows of the farmhouse showed colours that Leetha had never seen before, then came a tugging, deep inside, a yearning that frightened her.

Calli pointed in the other direction, at a big building opposite the farmhouse. Even at this distance, the smell of animals was strong. Big animals, grass eaters. Cattle? The strong, fast ones – horses?

A figure emerged from the darkness of the open doorway. Leetha was startled to see it was Gompers, his hair and his clothing awry. He barked orders at the guards. Soon, the guards were calm and orderly instead of running about and shouting.

Leetha saw then that Gompers was the most important person here. He was in charge and all the guards looked to him.

'Quickly now,' Gompers was saying. 'This barn is a satisfactory place. Bring the boxes from the rooms beneath the farmhouse before that woman's magic ruins everything. I won't have my work destroyed in a magical battle.'

A squad of guards trotted over to the farmhouse just as the ground shook beneath their feet. They hesitated, but Gompers shouted, 'Hurry!' and they plunged through the door. A few minutes later they came out carrying boxes, the larger needing two guards, one at each end.

They took the boxes into the animal building and returned empty-handed. Gompers immediately pointed at the farmhouse. With reluctance, the guards jogged back to the farmhouse, which had quietened but still showed dim violet light through the windows.

Gompers crossed his arms and waited.

'We should go back,' Calli whispered in Leetha's ear.

'No,' Leetha whispered. 'I want to see what is so worth rescuing.'

Calli winced as a high-pitched whistle came from the farmhouse. It made Leetha's skin prickle and, for a short moment, she was a child again, listening to the monsoon winds and hearing demons and sky-trolls arguing over the dead.

Two guards staggered out of the farmhouse with a large crate.

'Follow me,' Leetha said to Calli.

They kept to the shadows, hardly having to draw on their skills to remain unnoticed, such was the confusion. Many of the guards had assembled around the farmhouse, ringing it as her people would circle a balky pig. A gap was left for those carrying crates out of the building.

Calli found the side door to the animal building. Leetha grimaced when the rusty hinges creaked, but a noise boomed from the farmhouse – a vast, windy outpouring like the sigh of a mountain. Leetha rocked as it tumbled over her, and found it hard to keep her footing. Calli closed her eyes and groped for Leetha's hand. They stood shivering for a moment, then, together, they inched into the darkness.

The boxes had been stacked hastily. Some were made of metal, unlocked, but most were wooden with covers that were not nailed down. Gompers still stood at the entrance of the animal building, his back to them, a black figure outlined against the changing glow of the farmhouse. Leetha stared at him, for the shifting light made it appear as if Gompers were shifting, wavering, a little at a time, back and forth, not quite sure what his real shape was. She shivered and turned away. The man was a mystery, but for once her curiosity did not demand an answer.

Leetha and Calli climbed a ladder. They hid in the straw above the floor of the building, where they could peer through the cracks between the boards. The guards working below muttered under their breath as they stacked their prizes, but no-one protested aloud. Gradually, the flow of boxes slowed until, finally, Gompers dismissed the guards who went to join their fellows in the cordon around the farmhouse.

Gompers strode to the boxes. He unlatched one and withdrew a notebook. Leetha and Calli shared a look. It was one of the notebooks from the tests.

Gompers replaced the notebook and inspected the rest of the boxes, hands clasped behind his back. Leetha was startled to realise that he was humming.

At first she was not sure, but as the noise from the farmhouse died down she was left in no doubt. Gompers was humming some of the songs he had played her. Not the ones he had called 'opera'. He was humming the ones he had called 'popular songs'. The one on his lips had puzzled Leetha, for she did not know what a bicycle was, nor why it would be built for two.

Leetha had liked the song when she first heard it. It was happy, playful, light and loving. When Gompers hummed it, though, it became dreadful. He beat time with his fist against his thigh as if he were breaking rocks with a hammer. He had the rhythm perfectly but all joy was stripped from the song by his doggedness. He was nowhere near the heart of the song and it became a bleak thing.

Gompers finished his inspection. He had just dusted his hands together when Glass Face the guard appeared at the entrance.

'Mr Gompers? Sir? It's the Immortals. They've subdued the woman and they're calling for you.'

Gompers grunted and marched after the guard.

Leetha and Calli waited before they climbed down the ladder. Calli led the way and hid near the entrance, ready to give warning. Leetha busied herself looking through the chests and crates at the dozens and dozens of books, photographs and sketches. She could not read much of the writing, but the photographs and sketches made her tremble. Many were of her people, suffering, and not always because of hurt done to them. Sometimes they were sitting, crying, lost and alone, with no sign of being hit, or prodded or made to stand.

Then she found it. A small, black metal box. Leetha had long ago lost the paper that the young man had given her, but she recognised one of the words on the top: 'Sanderson'.

She took the box under her arm and waved to Calli. 'You can open this? Not now, later.'

Her cousin nodded. 'I hear children,' she whispered.

'I know.' Leetha shuddered. 'The sorcerers have them.'

The next day. Leetha watched through her barred window and saw big people working hard in the new buildings and in the old farmhouse.

Eventually, her people were taken out to one of the other new buildings. It was as Leetha feared: another workplace. This one had large doors that opened onto a wide, flat plain that extended to heavy woods beyond. While they stood in front of these doors, Gompers explained their tasks. He wore thick, uncomfortable garments again, but his hat was flat and brown instead of the tall black one he had worn in the city, the hat that meant he was important.

Gompers told them what was to be done and how they would be vital in constructing the tower the Immortals needed, but Leetha did not listen. She was looking at the world.

How far was it to the trees that ringed the grassy land? If her people could reach the woods, no-one would catch them. They would not be seen among the bushes and the leaves and the animals that must live there. Her people could live there, find things to eat. They would be free and safe.

She sighed. No, this was not their home and never would be. They could survive, for a time, but their home would be as far away as ever. They still needed help. Her job now was to help her people endure until it came.

She closed her eyes. They would come. She was sure of it.

Leetha opened her eyes. Gompers was still talking, still pointing past the farmhouse, still explaining about his concrete and steel.

From his face, she could tell that Gompers could see it already, the tower rising from its concrete base, higher than anything around it, reaching for the sky and then talking to the heavens.

Mannor would know. He would tell her. She would do what she had to. She would wind the wires. She would pack the hair. She would scramble around the metal tower and tighten the bolts and nuts. If she did, she would stay alive, and if she stayed alive she would lead her people home, when the ghost girl and the wild boy came.

TWENTY-NINE

Kingsley pushed back his cap and pointed with his cane. 'I think it wants us to go up the stairs.'

The myrmidon had led them out of the workshop and down the deserted street. Now it was now pointing with its nose at stairs that led up the side of the last building on the block. A little drizzle was falling and Kingsley began to regret his choice of walking stick over umbrella. He arranged his scarf around his collar to keep the worst of the damp away.

Evadne had changed into what she called her travelling outfit: a navy-blue sort of half-coat, half-dress with a few tassels that made Kingsley think of a uniform. With the narrow peaked hat she wore, it made her look formidable.

They had set off well-armed. Evadne had her Malefactor's Lament – a replacement for the Swingeing Blow that

239

had been lost when they were captured by the Immortals. Kingsley had a neat little electrical device she called the Shocking Pinch.

The rooftop provided a fine vista over this patch of the Demimonde and away to Southwark Bridge and the river, but the myrmidon left little time to admire the view. It hurried to the western edge of the building.

'Are you sure it knows where it's going?' Kingsley asked Evadne.

'Beanie might take a roundabout route, but he will get us there.'

Roundabout it was, and they needed a stop for a sandwich before they ended up on Drummond Street, facing the monumental and unmistakeable Euston Arch.

'So Beanie wants us to take a train, then,' Kingsley surmised. Crowds were entering the Euston Underground on their way home. This had forced Evadne to hide Beanie under her coat – a demure but practical black gabardine of Mr Burberry's. Kingsley was intensely uneasy about this, seeing it as akin to stuffing ferrets down one's trousers, but he restrained himself from commenting. 'How is he going to let us know exactly which train we should be on? Can he hold a pin in his mouth and jab it at a timetable?'

'Hardly.' Evadne she set off across the street and through the arch, leaving Kingsley to clutch his cap and hurry after her.

In the Great Hall, while Evadne read the destinations and departures aloud from the boards, Kingsley admired the allegorical statues. He divided them into those who looked as if they had forgotten something important and those who had slight headaches. A furious squirming under Evadne's armpit announced when she'd hit upon the correct train. 'Atherstone. A change or two along the way, but it's Atherstone we want.'

'Atherstone? North of Coventry?'

'Unless you know of another Atherstone, that's the one.'

'I'll buy us tickets. "Two and a rat, please, Mr Station-master", correct?'

'I hope you can overcome your antipathy towards myrmidons, Kingsley, really I do.'

Alone in their first class compartment, Kingsley practised with the pack of cards he'd slipped into his inner pocket before leaving the workshop – only fifty-one cards since he'd spun one to Christabel, but enough to go on with. Evadne patiently chose cards, reinserted them and then provided critiques that were detailed and, once he'd stopped wincing at how accurate they were, useful. After the first hour, she begged off and he was reduced to practising springing the deck from hand to hand, something that always benefited from drilling.

Evadne sat and juggled marbles with relentless rhythm, hardly even looking at them. Behind her pale blue spectacles, her eyes were distant and unfocused. Kingsley wondered what she was seeing.

Beanie the myrmidon sat on the seat between Evadne and the window. Occasionally he snuffled, but otherwise he could have been a rather tatty muff.

It was eight o'clock and well dark by the time they reached Atherstone Station. Kingsley purchased two chocolate bars and an apple, which he shared with Evadne, who nibbled distractedly as they followed Beanie. Wriggling with excitement, the myrmidon scuttled out of the station, past a signpost pointing to Fenny Drayton, and led them out of town and into the great and dark countryside beyond.

~❧ THIRTY ❧~

Kingsley trusted to the darkness. He ran through the woods, keeping an eye on the lights of the farmhouse a mile or so in the distance, and then crouched low. He was almost unbearably aware of the surroundings; the smell of the leaf mould underfoot was rich enough to make him dizzy while the cry of a fox, miles away, sent him spinning until he threw himself face-down near the trunk of an ancient chestnut tree. His heart was painful in his chest, thumping wildly.

Two thoughts came to him while he lay there panting: *I've ruined my jacket!* and *I must keep going before I lose the trail!*

Kingsley clutched his head in both hands. His civilised self and his wild self were pulling in different directions. The struggle hadn't been apparent in the headlong pursuit through the woods. He'd abandoned his civilised self in the thrill of the chase. He had prey ahead and he needed to chase it down. Now, though, his civilised self intruded: *And when I catch him, what then?*

Kingsley shivered, a spasm that took his whole body and racked it with shame and horror. He couldn't allow his wildness free rein like that. After all, his last lapse had resulted in his being beaten, chained and endangering both Evadne and himself.

His wildness had advantages. If not for it, he would never have been able to keep up with the faint trail through the woods. Its wariness, too, was useful – and he couldn't deny that his senses had improved since he'd acknowledged that his wildness was part of him. The world was richer when it was in the ascendant: everything was more alive, more imminent, more vital. It was easy to imagine abandoning the world of people, with its noise and stink, and fleeing to the wilderness. Even thinking of such freedom was thrilling. Losing himself in the forest or jungle, running wild and revelling in the touch of the world on his skin had an appeal that spoke to the deepest and rawest parts of him.

He buried his face in the leaf mould and was intoxicated by its earthiness. He filled his hands with it and felt tiny insects scurry across his skin, fleeing his disruption. The wild sang to him and he wanted to join it.

He lifted his head. *I can't.*

He couldn't desert Evadne, or his father, or his dreams of a life on the stage. He had a responsibility to see things through.

That's your civilised self talking. Surrender to the wild and you'll be free of such weakness. Surrender and we will find a place of freedom for us to roam.

Kingsley groaned. He rested his head against the roots of the old tree so that his nostrils were full of the earthy smell of damp bark. *I've given my wildness a voice and it's arguing with me!*

He made a fist and pounded the soft ground. It was more than stupid. The more he thought about it, the more he realised it was wrong. He wasn't two people. He was Kingsley Ward, who just happened to have a number of conflicting sides.

And doesn't everyone?

Evadne, he knew, struggled with her crusading spirit, the one that threatened to burst out at inopportune moments. Sometimes, a cool head was needed instead of an avenging fury. Mostly, she managed. Her crusading spirit never disappeared, though. It, in part, was what drove her. The inventive, capricious Evadne needed that zeal to help shape her life.

And then there was his foster father. Dr Ward's interests were many. If it weren't for his need for answers, he could have become a mere ditherer. He was never content to dip into a subject. He burned to wrestle with its implications and what they could mean for humanity.

Kingsley lifted his head. He licked his lips, then winced. He'd collected more bruises to add to what was already an outstanding assortment.

He was resolved, or at least as resolved as he could be, flat on his stomach in the darkness far from home. He would no longer deny his Inner Animal. It was part of him and he would welcome it – but he wouldn't let it dominate. Kingsley Ward wanted to be more than wild. He was a civilised being, but one who remembered the wild and what it meant.

Cautiously, he picked himself up. Evadne was bound to be worried. He brushed himself off absently and then crept around the trunk of the chestnut. He cast about for a moment, then sniffed. The trail led east, towards the remnants of an old hedgerow. He trotted in that direction, hands outstretched. He felt the breeze on his face, cool rather than chill. It brought the smell of Mallowside Farm to him – animal stables and dung – still strong despite being a mile or two away.

A few minutes later, Kingsley caught sight of the shadowy figure ahead – the man he'd been tracking. He had an urge to run after him, but instead he crouched behind a copse of hazel saplings and watched. The shadowy figure hunched and disappeared.

He sniffed, but the wind was blowing towards his prey. He scented nothing – but he worried that his prey might scent him.

Kingsley darted from tree to tree, getting closer in a circuitous route so that he was unlikely to be seen. When he came close enough to his prey, he eased himself into a damp hollow, lush with ferns, and gave no thought to the state of his clothes. With small, careful movements, he parted the ferns until he could just make out the figure a stone's throw away, lying prone, surveying the farmhouse.

Kingsley looked over his shoulder. Evadne was back there, waiting for him to report. If she didn't hear from him soon, she'd press ahead and startle this stranger. Kingsley didn't want that, and not because he feared for her. This stranger, his prey, could be a useful source of information. Kingsley wanted him in one piece.

He crawled closer. Each time, as he lowered his hands and knees, and before he put his weight on them, he knew what was there and judged if it were about to snap and alert his prey. If it were, he froze for a second or two, then shifted minutely to a more suitable spot.

It sounded complicated when he contemplated it – and when he did he nearly tangled his limbs and fell. He realised then that the entire process was better done underneath his notice.

Soon he came close enough to see that his prey was a big man. He wore a wide-brimmed hat and his boots were muddy. He was intent on the farmhouse, and was muttering to himself.

Kingsley patted his pocket. He had the Shocking Pinch, but he was circumspect about its effects, Evadne being notably evasive when he'd asked about them. He'd rather trust to a more direct approach.

Slowly, Kingsley stood. Then he ran, barely touching the ground, and leaped on the stranger. He used his full weight to drive the air out of the man's lungs, then he rolled and took him face to face in a great bear hug. He lifted, squeezing, and a snarl ripped from his throat.

Then he stared into the face of his prey, gasped and dropped him.

'Sorry, Father.' Feeling quite the fool, he extended a hand to the groaning Dr Malcolm Ward. 'I suppose I should have expected you here.'

Dr Ward eyed Kingsley askance as he stood and brushed himself off. 'And I suppose I should say I'm glad to see you, but it's hard to say that to someone who has possibly cracked a few of your ribs.'

'I had to subdue you. I thought you could have been dangerous.'

'I *am* dangerous, especially when someone I care about

has been abducted.' Dr Ward huffed a little, and fussed about for a moment. 'But I must say you've handled me easily enough. You've grown, Kingsley, quite considerably.'

Kingsley was immediately embarrassed at his foster father's appraisal and was relieved when he noticed Evadne slipping through the darkness towards them. 'Evadne, it's Dr Ward.'

Evadne had the Malefactor's Lament in one hand, her carpet bag in the other, and Kingsley's walking stick under one arm. 'Dr Ward! Of course you'd be here!'

'I suppose it's my fault.' Dr Ward took off his hat and slapped it into shape. 'I should have contacted you and let you know I was after the swine, but I couldn't spare a moment. If it weren't for that bicycle ...' He looked uncomfortable. 'I'll have to make it up to that poor butcher boy later.'

'You stole a butcher boy's bicycle?' Kingsley was shocked. Dr Ward was scrupulously honest.

'I had to steal it. He wasn't about to just give it to me,' Dr Ward said. 'With it, I was able to keep the Spawn creatures in sight and see which train they caught. They had a guard's van all to themselves, you know.' He glowered. 'Bundled Selene into it in most unseemly fashion, they did.'

'They must have organised that in advance,' Evadne said. She tossed Kingsley his walking stick.

'No, they simply swarmed aboard and threw the guard off just as the train was pulling out. The stationmaster was in a fearful bate about it, but the last I saw of him one of the swine was chasing him up the platform. I hope he escaped.' He clapped his hands together. 'I've been at my wits' end about what to do here, but now you've arrived you can go for some help. I'll watch the farm. The Agency is what's needed. The police would be outmatched, and I'm afraid these sorcerers are beyond the army, too.'

'We can send a message to the Agency,' Kingsley said, 'but it mightn't provide the sort of help you expect.'

'And why not? It mightn't be the most efficient organisation, but it should be equipped to confront such things, eh?'

'It's changed,' Evadne said. 'And, currently, the best that could be said for it is that it's ineffectual.'

'It's been run down,' Kingsley said. 'The operatives are working hard but the place is old-fashioned and poorly funded.'

'Hah! That's what you get when you run an intelligence organisation as if it were a gentleman's club. And what's Norris got to say about this?'

'Brigadier Norris retired. A Colonel Congreve-Knollys is in charge now.'

Dr Ward gazed into the distance, as if he were listening to a song he remembered from long ago – a song he hated.

'Father?'

'Congreve-Knollys. I thought I'd heard the last of him.'

'You know him?'

'Oh yes. We worked together in India. He's a rum fellow.'

'India.' The look Evadne gave Kingsley was so laden with meaning that he thought it needed special reinforcing lest it collapse under its own weight. 'The Immortals, Mrs Winter and now this Colonel Congreve-Knollys, all in India at the same time.'

'He wasn't a colonel when I knew him, of course,'

Dr Ward said, 'just an ambitious lieutenant. King's Own Light Infantry. Special detachment.'

'Special detachment?' Kingsley asked. 'Does that mean he was doing intelligence work?'

'He was, and he was reasonably good at it. A dab hand at languages, always knew who to ask about what was going on, but he had no idea about organisation. Couldn't keep his records and reports straight.' He snorted. 'Lucius would get lost in a map factory.'

'Why do you say he was a rum fellow?' Evadne asked.

'Because he managed to get ahead while bumbling about. Charming, always smiling, always polite and he managed to get on because he knew everybody. He knew who was arranging billets, who was handing out promotions, who was in charge of cosy assignments. And if he didn't know them, he went to school with their brother.'

'Sounds as if he hasn't changed,' Kingsley said. 'We met him at the Agency.'

'Excellent manners,' Evadne said, 'but I think he's found himself in a difficult position.'

'As leader of a substantial organisation?' Dr Ward said. 'I'd say so. He'd be in well over his head. Wouldn't want to give up, though. He's stubborn, especially where his own interests are concerned.'

'I think he's desperate to produce some results,' Kingsley said. 'Finding the Immortals would be a godsend for him.'

'Hrmph. So we might be helping Lucius here.'

'We're saving Mrs Winter,' Evadne said firmly. 'And the world.'

'He knew Selene, you know,' Dr Ward said. 'A long time ago. He couldn't believe it when she preferred me to him.'

Considering the romantic life of his foster father when young made Kingsley feel as if he were an eavesdropper. Out of respect – and not embarrassment at all – he moved on. 'As a first step, let's inspect this farm before making any decisions.'

Evadne was looking down the ridge. Kingsley saw her reach into her inner coat pocket and pull out a slender metal case. She opened it and extended a series of slots, accordion-like, each holding a set of spectacles. Evadne selected one, and swapped it with her current pair. 'That's better.' She looked around and tapped the rim twice before she was entirely happy. 'Mallowside Farm, as clear as day.'

'You can see in the dark with them?' Dr Ward asked. 'Remarkable. Where'd you get 'em? I wouldn't mind a pair meself.'

'Evadne made them,' Kingsley said.

'She did what?' Dr Ward stared at her. 'You did what?'

'With my eyesight, some knowledge of lenses was a sensible thing. I'll make you a pair, if you like, but I think we have a few things to do first.'

'Dashed decent of you, Evadne,' said Dr Ward. He pointed ahead. 'Before night fell I could make out a bit of what's going on down there. Construction, quite a lot of it, and it's been going on for a while. They've already laid out a large concrete area and the base of what looks like some sort of tower. Metal. Big girders. I think they're fabricating sections in one of the buildings behind the farmhouse.'

'Here?' Evadne frowned. 'Not in London?'

'You know what they're up to?' Dr Ward asked.

'We think the Immortals want to use a combination of wireless telegraphy and sympathetic magic to take control of a vast army of mind–controlled slaves. The country would soon be under their thumb.'

Dr Ward sagged. 'My stars. I'm going to sit down before my knees give out. I suggest you do too, and tell me everything.'

Evadne recounted their meeting the Agency, then Leetha, and the ruse with the Ficino Institute. Kingsley contributed. Dr Ward took it all in with a mixture of frank incredulity and growing anger. By the time Evadne had finished, he was ready to march up to the farmhouse and give everyone inside a robust thrashing.

'The beasts,' he fumed. 'I've come across plenty of nasty types in the Demimonde, but these beggars are prize winners in the ghastliness stakes. Who would have thought of using primitive magic on such a scale?'

'And why here?' Kingsley wondered.

Dr Ward was picking a leaf from his sleeve, but he stopped and shook his head. 'My boy, don't you realise where we are? Fenny Drayton is the geographical heart of England.'

Evadne had it a split second before Kingsley did and her eyes went wide. 'Locating a transmitter here gives them the best chance of reaching all of England.'

'So they could enslave the whole kingdom at once, instead of piece by piece?' Kingsley was appalled.

Dr Ward shook his head. 'How does Selene come into all this? She's no expert on wireless telegraphy.'

'They have one of those,' Kingsley said. 'Musgrave Gompers.'

The stream of invective that followed this was impressive and, in Kingsley's experience, unprecedented. His foster father was generally not given to extremes of passion, but the vehemence with which he described Gompers was evidence of the antipathy he had for the man. 'Musgrave Gompers,' Dr Ward said eventually. 'His working with the Immortals doesn't surprise me. He'd do anything to further his ends.'

Kingsley wasn't surprised that his father knew Gompers. He knew many, many people, in all walks of life. 'Tell us what you know of him.'

'Brilliant,' Dr Ward growled. 'But unscrupulous in the extreme. He's probably with the Immortals because they'd give him the opportunity to experiment in ways he couldn't anywhere else. Totally selfish man, but driven.'

'Selfish?' Evadne said, seizing on the word. 'Does that mean he could be bribeable?

'He's not driven by money.'

'Unlike Jabez Soames,' Kingsley said, 'which is unfortunate. You know where you stand with someone as greedy as Soames was.'

'And he's not driven by ambition,' Dr Ward added. 'All he wants to do is quell his fear.'

'Fear?' Kingsley said.

'Call it researching and experimenting if you like, but that's just dressing it up in pretty clothes. Gompers is afraid that he isn't human, that he's missing something vital that everyone else has.'

'That sounds like him,' Evadne said. 'The Musgrave Gompers I knew seemed to be searching for something. Fiercely, perhaps, with little thought of consequences, but searching nonetheless.'

'What an appalling way to live,' Kingsley said. 'Always doubting yourself like that? Wondering if you were human or not? It would drive me mad.'

'Quite,' Dr Ward said. 'Gompers has staved off collapse by turning his gaze to the question of humanity itself, as if to prove to himself that he is one of us.'

'That's sad,' Evadne said, 'but it doesn't excuse cruelty like he's unleashed on Leetha and her people. If he's as intelligent as you say, surely he can see how awful such treatment is?'

'He might be intelligent, but he isn't wise. Wisdom is intelligence plus insight plus compassion. Gompers is missing two of those qualities.'

Evadne went on to share her knowledge of Gompers with Dr Ward. Having heard all this before, Kingsley wandered a few yards away to the tree line, threw himself on his stomach, and studied Mallowside Farm. What looked to be the original farmhouse was still there and, judging by the light in the window, somebody was still awake. A yard separated the farmhouse from a scattering of dilapidated buildings – stables, a barn, workshops. Behind them came half a dozen bright new buildings, long and low, which looked like a military installation. While his night sight wasn't as acute as Evadne's enhanced vision, under the stars he could make out guards patrolling the perimeter.

'Kingsley,' Evadne called softly. 'Dr Ward wants to tells us something.'

'*Needs* to tell you both, my dear, not wants to.' The urgency in Dr Ward's voice made Kingsley worried. His father was the most self-possessed person he knew – at least, he had been until Kingsley met Evadne.

'Kingsley.' Dr Ward stopped, cleared his throat and started again. 'Kingsley, I may not have been entirely forthcoming about Mrs Winter. Not in every detail. Not fully.'

Kingsley shared a look with Evadne. 'We may have had an inkling of this.'

'Our side trip to St John's Wood wasn't part of our original plans.'

'We didn't think that you'd find much in the way of dialect studies in St John's Wood.'

'No.' Dr Ward looked away, towards the farmhouse, then back. 'You see, Mrs Winter and I, with everything that was going on with the Agency and the like ...' His voice trailed off, but then he rallied. 'Mrs Winter and I are married. You have a foster mother rather sooner than you expected.'

~ THIRTY-ONE ~

'You eloped?' Evadne said. 'Oh, how romantic!'

'Romantic?' Dr Ward looked puzzled. 'I suppose it was, but it was the practicalities that brought things to a head. The Hebrides idea was really Selene's way of getting us away from any hint of the Immortals, but when we were underway she pointed out the difficulty of travelling around the countryside together if we weren't married. Most innkeepers have a surprising regard for propriety, apparently.' He coughed. 'I'm sorry. We should have let you know earlier.'

'Never mind.' Evadne slipped her weapon through her belt, then took his hand in both of hers. 'Congratulations, sir. Every happiness to you.'

Kingsley seized Dr Ward's other hand and shook it vigorously, not giving a fig for the incongruity of the surroundings. 'It's wonderful, a fine thing.'

'So you can imagine that I'm more than eager to rescue Selene from these scoundrels, since she's my wife.'

'Sir, we were ready to act even before this news, but now ...' Kingsley raised an eyebrow at Evadne. 'Since we didn't get you a wedding present, can we count a rescue as a gift in lieu?'

'Nobly said, Kingsley, but I need to let you know that we're all in extreme peril.'

'Yes, the Immortals and their plans for a slave army, we know.' Kingsley reached for his weapon, the Shocking Pinch. When matters became heated, he didn't want to grasp it by the wrong end.

'I'm afraid it's far worse than that,' Dr Ward said. 'It touches on what else I haven't told you.'

Evadne stopped in her checking of her Malefactor's Lament. 'While I'm prepared to march blindfolded into the valley of death – in the right circumstances – I'd much rather step into anything dangerous with my eyes fully open.'

'Ah. Yes.' Dr Ward cleared his throat again. 'It's Mrs Winter ... Mrs Ward ... Selene, you see. She's very, very dangerous.'

The hair on the back of Kingsley's neck rose. 'This is your new bride you're talking about, or is it some other Mrs Winter we haven't met yet?'

'Oh, I don't mean dangerous to me. Or you two, most probably. But I'm afraid that if the worst comes to the worst here, the entire world could be in great danger from her.'

Kingsley had another of those moments, the sort he'd been experiencing often since his introduction to Evadne and the Demimonde, where he felt as if he were stepping deeper into a pool of water. Even when the water was

257

ankle-deep he'd been startled by the sensation. Now it was chest-deep he was somewhat accustomed to it but no less startled.

'Very well.' Dr Ward rubbed his chin for a moment. 'I have a story to tell you, one that you really deserve to know. It may take some time.'

'I hope we're not in any hurry,' Kingsley said.

'I think conducting a frontal assault on the Immortals' lair in the dark would be reckless.'

'I agree,' Evadne said. 'And since we're waiting, we can wait a little longer for some help I'll send for.'

She reached into her carpet bag and withdrew a wriggling furry shape. When she saw the barely concealed horror on the faces of both Kingsley and Dr Ward, she took Beanie off some distance and spoke to him in a low but urgent voice.

Kingsley glanced at his father. 'Myrmidons. Evadne made them from rats. They're quite appealing when you get used to them.'

'And how long before that happens?'

'In my case? Oh, a decade or two, perhaps.'

Evadne came back empty-handed. 'He'll be as quick as he can, the dear,' she said as she snapped her carpet bag closed. 'Now, Dr Ward, since this is a night for astonishing revelations, I'd say we're ready for yours.'

A few beech trees grew close together nearby. Kingsley and Evadne sat with their backs to one, huddled against the chill. Not far off, Kingsley could hear the small creatures going about their nocturnal business, hunting and being hunted. Momentarily, he wanted to join them, but the impulse passed quickly when he realised he'd rather be with Evadne.

Dr Ward faced them, his knees drawn up, his head bowed and reflective. Finally, he gazed at them and his spectacles glinted as his leonine head moved. 'Selene – Mrs Winter – comes from an unusual family. Her father was a colonel in the 65th Carnatic Infantry, and his family has been military for generations.' He chose his words carefully. 'It's her mother's side that has contributed to the situation in which we now find ourselves. They were Indian, high caste, and much given to mysticism of a particular sort.'

Kingsley became tense. He could remember little of India, and what he could was a cloth of many patches. Mostly he remembered smells, sensations, the feelings of being protected and cared for – in a way that was entirely non-human. He did have shreds of other recollections, too. These were night-time memories, for the greater part, things the pack experienced that were beyond their ken: shape changers; the sounds of music coming from under the ground; strange lights and movements that were a sign to run in the other direction. These phenomena raised hackles. They were unnatural, to be shunned.

This was part of his past, but it was a shattered, imperfect past. It was the sort of thing he desperately wanted restored to him.

'I've been in correspondence with some learned and informed people in India,' Evadne was saying. Kingsley shook off the fug of memory and paid attention. 'Many of them mentioned magic.'

'Selene's family have been scholars of magic for centuries,' Dr Ward said. 'They accumulated much wisdom in those years, but some of the family members decided that knowledge wasn't enough. They wanted actual magical power.'

'Coming close to power but not having it must have been tempting,' Kingsley said.

'To some. Selene's mother had the most overweening pride. She took herself away to a valley in the Western Ghats, all the better to perform rituals designed to attain this power.'

'Ambition?' Kingsley said. 'Hunger?'

'I don't know, but when magical power is at stake the consequences can be profound.'

'Did she succeed?' Evadne asked quietly. She was a ghostly presence in the dark, her skin almost luminous.

'She thought she'd failed,' Dr Ward said. 'This disappointment and the enormity of the ritual itself drove her mad.'

Kingsley grimaced. *Not something I'd wish on anybody.* 'It would have been wretched for Mrs Winter,' he said. 'How old was she?'

'She had not yet been born,' Dr Ward said. 'Her mother was with child when she performed the ritual.' Both Kingsley and Evadne gasped, but Dr Ward went on, doggedly. 'The woman did not know she was expecting at the time – and that's what I prefer to believe. Eight months later, Selene was born to a raving madwoman.'

'The poor baby,' Evadne said softly and her pain was so evident that Kingsley, without thinking, put an arm around her shoulders.

Evadne leaned closer into him. Kingsley held his breath but she didn't move away.

Dr Ward raised an eyebrow at this, but didn't comment. He went on with his story. 'Selene's father was shattered by the events, of which his wife had kept him ignorant. He recovered, though, and spent his life taking care of her and Selene.' He paused. The noises of the night – crickets, the soft soughing of the branches overhead – replaced his voice until he began again. 'This man was of the same scholarly persuasion, but he never had the lust for power that his wife had. In their home in the Ghats, he returned to his books, tended to his wife and raised his daughter. When his wife died, this man took his two-year-old daughter back to the family of the woman who had dared too much.'

'Normally, that would signal the end of a story,' Kingsley said at the dying fall in his foster father's voice. 'But I sense that there's more.'

Dr Ward nodded. 'Even though they were reclusive, this extended family of scholars, they were not unaware of the world. Soon after the child came home, it became apparent that they were being watched by creatures and people unsavoury.'

'That description would cover a great many things, here or in India,' Evadne said. Her hands were cold. Kingsley folded them into his.

'It would,' Dr Ward said. 'Many of these watchers were simply pairs of eyes willing to watch and report for a coin. Some were unnatural creatures born of sorcery.'

'Spawn?' Kingsley asked and had to quieten the uneasiness that was only partly a product of his Inner Animal.

'The description is consistent, although some may have been insane blends of animal and sorcery. Regardless, the elders in the community, through their wisdom, divined two things. The watchers were interested in the child and they were agents of the sorcerers we call the Immortals.'

'The ritual had drawn their attention,' Evadne whispered.

261

'Precisely. The community was afraid, but nothing happened. For years, the watchers were present, circling the enclave, but doing nothing. When challenged, they melted away. When confronted, they ran – but they always came back.'

Kingsley frowned. 'I'd never call the Immortals patient, despite their years. They flit from plan to plan, never settling long.'

'What you see as flitting may simply be the way they've learned to lay many plans all at once,' Dr Ward said. 'Many may never come to fruition, but some may, to our cost. They think in centuries, not hours.'

'So they can endure setbacks,' Evadne said. 'They simply shift their energy to another scheme that is already in train.'

'Not happily, I imagine,' Kingsley said. He had seen the rage and petulance of the Immortals. They weren't sombre and magisterial beings. He bit his lip. Perhaps their peevishness was a recent thing, a result of their body-shifting and extreme age?

Dr Ward shifted his position a little. 'Nothing happened for a long time. Selene was a happy child, and when her father died – worn out from the shock of his wife's betrayal – she was adopted by the entire community. She was adored, but she soon displayed an ability that nearly rent the community asunder.'

Dr Ward lifted a hand, struggling for words. Kingsley and Evadne were silent while he took off his spectacles and wiped his eyes. 'It is hard,' he said, 'imagining that poor child, shocking a community of intelligent, loving people with an ability she never asked for, an ability passed from an arrogant, unbalanced mother.'

'The power,' Kingsley asked. 'What was it?'

Dr Ward touched his jaw with a hand, as if the very words were painful. 'She has the power to open the way for gods.'

'You mean deities like the lar that she conjured up to save us.'

'No, not "conjured up", never that. She doesn't create them from thin air. That's more along your line. She simply *allows* a god to enter our world.'

'From where?' Evadne asked.

'From wherever it is the gods have gone.'

'Which is an explanation singularly empty of meaning.'

'It's the best I can do. Look around. We don't have the gods surrounding us any more. When I think about it, the world must have been swarming with them when it was young. So many little gods – gods of localities, gods of rivers and streams, gods for crossroads and trees and mountains and clouds, all deities with their own power and being. And that's not counting the big gods, the Olympian thunderbolt hurlers, the Asgardian giant killers. They're gods of an altogether different magnitude, but they've gone, too.'

'And your Mrs Winter opens a crack for them to come back?' Evadne said.

'It's more like she invites them. Very compellingly.'

'And she did this as a baby?' Kingsley pushed his hair back. 'That must have been unexpected.'

'As an infant, not a baby. She needed language to shape her will. Playing with blocks one day, she was frustrated. She asked for help in a way that allowed the god of the house – a long gone, long forgotten, very minor godling – to reappear and build a tower of blocks that stretched to the ceiling.'

'Impressive,' Kingsley said.

'And dangerous. She was startled. Fortunately enough, when she told the godling to go, it did. But not before it and its works were seen by the girl's ayah and a visiting scholar. The women knew they had seen something of great import, and brought it to the elders who soon determined what had happened. But it was too late. The child had gone.'

'Taken by the gods?' Evadne said, her hand to her mouth. She was upset – and increasingly furious. Kingsley squeezed her other hand. She looked at him sharply, then took a deep breath and leaned back against the tree.

'Taken by the Immortals.' Dr Ward paused and looked reflective. 'I have no evidence that the Immortals had been planning this all along, but I wouldn't be surprised. Perhaps they even organised to expose Selene's mother to hidden texts, tempting her like that.'

Evadne was trembling, but her voice was steady. 'They have little compunction when it comes to child stealing, so manipulating a whole family like this wouldn't be beyond them.'

'But they weren't stealing Mrs Winter to use as a vessel for themselves,' Kingsley said, 'were they?'

'No,' Dr Ward said. 'They raised her.'

THIRTY-TWO

Kingsley was angry. His early childhood was unusual, but at least the wolves had protected and defended him. 'Surely those creatures didn't raise her themselves. They must have handed the child to someone more ... more human.'

'As with your recollections of your early life, Mrs Winter's are cloudy, half-remembered and often shied away from. The Immortals wanted her to be obedient while still being able to exercise her power, and she had nurses who raised her as such. She was too important to damage, but some of the nurses were enthusiastic in their chastisement. Yet she survived and grew. When she was ten, she began to do the bidding of the Immortals, for she was told to obey them. She was strong in her power, but it was a fickle thing. The Immortals were afraid of what she could awake, and afraid she might not be able to close the door if something dangerous were allowed through. The tasks she was given were small and carefully circumscribed, watched by servants of the Immortals who were ready to destroy her if the summoned god went amuck.'

'Destroy her?' Kingsley said. 'Why? Would that close the way she'd opened?'

'That's what the Immortals decided.' He shook his head. 'So the poor child had to perform knowing that she could be killed at any time, just for doing that for which she was raised. It was inevitable that she was either going to break or to rebel. It is to my good fortune that, eventually, she rebelled.'

'What courage that must have taken,' Evadne said. 'To rebel against your whole reason for being.'

'She is an admirable woman,' Dr Ward said, then he looked embarrassed and hurried on. 'With the help of a minor trickster god she summoned, she fled and lost herself in the cities. Calcutta, Pondicherry, Dacca. She kept moving, doing what she could to stay alive. Eventually she fell in with a Colonel Winter of the Madras Light Cavalry.' He pointed a finger at Kingsley. 'A colleague of your father, or so I'm led to believe.'

'Colonel Winter was a spy?'

'He was an intelligence gatherer, as was your father. His work as scout took him into the Indian Demimonde as often as not, where he met Selene.'

'He rescued her,' Evadne said firmly.

'He fell in love with her first, then he rescued her, then he married her. They spent some time together, very happily. He worked for Army Intelligence and she discovered she had a calling as a school teacher.' Dr Ward paused before going on. 'Then they were trapped by agents of the Immortals who were chasing her. He gave his life to let her escape.'

'And how did you come to know her?' Kingsley asked.

A small, sweet smile crossed Dr Ward's face. 'In my time in India I heard stories of many things, and discounted most of them, miracles being a farthing a dozen in that land.'

'Most?' Kingsley asked.

'Most were just that: stories. Some were not. Some were exaggerations or distortions, but they hid a truth about a world where the rules of everyday life do not apply. A world where magic works and legends still walk abroad. A world that intersects, underlies and nudges against our own.'

'The Demimonde,' Evadne said.

'It's called many things in many places, but the Demimonde is as good as any. Wherever people go about their lives in their great diurnal round, there is a shadowy and encircling realm of otherness. Most people are unaware of it. Some are aware of it and shun it. Others pass back and forth and understand that both are parts of the human experience. Once apprised of it, I explored it to gather what I could.'

'Stories?' Kingsley said.

'Stories, tales, anecdotes and memories. More recondite knowledge too: languages and dialects long thought lost, crafts and practices forgotten in the mundane world.'

'But you've kept these secret. They don't feature in your writings,' Kingsley said, 'nor in your lectures.'

'One day, my boy, one day.' A chuckle. 'Although I may have to clothe them in the guise of fiction, as others have.

The world may not be ready for such knowledge, as Mr Wells has found out.'

'Mrs Winter was a story, then?' Evadne said. 'A damsel in distress?'

Kingsley had never thought of his foster father as a knight errant. He was fond of the old man, and grateful for his upbringing, but Dr Ward had always been a fusty dodderer, in his mind. *Hidden depths*, he thought.

Part of Kingsley, too, was responding to the tales of India. Surely there were still parts of that great land that were untamed, vast enough to become lost in, to roam free.

He shook his head angrily. *Enough of that*, he told himself.

'Mrs Winter was rather more than a story. The military intelligence operatives had a standing order to find her, to look out for her as a dependant of one of their own. As I was helping them at the time, I was aware of this. I had gone to a cave outside Chamarajanagar, drawn by rumours of a cache of pots with some highly interesting, potentially crypto-Dravidian scrolls. She was hiding in the cave. We made our acquaintance when she nearly stabbed me with a *bichawa*, but I was able to avoid the sting of the scorpion knife.'

'An unconventional introduction,' Evadne said, 'but it established that she was not a helpless waif.'

'Even though she looked like one,' Dr Ward said. 'She was bedraggled, gaunt and fearful of eye. Strangely, she looked both much older and much younger than her twenty years. And she was terrified that I was from the Immortals.'

Kingsley raised a finger. 'Why didn't she just call up some of these gods to help her if she was in trouble like that?'

'That was something else she was afraid of: the gods that she could sense all around her. She didn't think she could trust them, that they'd turn on her.' Dr Ward shook his head. 'Can you imagine living for so long with so much fear?'

Kingsley knew about fear. It was a great weakness for a professional escapologist, for it clouded the mind at times when it needed to be clearest. He also knew of it from the wild. In the wild, fear was as near as the noise behind the bush, the shadow in the tree, the movement unexpected.

'I explained that my intentions did not include harming her, and she told me part of her story,' Dr Ward went on. 'I could not leave her. After determining that the scrolls were merely last year's *Bombay Times*, we crept out of the cave to where I had left my horses. The journey to Bangalore was hair-raising, and is worth its own story one day, but it's enough to say that the scorpion knife had its chance to sting before we were safe.'

Kingsley's eyebrows rose. He had trouble imagining Mrs Winter as a knife-wielding beggar woman.

'She wouldn't have been safe, even in an army cantonment,' Evadne guessed.

'Indeed. That's why I decided she would be better in England.'

'Oh, that's why you offered to marry her,' Kingsley said, 'to make sure of her passage to England.'

Dr Ward took his time before answering. 'Kingsley, I offered to marry her because we love each other. She is a remarkable woman, unlike any I've met before.'

Well, she does have the ability to tell gods that they're welcome to drop in, Kingsley thought, *that's enough to put her in the basket labelled 'remarkable'.*

'Sorry, Father.'

'No need to apologise. You've always known me as a bachelor. Why would you think a romantic bone had ever existed in my body?'

'You can't predict when these things will strike,' Evadne said. 'And it's sometimes against one's better judgement.'

Kingsley swivelled his head and locked eyes with her. She held up her hand, the hand still intertwined with his, in a deliberate declaration that he took as a very fine thing indeed.

'Quite,' Dr Ward said. 'We made arrangements, but I was called away on a special assignment before we could depart. When I returned, she was gone.'

'You must have been distraught,' Evadne said.

'Distraught, afraid, desolate. I searched for her everywhere. I called in what favours I had among the military and the intelligence service. I looked for months, but it was as if she'd simply been swept off the face of the earth. I was willing to search until the end of days, but something else came up.'

Kingsley wondered what could be important enough to keep him from the woman he loved, but he saw Dr Ward's steady gaze. 'That's right, Kingsley. I found you.'

Kingsley straightened, and nearly banged his head on the trunk of the tree behind him.

'Raised by wolves,' Kingsley said. 'Baby me.'

'Baby you,' Dr Ward echoed. 'I was following a rumour of a miracle-working woman in the Kerala forest. Two workers flagged me down while I was riding past. They begged me to take you. I had no choice and by the time I'd left you, temporarily, at the Military headquarters in Madurai, I'd lost any hope of finding Selene.'

Kingsley was reeling. He'd cost his foster father his wife-to-be! 'You brought me to England.'

'And great joy you brought me, my boy. I couldn't have been prouder if you were my own flesh and blood. Fourteen years ago – nearly fifteen – it was. I had nearly forgotten my scorpion-stinging intended, when a letter arrived last year.'

'That must have been a shock,' Evadne said, with more than a touch of impishness. Kingsley scolded her with a look. She didn't take it seriously.

'I had to sit for some time after I read it. Then I re-read it again and again until I was satisfied that it was my own, dear Selene, alive after all these years. She had been taken by the Immortals and only recently escaped. She was on her way to our shores. I met her at Southampton and the rest you know.'

Weren't you suspicious? Kingsley wanted to ask, but he didn't – and not just to avoid embarrassing his foster father. He had an instant's insight when he glanced at Evadne and wondered how he would behave if she suddenly vanished and then reappeared many years later.

I doubt that my first reaction would be to ask some searching questions about affiliations with malevolent sorcerers.

'I think we're missing a few useful details,' Evadne said, 'but they can wait.' She looked towards the farmhouse. Smoke was coming from the chimney. 'So the Immortals have her again.'

'It was probably her actions at your workshop,' Dr Ward said. 'The Immortals would have noticed a magical disturbance in the ether. Selene was worried about such a thing – it was the first magic she'd performed since her escape, for that very reason. Hence our fleeing so quickly.'

'Do you have any idea why the Immortals want her?' Kingsley said. 'Specifically, that is. I imagine they're fond of having things just because they can, but a plan running over so many years indicates that they have something special in mind.'

'Part of the Immortals' interest in Platonism, or neo-Platonism to be more correct, is this notion of a superabundance of gods infesting the mortal realm. Selene fears that they are working up to invoking these deities, opening the door to them and bending them to their will.'

'Bringing back the gods,' Evadne breathed. 'If you can't be a god, then having a troupe of them as minions is the next best thing.'

'For them but not for humanity, I fear.' Dr Ward's voice was harsh. 'Every time she opens the way while the Immortals watch, they learn more about her ability. The more familiar they become with it, the more likely it is that they will be able to control the deities as they emerge.'

'She can't call on godly help without their knowledge, either,' Kingsley guessed. 'And she'll be watched constantly to prevent that, I imagine.'

'Almost certainly. While she's resourceful, I'm afraid it's up to us to get her out.'

Kingsley made a fist and bounced it on his knee. He stood, brushed off his trousers and surveyed the farm. 'Why did they have to come here?'

'We know that.' Evadne rose and joined him. 'Heart of England, large transmission tower, enslave the human race.'

'True, and a sleepy village is the perfect spot to do it. No interference from the busybodies of the city, a good place to get on with your own business as long as you don't draw attention to yourself too much.' He paused. Overhead, a wisp of cloud touched the moon. Was it a little lighter in the east? 'I think we should rest.'

A few objections came from both Evadne and Dr Ward, but they were mild and mostly from habit. They arranged themselves as best they could amid the beech trees, pulling jackets and scarves tight.

Kingsley wanted to sleep the wary half-sleep of the wolves, but he didn't dare come so close to his wildness. As a result, he immediately fell into troubled and alarming dreams.

THIRTY-THREE

Later that morning, Kingsley, Evadne and Dr Ward retired up the road a few miles towards Fenny Drayton. Evadne wanted a position a little removed from Mallowside Farm where they could rendezvous with those she'd sent for. Kingsley spied a stand of trees at the turn-off to Stoke Golding. The beeches were ancient and gnarled, and hazel and may bushes surrounded them in an untidy, but useful, tangle. As they neared the turn-off, Kingsley could smell burning – not recent – and the remains of a fire pit confirmed that the site had probably been used for many years.

Kingsley was relieved when, mid-morning, a caravan rolled along the road from the direction of Atterton, with the unmistakeable figure of Troilus at the reins and Lavinia standing and waving.

Kingsley was on his feet in an instant. Evadne held

out a hand for him to help her to her feet in a gesture probably unnecessary but certainly welcome. She was as bright-eyed and fresh-faced as if she'd just spent a night at the Savoy.

'The Trojans are here,' he announced.

Dr Ward stood gingerly, but he waved Kingsley off when he went to help. 'It's nothing, my boy,' he wheezed, 'just jolting the old body into action, that's all. A good galvanic shock would help, but I don't expect you have a generator on your person. No?' When he stood, he looked grim, but resolute. 'These helpers of yours. I've learned that nothing is too outlandish where you're concerned, but are you suggesting these are truly people from the ancient city of Troy?'

Evadne waved as the caravan neared. A second rounded the corner and was followed by three more. 'That would be foolish,' Kingsley said, having listened and learned. 'They're the *descendants* of those who fled the sacking of Troy.'

The tall figure of Troilus leaped down from the caravan, grinning broadly. 'We're seeking a place to build a new Troy, Dr Ward. And, as you can see, we haven't quite located it yet.' He stuck out a hand. 'I enjoyed your lecture on the origins of the species last year. Brilliant stuff. Ah, Evadne!'

Troilus swept Evadne up and swung her around, laughing. 'Glad I am to see you again!' he cried. 'My days are now better for it.'

He was wearing what Kingsley would have described as 'I'm a gamekeeper, not a poacher' gear – hard-wearing canvas trousers, knee-length boots, and despite the cool of the early day, a leather waistcoat over a white shirt with the sleeves rolled up to show the lush hair on his forearms. He wore no hat, as if daring the elements to do their worst to his dashing grey hair.

Evadne straightened her jacket. 'Troilus, I'm glad you're here.'

Lavinia caught Kingsley's eye and held out a hand. He took it. She steadied herself and alighted. She was in accord with her brother, in that her outfit announced that she was a lady gamekeeper and not a lady poacher: a no-nonsense tweed skirt with a well-buttoned jacket. She wore a hat over her black hair; round, it came down over her ears, and Kingsley wondered if it were as bulletproof as it looked.

'We are the Free Trojans, Dr Ward,' she said. 'We won't stop our search until we find the perfect place for New Troy.' She reached into the wagon, under the driver's seat, and handed a squirming bundle to Evadne. 'This is yours?'

Evadne cried out and took the myrmidon in her arms. 'Beanie! You are a clever boy!'

Troilus screwed up his face. 'True, that. I've never met a cleverer rat.'

Kingsley, Dr Ward and Troilus shared a look, and Kingsley was forced to revise his opinion of the New Trojan. If he was dubious about the myrmidons, he was obviously someone of perspicacity.

'You're lucky you caught us,' Lavinia said as the other Trojans clambered out of the caravans. Kingsley was pleased to see nearly thirty of them. 'We've just booked a steamer.'

Evadne's face fell. 'There's nothing for you here in England?'

'It doesn't appear so. Other places beckon.'

'I've a mind to try some of those South Seas,' Troilus said. 'None of us Free Trojans have been out there. Maybe it's the place for us.'

'But you don't mind helping us?' Kingsley noticed several of the Trojans were checking rifles.

'We owe Evadne,' Lavinia said simply. 'Whenever she needs us, we'll be there.'

'It'll just take a long time to get here if she asks while we're in the South Seas,' Troilus added. 'Now, what're we in for this time?'

As Evadne explained, both Troilus and Lavinia grew stony-faced. When she finished, Lavinia eyed the road that led to the farmhouse. 'The Immortals. This explains the missing children in the district.'

'Missing children?' Evadne covered her mouth with a hand.

'We stopped in the village,' Troilus said. 'Bleak, the people were. Three children have disappeared in the last few weeks.'

Kingsley was watching Evadne closely. At Troilus's announcement, any delight at the arrival of the Trojans drained away. Grief touched her but was quickly hidden behind steely-eyed fury. He took her arm. She was trembling.

'It's not as if we needed another reason for going against these monsters, but you've provided one,' he said. 'We'll rescue them, too.'

He felt Evadne relax, just a little.

'With all this, I can't say we're overjoyed at the prospect of putting ourselves up against these Immortals,' Lavinia said, 'but there you have it. We're armed well enough.' She gestured to the rest of the Trojans, who had stood their rifles in bunches of three, and were now starting a fire.

With tea in mind, Kingsley hoped. 'And we have some heavier stuff ready in the back.'

Evadne craned her neck. 'Really?'

'Under the floorboards we have a light cannon and a Maxim gun. They'll take a while to assemble, but they're yours if needed.'

'Now, look here,' Dr Ward bristled, red in the face, 'I'm not having this place become a battleground. Too much at risk.'

'And what would that be?' Troilus asked.

Dr Ward glanced at him to see if he were joking, but Troilus's sunny face made him subside. 'My wife is in there somewhere.'

'Oh. You know where?'

'Not yet.' Dr Ward dropped into what Kingsley always thought of as his lecturing mode. 'The farmhouse is surrounded by new outbuildings and a large barn.'

'These'd be on the other side, away from the field we're going to set up in?'

'That's right.'

'But you don't know which of these many buildings your wife is in.'

'Not as yet.'

Troilus shrugged. 'With the right sort of surprise and firepower, some of our lads should be able to storm the whole lot. We'd hardly work up a sweat.'

'That's the worst thing to do. You'll start a battle. There are children, foreigners, my wife.'

Kingsley took his father's arm. 'It's all right. They haven't heard our plan yet.'

'You have a plan?' Troilus perked up. 'Righto then, time to share, I think, around a nice cup of cha.'

278

Under the sceptical but friendly gaze of the Trojans, Kingsley laid out his thinking. 'It all depends on Gompers,' he began. 'It appears as if he's managing the affairs of the Immortals, at least where this wireless telegraphy is concerned.'

'Gompers?' Troilus said. 'Big bloke, rude, white mutton-chops?'

'That's him,' Evadne said.

'He's the main man, then. The people in the village say he's been coming and going for nearly a year, now; buying, selling, organising deliveries. They don't like him but they like the money he's been spreading about.'

'Father, you know him. Can you tell us anything about his upbringing?'

'Eh? Little boy Gompers?'

'That sort of thing. Where was he raised?'

'Belgravia. His family was very well-to-do. From there straight to Cambridge where he stayed until the Olmsley Affair, after which he was stripped of all of his honours, his positions and his career.'

'No time spent elsewhere?'

'What are you driving at, my boy?' Dr Ward said. 'Why are you so interested in Gompers's life? He's a bad egg, that's what he is, and a dangerous one to boot.'

'I want to know if he's a city person rather than a country person.'

Dr Ward snorted. 'I doubt he'd know a dandelion if it bit him. He's citified to the bone. Prefers the inside of a library or a laboratory. This must be a great shock for him, fresh air and the like.'

'That's what I was hoping.' Kingsley pointed at the

farmhouse. 'This plan of the Immortals' needs some secrecy if it's to succeed, doesn't it?'

'Most definitely.'

'So, as long as I'm correct, Gompers would do just about anything to fit in with the local way of life without really knowing what the local way of life is.'

'I see,' Dr Ward said. 'The Immortals won't let anything interfere with their task, though. At anything untoward, they'd take lively action.'

'Naturally,' Kingsley said, 'but that necessitates knowing that something untoward is going on. Being out of his element, how can Gompers judge what's untoward and what's . . . toward?'

Evadne made a classic gesture of prestidigitation, tumbling her hands together and then separating them with a flourish. 'Deception and misdirection culminating in an astonishing resolution?'

'You've intrigued us, Kingsley,' Lavinia said. 'Tell us more.'

Kingsley soon realised, as he answered questions, revised small points and rebuffed criticisms, that his wildness and his rationality were working together. He had to draw on all his powers of persuasion, intelligence and anticipation – he was in the realm of civilised Kingsley – but his wildness kept him aware of the people around him. He was alert to unspoken objections, half-formed arguments and the wordless connections between those who were judging his plan. Hardly realising it, he was aware of the bonds of deference and obligation, of responsibility and duty that allowed him to guess who would speak first and who would support whom.

The more he had to adjust his plan in response to the Trojans, the more he appreciated the honing of intellect that civilisation had provided. The more he had to acknowledge their hesitations and to gain their support, the more he was grateful for the perception of intangible bonds that his time as a pack member brought him. Both came from his past, his upbringing, and both belonged to him.

Eventually, he finished. He sat back on the stone he'd drawn up to the fire. He inspected the faces of the Trojans. Most were nodding. Some had that faraway look that spoke of imagining themselves in the situation Kingsley had described.

Troilus took out a knife, opened it and began paring at a fingernail. 'That, my friend, is a plan that shows a devious and crooked mind.'

'I'm sorry,' Kingsley said. 'It was all I could think of.'

He pointed the knife at Kingsley. 'I meant it as a compliment.'

'Life on the road means you have to develop a fine sense of the devious and crooked,' Lavinia explained, 'if only to meet it head on.'

Dr Ward, however, wasn't so easily won over. 'So that's it?' he said, arms crossed on his chest. 'We're going ahead with Kingsley's scheme?'

'What is it, Father? From everything we've seen, everything we've learned, Gompers is the key. We separate him from the Immortals' installation and we should have a chance to get in and perform our rescue.'

'That much is reasonable, my boy. I don't want to appear to be carping, but the rest sounds outlandish, preposterous even.'

'It is. This whole situation is preposterous and it needs a preposterous solution.'

Dr Ward went to speak, then grasped his chin and thought furiously for a moment before bursting out laughing. 'Kingsley, you *have* grown! You saw the way forward much more clearly than I did, dear boy, much more clearly. I, the old bull, give way, and I acknowledge that I was being a duffer.'

Evadne stared at him. 'I'm sorry, I think I've missed something.'

Dr Ward stood, still chuckling. 'My dear, it's like this. In the wild, there comes a time when the old bull who leads the herd is challenged by a younger bull. They lock horns, or trunks, or tusks, or whatever they fight with. Sometimes it's merely posturing, sometimes it's violent and bloody. The winner becomes leader of the herd again, or for the first time.' He slapped his own forehead. 'I was too caught up in my own feelings to realise. I saw a young bull challenging my authority, and I was resist-ing – regardless of whether bull boy here had a good idea or not.'

'Dr Ward, you should have accepted that his plan was a good one. I wouldn't be going along with it if it weren't.'

'An excellent point.' He clapped his hands together. 'Right, what's my part in all this?'

THIRTY-FOUR

'Can I borrow the field glasses?' Kingsley asked Evadne as they lay on their stomachs on the slight ridge that overlooked Mallowside Farm. Their observation point was in the middle of a stand of elders, well screened from view.

Without speaking, Evadne handed the binoculars to him. The sun was high in a sky that looked as if it had never seen a cloud. Kingsley was grateful for the visual aids the Trojans had ferreted out of the endless hidden chambers and hidey-holes of their caravans.

Kingsley was apprehensive when the caravans rolled up to the farmhouse, but when he saw the man who opened the door, he knew that they'd entered a crucial phase of the plan.

Musgrave Gompers. The man looked out of place in what he must have imagined were farmer's clothes

– heavy trousers held up by braces over a checked shirt, a leather waistcoat and a cloth cap. They clung to him as if they weren't sure of their welcome. Gompers looked uncomfortable just standing there.

Kingsley looked through the field glasses again. Gompers's face was hard, but not angry. He was resisting the Free Trojans, but he was doing it calmly. Troilus was joined by Lavinia, and she began pointing down the road to the village and shaking her head.

This was the vital moment. Those at the farmhouse needed to believe that the Trojans were travellers who traditionally camped in the field near the wood, year after year, and were a commonplace part of the annual round in this part of the world. Kingsley could already hear Troilus laughing and declaring that it was an established practice here, then asking Gompers if he needed any watches, or jewellery, or silver snuffboxes.

If Gompers confused the Trojans with the Rom – the gypsies – that was good. Troilus wouldn't disabuse him of that. The important part was to convince Gompers that interrupting local traditions would cause controversy up and down the dale. Tongues would wag, gossip mongers would mong, attention would come down on Mallowside Farm from all directions – the last thing that Gompers, or the Immortals, would want.

Give in, Gompers, Kingsley urged silently, *give in*.

Then it was done, as quickly as that. Gompers shook his head, but the way he jabbed a finger in the direction of the field suggested that he was doubting his own sanity in granting access. Troilus grabbed the old man's hand and pumped it vigorously. Kingsley hoped he wasn't overdoing it.

'Phase One is successful,' he breathed and handed the field glasses to Evadne. 'Now, it's time for a show.'

The Trojans took their caravans to the field, a quarter of a mile or so from the nearest of the farm buildings. Within minutes, a fire was roaring away and washing lines were strung from the trees just over the fence where the woods proper began. The field had a gate of its own opening directly onto the road to the village, which the Trojans had used after the negotiations with Gompers. They had neatly arranged the caravans to block the fire and the nearest part of the woods from any observers at the farm.

Kingsley, Evadne and Dr Ward slipped from the woods to join the Trojans who had gathered about the fire. Kingsley approved of the way the Trojans moved about, entering the caravans singly or in small groups, so that the conclave around the fire was a constantly changing, shifting array, hard to keep track of if anyone was observing. The only constants were Troilus and Lavinia – and now Kingsley, Evadne and Dr Ward.

They stood for a moment, enjoying the fire. 'You had no trouble at the farmhouse?' Kingsley asked.

'No trouble at all,' Troilus said. He spat into the flames. 'Lovely bloke, that. Lovely.'

'Lovely?' Kingsley echoed.

'Lovely,' Troilus echoed. 'For a heartless lunatic, that is. It's in the eyes, you know. They don't smile when the rest of his face does.'

'That would be our Mr Gompers in a nutshell,' Evadne said lightly, 'as long as you add "capable of boundless cruelty". Kingsley darted a look at her. She resolutely refused to meet it.

'Have you sorted out the staging?' Kingsley asked, aware that he could have a problem on his hands with Evadne, but knowing that the planning of Phase Two couldn't be delayed.

'We always pack tents for stalls or fortune telling or the like,' Lavinia said. 'We'll use those, some barrels, and some boards we have in case of repair.'

'It'll get done, all right,' Troilus said, 'but what about your part of the business?'

Kingsley looked across the open expanse of the field to the road. 'That, as we say in the world of the theatre, will be a matter of timing.'

Kingsley had hoped for another wagon along with the Trojans, and had been disappointed when it hadn't arrived. *I suppose I shouldn't have relied on the rat creature*, he thought, but he knew he was being unfair. The myrmidon had found the Trojans as well as completing its other messaging, which was nigh on a miracle. To find Finny as well was a hope too far.

'If we have to,' Evadne said, coming to his side and scanning the road as well, 'we'll extemporise.'

'Of course,' Kingsley said. With a flourish, he produced a back-palmed nine of diamonds. 'From nothing, we will produce something.'

The rest of the day was given over to carpentry and stage management. Kingsley made sure that his foster father was fully involved, even to the extent of putting him in charge of the set construction. It meant he had to suffer Dr Ward endlessly ordering 'Up a bit', then 'To your left' and 'Down a bit', but it kept him from brooding or, worse, going off on his own on a well-intentioned but poorly timed spot of scouting.

The physical work gave Kingsley time to analyse his plan over and over. Had he forgotten anything? Had he considered all possibilities?

He also had time to wonder about the strange tiny woman, Leetha. Kingsley was conscious of how seriously Leetha had taken the promise they'd made. He was determined to do what he could to help her.

Kingsley kept Evadne close. He was worried about her shifting into the reckless crusading mode she was prone to when those who harmed children were nearby. She assured him, many times, that she'd overcome such tendencies, but he knew that her zeal was deep-seated. She threw herself into the job of erecting the tiny stage with such aplomb that Kingsley was taken aback when, late in the afternoon, he realised he hadn't seen her for some time.

He straightened, ignoring a twinge in his back. 'Have you seen Evadne?' he asked Dr Ward.

'That board is a touch too long,' Dr Ward said. 'You'll need to saw another inch off it.'

Kingsley handed the saw to Dr Ward. 'Evadne,' he repeated. 'Have you seen her?'

Dr Ward waved vaguely. 'She went off. An hour or so ago.'

'In which direction?'

'That way.' Dr Ward pointed towards the farm buildings. 'She was with Lavinia.'

Kingsley was already on his way by the time Dr Ward completed his observation. *With Lavinia*, Kingsley thought. *That's good. That's not so bad. That should be all right.*

He had just reached the caravans when Lavinia opened the rear door of one and came down the stairs. Kingsley brought himself up short and nearly pulled a muscle in his back. 'Thank goodness,' he said. 'Evadne. Have you seen her?'

A low, throaty laugh came from the top of the stairs. At the open door stood an elegant redhead, green-eyed behind her clear spectacles and abundantly freckled. She wore a flouncy skirt, a peasant blouse and a startling bright green scarf around her neck. 'Kingsley,' she said. 'Where on earth are you going?'

'Evadne,' he said. While Lavinia laughed, he held out a hand. 'My, how you've changed. Again.'

Evadne swayed her way down the stairs. She had a brace of fine gold chains around each wrist and they tinkled as she descended. 'If we're encountering Gompers, I thought it wise to don a wig,' she said. 'I don't want him recognising me.'

'And it's not just because you like dressing up?'

'Pish!'

'Not that you don't do it well. So delightfully, in fact, I'm ruing the fact that I don't have a camera with me.'

'And you?'

'No beard and no limp, so I don't think he'll associate me with the institute. While I'm working here, I'll keep my hat on and I'll scowl, thus disguising my custom-ary sunny disposition.' Kingsley had rescued the hat from the Trojans' rubbish heap. The colour was between brown and grey, and mostly provided by the dirt that had impregnated it.

Movement on the road caught Kingsley's eye. 'I think we won't have to extemporise at all, Evadne. Finny's here.'

∽ THIRTY-FIVE ∽

'It's a long time since I've been out this way,' Finny said as he climbed down from his motor van. 'Not since the Lord Stoathaven business.' He plucked at his braces. 'Nothing makes me happier than taking a lot of money from a greedy man who thinks he's doing something a bit underhand.'

As much as he would have liked to hear about the Lord Stoathaven business, Kingsley refused to be distracted. 'You brought everything?'

A cigar had appeared in the corner of Finny's mouth. He slapped the side of the van, right under the 'Chas. Trevelyan and Sons, Cabinet Makers' sign and the canvas rippled. 'Easily done, my lad, easily done. Once I gathered what your ratty friend was on about, things went quick smart. Sharp little fellow he is, pointing stuff out with his nose like that.'

'He's not my ratty friend,' Kingsley said. He lowered the tailgate. 'The ebony box is in here?'

Finny grinned. 'I said I brought everything, and everything is what I brought.'

Inside, the rear of the van was jam-packed, shrouded in heavy drop sheets, with some floorboards projecting along one side. While Kingsley studied Finny's delivery, Lavinia and Evadne strolled over, with Troilus joining them. Kingsley had to reassure a goggle-eyed Finny that the redhead was, indeed, Evadne.

'Lavinia,' Kingsley said, 'I think it could be time to brace Gompers about this evening.'

'Do you really think he'll accept that he has a role in proceedings?' Evadne asked.

'That's what I'm hoping,' Kingsley said. 'He's on unfamiliar ground. He doesn't want to create a fuss for his masters, so he should be willing to be persuaded that the landlord of Mallowside Farm has a traditional role in the night's festivities. And I'm also relying on Gompers's penchant for theatre going.'

'You still think you can get him to be an audience volunteer?' Troilus asked.

'Selecting and persuading reluctant audience volunteers is part of the repertoire of any stage magician. Firstly, let's see if we can get him here tonight. Lavinia?'

'She has the family silver tongue,' Troilus said and he beamed at his sister. 'She'll have him here and ready to dance a jig.'

Kingsley found that going about normal business while trying to appear unsuspicious and also planning something highly dangerous was not an easy task. Even such simple jobs as standing around the main camp fire induced a self-consciousness that was almost crippling, but he summoned his stage persona and pretended that he was in performance all afternoon.

His equanimity was further tested by Evadne's presence in her flame-haired glory. She laughed and chaffed with the Trojans, and the male Trojans were particularly attentive. Kingsley wasn't sure it would have been any different with Evadne in her normal guise, as attractive as she was, but her startlingly different appearance only made things more apparent.

When it came to rehearsing their performance for the evening, he was disconcerted again and again when he turned around expecting silver-haired Evadne only to find a flame-tressed stranger regarding him. An extra puzzler was that they'd decided that Evadne should avoid juggling, just in case Gompers had a good memory for performers. Instead, she relied on her dazzling presence, and substituted some tumbling, which was both elegant and eye-opening.

'That's pleasing,' she said breathlessly after she completed her first stunning series. She had entered the tiny stage left with a cartwheel, which transformed into a laid-out front somersault landing by Kingsley's side, a hand resting lightly on his shoulder while she gestured at what would be the audience, her beaded dress still swaying from her exertions.

'I didn't know you could do that,' Kingsley said after he'd composed himself sufficiently. He had an array of coloured scarves in his hands that were going to be used for something or other.

'I thought I may have forgotten,' she said and shrugged.

'I used to do a fair bit of tumbling, but I decided to concentrate on juggling when an agent said that some theatre owners find lady tumblers unladylike.'

'Unladylike?' Kingsley said. 'I thought it supremely athletic, but never unfeminine. Elegant, powerful and charming.'

Evadne favoured him with a quizzical smile. 'It could find a place in our Extraordinaires act?'

'Oh, most surely.'

'Kingsley, you are an original.'

'I do my best.'

The next heart-in-mouth moment came after the Trojans lit the camp site with flaming torches, making it a barbarous fairyland. In one of the caravans, Kingsley dressed in an outlandish costume, concocting an flamboyant blend that was part-Oriental, part-Arabian and part-Cossack. Billowing purple trousers, a silk shirt and an orange sash around his waist was the beginning of the ensemble, but it was the furry hat with long earflaps that completed the effect.

From the steps of the caravan, he watched Lavinia, garbed in exotic peasant gear as well, make her way along a path beaten through the grass of the field. More torches had been spaced on either side to light her way in the gathering twilight.

Be good, Kingsley thought. *Be convincing.* Even though her afternoon entreaties had been well received, this was the crucial time. Would Gompers be biddable? In her visit just after lunchtime, Lavinia had impressed upon him the importance of the man of the manor coming to the night's revels and how it was a tradition that had never been broken in two hundred years – and then by Black Jack Rosebury, whose name was infamous in the district. Lavinia's blandishments plus the music and lights from the campsite would tempt any normal man – and surely it would tempt a man interested in what made up normal men.

Lavinia disappeared around the corner of the farmhouse and Kingsley began his final preparations, while trying to ignore the doubts and misgivings that battled for possession of his mind. Before every performance, Kingsley undertook mental rehearsal as much as physical rehearsal. His fingers twitched as he went over the card tricks they'd agreed on. With such a small audience they would be most apt. The scarves and rings were also mandatory as they were showy and effective. Then it was the time for a neat rope escape, when Kingsley hoped a modicum of audience participation could be established as de rigueur.

Then would come the final trick. The Astounding Ebony Box.

A quarter of an hour later – measured by Kingsley's near constant referrals to his pocket watch – Lavinia reappeared. She was leading Gompers and a small company of guards down the path towards the camp. She had her arm linked with his and, as they neared, Kingsley saw Gompers's hard eyes taking in every detail of the Free Trojans.

Lavinia, Kingsley thought, *you are a marvel.* He promised himself that when all was done and successful – he refused to countenance any other outcome – he would find the largest bunch of flowers in southern England and present them to her in admiration.

Despite his relief, he saw how Gompers surveyed the camp. He scanned the whole area suspiciously and Kingsley was glad he'd taken Finny's maxim to heart: *the best way to stop someone detecting a fake is not to be a fake.*

The camp was a real, living gathering. They were putting on a proper show here tonight, with everything Evadne and he had learned about performance. Nothing was out of place, or unsettling, or awry.

There's nothing up our sleeves, Kingsley thought, *I just hope we have an appropriate 'Hey Presto!'*

The guards with Gompers weren't armed, which Kingsley took as a good sign. They weren't quite bodyguards, but nor were they a bunch of lads looking for a fun night on the town. They had clearly been ordered to be watchful.

No matter. Kingsley checked himself in the narrow mirror near the door of the caravan and decided he looked distinctly piratical. *We'll win them over.*

A pig was rotating on a spit when Kingsley emerged. It was an essential part of the ruse, Troilus had insisted, helping to create the proper atmosphere of rustic carousery. Kingsley was sure most of Troilus's motivation was a partiality to pork, but he had to agree that with the mouth-watering aroma, the sound of accordion and fiddle, the torches and paper lanterns and the empty but beckoning stage with its wings draped with canvas, the stage had well and truly been set.

Finny was standing next to the stage, one arm propped on a barrel. He still had his bowler hat and cigar, but he, too, had dressed for the part. Even though he looked uncomfortable in his heavy purple coat over loud checked trousers, he managed to tip his chin significantly before looking away from Kingsley.

Gompers and his underlings followed Lavinia between the caravans. Gompers didn't show the signs of someone who'd been hauled over the coals by maniacal sorcerers, but he did look weary. The relocating of the Immortals and their resources in such a short time must have been a substantial drain. Kingsley thought he saw signs of impatience, and hoped that Gompers was wanting the performance, that it could fit in with his explorations of humanity.

Evadne was in the thick of things. She was handing out plates of food, laughing and smiling, while the Trojans milled about. An open area had been left between the fire and the stage. Troilus was up on the boards lighting the lanterns that hung from the rough and ready proscenium. When Kingsley saw Gompers standing in front of it, oblivious to the pork wrapped in bread someone had shoved into his hand, he thought they might have a chance.

Kingsley eased his way through the Trojans, noting how well they were undertaking their dual tasks of carousing and making sure Gompers and his underlings were caught up in the festivities. He slipped between two tents and hurried to the rear of the stage. Dr Ward was waiting for him. A lantern was suspended from the bough of an enormous oak that overhung the fence, a guardian of the woods beyond.

'He's here?' Dr Ward asked. He would have looked out of place at the campfire. His tweeds and deerstalker were far too sombre for the revelries, but he had insisted they were, as he put it, 'ideal rescuing gear'.

'He has, and he's ready for it, I'd say.'

'I'll go scouting then.'

'Be careful.'

'My boy, I prowled around some of the wildest parts of India long before you were born. Never so much as a scratch.' At Kingsley's look of scepticism, he added. 'Well, a few scratches, perhaps, but I was a top class prowler, nonetheless.'

Kingsley held out a hand. 'Good luck, Father.'

They shook. 'It's all a matter of timing, now,' Dr Ward said, and then disappeared into the woods.

∽ THIRTY-SIX ∾

Finny slipped through the canvas. 'It's time, my lad. Everyone's in position.'

Evadne eased past him, her eyes shining in the lantern light. 'We have a show to put on, Kingsley. I hope you're ready.'

'I am, and there's no-one I'd rather put it on with than you.'

She stood on tiptoes and gave him a peck on the cheek. 'And I'll say the same to you.'

Kingsley could feel the spot on his cheek where Evadne's lips had touched rather more than he could feel the rest of his body. 'Even though it's dangerous?'

'Especially since it's dangerous. We're a good team, Kingsley.'

'That we are.'

A drum roll. Evadne caught his arm and turned towards

the wings. They could hear Troilus's voice. Evadne came so close Kingsley could feel her heartbeat; it was racing even though her face was calm.

He's good, Kingsley thought as Troilus continued his introduction. He covered Evadne's hand with his. *He could do this for a living.*

'For one night only,' Troilus stretched out the moment. 'Fresh from engagements in the mystical east and the mysterious north, I am delighted to give to you, I'm honoured to give to you, I'm humbled to give to you ...' He faltered and looked to the ramshackle wings. 'Who exactly *are* you?'

Kingsley stared. They hadn't thought of *names!*

Evadne saved the day. While Kingsley stood there, she pushed past him, flipped her way to the front of the stage and stood with her hands on her hips. 'Hello everyone! I am the Amazing Serafina and this is Zoltan the Magnificent!'

Kingsley followed Evadne's lead. He bounded onto the stage, roaring like a lion. A relieved Troilus leaped into the wings.

Kingsley gave silent thanks for his height and the width of his shoulders. Done up as he was, no-one would think he was only months past his seventeenth birthday. He strutted about the stage as if he'd lived decades with a whip coiled on his hip, a gold earring in each ear, and an oiled moustache as broad as a bicycle handle. While the accordion and fiddle quickly swung into a mishmash Hungarian peasant tune, he glowered, he slapped his hands together, he poked at the stage setting and he stomped his boots while Evadne stood, amused.

The audience loved it, and Kingsley thought only

part of it was the guaranteed reception they'd rehearsed earlier. Trained as he was not to look at the audience, this time he had to keep an eye on Gompers, to make sure he was – at least – tolerating the performance.

He was. While he may not have been beaming, or whistling, or cheering as everyone else was – including his guards, who had all taken a shine to Evadne – Gompers was standing in the front row. His arms were crossed and his features set in what Kingsley hoped was a neutral and receptive arrangement.

Kingsley concluded his bravado-filled entrance by coming to Evadne's side. He stood, feet well apart, hands linked behind his head and scowled. 'This is a night for magic,' he bellowed. 'So magic I do for you.'

This time, when he slapped his hands together, he was rewarded with a flash and puff of orange smoke, thanks to the striker and the flash paper he'd had down his collar and retrieved while his hands were behind his head. The audience gasped and Gompers actually jumped, before looking about suspiciously.

Excellent.

Evadne tumbled and cartwheeled. Kingsley produced cards from thin air and made them vanish again – his back-palming practice had been successful – then he had some fun simply skimming them over the heads of the audience, spinning them wildly with a snap of his wrist. Producing a chain of multi-coloured scarves was pretty but hardly taxing; it was made more entertaining by Evadne's whirling as he produced them, winding them around her body as she spun. Kingsley noted that Gompers applauded carefully after Evadne's lissom and colourful curtsey.

300

Kingsley waved her aside and then swaggered to the centre of the tiny stage. He glowered at the audience. 'I need some hearty men,' he growled. 'Men who are strong, powerful, full of blood and nerve!' He bent and swept an arm over their heads. 'Who among you is big enough?'

Ready for this, the Trojans clamoured for the chance. 'Good!' Kingsley threw back his head and laughed. 'There are men among you yet!'

He held out a hand. With her juggler's precision, Evadne tossed a coil of rope. Without looking, Kingsley opened his fingers and snapped them shut when the rope struck them. 'Here! Good rope! Strong rope! Rope to tie a giant!'

He threw it to the nearest of the Trojans. 'Come, all six of you, tie me up! Use all the knots you can! Zoltan the Magnificent defies you!'

Wild applause greeted this sally. After that, the act ran smoothly. So smoothly, that Kingsley had time to wonder if Dr Ward could have reached the farm buildings and begun his reconnaissance.

Kingsley kept up his taunting. As with most rope-tying escapes, the audience volunteers began well, concentrating on wrapping the rope tightly and fastening it at each round with complex knots, but all Kingsley had to do was keep his chest well expanded and his shoulders flexed. When he relaxed, the slack created was enough for ninety per cent of the escape.

As usual, the volunteers eventually fell back on simply winding the rope around Kingsley from neck to ankle, finishing with a knot behind his back. Of course, if they had started with him in the middle of the rope and then used both ends for knots, things would have been much more difficult, but such was rarely the case.

'Back!' Kingsley roared when they were done. He flexed a little, felt sufficient slack and then did his best to show signs of dismay. After that, the escape was mostly showmanship.

The audience was delighted by his feigned distress. He wrenched himself about in a manner designed to be dramatic and to signal that the ropes were fiendishly well tied. As Kingsley staggered and heaved he actually had to be careful not to let them slip over his shoulder, lest the whole tangle fall loose.

After some apparently fruitless effort, Kingsley fell with a crash so alarming that he momentarily worried about the soundness of the afternoon's carpentry. He rolled about, roaring his imagined frustrations, adding grunts and exclamations of pain for good effect.

Matters were made more difficult when he caught sight of Evadne, off stage. She had one hand clamped over her mouth, while the other held her stomach in an effort to muffle her giggling. Of course, the infectiousness of this caught him, and it took a supreme effort to prevent himself from bursting out laughing himself.

Concentrate! he admonished himself and he rolled away so he couldn't see her.

When he judged that enough was enough, Kingsley wrenched his arms around, rose to all fours and shook like a dog emerging from a swamp. Then he sprang forward and left the ropes behind him.

'Free!' he roared. 'People may live in chains, dreaming of freedom, but Zoltan the Magnificent makes the dream come true!'

The applause was wild. Gompers joined in, but his clapping was almost mechanical in its regularity.

302

Kingsley held up both hands. 'Easy, my friends, easy. Now is the time for a mystery.' He shook his head. 'Zoltan has travelled far, seen much. What I bring to you is something that is beyond the beyond, something that cannot be known.' *Meaningless, but atmospheric.* 'Many have sought for the secret I am about to show you, but few have seen it. You, my friends, are the lucky ones. Serafina, the box!'

Evadne wheeled the ebony box to the middle of the stage, near the rear, centring it over the discreet mark they'd measured out earlier. She opened the front door to display a red interior, totally bare and unadorned. She closed the door and spun the cabinet around on its casters, thumping it with a fist, to show that it was solid on all sides.

Kingsley was proud of the ebony cabinet. Evadne and he had laboured over it in between engagements, on and off, for months. The red oriental script on each side had been carefully chosen from one of Evadne's oldest books, and it was her steady hand with a fine brush that had painted the script on the lacquered ebony. The cabinet of mystery was a classic, but thanks to their combined skills, Kingsley was sure he had a twist that would surprise.

'This cabinet is a mystery of mysteries,' he said, adding to the drama while giving the Trojans who were moving through the audience more time. Three key figures were arranging themselves behind Gompers. 'Its secrets have puzzled a thousand scholars, a hundred thousand scholars, all scholars everywhere!' *Hyperbole is best done large.* 'But now, to test the cabinet – the cabinet of fear, the cabinet of horror, the cabinet of the riddle of the universe – we need a volunteer!'

Cheers, whistles, shouts, and the three key Trojans sited directly behind Gompers gave the man a hefty shove in the back.

Amid laughter and more cheering, Gompers staggered forward and barely caught himself on the edge of the stage. While he looked up angrily, Kingsley roared: 'We have a hero who cannot wait to challenge the cabinet! Applaud him! Cheer for him! Honour him!'

This was a crucial moment. Kingsley was relying on the mightily powerful effect of the crowd. It took remarkable steadfastness to stand back and resist the crowd, to look around and say 'No, I'm not doing it'. If Gompers walked away, the plan would be ruined.

Gompers glared at Kingsley for a moment, then nodded. Kingsley stifled a sigh of relief, then gestured. Gompers stalked to the stairs on the side of the stage. He mounted them and came to Kingsley's side. 'You are brave, my friend,' Kingsley said, 'are you not?'

Gompers sized up Kingsley, but did not respond. He was no pliant volunteer. He stood, eyes narrowed, a reluctant participant. Every inch of him was saying 'Get on with it'.

'But just how brave are you?' Kingsley went on.

Gompers snorted.

Kingsley held out a hand and came back with a long, curving sword that Finny had thrust on him from the wings. 'Brave enough for this?' Kingsley said.

Gompers was unmoved as the crowd roared and, for a split-second, Kingsley thought the man was going to turn and march away. The momentum that the crowd imposed on him had its way, however, and he gave a single, sharp nod of acceptance.

Kingsley gestured with the sword and Gompers stepped up to the cabinet. He looked at Evadne, who smiled and opened the door.

Gompers touched the door of the cabinet. He ran his fingers along it. Kingsley tapped him on the shoulder with the sword. 'Inside, hero!'

Gompers shuffled around and faced the audience. He crossed both hands over his chest and stepped backwards into the cabinet. He stood there, with a scowl not far from his face.

'Glorious!' Kingsley roared, then he seized the door of the cabinet. As he went to slam it shut, he paused for an instant, for Gompers had lifted a finger and fixed him with a look. 'This is good for me,' he said.

Kingsley blinked. He closed the door. He shrugged and addressed the audience. 'Now, for the miracle!'

He paced, slashing the sword through the air and glaring at the cabinet as if it were his worst enemy. He growled, he snarled, he glowered. He stamped his feet, he grimaced, he would have plucked at his beard if he'd had one. Then he brandished his sword and went to lunge at the cabinet with it – but he stopped short. 'No,' he said, 'you have seen that before. It is much too easy!'

Instead, he took a step back and pointed at the cabinet. With a crash – provided by Finny behind the stage – the cabinet disappeared.

Kingsley loved this moment in stage magic: the silence. If an illusion were performed correctly, with the perfect blend of preparation, suspense, theatricality and audaciousness, the final flourish always produced a momentary stillness before the applause, a collective expression of wonder and disbelief. Only silence was the appropriate measure of the mystery made real in front of them.

Of course, it needed to be followed by thunderous applause – and it was.

The ebony box was another product of Evadne's inventiveness. Thanks to the arrangement of springs, levers and hinges, the box had folded in on itself: sides first, then the top plunged straight down so all that was left on the stage was a slim black rectangle a few feet square and a few inches in height. Kingsley let the applause roll on, then he gestured grandly at the flat black tile. Instantly, it sprang up and resumed its shape and size.

Evadne flung the door open to reveal the interior was empty.

More applause, more thunderous than the last, and the musicians – on cue – struck up a lively mock peasant tune. The whole audience cried out and joined in, sweeping Gompers's underlings into a wild and abandoned dance.

Kingsley took Evadne's hand, kissed it, and they bowed. 'What a team we make,' he said out of the corner of his mouth.

She squeezed his hand.

THIRTY-SEVEN

Kingsley and Evadne hurried through the makeshift wings. They barely glanced at the gagged and bound Gompers who was in the keeping of Finny and a pair of well-armed Trojans. Kingsley was pleased to see that he could tick off Phase One. Then the music ended and Kingsley ticked off Phase Two, which was confirmed when they saw Gompers's guards standing with hands up, surrounded by more armed Trojans. Some of the guards still had tankards of ale in hand, others had mouths full of food. 'Tie them,' Kingsley ordered. 'Properly.'

He darted into one caravan while Evadne went into another. Kingsley ripped off his stage costume and quickly dressed in something more practical – serge trousers, shirt, woollen jacket – and emerged two minutes later with his walking stick to find Evadne waiting for him. She'd stripped off her wig and her hair was wild and loose. Kingsley had half a second to admire her practical but stylish change of outfit before she seized his hand and they were off.

The farmhouse was dark and of Dr Ward there was no sign. The lock proved only a momentary barrier. Kingsley had it open as quickly as if they'd turned a door knob. They stepped into an unlit kitchen so ordinary that Kingsley thought it could serve as a museum piece: 'The Rustic Kitchen'. An abundance of humble wood in dressers and beams. Some china proudly on display on shelves. A hulking great iron stove large enough to cook for a horde of barbarians, and six uniformed guards sitting at a large wooden table, enjoying mugs of tea.

Since there was no possible way of hiding, Kingsley cried out and held his cane at the ready. The guards, dumbfounded by this sudden disturbance, were still motionless when Evadne brought her Malefactor's Lament to bear.

With a solid metallic *thwang*, a fine mesh shot from the barrel of the outrageous firearm. It flew across the room and enveloped the guards before they could get to their feet. Immediately, they sagged bonelessly and their heads met the table. One started to snore like a sailor.

'They're asleep?' Kingsley looked at Evadne, who was twisting a brass knob near the trigger of the pistol. 'What sort of lament is that?'

'A non-lethal one. I prefer to think these are blameless hirelings. Or ruffians who may benefit from a second chance, at least.'

A staircase against the east wall led down and, with no other obvious option, Kingsley and Evadne charged down it only to meet an iron door with a much more challenging lock. This one needed both of Kingsley's better lock picks and fifteen seconds before they were through – only to be confronted by as drastic a contrast in interior design as Kingsley could imagine.

'They've been preparing this place for months,' Evadne breathed. 'Years, perhaps.'

All Kingsley could do was agree as he surveyed the three arched corridors stretching into the distance. Walls, floor and ceiling were clad in gleaming white tiles. At regular intervals, bold electric lights studded the arched ceilings. The light they cast rippled along the shininess of the tiles and made the corridors look like tunnels boring through the heart of a glacier.

Kingsley was frozen, too, by imagining the busyness of the Immortals preparing dozens of redoubts or hideouts or refuges across the length and breadth of the country. He realised, then, that he'd been underestimating the Immortals. He had been lulled by their peevishness. Partly because of their aspect of petulant children, they were easy to dismiss as simply mischievous. Estimating the energy and planning that must have gone into this underground lair forced him to revise his opinion of them. They were malevolent in a way that came from long-learned patience.

Evadne cocked her head. 'Listen.'

Kingsley didn't have to. He'd already heard the music that was echoing down the corridor directly in front of them and he was struggling not to respond. The music was erratic and swirling, faint and fainter, and it was wild in a way that made his blood surge. Instantly, he was battling an urge to abandon everything – cares, responsibilities and the trappings of civilisation – and to find the true wilderness in which to live.

'Don't,' he said, through gritted teeth as Evadne took a step forward. He took her forearm. 'It's calling to me.'

Kingsley had never before thought of music as wild. Music was a product of culture, of civilisation, at all levels. In grand chambers full of gowns and tiaras, in taverns and churches, around campfires and workplaces. Music was an expression of people communicating with people.

This music, however, was different. It was primitive and it roused his wildness as much as the smell of blood did. It spoke to him of running free, of roaming the open plains and prowling through the jungle. It was full of danger, too, of the thrill of the chase and the fear of being prey.

His Inner Animal was responding. His breath was coming in short, sharp gasps. His hands were clenching into fists and his nails cut into his palms. He trembled.

Kingsley staggered. Evadne caught him and held on. 'The music's gone,' she said. 'Are you all right?'

'It hasn't gone.' Kingsley could hear it, faint and distant. More than that, he could feel it lodged in his bones, in the back of his throat, and in his mouth was a taste he couldn't ignore.

'We'll withdraw,' Evadne said.

'No.' The effort hurt him. 'We must go on.'

'Which way?'

He pointed towards the source of the music. 'That way.'

With steely strength, Evadne shuffled him around until he was facing her. She took both his arms at the elbow. 'Are you being heroic?'

'I hope so.'

'Are you in danger?'

'If I start howling, we'll know.' He shook himself. The unsettling sensation was easing.

'I'll remember that.' She studied him, frowning slightly, her pinkish gaze magnified by her spectacles. 'I hope you're not doing this just to impress me.'

He rubbed the back of his neck. He might have pulled a muscle there, straining against the music. 'I don't do things *just* to impress you, although I hope you have been impressed on the odd occasion.'

She squeezed his arms and let them drop. 'I've been impressed. On more than the odd occasion.'

Kingsley used a finger to ease his collar, which was feeling unaccountably tight. 'And that's a matter for another day, correct?'

'Correct.'

THIRTY-EIGHT

The music is coming through the walls, Kingsley thought as they crept along the corridor. He glanced at Evadne, but she showed no signs of hearing. She had her Malefactor's Lament and a determined look that Kingsley feared might presage righteous fury.

Kingsley gripped his walking stick and concentrated on denying his wolfishness.

For that was what it was coming to. The music spoke directly to his wildness, the wildness he thought he'd accommodated, cultivating it as if it were a precious seedling. And like a well-nurtured seedling, it was growing. Inside, he was a ferment, waiting to howl at the moon, the stars, at any enemy who dared to cross his path.

He gritted his teeth. *Wildness cannot dominate me*, he thought, *for it is who I am.*

The corridor brought Kingsley and Evadne to the middle of a large chamber, eighty or ninety feet to their left and right and about that in breadth. It was entirely clad in white tiles apart from the wall to their left, which was raw rock. The ceiling was a lofty curve, fifty feet or more at the highest point of the arch. Giant electric lights shone down and made the whole place as bright as day.

The wall opposite had five niches. Two of them were occupied by Platonic solids – the three-sided pyramid and the cube, each three feet in diameter. Kingsley had seen them before, under Greenwich. Before he could point this out to Evadne, and share his satisfaction that the Immortals hadn't obtained any more of the magical objects, she gasped.

At the far end of the grand chamber a mass of Spawn was trying to hold its ground against a band of women who were tearing them to pieces. The Spawn were protecting the Immortals, who were standing on their throne, chattering and gesticulating, gibbering with anger. Slowly, though, the Spawn were being annihilated, rent apart by a score or more of bare-handed women of all ages, sizes and shapes, skin and hair colours, clad in animal skins or ragged robes and crowned with ivy wreaths. Their expressions were ecstatic; they sang as they grappled with the hideous Spawn. Some were playing on pipes and drums.

They were all laughing as they committed savagery.

Evadne gripped his arm and pointed. The wild-eyed Mrs Winter was prominent in their midst, one arm dripping blood from a long shallow gash.

Behind them, emerging from the rock wall, was a gigantic glowing cloud. It towered high, bending where it met the ceiling.

It, too, laughed.

Evadne nearly went to her knees. Kingsley sagged as the laughter rolled past them and over the mayhem. The mirth was ancient and it was arrogant. It was the amusement that came from seeing others in pain or in distress. It was the delight that enjoyed a diversion from boredom. It was merriment without compassion.

It was then that Kingsley knew they were in the presence of a god. It was oozing from the rock and it had made Mrs Winter – the woman who had summoned it – mad.

Kingsley was sweating and trembling, for the presence of the wild god was making him forget everything about civilisation, rationality and culture. His Inner Animal responded to the air of reckless abandon – the liberation – that the god was bringing. Its breath was the wind off the grasslands, the breeze in the treetops and Kingsley greatly wanted to be part of it.

Desperately, he swung to Evadne to find that she was running towards the Immortals, firing her outlandish pistol as she went. This time it crackled, bolts of lightning lancing from its barrel.

A firearm for all seasons, Kingsley thought. He took a step after her, then the music ran into him. It wrapped itself around his heart, squeezed and when it let go Kingsley was taken up in a torrent of wildness. He fought it, fists clenched and shoulders hunched, his walking stick held as a shield in front of him, but he was overwhelmed by the music, the exhilaration and the smell of blood. He

314

flung his walking stick aside, tore off his tie, threw back his head and howled.

Free! I run free!

A hand dropped on his collar. He was jerked to his feet and twisted around to come face to face with Dr Ward, who grabbed his lapels and shook him as if he were a naughty puppy. 'Kingsley! We don't have time for that now! Selene and Evadne need our help!'

It was like a dash of cold water; Kingsley flung off the intoxication that had seized him. 'I'm sorry, sir,' he shouted over the ululating chorus of women and the snarling of the Spawn – who had divided their numbers and were moving on Evadne as well as doing their best to keep the madwomen away from their masters.

'They're the Bacchae!' Dr Ward cried. 'The wild followers of the god Bacchus! Must've been a Roman settlement hereabouts with wine production. Mrs Winter has invited him here to combat the Immortals!'

'Get to her!' Kingsley shouted over the pandemonium. He scooped up his walking stick. 'I'm after Evadne!'

Evadne had been backed against the wall by a dozen Spawn. A handful were heaped in front of her, scorched by the crackling discharge of her Malefactor's Lament. Kingsley leaped into the fray from behind. He swung his walking stick hard, aiming for knees and ankles. One Spawn toppled, howling, and then Kingsley lashed out again to bring another down. Four or five then hurled themselves at him.

Kingsley was plunged into the confusion where time goes both slowly and infinitely quickly. He plucked his Shocking Pinch and used it left-handed, yelling in triumph when the Spawn reeled away, smoking wherever touched by its prongs. In his other hand, his walking stick was never still. He sized up targets, jabbed at faces and throats, slashed and took them on knees and elbows. He took charges and shouldered them aside, caught blows on the outstretched walking stick, elbowed, punched, kneed and suddenly he was through the press and facing a dazed and panting Evadne. He, too, struggled for breath, but in the brief moment of respite he held out a hand. 'May I have this dance?'

She stared at him for a moment, still struggling for breath. Her eyes were wide and two spots of red bloomed in her cheeks. 'Oh. Oh my.' Then she put one hand to the side of her face. 'I lost control again, didn't I?'

'In a manner of speaking.'

'I'm sorry.'

'I know, but you haven't answered my question.'

Evadne looked quizzical for a split second, then she had it. 'Dance? I was hoping you'd ask. Of course I shall.'

'And damn professional conduct?'

She nodded solemnly. 'Damn it to hell.'

The Bacchae had dispensed with most of the Spawn guarding the Immortals. They were spreading in a tumbling, riotous wave. Dr Ward was circling the mob and looking for a way to Mrs Winter but he was driven back again and again by the fierceness of the women. As they fought, they continued to dance and sing their wild, wordless song.

The Immortals were using their magic to move the throne behind the remaining Spawn. It wasn't long before the throne was backed against the far wall, in front of the niches that held the cube and the three-sided pyramid – which were now rotating slowly.

'There.' Kingsley had to lean in close to Evadne's ear to be heard. 'The Platonic solids. Malefactor's Lament.'

One of the many things he admired about Evadne was her quickness of apprehension. He didn't have to repeat himself or explain what he meant. They ran, skirting the dwindling numbers of Spawn. Kingsley had his faithful walking stick in one hand and he did his best to stay slightly ahead of Evadne in their headlong charge, with the dim thought of being a better, closer target than her if anyone dashed at them.

In the wild mish-mash of noise, the screeching of the Immortals was only evident when Kingsley and Evadne drew within ten yards. Then one of the sorcerers – Forkbeard – caught sight of them. He flailed a bloody, bandaged hand and almost fell off the throne, but he caught the attention of the Immortal next to him, Jia.

Evadne didn't have to be told. She loosed a round from her pistol. The bolt of crackling power lashed at the rotating cube where, with a sound like the world coming apart, its eye-singeing glare was met with a bolt that could have come from the heart of the sun.

Kingsley became aware that he was lying on his back, drifting through the air and thinking: *This is comfortable* and *Why, it's so quiet!*

Then he hit the floor.

The impact drove all the air from his lungs. He slid, kept sliding, and when he finished sliding, he lay and spent a horrible moment or two remembering how to breathe. What felt like a few lifetimes later, his body finally lurched into normality. He sucked in a huge gulp of air and loved every smoky, greasy particle of it.

Evadne was at his side, kneeling and helping him to his feet. 'What happened?' he asked and could barely hear himself past the ringing in his ears.

'You threw yourself in front of me as a shield.'

He blinked, and rubbed his forehead with the heel of a hand to cover his bemusement. 'I know that, but what was I shielding you from?'

'The cube exploded.' She gestured with the Malefactor's Lament. 'It wasn't altogether a mundane explosion. Mostly magical, I think. Some phlogiston involved, I wouldn't be surprised.'

Three child-like forms lay in the ruins of the throne. The cube had disappeared. The pyramid solid was dull and resting on the bottom of its niche.

The Bacchae resumed their singing and the silence was broken. They gaily returned to their dismembering of the remaining Spawn, who had all fallen senseless to the floor. 'It happened when the Immortals were stunned by the explosion of the cube,' Evadne said when she saw the direction of Kingsley's gaze.

Kingsley held up a hand to shield his eyes. The radiance behind the dancing, dangerous women was larger and brighter than before, pouring from the rock wall into the room like a misty avalanche. Kingsley could now make out a giant form, a man with curly hair reclining amid vines and grapes, and smiling at the celebrations of his followers.

The Bacchae had grown bored with the limpness of the Spawn. Their merry savagery dwindled. Their dancing and song slowed.

One of them saw Dr Ward, who was trying to approach from the side. She pointed and cried out. Her sisters, with expressions that could only be that of joy, abandoned the Spawn, and danced towards him hand in hand, glad now they had more prey to amuse them.

Dr Ward didn't flinch at their approach. As they cavorted towards him he stood still, his hands behind his back. Kingsley ran, Evadne close behind, but they were never going to reach the Bacchae before they encircled the old man. Kingsley cried out, but it was Mrs Winter herself who was at the vanguard of their antic advance. She neared, singing and dancing, arms floating, the pale, insipid blood of the Spawn dripping from her nails, her own blood streaking her arm. Her eyes were quite, quite mad.

Dr Ward waited until she was only a yard or two away. Then he tossed a golden ring high into the air.

Like birds, all the Bacchae goggled at the shiny thing as it soared, spinning and glinting. Mrs Winter was open-mouthed as it crested and then began to fall, still spinning, still glinting. Then she stood on bare tiptoes, reached out and plucked it from the air.

'Your wedding ring,' Dr Ward said while she was admiring it, 'and a pre-emptive apology. I'm sorry for what I'm about to do.' He took a step and punched her on the point of her jaw.

~ THIRTY-NINE ~

Mrs Winter's eyes rolled back. She crumpled, but Dr Ward caught her. He straightened to find the Bacchae still singing and advancing on him. 'Oh, I say.' He jerked his head up and blinked at the glowing god behind the Bacchae. He was still drifting towards them, growing more solid and more ominous as he came. 'I'd hoped you'd be gone.'

Kingsley bowled into the Bacchae and sent them scattering. *I'm still not accustomed to fighting women*, he thought, even as one rolled to her feet, laughing, and clawed at his eyes. He sighed and swept her feet out from under her with his walking stick. She fell and then Evadne cried out, 'Back away, Kingsley!'

He didn't argue and bounded away just as a blessed *thwang* sounded from behind him. A gauzy mesh, larger than the one Evadne had deployed on the guards in

320

the kitchen, spun over his head and dropped over the Bacchae. Within seconds, they were all asleep.

An angry moan, loud and painful, came from the golden cloud. Dr Ward was struggling to hold Mrs Winter, so Kingsley scooped up the woman who was now his foster mother. 'Now, we run.'

'I don't think we'll be allowed to,' Evadne said. She reached for Mrs Winter's ear and cruelly twisted the lobe. Mrs Winter's eyes fluttered open. Kingsley nearly cheered when they had no trace of madness. 'Malcolm?'

'My dear,' Dr Ward said, 'I'll explain later, but can you possibly close the way you opened and make sure that Bacchus is on the other side?'

Mrs Winter stood, swaying a little, and supported by Dr Ward. 'I'm sorry for all this,' she said. 'I tried to invite little local gods to help me escape, but the Immortals defeated them. I had to invite a more powerful being.'

The god was still cloudy and indistinct, but Kingsley made out two immense hands coming together. He had just enough time to shout 'Cover your ears!' and the whole chamber shook with the sound of thunder.

The Bacchae woke. Within seconds they'd risen and shredded Evadne's net with hardly an effort.

'That's not meant to happen,' Evadne said. Kingsley's ears were still ringing from the godly thunderclap, but he shepherded the others back towards the corridor, away from the wild women.

Instead of advancing, though, the Bacchae withdrew, singing a song that was almost a dirge. They gathered in front of the glowing cloud of godhood and puissance. They smiled languidly, as if they'd just had the most super time on a picnic, and were now looking forward to some

321

real fun. Some reclined, others sat, others wafted about with sinuous steps. All of them looked as if they were listening to music they loved.

Kingsley heard it too.

It called to him, tickling under the skin. It asked him to abandon all restrictions and laws, to join them in the free, exhilarating wildness.

I won't, he thought. He glanced at his father, at his new mother, and at Evadne. *I can't*.

With that, and without moving a muscle, he rejected the siren call of the Bacchanalian extremes of abandon, but not without regret. He couldn't deny the appeal of the heedless, headlong rush into the untamed.

Mrs Winter pushed past him. She dropped her head for a moment as she flexed her hands. When she lifted her gaze and addressed the golden cloud of godhood, Kingsley once again could not focus on her. As when she performed her magic in their Southwark workshop, Mrs Winter was blurred, as if two of her were standing so close that they overlapped. 'I thank you,' she said in a voice dark and deep. 'I was in need and you came.'

In response, from the roil of golden cloudiness came something that could have been the wind or may have been a godly sigh. Kingsley reached out for Evadne's hand only to find she was reaching for his.

Mrs Winter spread her arms wide. 'I know it has been long since you were asked back here. It is time to return, nonetheless. With my gratitude, I shall open a way for you.'

A boom like an indistinct echo and another sighing of the wind in a thousand trees. Then laughter. Haughty, cruel laughter. The Bacchae rose to their feet, threw their heads back and began to dance again.

'My dear?' Dr Ward said. 'Does that mean what I fear it means?'

Mrs Winter was grim. 'We have a god on our hands who doesn't want to go home.'

'Ah,' Dr Ward said. 'That would seem to be a problem.'

'This is why we hesitate to invite the old gods back,' Mrs Winter said. The jewel in the side of her nose flashed. 'Once unleashed, it can be difficult to slip the collar back on.'

Kingsley could already imagine the unearthly figure of Bacchus striding down Pall Mall, with his Bacchae laughing and singing while they tore people apart. No-one could stand in their way – and he suspected that their madness was infectious.

Kingsley had Evadne's hand. On his other side were his foster parents. In front of him was a god and its bloodthirsty followers. He was afraid, but he had a plan. It was foolish and desperate and poorly conceived, but he decided that if there were ever a time for a foolish, desperate and poorly conceived plan this was the moment.

Kingsley and Evadne backed away from the dance of the Bacchae as it spread and became an erratic but unmistakeable advance. Dr Ward and Mrs Winter retreated as well while the golden billowing behind them continued to take on more substance. Kingsley touched Mrs Winter's shoulder. 'Can you open a way anywhere you like?'

'Within reason. I must be able to see the location for the opening, and see it well.'

Several of the Bacchae had pipes and were playing what Kingsley could only describe as skirls. 'How quickly can you do it?'

'It takes me a little time to perform the invocation. A minute?'

Too slow. 'Can you perform part of the invocation and drop the last bit into place quickly?'

'I'd never thought of doing that, but I suppose so. There's no reason why not.'

'Good. So if I get that god thing to follow me, you could crack open a gate just behind me?'

Her dark eyes were sceptical. 'You're asking me to do something I've never done before.'

'I haven't battled an ancient god before, and I don't think London has had an ancient god striding along Pall Mall before – but never mind that. Let's accept that it's a time for firsts.'

'But what makes you think the god will follow you?'

'He follows his Bacchae, doesn't he? I'll just get them to follow me.'

'What? How?'

'They followed you, didn't they?'

'But I was one of them!'

'So shall I be. Now, Evadne, Father, pull back, I'll need some room.'

Dr Ward took Mrs Winter by the arm. She was reluctant, but he was insistent. Together they hurried towards the mouth of the corridor.

Evadne didn't. She stood there. 'This is where I should beg you not to, isn't it?'

Kingsley glanced at the advancing horde. The music was louder, their faces more ecstatic. An enormous vine-leaf wreath had taken solidity and shape in the golden cloud. It hovered nearly twenty feet above the ground, crowning a form that was rapidly becoming solid itself. 'It's customary,' Kingsley said, 'or so I understand.'

'You're going to surrender yourself to your Inner Animal.'

'In essence, yes, but that really doesn't make much sense. I'm going to surrender myself to myself.'

'You know what I mean.'

'I do, and here's where I get to plead that it's the only way, and you should save yourself and such things.'

'I'm going to and you're going to too.'

He parsed it. 'That actually makes sense.' He looked at her quizzically. 'You're not going to talk me out of it?'

'No, even though my heart's in my mouth, and I'm feeling as if this could be the end of my world if you don't come back.'

Kingsley, on the spur of the moment, surrendered himself in another way and gave in to impulse. He kissed Evadne on the cheek. 'Let's have tea at the Savoy again when this is all done.'

She smiled and Kingsley's heart was hers. 'That's starting to become a tradition.'

'One that I hope to share with you for many years to come.' He paused. 'I said that aloud, didn't I? I didn't just think it?'

'I'm glad you didn't keep it to yourself.'

He kissed her on the lips this time. 'We'll invite Mr Kipling, too,' he said, then he sprinted to the right, away from the madcap women.

As he drew nearer to them, he let himself become wild.

It was as if a long-dormant volcano had decided to make up for lost millennia. He put aside his feeble humanity,

325

purging himself of his frailty, his pathetic scruples and manners, his mealy-mouthed culture. He spat out his civilisation. His whole body was seized by the spirit of the forest. He kicked off his shoes, ripped his jacket away and hurled himself forward in a great bound, rolling and coming to his feet just in front of the Bacchae. He stretched his neck back and howled until his throat was raw.

This was good. This was right. This was how it should be. He snarled a challenge at the women. They stopped their advance, still laughing and pointing and humming fragments of songs that were older than civilisation.

And Kingsley knew the songs. Every wild thing knew the songs of the earth, the songs of the jungles, the songs of the deserts and the mountains and the places untamed and untouched by humans, the places he truly belonged. When he growled, rumbling deep in his chest, it was the sound of contentment rather than anger.

The Bacchae, as one, rushed at him, mad-eyed and trilling, but Kingsley didn't move. They embraced him, cooing and humming, laughing and singing. They recognised him. He was one of them.

He threw back his head and howled again. The Bacchae cheered. They linked arms and danced around him. He howled once more and smelled the woods, the spray off the waves, the grass of the open plains. He smelled sweat and he smelled blood. He smelled wine and abandon. He smelled pain and food. He saw the night in their eyes, when hunting was good, and the twilight, too, when prey was waking. They hungered, as they always did, and he hungered too. Deep in his belly was a void to be filled, a void that needed flesh, hot and bloody, the flesh of the living.

He shook his head and saw, beyond the Bacchae, that the great god of wine had a companion: a goat-hooved and horned god playing on a pipe the music that enflamed the heart and the soul.

We should be running through the trees, he thought dimly, *leaping streams, chasing prey, hunting the tasty!*

The goat god pointed. Kingsley whirled to see what he was pointing at.

So weak and helpless, huddled, three of them.

Prey.

He held up a hand to hold back the Bacchae. He took a step, a light step, nothing to frighten the prey into running, not sideways, not direct. Then another. Then one more.

He halted and shook his head, which was thick and heavy. Those in front of him weren't prey. They were his pack, and he knew that he had to protect them.

With that, he was suddenly thinking much more clearly. He needed to do more than protect them. He had a plan he needed to carry out.

His thoughts became clearer still. He could still feel the ecstasy that the gods were bringing with them – wildness both like and unlike his own. It had the exhilaration, the sense of giddy freedom and boundaries unlimited, but it was overlaid with a cruelty he shrank from. No, not cruelty itself, but a *delight* in cruelty, and he knew he didn't want to be part of it.

Ahead, forty feet away, were Evadne, Dr Ward and Mrs Winter. They were backed against the wall, a few yards from the entrance to the corridor. Evadne was staring at him aghast, and it hurt.

He wanted to give them a sign to let them know that they were safe, but he couldn't risk it. He had to work with his wildness to convince the Bacchae he was still one of them.

He let his body relax and lowered his shoulders. The smell of sweat and blood grew sharper. When he loped towards Evadne and his foster parents he knew he could keep up this long, striding gait for days.

The Bacchae behind him followed, whooping and singing, dancing and whirling. They dragged Bacchus and Pan along with them to the feast.

Kingsley was about to attempt another howl when he staggered and went to his knees. Shrieks came from behind him, then a sound like a mountainside falling away. The floor shifted, dizzyingly, and he spread himself face-down, looking for any solidity at all. Behind him, he could feel the world slipping. It pulled at him. The women shrieked and cried with frustration and anger.

He risked a glance over his shoulder. A void had opened in the air, a crack between here and somewhere else. Around him, the world groaned in pain.

The gods were no longer merry, and neither were their followers. They were being pulled towards the rent in the fabric of the world like smoke up a chimney. Fascinated, unable to look away, Kingsley saw their godly substance shredding, whipping away into the void faster and faster, fading and diminishing as their followers whirled away with them.

And he was being drawn there, too.

'Kingsley!'

Evadne was in front of him, her hand extended. He lunged for her as the void snapped shut behind him.

Kingsley lay in Evadne's arms. He groaned and looked about. Countless fine cracks ran across the white tiles of the floor, as if it had been hit with an enormous hammer.

The gods and their Bacchae were gone.

'Another successful escape?' he asked.

Evadne kissed him. 'A brilliant performance.'

As it seemed the right thing to do, he kissed her back. When he was able to pull himself away, he gazed at her for a long, still moment, admiring her false freckles, while the smell of wine and ivy lingered in the air around them.

~~ FORTY ~~

Dr Ward held a trembling Mrs Winter and dabbed at her bleeding forearm with a handkerchief. They accompanied Kingsley and Evadne as they picked their way through the already melting bodies of the Spawn to where the Immortals lay, unmoving, in the ruins of their throne.

Perhaps unusually for someone his age, Kingsley had now faced death a number of times. Many of the situations were self-imposed, as part of practising for his stage performances, but he was well acquainted with the rush of terror that signalled the moment when mortality's end was only seconds away. Therefore, he also knew the joy that came from defying death, from coming close but stepping away – sometimes with a grin, sometimes with a bowed head.

However, he had no truck with the romantic notion of challenging death making one braver, or wiser, or stronger.

He knew death was implacable and cared nothing for challenges, or dares, or even last-minute bargains. Death was the final winner.

'I'm sorry,' Mrs Winter said as they took in the sobering sight. Without the animation of their magic, the Immortals were children, free of the vile intelligence that the sorcerers lent them. Mrs Winter had a hand clenched in front of her, as if caught in the process of pushing the scene away. 'I shouldn't have asked the god to step through. Even though I needed help, I should have known better.'

'You were desperate,' Evadne said. Her voice was low and raw.

'Desperate?' Mrs Winter smiled. Kingsley saw a history of pain and torment in that smile, but he also saw the fortitude born of such ordeals. 'Oh, facing these Immortals again took me well past desperation. That horrid Gompers man was trying to convince me to become part of the Immortals' organisation again. He was ill suited to sweet-talking, let me tell you. A hard, unseemly man.'

'Whose fate we need to decide,' Kingsley said. 'We have him prisoner.'

'Let's see how he enjoys being on the other side, for once.' Mrs Winter took a deep breath. 'And I really must apologise for how I treated both of you when we first met.'

'You saved us then, too,' Kingsley said, somewhat uncomfortably.

'I didn't think I could trust you. I thought you had the taint of the Immortals on you.'

'We had encountered them, and fought them,' Evadne said. 'As we did here. Perhaps that's what you were sensing.'

'I see that now,' Mrs Winter said. Her voice was small. 'I was mistaken.'

Dr Ward squeezed her shoulders. 'After what you've been through with them, my dear, no wonder you're suspicious.'

'I see them everywhere,' she whispered. She looked up at him. 'I knew you'd shift heaven and earth to save me.'

'Just heaven and earth?' Dr Ward said. 'You under-estimate me.'

Any lingering notion Kingsley had that this was a marriage of convenience vanished at the look Dr Ward and Mrs Winter shared. To analyse that look was to diminish it, but Kingsley couldn't help but see respect, admiration, patience and a dozen other emotions wrapped up together in a moment where words were superfluous.

Kingsley crouched and touched the neck of the nearest Immortal, a pathetic figure dressed in white robes like a classical priest – and he reared back. 'He's still alive.'

Evadne hissed. She took out her Malefactor's Lament and trained it on the three tiny forms. 'What about the others?'

'They're barely breathing, but they are alive.'

'What are we going to do with them?' Dr Ward asked, shifting slightly so he was between Mrs Winter and the Immortals.

Kingsley looked around. Evadne had her fearsome firearm ready, and she'd caught a corner of her lip in her teeth.

Mrs Winter was grim. 'We kill them, of course,' she said. 'I wouldn't have thought there were any question about it.'

Kingsley rose, wiping his hands on his trousers. 'They're helpless.'

'That's the best time to do it,' Mrs Winter said. 'It may be the *only* time to do it.'

'We can't,' Evadne said in a voice like glass. 'Part of me wants to, but we can't. Not if we want to be better than they are.'

Mrs Winter appealed to Dr Ward. 'Malcolm? You understand, don't you?'

'I do, my dear, but I'm afraid I can't support you on this. Will you forgive me?'

Mrs Winter looked away, but her face and voice were steady. 'How could I not forgive my rescuer?'

Then she began to sob. Dr Ward put his arm around her and together they walked slowly towards the corridor.

Evadne was breathing hard. Her free hand was clenched. 'So what do we do with them while we find the missing children?'

'I'm sure no lair of the Immortals would be complete without a cell or two.'

Voices and the sound of boots echoed from the entrance to the corridor. Uniforms swarmed into the chamber, forcing Dr Ward to push Mrs Winter behind him. Evadne whirled at the commotion and tried to keep the Immortals under the attention of her firearm while taking in this new threat.

'No need,' Kingsley said, steadying her with a hand on her arm. 'I think they're friends, here at last.'

The leader of the twenty or thirty uniformed troops, a smartly turned out young woman, took one look at Dr Ward and Mrs Winter and ignored them. The troops marched directly to the ruined throne. The leader snapped off a smart salute. 'Quite a pig's breakfast you've made of this, haven't you?'

'Hello Christabel,' Kingsley said. 'It's good to see you. You brought a few extras, too? Excellent.'

'Arrived just after the nick of time, in true Agency fashion,' Evadne said with something approaching her normal insouciance. She tucked away her Malefactor's Lament and Kingsley relaxed, finally.

We might have put a very tense moment behind us, he thought.

'Sorry,' Christabel said. 'Just as we got your message, Congers and Buckers tracked us down. I think they're close behind us.'

Kingsley shrugged. 'Well, it's too late for them to get in the way.'

Evadne bit her lip. 'You'd be interested in taking these horrors away, though, wouldn't you? Please?'

'These are the Immortals? Rather.'

'You'll be able to keep them restrained?' Kingsley asked.

'We have some very special places at HQ, just for types like these.' Christabel signalled to her unit. Three operatives broke ranks and scooped up an Immortal apiece. 'This might make Congers and Buckers overlook this unapproved jaunt.'

'I'd say there's a medal in this for you,' Kingsley said. He frowned. 'I smell burning.'

He sprinted for the corridor mouth. No smoke hung in the air there, but the smell was strong. He pounded along the white tiles until he reached the stairs. The smell was stronger. He leaped up the stairs two at a time and burst out of the kitchen.

Outside, in the pale light of dawn, the outbuildings

were on fire. The Trojans were swarming towards the conflagration, summoned by the smoke.

Evadne hurried out of the farmhouse and stood with him, aghast, shielding her eyes from the heat and the smoke. 'The children!' she cried.

Kingsley had to hold her back. No-one could have survived in the inferno that was gleefully consuming each building. He was sickened, not just for the children, but for Leetha's people. The significance didn't escape him, either, that in titanic struggles, it was the little people who always suffered most.

'I've failed,' Evadne said. 'Again.' Tears hung on her cheeks.

'I'm sorry.' Kingsley was aware how weak that sounded, but he needed to say something before events overtook them. 'We have the Immortals,' he said and immediately knew how inadequate it was to point this out.

'I don't care about them,' Evadne cried. 'I had to save the innocents.'

Kingsley took her into his arms. She sobbed and he didn't speak, for no words were good enough. Evadne's burden was a self-appointed one and it was almost crushing her.

He vowed to do what he could to spare her from it.

Christabel and the other Agency officers were trooping out of the farmhouse with three inert bundles, heading for a line of black Daimlers parked on the driveway. The Trojans were nearing. Troilus and Lavinia were hailing. In the distance, through the darkness and the smoke, Kingsley could make out the headlights of an approaching motor car. He realised that the villagers must have noticed the smoke of the fire.

'Let's see what we can find before everyone makes it impossible,' Kingsley suggested. 'Maybe the children escaped before the fire.'

Evadne struck away her tears with a fist. 'I appreciate that, Kingsley, even though it's a forlorn hope. Let's do it for thoroughness rather than with any expectation of a cheery outcome.'

The lapel of his jacket was wet with her tears. She dabbed at it, but he didn't mind.

The wind was coming from the north-west, driving the fire towards the field where the Trojans had set up camp. The barn was the only one of the outbuildings to have escaped the fire, but it wouldn't last long unless something was done.

The roar of the flames was deafening as they picked their way around the west side of the new buildings. The roof of the northernmost building crashed as they neared and it sent up a fountain of sparks.

Kingsley held his tongue. Any comment about nothing being able to survive was superfluous. Evadne stood with her back to the wind, her hands in the pockets of her skirt, and surveyed the scene miserably. He stood next to her. No matter how much he wanted to put his arm around her he sensed that this was not the time. She was confronted with what she saw as proof of her failure as a protector of children, a failure that harked back to the loss of her sister on her watch. This was where he wished he had a special kind of magic: the sort that could convince Evadne that it wasn't her fault and that the burden of guilt she carried could be laid down.

We all have our burdens, he thought, *but I wish I could*

take Evadne's away from her. He blinked, then, and wiped his eyes. *It's the smoke. That's all. It's just the smoke.*

Then, just to let him know that his Inner Animal was still with him, he felt a prickle at the back of his neck. Someone was watching them.

He turned slowly but saw nothing. A few yards away were some straggling bushy roses, some daisies, the remnants of a garden in sunnier days.

He squinted. Then looked harder. A face was peering out from behind one of the roses. A small face. 'Leetha!' he cried.

Evadne whirled. She too cried out when Leetha stepped from behind the rose – she was holding the hand of a small child.

'We took the children away,' Leetha explained. She winced and shielded her face from the flames. 'We like fire, but sometimes we like it too much.'

'You lit the fire?' Kingsley said. More of Leetha's people crept out from the garden. They were shepherding five other very bewildered children. Kingsley was puzzled as to how he hadn't seen them. There wasn't enough cover. Had he simply not noticed them, bound up in Evadne's grief as he was?

'Hiding is something we can do, so we did,' Leetha said. 'We heard the magic below the ground. We thought it was a chance for us to run away.'

Kingsley put aside questions of how far they could have run. Evadne was crouching and talking in a low voice to the children, two boys and four girls. None of them could have been older than five. They were dazed. They stared at the flames, Leetha's people and at the world in general, almost as if they weren't sure it were all real. Kingsley wondered how they would remember this, if at all. A dream? A story?

Leetha nudged him. 'Your book, the one you asked us to find? You did not say there were two of them.'

She held out a pair of small volumes bound in scarred brown leather. Kingsley's heart lurched. 'I beg your pardon?'

'We found them, we hid them, we bring them to you as you wanted.' She looked at him. 'They must be precious.'

'I —' Kingsley's words tripped over each other. 'I thank you,' he said.

He wondered what, exactly, Leetha had found. Had his father written another volume? If so, why did the Immortals have it?

The first book bore the words stamped into the leather, the words he'd seen a hundred times in his memory: 'Major G Sanderson.' The other book though …

He shuffled the two so the mystery volume was on top. It had had a hard life, to judge from the stains and the scratches in the leather. The cover was worn, the title hard to read. He riffled through the pages, and raised an eyebrow when he saw that it wasn't a printed book — it too was handwritten.

Then he returned to the cover and peered at the letters stamped in the leather. The world spun around him.

The Diary of Mrs Greville Sanderson While in India.

It was his *mother's* journal.

He had no idea how long he stood there. It might have been a hundred years, it might have been a geologic age or two. He was only brought out of his reverie by Leetha's tugging on his sleeve. She pointed at the word 'Sanderson'. 'They both had this so we took them both,' she said.

'You did the right thing,' Kingsley reassured her.

Leetha gazed at Evadne, who was assuring the children that she'd take them home. 'We too, want to go home,' Leetha said to him. 'Our bargain.'

He tucked the journals in a pocket. 'The East Indies?'

A motor car had turned off the road, and Kingsley wondered if it was the one he'd seen earlier. It was roaring up the lane towards the farmhouse and the half dozen motor cars that Kingsley assumed had brought Christabel's force. The shape suggested it was a Daimler, like the others.

'Java.' Leetha shrugged. 'Flores. It means nothing to us.'

Java? Kingsley looked back to see the Trojans had reached the farmhouse and were milling about with Christabel and her people. The black Daimler was close.

'Can you wait here?' he said to Leetha. He took Evadne's hand and they hurried to where Dr Ward and Mrs Winter had emerged from the farmhouse, just as the black Daimler pulled up. The door banged open and Colonel Lucius Congreve-Knollys leaped out of the passenger side. His hat flew off with the force of his exit, but he didn't pay it any attention. 'Ah, Selene!' he cried. 'Are you all right?'

Mrs Winter stiffened. 'You've never cared if I'm all right or not, Lucius, but I'm perfectly well thanks to Malcolm and his young people.'

'Lucius Congreve-Knollys,' Dr Ward growled, 'still bumbling about?'

'Hello Malcolm,' said Congreve-Knollys. 'Just doing my job, that's all.'

Buchanan emerged from the motor car, holding his hat on. He spied Christabel. 'Hughes. What's going on here?'

'We have the Immortals, sir, and Gompers.'

Congreve-Knollys gave a yelp of triumph. 'I assume that means their plans have been disrupted? Wonderful!'

'You have fine people working for you,' Kingsley pointed out. 'I hope they'll receive appropriate recognition.'

'Eh? Oh, of course, of course.'

'So it's all gone well despite you, Lucius,' Dr Ward said. 'You're a lucky fellow, as ever.'

Congreve-Knollys laughed, but Kingsley thought it as shaky as a gingerbread tower. 'I'll get you a nice new set of garden tools, Malcolm,' Congreve-Knollys said. 'You've been raking over the past for so long I'm sure at least one of them is worn out.'

'And how's your record-keeping going, Lucius? I imagine any organisation run by you wouldn't know what it's done, or doing, or about to do.'

'I have people for that,' Congreve-Knollys said airily. 'Still working alone, are you Malcolm? Solo, unhindered, unique? *Natura il fece, e poi ruppe la stampa?*'

While his father and the head of the Agency for Demi-monde affairs continued their spat, Kingsley caught the eye of Troilus, who was enjoying the verbal stoush. The Trojan waved him over. 'They don't half know a lot of words,' Troilus said. 'Someone should be writing this down.'

With a shake of his head, Congreve-Knollys turned and strolled off, leaving a fuming Dr Ward behind. Troilus looked disappointed.

'On another matter entirely,' Kingsley said to him, 'do you remember your notion of a south seas journey?'

'It's a notion that's firmed up a fair bit since we've been here,' Troilus said. 'We think it might be a good time to leave this part of the world, things being how they are.'

'D'you feel like taking a slight detour along the way? With some very special passengers?'

'Where would you be thinking of?'
'Java.'

Kingsley had just reached Evadne, who had handed the children to overjoyed villagers – who had indeed been attracted to the farm by the fire – when Congreve-Knollys approached, smiling, with Buchanan at his side. 'Well, this has worked out splendidly, hasn't it?'

'I take that as a special thankyou,' Evadne said. 'We're happy to have done your work for you.'

Dr Ward strode up, with his new wife on his arm. Congreve-Knollys beamed at Evadne. 'I can't let you take all the credit, Miss Stephens. I must humbly insist on a portion of it belonging to me.'

'To you, CK?' Dr Ward said. 'What did you do? Hold a cocktail party to tell people you were hot on the trail of the Immortals?'

Congreve-Knollys shook his head. 'I love it when you try to joke, Malcolm. It makes the rest of us look much funnier.' He cleared his throat. 'When a leader has few resources, it's a test of that leader's capabilities, his capacity for innovation and unorthodox methods.'

'He's talking about himself, my dear,' Dr Ward said to his wife. 'I'd feel sorry for him if he weren't so ludicrous.'

Congreve-Knollys ignored him. 'I knew that the Agency couldn't hope to find the Immortals, let alone defeat them. So I had to enlist those who could.'

Evadne shrugged. 'As I said, we were happy to help.'

'But you may not have been as happy if you hadn't

been confronted by the re-emergence of the Immortals in a rather dramatic way. And, just in case you needed anything to convince you, if the Immortals had a highly desirable item of yours, one that you'd been looking for, one that meant a great deal to a young man who could be useful in confronting the Immortals.'

'You?' Kingsley stared. 'The journal?'

Congreve-Knollys turned his hands over. 'Let's just say that I still had enough friends in India to procure this journal and send it to you as if it were coming from that known confederate of the Immortals, Jabez Soames. Then it was a simple matter of letting it be known in the Demimonde when it had landed in your possession. Arranging things so that the greatest foe of the Immortals was pitted against the Immortals was quite a brainwave, I think.'

'That sort of organisation from you? I don't believe it,' Dr Ward said flatly.

'It's only a letter or two, dear,' his wife said. 'Getting other people to do his work for him.'

'I think they call it "delegation" these days,' Congreve-Knollys said. 'A tasty word. I like it.' He clapped his hands together. 'I can't take all the credit. It was Buchanan here who suggested that Mrs Winter – sorry, Mrs *Ward* – could be a useful element in this strategy.'

Congreve-Knollys, for the first time since arriving at Mallowside Farm, looked uncomfortable. 'Since this matter of the Immortals was looking pretty dire, I wanted to make sure that my scheme was foolproof. I remembered how old Malcolm had been sweet on you, Selene, so I assisted your escape, then expedited your journey to England so you could meet up with him again. I reasoned that the Immortals would grab you again and give more reason for Miss Stephens to rage against them, since she and your son are such a pair. And, yes, well, that part of the plan didn't quite work out as I'd hoped, but one can't have everything. The things one has to do, eh? Especially where the safety of the realm is concerned.'

Kingsley was astounded, and from the faces of those about him, so were Evadne, Dr Ward and Mrs Winter.

'You fool,' Kingsley said. His hands had curled into fists. 'Evadne – and I – need no extra spur to rid the world of the Immortals. Your silly plotting simply endangered everyone.'

Dr Ward had adopted a rigid calm. 'And, Lucius, you actually put into the Immortals' hands the very thing they needed to complete another plan to dominate the world.'

Congreve-Knollys blinked. He started to speak, but he faltered and stopped. He looked decidedly sick.

Dr Ward pressed on: 'You really didn't think this through, did you, Lucius? Not all the way. Shoddy stuff, as was always your wont. It wasn't your planning that brought about success today, it was the efforts of these young people.'

'And a fair share of luck,' Mrs Winter said. She glared at Congreve-Knollys.

Kingsley noticed that Christabel and a few of her fellow operatives had gathered. She looked unsurprised at the turning of affairs.

Congreve-Knollys rubbed his forehead. 'You don't understand how difficult it's been, trying to protect the country while our budget grew smaller and smaller. Desperate times, all round.' He drew himself up. 'I may be incompetent, but I'm no fool. I can see that my time at the Agency is done, and I won't stand in the way when the perfect head of the department is at hand.'

Dr Ward frowned suspiciously. 'What are you on about, Lucius?'

'Now that the country is safe from the Immortals, I'm resigning. And I'll recommend that you, Malcolm, are appointed head of the Agency for Demimonde Affairs.'

Before anyone could respond, Congreve-Knollys turned on his heel and, after gesturing to Buchanan, strode to the Daimler and roared off.

'Typical Congreve-Knollys,' Dr Ward fumed. 'Move on and leave a mess behind for someone else to clean up.'

'He might be right.' Mrs Winter touched the jewel in the side of her nose. 'You might just be the man for the job.'

'You think so, m'dear?'

'I know of no-one better.'

'Do you think Congreve-Knollys will get his knighthood?' Kingsley asked Evadne.

'Almost certainly.'

Kingsley took a deep breath of smoky air. Troilus, Lavinia and their people were introducing themselves to Leetha and hers. Dr Ward peered in their direction, acutely curious. When his new wife saw this, she dragged him over to meet the tiny strangers.

Christabel approached.

'What now?' Kingsley asked her.

'We'll take the Immortals and Gompers to Agency HQ. We'll bring Gompers's underlings to the Agency for questioning as well. We'll cordon off this place to keep the villagers away. We'll take photographs, pick over the ruins and see what we can discover. Then I imagine another fire will break out. Even bigger this time, with nothing left at all. And you?'

'Oh, a theatrical revival – in a personal sense – is high on my list.'

Evadne nodded towards Dr Ward and Mrs Winter. 'But first, we have some newlyweds to celebrate,' she said.

~ FORTY-ONE ~

'Twenty-one, twenty-two, twenty-three ...'

Kingsley ignored Mr Kipling's chanting and concentrated on wrenching the arms of the straitjacket over his head – without setting the rope tied around his ankles swinging too much. The Jaws of Death would crash shut at the slightest touch, so his struggles had to be contained to a narrow sphere of endeavour.

'Twenty-six, twenty-seven – get ready, Evadne – twenty-nine, thirty, now!'

Evadne, all aspangle in green sequins, flung her sabre. It took all her juggler's finesse to make the blade fly straight and true, but it sliced the rope perfectly before thudding into the rafter.

Kingsley was ready, thanks to Mr Kipling's adroit use of the stopwatch. An instant before the sabre struck, he ripped off the straitjacket. Then, still upside down, he swung his arms to gain momentum. Remembering Evadne's tumbling instructions, he tucked in his chin and somersaulted through the air. He landed in front of the Jaws of Death on one knee, with his arms outstretched triumphantly. Then he dropped his left hand in time for Evadne to cartwheel in and grasp it as the trap crashed shut.

Together, they bowed while the workshop echoed to Mr Kipling's applause.

'Outstanding!' he cried. 'Magnificent! Your best yet!'

Kingsley was breathing hard, but not panting. He glanced at Evadne. She was unruffled. 'Evadne?'

'A fine display of singlemindedness and showmanship. Just what we need.'

Kipling stowed his stopwatch in the pocket of his surpassingly tweedy Norfolk jacket. 'And your performance begins next week? You'll be a sensation!'

Kingsley bowed again. 'We're aiming to be the toast of Edinburgh.'

'And to move up from the bottom of the bill,' Evadne said. She threw Kingsley a towel. 'I won't abide being below a man with a monkey doll.'

'Jolly Jimbo is the best primate ventriloquist in the land.' Kingsley wiped the sweat from his forehead. 'He can make that monkey dummy talk while he's eating a banana.'

Evadne shuddered. 'Monkeys are human enough without talking.'

It was Evadne's mysterious friend Lady Aglaia who had come to the rescue of the Extraordinaires. A letter was waiting for them after their interminable Agency debriefing. Lady Aglaia had learned of a two-week engagement at the bottom of the bill at the Edinburgh Empire Palace. Apparently, she'd been chatting with Oswald Stoll, the owner of the Stoll circuit and one thing led to another. He had a word with Edward Moss and, with four shows a day to fill, he found a spot for them in Edinburgh. A small beginning, it was. Kingsley was grateful – but he had an inkling that, being so low on the bill, the Extraordinaires and the Jaws of Death were bound to dazzle the Edinburgh crowd.

Kipling clapped his hands together and rubbed them. 'And now, it's off to the Ritz for afternoon tea, as planned.'

Evadne stopped on the way to change. 'Not the Savoy?'

'I thought we'd try this newish place. People say it's splendid.'

'I'm sure it shall be,' Evadne said. 'And thank you, Mr Kipling, for organising this celebration.'

The writer shook his head. 'No, I'm the one who should be doing the thanking. I've been part of an adventure, thanks to you and Kingsley.' He chuckled. 'While exhilarating, the last few weeks have reassured me that I'm much better at writing about adventures than participating in them.'

The fortnight since the capture of the Immortals had been a hectic resumption of normal life. As well as organising a huge bunch of flowers for Lavinia, Kingsley had thrown himself into rehearsing and – inspired by the work they'd put in on their bogus Ficino Institute – he'd cleared out the basement of the workshop and divided it into living quarters. It had been Evadne's suggestion to use Japanese paper walls and even though Kingsley had been sceptical, he had to admit that the result was extremely stylish – and easy to construct.

The bathroom was taking a little longer to install, even with help from some of Finny's tradesmen. Partly it was the normal complexities of plumbing and drainage, but proceedings had hit a snag after he'd put his foot down when white tiles had been suggested to finish the walls and floor. After the confrontation in the underground lair of the Immortals, he had an aversion to white ceramics.

Evadne and he went to their separate rooms. While Kingsley was searching for a clean tie, he stopped, looked around, and had one of his many moments of wonder.

This is astonishing, he thought, *this life we're shaping for ourselves*.

A young woman and young man sharing living facilities was an extremely Bohemian arrangement, but since Evadne hadn't spent a moment worrying about the matter, Kingsley was doing his best not to. It was economical, for one thing, as Evadne had pointed out. Kingsley was able to move out of his Pimlico rooms, thereby saving money. It was practical, too, as he saved time moving between rehearsing and home.

Kingsley had noted that Evadne hadn't closed down her retreat under the White City, but he decided raising such would be poor form, mostly because Evadne would have a very good reason for keeping it. Probably because of the heavy industrial facilities she had there. Or the view. Or the prestigious underground address.

One drawback was that he needed to grow accustomed to having myrmidons trundle around. He had, to the extent that he didn't leap into the air and cry out whenever one hove into view any more. He thought it a solid improvement.

As for more delicate matters, Kingsley was uncertain about the state of affairs. On the whole, he was much gladder to be around Evadne than not, and she seemed to reciprocate. Without discussing anything at all, apart from stage matters and various forms of armed and unarmed combat, they'd established a new and quite marvellous understanding. They were the Extraordinaires. They were also Evadne and Kingsley.

As he adjusted his collar in front of the cheval mirror and considered this sensitive subject, he came over all strange. His heart bumbled around inside him like a moth inside a lantern. His knees were weak and he was sure he'd forgotten how to breathe.

Evadne and Kingsley. I suppose that would make us a couple.

He had to sit on his bed, lest he find himself on the floor.

This hadn't been a sudden plunge into romance. Nor was it a considered thing where he'd tallied up advantages and disadvantages. He was tempted to say that it crept up on him and took him unawares, but that would be an untruth. Ever since the first time he'd seen Evadne Stephens, he had dreamed about her. These dreams were pleasing but her capriciousness had kept him at a distance. She was kind, she was fun, she was stunningly good-looking, but she was also challenging, impulsive and decidedly prickly at times. When she had declared that a professional partnership needed a degree of distance he'd agreed with some relief, but it was a relief tinged with regret. Ever after, circumstances had been conspiring to breach this wall of professionalism, assaulting his battlements of detachment, besieging his fortress of friendliness. The events of the last few months had been trying enough without his also laying his feelings bare. In extremis, they had both found what was important and had declared it through their actions.

'Kingsley.'

Evadne stood in his doorway, a picture that took away what little breath he'd managed to regain. She was wearing some sort of pale blue Oriental coat over a black dress. The coat looked heavy, with elaborate embroidery and gold braiding. She wore a hat, too, smaller than most hats Kingsley had seen women wearing lately, almost a miniature fez. 'It's a Mandarin coat, Kingsley. A perfectly delightful old woman sold it to me a few years ago. I wear it too seldom, so I thought this the perfect time. Come here, your tie is crooked.'

'That's because it's ashamed at not being able to meet the standard you set, which is exceedingly high.'

'Fumbly and awkward, but still a compliment. Good.'

'What I meant to say is that you look overwhelmingly lovely. It's not just your clothes, although the fact you chose them shows your exceptional good taste. It's your bearing and your manner, which are striking in their own right.'

She finished adjusting his tie and stood back, smiling broadly. 'That's better.'

'The tie?'

'And the compliment. Detailed, thoughtful and eloquent. I could live with that.'

He took her hand and kissed it. 'And I couldn't live without that.'

The Palm Court at the Ritz had so much style that Kingsley thought it could give its excess to less well-appointed hotels and London would be the better for it. It sparkled, a song of pale walls, many mirrors and gilt.

Kingsley's foster father was resplendent in his morning dress, with a soft grey waistcoat for a touch of individuality. He rose, smiling, when Kipling, Evadne and Kingsley entered. 'We've ordered tea. Hope you don't mind.'

Kingsley seated Evadne, and when he sat he was next to Mrs Winter. Mrs Ward. The woman who married his foster father.

This is foolish, he thought and he decided a direct approach was best. 'I'm sorry,' he said to her. 'I still don't know how to address you.'

She rested her chin on her hand for a moment, amused. She had a white silk wrap over a dress of palest yellow satin. Her hat was a tight black turban. 'How would you *like* to address me, Kingsley?'

'That's only half of it. How would you like to be addressed?'

'Oh my. We're in danger of foundering on our own over-solicitousness. The name I have that is least under dispute is "Selene".'

Kingsley felt a little awkward, calling an adult by her first name. Yet the alternatives were even less comfortable. 'Selene is a charming name. I'd be honoured to use it.'

Evadne, on his left, leaned across. 'Since we're talking about names, Selene, have you thought about my offer?'

Kingsley noted that Evadne had none of his hesitation in using an adult's first name. He added an abundance of self-possession to the list of things he admired in her. 'What offer?'

Selene touched his wrist. 'Evadne has an intriguing opportunity, but I'm afraid I must decline.'

Kingsley looked across the table. Mr Kipling and his foster father were discussing something that entailed their heads being close together with quite a few furtive looks being cast at the other patrons of the Palm Court.

Probably something to do with the safety of the realm and my father's new job.

Despite blustering and refusing and arguing, Dr Ward had ended up as the new head of the Agency for Demimonde Affairs, mostly because his wife had declared that she was happier in a country with good protection from Demimonde devilry, and no-one could do a better job than her husband.

'But you'd be splendid,' Evadne was saying to the new Mrs Ward. 'Someone with your calm, your aplomb.'

'Not to mention my easy way with any gods who might be in the area? No, sorry, Evadne, your terms are too onerous.'

Kingsley tapped his teacup with a spoon. 'And here's where I'll interrupt and ask "what's all this about?" instead of listening hard and trying to make sense of what you're both talking about.'

'I've asked Selene to be the new Mrs Oldham,' Evadne said simply. 'She *has* been a school teacher and I'm sure she could manage the girls.'

'Oh, I'm sure I could,' Selene said. 'In fact, I'd love to. It's just that having only recently taken on a new name, I couldn't possibly throw it aside and take another.'

Kingsley dabbed at his lips with a napkin. 'Everyone in charge of Mrs Oldham's School for Girls must take on the name of "Mrs Oldham".' He frowned at Evadne. 'I think "Mrs Ward's School for Girls" has a fine ring to it.'

Evadne threw her hands up in the air. 'Oh, very well then. It'll mean having to get a new brass plaque, though.'

353

Kingsley pointed at her with the teaspoon he still had in hand. 'I'm sure you have a Demimonde friend who can do such work.'

'Of course.' She leaned across Kingsley again. 'Mrs Ward's School for Girls it is.'

Evadne and Selene shook hands, elegantly.

'I say, Kingsley, Evadne, have you heard the news?' Mr Kipling was gesturing across the table. 'Dr Ward has just told me that Buchanan wants to stay on in the Agency.'

'What?' Kingsley said. 'I thought he'd want to go when Congreve-Knollys left.'

'He says the filing system needs a complete overhaul,' Dr Ward said. 'And procurement is in a shambles.'

'You could do worse, I suppose,' Kingsley said. 'But whatever you do, spend some time with Christabel Hughes, Father. She'll tell you what's really going on in that place.'

'Hughes? The youngster who was at the farm?'

'That's the one.' Kingsley thought about having another salmon sandwich. 'And the Immortals. Any thoughts about what you'll do with them?'

'The same as Gompers. Keep them locked up. Oh, someone will probably want to study them, try to work out where their power comes from, but I think that might be a very dangerous road to go down. I'd be happy if everyone simply forgot about them.'

And that's enough shop talk. Kingsley signalled to the waiter who had been alert for the cue. An instant later, half a dozen of his white coated colleagues were serving champagne to the table. 'This was meant to acknowledge your wedding,' Kingsley said, his glass raised in a toast, 'but to that I'll add congratulations to Selene on achieving the distinction of superseding Mrs Oldham, and to my father on his new position as head of the Agency for Demimonde Affairs.'

'I probably won't last a month,' Dr Ward said. His attempt at gruffness was short-lived, however, when he spied the waiter approaching. 'Ah, cucumber sandwiches, my favourite! It's the mint, you know, that makes them so appetising.'

A few delightful hours later, Kingsley and Evadne left, making their apologies. Outside, the weather was caught between drizzle and not. 'Shall we walk?' Evadne said.

'What about your Mandarin coat?'

She pointed at the man on the corner. 'Such times were made for umbrella sellers.'

Arm in arm, they walked down St James's Street towards Pall Mall.

'Dr Ward asked me if you'd finished reading the journals,' Evadne said. 'The two journals.'

'I haven't found the proper time.' It was odd, but after seeking his past so avidly, now that he had the journals, Kingsley had been reluctant to read either of them.

'Mind you,' Evadne said, 'he didn't actually ask to read either of them, even though his interest was palpable. I think he's wondering how you'd react to a request.'

'Favourably. I owe him so much.' *We share a past already. Now it's a larger one.* He hesitated, then he decided he had to share. 'I nearly ran away, you know, several times over the last year.'

'Ah. I wondered. You had that look about you.'

Kingsley really wasn't surprised she'd noticed. 'What sort of look?'

'I'd come across you gazing into the distance, but it was a distance that looked infinitely preferable to the place you found yourself at that moment.'

'That describes the feeling perfectly.'

'And now?'

'Nowhere is preferable to where I find myself right now.'

'I'm glad.'

He squeezed her arm. 'Have you packed the dodeca-hedron off to the Agency yet?'

'Not yet. I have a few experiments of my own to do first. Then I'll decide. Even with your father in charge, the Agency is still the Agency.'

They reached the Embankment. The day was beginning to draw in. 'We have so much packing to do, Kingsley. Are you sure we'll be able to catch the Edinburgh train in the morning?'

'The only trouble catching a train is getting someone to throw it to you,' Kingsley said.

Evadne tapped his arm with a gloved finger. 'If you were any more arch we could build a bridge out of you.'

Kingsley shook his head. 'I am now truly put in my place by the supremo of witticisms. I accept that my role is to be the strong and silent partner.'

'Oh, no, not silent. That's far too dreary. Just do your best to keep up.'

Kingsley could think of nothing more agreeable. He took her hand in his. 'I shall.'

~❧ FORTY-TWO ❧~

Later that day, replete after the sumptuous tea, Kingsley settled in their now secure workshop and started reading his father's journal. The experience was a strange one.

Before he began, he propped the battered photograph, the one Evadne had found for him, on the table in front of him.

He couldn't remember his true father at all, so he was looking for the man with every word. He wanted to touch the flesh and blood that were his, but the more he read the more the man eluded him. Kingsley tried to reconstitute the man from such entries as 'Water courses in NE unaccountably dry' and 'Chota Lal – disappeared'. Lists of dates and distances travelled were there aplenty, but the only picture that came was of a man of duty – an observant man, sharp, curious and organised.

Gradually, he learned that his father had been reporting

357

to the Indian branch of the Agency, as well as to the normal military intelligence authorities. It shouldn't have surprised him, but it did. His father was not only involved with politics, but he was involved with monitoring events in the shifting world of the Demimonde.

The journal was a field diary, a compendium of notes taken while on mission, and by rights should have been handed in with a full report of findings. The fact that it hadn't made Kingsley sure that his father – Greville Sanderson, British spy – had come to an awful end.

Kingsley paused for some time before reading the final entries.

His father had become aware of rumours concerning vile practices in Kerala, near Ramakkalmedu. In the methodical, organised manner Kingsley was becoming accustomed to, his father had travelled south and set about collecting information, assuming the guise of an official from the Forestry Service. This allowed him access to all sectors of society, from the lowest timber workers to the merchants and to the British officials. His pretence was aided by the presence of his heavily pregnant wife, Alice, who was loved by all around her.

It was in mentions of his wife that Greville Sanderson's military bearing slipped. His adoration for the woman who was Kingsley's mother seeped through his stiff prose. He respected her fortitude, admired her intelligence, and loved her kindness. Kingsley wept when he read the hesitating description of how his mother carefully selected servants with families, and insisted that the families came to live with them to share in their comfort.

Sanderson had assumed, at first, that the rumours of evil practices could be hinting at the reawakening of the dreaded Thuggee cult, the mad murderers dedicated to the goddess Kali, but soon it became apparent that this wasn't the case. Unspeakable rites were taking place, but they had nothing to do with the Thuggees. This was something new.

In a land as ancient as India, with its multitude of people and its panoplies of histories, novelty was rare. Almost everything that was done had been done before, in one way or another. Yet Greville Sanderson was sure he had uncovered something new, in the most hideous way.

Sadly, the disappearance of children was not an unknown thing. Illness and accident took many young lives, while poverty and hardship forced appalling decisions on some families. Yet the wave of child disappearances in the area centring on Ramakkalmedu was enough to cause disquiet, especially when considered alongside other events in the area.

Greville Sanderson discovered evidence of large groups of people gathering in the forest at night. They went to witness abominable acts designed to give expression to the basest aspects of humanity. Acts of blood and death brought crowds together to wail at the sky, and when morning came, those who perpetrated the acts disappeared, leaving those who'd come to watch sickened, dismayed and ashamed – but hungering for the next time.

While this was happening, elsewhere in the region strange excavations were being undertaken. Rumours abounded of mysterious objects being dug up from deep in the forest, objects that sent many diggers mad simply to look upon.

Greville Sanderson had no choice. He donned a disguise and joined a midnight meeting.

Later, writing in the safety of their house in Ramak-kalmedu – the house overlooking the forest – he detailed in careful prose the outrages committed upon animals and people, documenting them for his superiors. His horror became a cold fury as he promised to bring the perpetrators to justice.

Kingsley almost cried out when his father described these perpetrators: three youths who commanded a legion of unliving minions.

At this point, Kingsley stopped reading to order his thoughts, and to cope with the press of emotion. He needed several deep breaths and the application of a hand-kerchief to his eyes, but his thoughts were more difficult to deal with. His father had encountered the Immortals. When Evadne and he had run up against the sorcerers and their Spawn, there were hints that the unspeakable creatures had spent time in India, and that they had only come back to London recently. Soames, their human go-between, had been arranging shipments containing substantial magical worth. Had this anything to do with the objects being dug from the Indian forest?

Kingsley turned the page to find the next entry was the last. It was brief and shocking in its informality. For the only time, Greville Sanderson wrote in the first person. Kingsley, reading the fateful, final words, was hearing the voice of his father.

'They have found us. I have barred the door and will hold them off. Alice has the baby. A trusted servant is taking them into the forest. God have mercy on their souls. I love them both.'

Kingsley closed the journal. He sat there in the basement, alone with his thoughts, for a long time.

Then he opened his mother's journal.

~ FORTY-THREE ~

Leetha did not like being on the deck of the ship. So much world on either side and none of it to stand on. Despite having Lavinia and Troilus beside her, she was deeply uneasy at the expanse of water; never solid, never still. The weather, though, had steadily grown warmer and warmer as they had travelled, and more like that of their home. This was cheering.

They had been journeying for many days, and yet she was still not happy with the motion of the vessel. The way it moved, side to side, end to end, was too unsteady for her. Even though the ship was taking them home, she knew that her gratitude to it would be only mild.

She had been glad of the skill of the shipmasters. They had prepared comfortable quarters for her people and her. The captain had also discussed their special requirements with her. Large rooms, bedding on floors, no locks, as many of the round windows as they could have.

Home.

'What will you do when you get home?' Lavinia asked Leetha. The wind ruffled the hair of the Trojan woman. She swept it away with an easy hand.

Leetha knew. She and her people would withdraw. They would lose themselves and retire from the world. They did not want to be part of it, not if it was as they had seen. They would remain hidden, overlooked. 'We shall be together,' she said. 'We shall live our lives.'

'Like us,' Troilus said. He nudged his sister. He swept an arm over the ocean. 'While we're roaming, at least we have each other.'

'And all your people, are they happy?' Lavinia asked.

'All those who came with us,' Leetha said. 'They are impatient, now.'

Then she remembered Mannor. He and a few of his friends had decided to stay behind. It was a shock to many, but Leetha was not surprised. Mannor had been fascinated by the workings of the big people. Leetha would never stop anyone who wanted to learn, and the ghost girl – Evadne – promised that she would find Mannor and his friends a place where they could be safe and be taught the ways of working with metal and electricity.

'And what about you?' she said to Troilus and Lavinia. 'Where are you bound?'

'Home,' Troilus said. He grinned. 'Wherever that is.'

Leetha looked at the wide world around them. 'You will know it when you see it,' she said and she was as certain of this as anything in her life.